The Mysterious Double Death of Honey Black

Lisa Hall is the #1 bestselling author of six psychological thrillers, including *Between You and Me*, *The Perfect Couple* and *The Woman in the Woods*. Lisa lives in a small village in Kent, surrounded by her towering TBR pile, a rather large brood of children, dogs, chickens and ponies, and her long-suffering husband.

LISA HALL

THE MYSTERIOUS DOUBLE DEATH OF HONEY BLACK

CANELO
US

San Diego, California

Canelo US
An imprint of Printers Row Publishing Group
9717 Pacific Heights Blvd, San Diego, CA 92121
www.canelobooksus.com

Printers Row Publishing Group is a division of Readerlink Distribution
Services, LLC. Canelo US is a registered trademark of Readerlink
Distribution Services, LLC.

This edition originally published in the United Kingdom in 2023 by
Canelo.

Published in partnership with Canelo.

Correspondence regarding the content of this book should be sent to Canelo
US, Editorial Department, at the above address. Author inquiries should be
sent to Canelo, Unit 9, 5th Floor, Cargo Works, 1–2 Hatfields, London SE1
9PG, United Kingdom, www.canelo.co.

Publisher: Peter Norton • Associate Publisher: Ana Parker
Art Director: Charles McStravick
Editorial Director: April Graham
Editor: Traci Douglas
Production Team: Beno Chan, Julie Greene

Library of Congress Control Number: 2023948760

ISBN: 978-1-6672-0659-2

Printed in India

28 27 26 25 24   1 2 3 4 5

For Karen

and for Peg

Prologue

As she opens the door, her face split in a wide grin, I'm not 100 per cent sure I'm going to do it. And then she hands me a glass of champagne and opens her mouth.

'What is it? Is it about me? Are they out there for me?' Her hands press against her mouth in glee.

'You?' I shake my head, my throat fizzing as I throw back the drink and place the glass on the coffee table. 'It's always been about you, hasn't it?' A spark ignites, and my vision shimmers with the heat of my rage. 'What about me? Did you ever think about me? About what you have done to me?'

She frowns, gives a tiny shake of her head. 'I don't…'

'You never did.' Venom pours from my lips, as if a cork has popped from a bottle. 'All you ever see is your own face reflected back at you, you never think about the way the things you do, the decisions you make, affect things for other people. Ruin things for other people.'

'There's nothing wrong with being ambitious. You've said that before to me. I don't understand why you're—'

'You did this, Honey. Everything that happens now is because of you.'

It's surprising how easy it is, in the end. The way the knife slips between her ribs without resistance, her eyes widening as her breath comes in a tiny gasp, sticking in her throat. I was expecting some sort of struggle, for my shaking hands to drop the knife, sending it scuttering across the floor. For the blade to scrape against bone. For her to see what was coming and try to fight back, but she doesn't. Even as I draw back my arm, she doesn't make a sound, my name hovering on her lips as her brow creases in confusion before I plunge the knife in, slicing through the thin silk of her dress, through her perfect, creamy flesh. Her mouth drops into a perfect 'O', one hand fluttering towards her chest as she raises her eyes to mine. And then she slumps, awkwardly, heavily, stumbling back towards the chaise longue, a circle of claret growing on the front of her pale pink dress.

Her eyes close as her body hits the back of the chaise, causing her to lean drunkenly. Stepping closer, avoiding the crimson splashes that mar the plush carpet, I reach for her shoulders and lay her prone on the chaise, settling her hands across her lap. I loved you once, I think, my eyes drinking in her waxy, still features. I loved you before I hated you. She looks angelic, sweet, the way her fans think she is in real life. She's none of those things.

Snatching up the knife from where I dropped it, I step away from the mess that used to be America's latest sweetheart, pausing at the door to rearrange my features into a more suitable expression. Honey Black got what was coming to her. And revenge has never tasted sweeter.

Chapter One

Rumours. Gossip. Lies. Not to mention glamour. As I approach the Beverly Hills Hotel, I can't help but feel a flicker of excitement in my belly, the early morning sun reflecting off the pale pink walls of the exterior and casting a warm glow across the immaculately kept entrance, with its plush red carpet and waiting valet. I skirt around the edge of the building, past the neatly trimmed hedges that keep the hotel residents from prying eyes, unable to stop myself from brushing my fingers over the rosy walls as I arrive for my housekeeping shift, as if the scandal and glamour will soak in through my fingers. All I've ever wanted my entire life was to be here, in Hollywood, home to some of the best movies ever made.

'Morning, Lily.' Eric, my supervisor – and probably my best (and only) friend in LA – is waiting for me as I hurry in through the back entrance, tucking my phone into the pocket of my uniform, and tugging my hair into a ponytail.

'Morning, Eric.' I flash him a grin, aware of the way he quickly glances over me. While I would like to think that it's because he secretly fancies me (Eric is supremely hot – 100 per cent California gold, with swishy dark blond hair, a surfer's body and green eyes that can see into your soul), I think it's more likely that he's just checking I am presentable before I head up to my floor. The Beverly

Hills is a stickler for perfection, and with good reason. You don't become *the* hotel to the rich and famous without high standards.

'Hey Lil, I need you to help me out today.' Eric's voice is muffled as he digs in the store cupboard. The service area is unusually quiet – even the door to the laundry is tightly closed – and I realise that it's just us in here. 'We're super short-staffed and I really need a hand. Paulina and Maria are out sick, so I have no one to work the first-floor suites.'

'And you want me to do it?' I feel a twitch of anticipation, my lips already beginning to curve into a smile. The suites might not be the movies, but they're a step closer. All the celebrities stay in the bungalows or in the suites, and Eric warned me when I started working here a few months ago that you have to work your way up. I never thought I'd be here long enough to work the suites, if I'm brutally honest, I thought I'd have a job in production by now. At least, that was the plan. But I don't. And who knows? Tarantino could be up there right now, wishing he had fresh, new talent for his production team. 'Sure, I'll help.'

Following Eric and his laden trolley, we work briskly together, starting with the junior suites. The buzz of anticipation grows in my stomach as I scrub, and fold, and straighten – housekeeping isn't a glamorous job, but the suites... now they, and their occupants, *are*.

'So,' Eric says, as he wipes over the mirror in the bathroom in one of the smaller suites, and I straighten the sheets on the bed. 'How are things with Rex?'

I pause, my heart sinking, as I renew my sheet-tucking with more vigour. 'Honestly? He's a cheating asshole.' I flap out the duvet viciously.

'Really.' Eric doesn't sound surprised. Eric Jardine thinks Rex Crawford is an asshole, full stop. And Rex is wildly jealous of any time I spend with Eric outside of work, even though Eric is literally the only other person in my LA life besides Rex, my boyfriend. *Ex*-boyfriend. 'Wanna talk about it?'

'Not really.' My eyes smart and I blink. 'It's over.'

'I'm sorry, Lil.'

'Shit happens.' I punch a pillow back into shape and throw it onto the bed.

'So… what will you do now?' Eric's voice is muffled beneath the roar of the bath tap before the water is shut off abruptly. 'Will you go back to London?'

'London?' I shake my head. Eight months on, I still get sharp pangs of homesickness when I think of certain things at home, but I definitely don't want to go back. 'No, I won't go back. I didn't come to LA for Rex, Eric. I came for work. For the movies. You know that.' Even though it's harder to get a position as a production assistant than I first thought, despite a first-class degree from the London Film Academy.

Eric lays down his cloth and steps out of the bathroom towards me. 'I always thought Rex was a bit of an asshole.' He grins at me, and I can't help but grin back.

'Really? You never said.' I roll my eyes.

'Listen, I was wondering…' Eric clears his throat. 'They're holding an anniversary showing of *Kentucky Queen* at the Grauman Theatre… I was wondering if you wanted to go and see it?'

'I've seen the poster outside the theatre!' I say. I've walked past it every day for weeks, hoping to go and see it but knowing that Rex wouldn't want to. 'How did you know I'd want to go? *Kentucky Queen* is one of my favourite movies. Jessica Parks is fantastic in it, but it's Honey Black who really steals the show.'

'You might have mentioned liking old movies once or twice,' Eric says, his eyes crinkling at the corners, before he grows serious. 'Or like, six or seven times. In fact, I'd say you're a walking encyclopaedia for the movies. Got a question about an obscure movie from 1942 that only three people in the world have ever seen? Dial 1-800-Lil for answers!'

'Shut up, you idiot,' I laugh, shaking my head. 'I'm not an encyclopaedia. More like a half-loaded Wiki page.'

Eric rolls his eyes and smirks. 'So, tomorrow night, maybe? If you're not busy?'

'Not busy,' I say.

'Cool,' Eric says, the air growing thick between us. 'Speaking of Honey Black,' Eric says, and the moment passes. 'We only have one suite left on this floor. Come on, follow me.'

I follow Eric along the carpeted hallway with its familiar banana-leaf wallpaper, as he leads me to a room with a plaque on the door reading 'Paul Williams Suite'. He gives a quick tap on the door before he lets us into a room that is plush even by Beverly Hills standards.

'Crikey.' I have to stand for a moment and soak it all up. It's a suite, obviously, but there's a bar in the corner, a bottle of champagne and two saucers standing on it. Alongside a beautiful brick fireplace, there is a piano, and a chaise longue sofa, with bucket-style armchairs. I walk through to the huge bathroom and then into the bedroom with its luxury king-sized bed. There is a deliciously retro feel to the whole suite. 'This place is amazing.'

'Isn't it? This is one of the most popular suites in the hotel – and one of the most expensive.' Eric is already snapping on a pair of gloves and preparing his spray bottle of cleaner. 'It's named after the guy who designed it back in the 1940s.'

'Is that the Paul Williams on the nameplate?' I run my fingers over the piano and wish I'd learned to play.

'That's the guy.' Eric seems hurried and distracted now, no trace of his usual friendly demeanour, as he quickly spritzes over the table with sanitiser. 'You never heard of him?'

'Nope.'

Eric sighs and pauses in his cleaning. 'Paul Williams was a well-known African-American architect. He built houses for Frank Sinatra, Barbara Stanwyck, Lucille Ball… he was kind of a big deal round here in the Forties and Fifties. He designed this suite and gave the hotel a revamp back in the late Forties. That's why the outside walls of the hotel are pink – he decided on it. And the wallpaper in the hallways.'

'I love that wallpaper. How do you know all this stuff?'

Eric shrugs. 'I just find it interesting, all the old history. There's been someone in my family working at the Beverly Hills Hotel for decades, right back to my great grandfather. He had a thing with a British girl once, you know.'

'Yeah?' I raise an eyebrow.

'Apparently she was a firecracker.' Eric winks, and the atmosphere shifts slightly. 'Anyway, this room has been kept the same since Paul Williams first designed it. This room is exactly as he had it decorated in the Forties, even down to keeping the bottle of champagne on the bar.'

'Wow.' I knew the hotel liked tradition – our uniforms have barely changed for decades – but now there is the sensation of stepping back in time, of finding myself in a bygone, simpler age, as I run my fingers over the fabric of the sofa, wondering about all the people who must have sat here.

'Come on, Lil, you'll have plenty of time to gawp at this place later. Let's just get it done and get out of here.' Eric rubs his hands together, as if all business, but there is something anxious around his eyes.

'What is it?' I ask. 'Why don't you want to be in here?'

Eric peels off his gloves and throws them into the bin. 'You're a movie fan. You know about Honey Black, right?'

'Yes, of course.' I think for a moment, remembering the movie poster outside Grauman's Chinese Theatre. 'Of course I know Honey Black. Like I said, *Kentucky Queen* is one of my favourite movies. My mum used to love watching old movies on a Sunday. It was her who got me hooked on them.' I am assaulted by the memory of my mum, standing at the ironing board, discreetly swiping at tears as she watched old black-and-white movies enveloped in a cloud of laundry-scented steam. 'Honey Black was murdered, wasn't she? Here, at the hotel.' Scandals like the death of Honey Black are partly why I was excited to get the job here at the Beverly Hills, as morbid as it sounds, and I feel it again, that familiar buzz of anticipation, a crackle of expectation on the air. 'Wait a minute.' I spin around, taking in every inch of the hotel suite. 'It was here, wasn't it? She was murdered right here, in this suite.'

'Yeah,' Eric says. 'Right here in this very room, on the twenty-fifth of June 1949. I should have known you would know all about it, Miss Hollywood. Is there anything you don't know about the movies, you big encyclopaedic dork?'

'Very funny.' I swat him on the arm and let out a long breath, as goosebumps ripple along my arms.

'The story is that she was found over there...' Eric points to the chaise longue, 'with a stab wound right through her heart. She had been filming a new movie, *Goodtime Gal*, and was staying here. Whoever did it stabbed her once and left her to die, on the night before her twenty-first birthday.' He glances around the luxurious suite, before his eyes come to rest on my face. 'Scary, right? That something so terrible could happen here, in a place where Honey should have been safe.'

'I read about it.' I pause for a moment, thinking over Eric's words. 'Years ago, in one of those books on Hollywood scandals.' The story had stuck with me, because she was one of my mum's favourite movie stars. 'They never found her killer, did they?'

'No. Never found them. Whoever killed Honey Black got clean away with it. They say it was someone connected to the movie, but there were never any formal arrests, there wasn't ever enough evidence.'

'I remember,' I say, 'they thought the director of the movie she was working on might have had something to do with it, and it all got hushed up.' I frown, trying to remember what else I had read in the scrappy two paragraphs dedicated to her demise in the flimsy borrowed paperback.

'That's right,' Eric says. 'Completely covered it up. But the fact that she let her killer into her suite...'

'Means it *must* have been someone she knew.' The idea of Honey Black − a girl younger than me − letting someone into her suite, someone she trusted, for them to brutally murder her makes the hairs stand up on the back of my neck. 'Poor Honey, how utterly terrifying.'

I glance around the room, my eyes drawn to the chaise, and I imagine her lying there, cold and still. 'It must have been quite shocking; a movie star dying so violently like that. It's a wonder they managed to hush it up so well.'

'She was Hollywood's newest movie star,' Eric says, stepping closer and lowering his voice as if afraid of being overheard. 'She had a secondary role in *Kentucky Queen*, and she blew the audiences away. They say *Goodtime Gal* would have put her up there with Rita and Jane. But she was murdered before they could finish it, and the idea that maybe the murderer was involved in the movie... like you said, one of the initial suspects was a successful, powerful movie director, hence the reason the whole thing was hushed up as much as possible. Tinseltown isn't exactly scandal-free, but a murder is a hell of a lot more scandalous than Spencer Tracy having an affair with Katharine Hepburn.'

I see now why Eric wants to hurry through cleaning the suite. There is something else now, under that retro vibe, something desperately sad and almost a little creepy, as I find my gaze wandering back to the chaise where Honey was supposedly found, half expecting to see the imprint of her body etched into the fabric.

'I hate cleaning in here,' Eric says suddenly. 'Every time I come in, all I can think about is Honey. Lying there in her own blood, cold and blue. I always think I can hear things in the bedroom and sometimes...' he pauses a moment, his eyes never leaving mine, 'sometimes things have moved, when I've only left the room for a few seconds.'

'Shit,' I breathe, rubbing my hands over my arms to ward off the chill that has descended on me, before giving a nervous laugh. 'I'll do it today,' I say, before I've thought it through. 'You go, and I'll finish in here.'

'No, Lily, I can't leave you in here on your own.'

'Why? Are you worried' – I glance theatrically over my shoulder – 'that the *ghosts* will get me?'

Eric tuts in annoyance. 'Come on Lily, it's not funny.'

'Sorry!' I hold up my hands. 'Honestly, I'm sorry. I didn't mean to laugh at you. Please, let me do it today if you feel uncomfortable. I don't believe in any of that crap.'

'You don't?'

'Hell, no.' There can't be an afterlife, because if there was surely my mum would have let me know. She would have come back to see me, wouldn't she? 'No such things as ghosts.' As I say the words, the hairs on the back of my neck lift slightly, as if there is a draught nearby.

'Really? Are you sure?' Eric asks, but he's already packing his things onto his trolley and passing the protective latex gloves to me.

'Of course. What are friends for? You go, I'll be fine.' *What's the worst that could happen?*

-

As soon as Eric leaves, I regret making the offer. Wiping over the large, ornate mirror in the bathroom I keep my eyes on the door reflected back at me, convinced I will see someone flit past in the room behind, my heart beating double time in my chest, but there is nothing. *No such thing as ghosts, Lil.* Even so, I can't help picturing Honey looking into this same mirror, her smooth reflection staring back. *It's a story, that's all.* There is nothing haunted about the suite, despite its awful history. It's just a story, a tale that has probably been exaggerated over time, embellished by the fact that Hollywood tried to cover it up. And while I feel sorry for Honey Black, I doubt she is spending her endless days haunting the chambermaids of the Beverly Hills Hotel. If I were her, I'd be swanning around in heaven, flirting with Clark Gable and Marlon Brando.

'Sorry, Honey.' I shake my head, as I swipe my cloth around the shining sink. 'I just don't believe it. I'm sure you've got better things to be doing than hanging around here.'

I move on to the bathtub. Turning on the taps, I am leaning over the tub to scrub the enamel, the fresh lemon scent of cleaning fluid filling my nose, when I feel it. Something like a hard push at the base of my spine, and I lose my balance, cracking my head on the tiled wall as I fall.

Everything goes black.

Chapter Two

Ouch. Pushing myself up into a sitting position on the chilly floor of the bathroom, I raise my hand to my head, fingers probing until they find a lump. *Blimey. I must have really cracked my head.* Looking at my fingers, I let out a breath when they come away clean, no sign of blood. *Wait until I tell Eric about this.* Carefully I roll over onto my knees and hold three fingers in front of my face. Definitely three. Although I know how many fingers I am holding up as I'm holding them up myself, so I'm not sure how accurate my check for concussion is. I hoist myself up using the bathtub for leverage and as I pause there, something bubbles to the front of my mind. *Did I feel a shove as I leaned over the tub, right before I cracked my head?* I hold my position for a moment, feeling uncertain. There was no one else in the suite while I was cleaning, Eric left before I even reached the bathroom, and I would have heard if someone had come in. *Maybe it was the ghost of Honey Black.* I shake the thought away, wincing as I stand upright. Glancing in the mirror I see the small lump that has formed above my temple, and hastily rearrange my dark curls a little to cover it. Maybe I won't tell Eric what happened.

There is no sign of the cloth I was using, and I step towards the bathroom door to check the bedroom, just as the door to the suite slams closed. *Shit.* Checking my watch, I see it's almost three o'clock. I've been in here for over half an hour. Eric will go mad over the time I've taken – he's made it clear that we are to be in and out of the rooms as quickly as possible to avoid disrupting the guests. *Please don't let me get fired.*

Slowly, I push open the bathroom door and creep along the thickly carpeted floor, sneaking past the bar, before catching sight of a woman in the lounge area, her back to me. *Oh yikes, I really am for it.* My only hope is to get out as quickly and quietly as possible. She stands at the window, the suite telephone pressed to her ear. A cascade of blonde hair tumbles down her back and she wears a pencil skirt and heels, not the familiar pink housekeeping uniform. *Definitely a guest.*

I am halfway across the room when the suite door flies open again, and another woman hurries into the room, her face flushed.

'Please,' she says, breathless and flustered. 'Just put the telephone down and we can discuss this.'

Aware that neither of them have noticed me, I slip back towards the bathroom, my heart hammering in my chest as I peer around the door frame at the scene in front of me. The blonde woman puts the phone down and turns to face the other.

'Give me one good reason why I shouldn't call him right now,' she says, raising her chin. There is something in her expression that is familiar, something I recognise that I can't quite put my finger on.

'Oh for God's…' the other woman tuts. 'I don't get paid enough for this; do you know that? I'm here as your PA, not your mother, not your… your slave. I work very hard every day, trying to stop you from making ridiculous decisions—'

'Having that man thrown off set isn't ridiculous.' *Set*. The blonde woman must be an actress, that's why she seems familiar. The women face off against each other, neither of them willing to back down. I hold my breath, unable to look away from the scene that plays out in front of me, wishing I'd had the foresight to hurry out of the suite, instead of scurrying back to the bathroom.

'You are impossible, do you know that?' The other woman – younger, and with an air of mild disgust – looks at the actress with undisguised dislike written all over her face. She wears a vintage dress, and she holds a pair of white gloves in one hand. Both of them look as if they have stepped off a movie set, their clothes lending an old-fashioned air to the scene, which makes sense if they are in the business, I guess.

'I do know that,' the actress smirks. There is a faint Southern twang to her voice, overlaid with something else, something less lyrical, as though she is trying to disguise her accent. 'But I would rather be impossible than lily-livered. I explicitly told you I didn't want him around, and you let him on set. Maybe I oughta get you a little chicken suit to wear, seein' as how you can't stand up to anybody that tells you no, unless it's me, of course.'

It's mean, but I can't help the bubble of laughter that escapes my lips at the thought of the sour-faced girl in a chicken suit. Regret hits immediately, when both women whip their heads round to look at me.

'Who are you, and what are you doing in this suite?' Sour Face asks, her anger directed at me now, as she steps forward, her hands outstretched.

'I… I was just—'

'Wait a second,' the actress says, pushing Sour Face to one side. 'You the housekeeper, sweetie? I thought you'd'a been done by now.' She frowns.

I nod, adrenaline leaving me oddly shaky. 'Sorry, I didn't mean to listen in, I was just leaving, and I saw you and I panicked—'

'You need to leave, immediately. Before I call security.' Sour Face grasps at my arm, tugging me towards the hotel suite door. 'This is unacceptable. Who is your superior? I'll be reporting you for this, you see if I don't.'

My temple thuds, and I raise a hand to the lump there. *This isn't my fault.* I was injured, while cleaning this suite. If I hadn't fallen, then I would have been long gone by the time this angry, tart young woman arrived. 'Fine. His name is Eric Jardine.' *So long, Beverly Hills Hotel. So long, any chance of meeting a director and living my dream.* 'Just one thing before you chuck me out and get me fired.' *In for a penny and all that.* 'I'm sorry,' I say to the actress, her face so familiar but no name springing to mind, 'but I agree with you. If someone had let a man on set who I explicitly asked not to be there, then I would be completely furious.' I resist the urge to throw a smug grin towards Sour Face as she marches me towards the door. She throws it open, before grasping my arm tightly again, shoving me into the corridor.

'It's OK,' I say, with more bravado than I really feel. 'I know the way.'

'Wait.' The actress appears at the door, her eyes never leaving my face. 'Annabel, let go of her arm.' She steps forward, her mouth quirking into a smile. 'You'd be furious too, huh? I guess you'd never let him on set in the first place?'

'Of course not. Not if he wasn't wanted.'

16

'Huh. How about that?' The actress glances at Sour Face – Annabel – before turning her gaze back to me. 'Oh sugar, I can tell we're going to get along just fine. What's your name?'

'Lily,' I say. 'My name is Lily Jones.'

'*Lily*. And you're *British*! What fun. You know what I think, Lily? I think you'd make a much better PA than Annabel.'

My breath stops in my throat, and I keep my eyes on the floor, as Annabel turns a furious gaze on the actress.

'You can't do this! I'll call Leonard!' Her voice is high-pitched, the acidity hitting a biting, lemony tone.

'You call him. I'll let him know you put my safety at risk today.' The actress turns to me. 'How about it, sugar? You wanna work in the movies?'

'Um, I think so. I mean, yes please. But—'

'Thanks Annabel, but you're fired.' The actress marches past the now blotchy, red-faced young woman to where I stand, linking her arm through mine as she guides me back towards the suite. She closes the door in a blinking, speechless Annabel's face with a smile. 'Welcome, Lily. I hope you'll be more of a pleasure to work with than old sourpuss out there.' She laughs, a tinkly, showbusiness laugh.

My heart skips a beat even as guilt tickles at the back of my mind. The guilt doesn't last long. Annabel wanted to get me fired… and this could be my chance to finally break into the movie industry, after eight long months of phone calls, online applications, and failed interviews. I could step into the PA's shoes, help this woman out, and carve myself a route into the movies. *I couldn't, could I? Yes, I could. As long as there's not too much secretarial stuff involved.*

17

I can type at the speed of light on my phone, but filing is another matter.

'Yes, me too. I mean, of course. Thank you.'

The actress eyes me closely, running her eyes over my unruly dark curls, and the pink housekeeping uniform that doesn't quite fit properly over the bust. 'If you're going to be my PA you've got to look the part. Y'all need to get yourself changed into something a little more appropriate. I can't have you going outside like that, people will think I've hired the help.'

'Absolutely. No problem.' I nod frantically, my mind already burrowing deep into the tiny closet of clothes in my miniscule apartment, searching for something to wear. This feels like a scene from an old movie, the *right place, right time* scenario. This kind of thing doesn't usually happen to girls like me.

'Good. I'll call Leonard and let him know I have a new PA.' She winks at me and reaches for the telephone.

'Just one thing,' I say, my pulse fluttering as I swipe my sweaty palms discreetly over my skirt. 'What should I call you?' I haven't actually outright said I don't know who she is.

'My name, of course,' the actress says. 'You can call me Honey. Honey Black.'

–

As the woman starts to shout into the telephone, I gesture towards the suite door, already pulling my phone from my pocket. *Honey Black? Did she say Honey Black? I think I must have hit my head harder than I thought, because I'm not sure I heard her right.* I'll call Eric and tell him I'm really sorry, but I can't work at the hotel as a chambermaid anymore... I'll offer to pick up the bill for the movie tickets for *Kentucky Queen*, and maybe I could even spring for dinner after? If I'm going to be PA to a movie star, then the least I can do is treat him to some Mexican food. Hurrying out into the corridor I jab at my phone screen, but it stays resolutely blank. *That's the last thing I need.* Shoving it back into my pocket, I hurry along the hallway into the lobby, not worrying about being spotted in my uniform, but my footsteps slow as I enter. Everything seems… off, somehow. Different. As if the hotel has been spruced up overnight. I pass the Crystal Ballroom, my feet silent on the thick carpet, as I make my way towards the front entrance. I don't recognise the man on the reception desk, where Lyle usually works until five. This guy wears his hair slicked back and sports a thin pencil moustache that gives him an old-fashioned air. I hope Lyle hasn't moved on. Two women hurry across the plush carpet, both in vintage dresses similar in style to the one Annabel was wearing, and I turn my head to watch them pass. There must be a big budget movie in town, clearly set in the 1940s. It must be big budget, if the actors are staying here, wandering around in their costumes. I feel a buzz of excitement as I realise the actress in the suite was wearing vintage clothing too. Could I be working with her on some big Hollywood blockbuster? Maybe they're making a biopic of Honey Black's life, and my new boss was staying in character. I can't stop the grin that marches across my face as I step out onto the red carpet, and along the enclosed hedged sidewalk onto the street. That's when my footsteps slow completely and the smile drops from my face.

Everything is different. Not just the people, in their vintage clothing. I blink, the bright, harsh sunlight of a Hollywood afternoon beating down on my head. The hedges that line the street, shielding the hotel from view, are smaller somehow. Not trimmed, but *younger*. As if they haven't fully knitted together yet. I turn back, to look at the hotel. The pink of the exterior walls seems fresher, cleaner. Palm trees line the sidewalk, swaying in the light breeze, but they also seem different, as if they haven't yet reached the dizzy heights of the top floor hotel rooms. Turning back to the street, it too looks changed from when I entered the hotel this morning. There are fewer houses, and as I turn to peer out towards Sunset Boulevard, to where just this morning the traffic was backing up as commuters fought their way to the opposite side of the city, the roads are almost empty. It seems cleaner. Less shabby. Shaking my head, I turn back to Sunset Boulevard, beginning to walk on legs that feel slightly numb towards my apartment, but I only manage a few steps before I slow to a stop. Cars pass slowly, and I have to blink, pressing my hand to my mouth. Vintage Cadillacs, two of them, pass me, followed by a black Ford, its bumper a grin below the perfectly circular headlights. The driver tips his hat – a trilby – in my direction with a smile, cigarette clamped between his teeth. I lift a hand, watching him drive past, before shaking my head. Something isn't right. I must have really hurt myself when I hit my head, because this isn't the Beverly Hills that I know. Surely no movie studio would have a budget so big that they could turn the exterior of the hotel, the very streets that surround it, into a scene from the 1940s. Could they? I swallow hard, suddenly feeling nauseous, my hand going to the lump on my head, as I let myself sag against a large blue container on the sidewalk.

Looking down, I see it's a newspaper dispenser, some-thing I'm sure wasn't there this morning. They must be really going for this authenticity thing. It's full, and I scan the headlines, my eyes running over the black ink, once, twice, three times.

TRUMAN SPEAKS ON HOLLYWOOD BLACKLIST OVER RED SCARE

Truman? As in Harry? I blink, my eyes returning to the page in front of me. A smaller headline runs in the bottom left-hand corner.

SINATRA HITS THE HIGH NOTES! FRANK WOWS THE CROWDS

'You OK, honey?' A hand on my arm makes me jump, and I raise my eyes to see a woman in a familiar pink uniform. *My uniform.* Her auburn hair is curled into victory rolls, her face bare of make-up. 'You look kinda pale.'

I blink, then nod. 'I'm... fine, thank you. Just a little hot.' I glance down at the newspaper headlines again.

'You just finish your shift? Or you just starting? I can walk in with you if you'd like, I start in fifteen minutes.'

Air whooshes out of my lungs in a relieved sigh. Of course, it's just a movie. Something big, I guess, to have the whole hotel involved. But if it's just a movie, how did they... I take another look at the woman in the housekeeping uniform in front of me. 'You work here? At the hotel?'

She gives a quick nod. 'Housekeeping. And I'm going to be late, so...'

I look down at her feet, next to mine. She wears dated – *very* dated – slingback sandals, beige and clumpy. They look old-fashioned next to my Converse trainers. 'I like your shoes,' I say.

'You do?' She frowns. 'They're just work shoes. I got them for $1.75, which my mom said was expensive, but you know, after rationing ended everyone went a little crazy. I'm sorry, I have to go. Will you be OK?'

'Sure. Thanks.' *Rationing?* I run my eyes over the victory rolls in her hair as she leaves, and then let my gaze fall on the date at the top of the newspaper. Saturday 11 June 1949. *What. The. Fuck?* Am I dreaming? Did I knock myself unconscious? Am I *in a coma?* Bloody hell. I pinch myself hard, grasping my forearm between finger and thumb, pinching until my skin is red and raised. But nothing changes. I am standing on the corner of Sunset and N Crescent. I am looking back at a fresher, newer version of the hotel that I love. I am in 1949.

Chapter Three

What the fuckety fuck is going on? I watch the housekeeper walk away in her ugly, old-fashioned shoes, as another vintage Ford rolls past, before closing my eyes. *This can't be happening.* The headline of the newspaper glares up at me and I fumble in my pocket for a coin. I'll get a paper, and when I open the pages they'll be blank, I tell myself, it's just a prop. But all I have in my pocket is a mobile phone that still stubbornly refuses to come to life.

I'm definitely in a coma. That's it. I hit my head so hard that I put myself in a coma, and none of this is really happening. My brain has brought me here to 1949, because of my mother. I'm still grieving, my heart aching for her every morning when I wake up and remember she's gone, and what better way for my brain to try and help me heal? Of course I would end up here in 1940s Hollywood, a place where we spent every Sunday afternoon for years. My fingers find the lump on my forehead, pressing gently, and the wave of nausea that follows tells me this is real.

'I'm crazy then,' I whisper to myself. 'If I'm not in a coma, then I must have gone stark raving bonkers, because none of this can be happening.'

I can't stay out here. The ground feels uneven beneath my feet, and I press my hand against the newspaper dispenser, the metal warm beneath my palm, in the hopes of grounding myself. It'll only be a matter of time before someone calls hotel security, but I can't go home, because I don't think my apartment block exists yet. Clapping my hand over my mouth, I glance up at the window to the Paul Williams Suite as I make my way on autopilot towards the back entrance of the hotel, picturing Honey Black looking out as she makes her phone calls. *Honey Black.* Oh God, the actress said her name was Honey Black. Maybe I'm not going mad, and maybe she's not deluded, or playing a character. Maybe she said her name was Honey Black because *she is Honey Black.* Safely back inside the hotel, I pause then, pressing myself against the wall outside the hotel laundry as the floor tilts dangerously beneath my feet.

I open my eyes the tiniest bit, peeping out on to the silent, empty corridor expecting to see something, anything that can tell me this isn't happening, but all I can see in my mind's eye is that date on the top of the newspaper. I squeeze my eyes tightly closed again, as the room whirls around me, my stomach swooping and diving as a faint ringing clamours in my ears.

Don't faint, Lily. Whatever you do don't faint. I force my eyes open again, my hand pressing down on the handle of the door to the laundry room. It swings open and I slide inside, a blast of warm air hitting my face as I flick the lock closed. Racks of clothes hang around the room, all freshly laundered and ready to be returned to their owners, the hot air scented with something light and cottony. The sight of the garments makes my head spin, as I take in the swing dresses, the tailored jackets, the ballgowns. Dresses with distinctive wide necklines, gloves to match, reams of fabric pressed tightly together. Vintage, every one of them. *Not vintage, Lil. Contemporary and modern. They'll be vintage one day, but not yet.* I swallow hard, nauseous again, and scrub my hands over my face. I have to pull myself together.

I hit my head. I woke up. There was a woman who called herself Honey Black in the room, and when I stepped outside, everything was different. The newspaper said it's 1949. I run through everything, trying to piece it all together, and still the only thing I can come up with is that I'm in a coma, I'm crazy, or... I really am in 1949, and the woman in the Paul Williams Suite really is Honey Black. And if she is... realisation dawns and I have to draw in a series of deep breaths until I am light-headed. If she is, that means in two weeks' time, someone out there is going to try to kill her.

'Hello?' A brisk knock comes from the other side of the door. 'Someone in there?' The voice outside is clear despite the barrier between us. *I don't think I am unconscious.*

'I'll just be a minute,' I call back.

'This door shouldn't be locked,' the voice murmurs, as if the person outside is pressing themselves against it.

'Two minutes,' I say, desperately. 'I'm just... delivering some laundry.' My heart pounds in my chest, my breath coming in tiny gasps, as the knocking comes again. I take a deep breath, snatch up a dress, and open the door. 'Hi,' I say to the squat-looking man in front of me. Before he can say anything, I say, 'just dropping some laundry off.' I hold up the dress. 'For a very high-profile guest. Top secret, you know. Very important that no one knows she's here.' And I slam the door closed again, leaning against it with my pulse pounding in my ears until I hear him move on.

What on earth do I do? Even if this is a wild delusion, some crazy coma dream, I can't hide out here until I wake up. The thought of running away crosses my mind, but where would I run to? Where would I go? Nothing outside is as it was this morning.

Honey is still waiting for me to return from my apartment. My apartment that isn't even built in 1949. I scan the racks ahead of me, knowing I have no choice. I can't hide out here, and I can't go home. I simply have to… go along with things, starting with borrowing something to wear.

I rifle through the racks, searching for something in my size, tugging the clothes free. Everything is so *tiny*, and I despair of finding anything even remotely close to my size, before I spot a blouse tucked away at one end of the rail, squashed between the feather boning of two – honestly quite fantastic – gowns, their voluminous folds of tulle almost hiding it completely. The silky, blush pink satin is cool between my fingers, and I feel my belly give another ominous roll. I've never had a dream where everything felt this real before. I strip off my uniform with shaking fingers and pull the blouse on, before stepping into a classic A-line skirt, and sliding my feet back into my old, battered Converse. There aren't any shoes in the laundry room, so there's not much I can do about them. Raising my eyes, I see my own face reflected back in the spotted glass of the mirror on the wall to the side of the racks. My chestnut curls are unruly, hints of red glinting under the dim yellow light, and I raise a hand to smooth them down, then press my hands to my cheeks. My face is pale, a waxy, flat shade of cream that I don't think is anything to do with the lighting in here, and I pinch my cheeks hard, pressing pink blooms into the skin there.

This is definitely not a dream, a persistent voice insists in my head, as my eyes smart at the pinching of my cheeks. A voice that sounds suspiciously like my mother. Stepping away from the door, I follow Dorothy's lead and cautiously click my heels together. Any movie fan knows this is the sure-fire way to get home – but the room remains unchanged, the clothes still hang eerily silent around me, and I can still hear Honey Black telling Annabel she is fired. *Lily, this isn't a dream.* I press my hand to my mouth, holding in the yelp that lurks in my throat. If this isn't a dream, if I'm not crazy, then I really am here, in the Beverly Hills Hotel, two weeks before Honey Black is going to be murdered. My knees turn to water, and I sink slowly to the floor.

–

'Well, don't you look the cutest?' Honey arches an eyebrow at me as she opens the suite door, the missing Paul Williams nameplate glaring in its absence. I give her a wobbly smile, my legs still blancmange soft. 'I'll give you your due, you have good taste in clothes. That blouse goes perfectly with your dark hair – in fact, I have one just like that. Give me a twirl!'

Oh God, don't tell me I nicked her blouse. Obediently I turn in a wobbly circle, feeling vague and disconnected as my eyes follow the line of the room. It's still the same suite I entered with Eric earlier this afternoon, but now I see little signs of occupancy that weren't there before. Balled-up tissues in the waste basket, an empty coffee mug on the piano, Honey's heels, slipped from her feet and laid at the end of the chaise, where she moves to now, lowering herself into a reclining position. I walk towards the table, half hopeful, half fearful of seeing the date on the newspaper that sits there. *How can this be happening?* I surreptitiously pinch the skin on the back of my hand this time, but everything stays the same.

'How about we run some lines? You wanna grab my script for me?' Honey wafts a hand in my direction, and I fumble with the papers on the table, scrabbling through until I get my hands on the thick, chunky pages. As I run my eyes over the title page, I feel a jolt, like a bolt of electricity running through my fingertips. *Goodtime Gal. The movie that was going to catapult Honey to the top of her game. Until she died.*

'Well? You got that script there, sweetness? I really need to get to work, things did *not* go well today.'

'Yes. Here.' Handing it to her, I can't take my eyes off her. The perfect golden waves of her hair, that flawless, creamy skin that I've only ever seen in black and white before. Her eyes are a brighter shade of blue than I imagined. She thumbs through the pages before realising I am still standing in front of her.

'Could you not stand over me?' Honey lowers the script and stares up at me. Heat flushes up my neck towards my face.

'Sorry.' Twisting my hands together, my mind still swirls on a loop. *Crazy? Or coma? Or something too impossible to imagine?*

'I can't concentrate with you standing over me like that.'

'Sorry,' I say again, inwardly cringing. 'I could make some tea? If you wanted some.'

'Sure,' Honey snaps, before her face softens. 'Don't be such a frightened rabbit. I don't bite. Sure, I'll have some tea. Then maybe you can test me on my lines?'

'Of course.' I muster up a smile, feeling muzzy-headed and strangely out of my own body. Realising there is no means of physically making tea, I call down for a pot and then wander over to the window, pushing aside the thick curtain to peer past the small patio area and out to the city. A car slows as it reaches the entrance, a red convertible – the kind I've only ever seen in old movies – and I glimpse the driver, a handsome man with thick black hair. He pulls up, and his passenger leans over to kiss him before slipping out on the sidewalk. As she steps away towards the hotel, a scarf covering her hair, I realise she looks a little like Ingrid Bergman. *Maybe it is Ingrid Bergman.* I pull the curtain across and press my face into the heavy fabric, before peering out again, the overwhelming sense that this isn't really happening making my head feel light and swimmy. The woman is gone, and the car is turning back out onto the main street again. I lean my head against the cold of the windowpane, running my eyes along the street opposite. It looks as it did when I stepped out earlier. Fresher, as though... as though everything is newer. Maybe seventy years newer. *Oh yikes.*

I move to the pile of newspapers, flicking through the pages and running my eyes over more headlines that don't mean anything to me. There is no mention of Trump, of the election that is due the following year. No mention of Meghan and Harry, and baby Archie. Nothing, in fact, that I can relate to at all. My eyes go to the date at the top of the newspaper again. Saturday 11 June 1949. I have an overwhelming instinct to google 1949, so strong that my hand goes to my pocket and I pull out my phone. The screen stays blank, and I clap my hands to my mouth to hold back the wave of hysterical laughter that threatens to bubble up out of my throat. Swallowing hard, I shove the phone back into the pocket of my skirt and straighten the newspapers before perching on the edge of the bucket armchair close to the chaise, pressing my feet into the plush carpet in an effort to ground myself.

'Are you OK? You don't look so good.' Honey frowns as she looks me over.

'I'm a little… hot. It's a bit stuffy in here.' I fan at my face pathetically, realising that I actually am feeling hot. And bothered. And slightly concerned that I'm having a mental breakdown.

'Isn't it?' Honey sits up, reaching for a glass of water and handing it to me, her fingers lightly brushing mine. 'Here, have some water. I'd love to keep those doors open and sit out on the patio, but Jean wouldn't approve – she's always antsy about the press, even here – and I just know she'd run back to Leonard and tattle on me.' She takes a sip of her own water, eyeing me over the rim of her glass, her mouth twitching. 'Jean's no fun.'

'Jean?'

'Jean Lawrence.' Honey lays the script in her lap. 'Leonard's assistant, although she's more of a gatekeeper, and boy, does she let people know it.' She rolls her eyes.

'Leonard?'

'Langford. You know, the director?' Honey gives me an odd look. 'You are alive, right? You must have heard of Leonard Langford. He's the best director there is.'

'Of course, sorry.' I give Honey a weak smile and sip at the icy cold water, grimacing as it slides down my throat. *This is real. This isn't a dream. Oh, blimey.*

'These lines won't learn themselves. You ready?' Honey flips through the script until she finds the page she's looking for. 'I need to be perfect, you got that? Absolutely word perfect.'

'Sure.' I nod, placing the water back on the table. If this isn't a dream, and I really am here in 1949, then I need to suck it up and figure out exactly what is going on, and why I'm here, even though the very thought of it makes my head spin. I'm going to have to try to fit in the best I can, and that means bringing out the old Lily. I need to bring out the strong, capable Lily, who nursed her mother through a terminal illness, who worked double shifts in the supermarket while writing her final year university dissertation, who packed a single suitcase and headed for Hollywood. The Lily who had a dream and went for it.

–

We run through the lines until I am confident that I could probably perform any of the other parts alongside Honey, but it isn't a chore. Even just practising in her hotel room, there is something luminous about Honey as she takes on the persona of Sofia Budd, the gal who is the focus of *Goodtime Gal*. She has a star quality, and I am in awe of her as she paces the thick, luxurious carpet, her arms gesturing, her face taking on all the emotions she is acting out, pausing only to sip at the tea that arrives from room service. A shiver runs up my spine as I realise that this movie is going to be the one that makes her a star – after this Honey Black will be the name on everybody's lips. Until I remember that it's not going to happen, Honey will be murdered before the movie is made.

'Phew.' Honey throws herself on to the chaise, fanning herself with her script. 'I think I got that right on the nose, wouldn't you say?' She smiles, but there is a wariness to it, as if she's not entirely sure.

'*Absolutely.*' I'm amazed at her lack of confidence. I wish I could tell her my mother thought she was incredible, that she would watch *Kentucky Queen* over and over. Will watch. God, this whole thing is so confusing. 'Honey, you were fantastic!'

'Do you think?' Honey presses her hand to her mouth to smother a smile. 'Leonard says this is it for me, my chance to make it to the big time. I had a part on one of Jessica's movies – Jessica is the real star round here, let's be honest – and Leonard was so pleased with me he asked me to do a screen test and now here I am, in Hollywood. Living my dream.'

Hang on. Leonard Langford is the director of this movie? And it's just two weeks until Honey is found murdered? Eric's words echo through my mind, and I find myself suppressing a shiver. 'Jessica?' *It can't be.*

'Jessica Parks, who else? You must have heard of her; she's a superstar. Everyone knows Jessica. You know she got the part of Carla in Leonard's last big movie? Apparently,' Honey leans in close and lowers her voice, even though we are the only two in the room, 'the part was meant to go to Ingrid, and Jessica snitched it from right under her nose.' She lets out a shout of delighted laughter. 'I was so pleased for her; she's been such a good friend to me. Poor old Ingrid, but that's just how it is here in Hollywood.'

'I've heard of Jessica Parks.' Jessica Parks is one of the biggest movie stars of all time, up there with Audrey Hepburn, Rita Hayworth and Marilyn Monroe, but of course, I don't say that. '*Kentucky Queen*, right? She was Carla in *Kentucky Queen*. I saw...' *your name on the poster*, are the words on my lips, but I can't get them out. *Was it only a few hours ago that I agreed to go to the movies with Eric?* The spinning sensation returns – *Crazy? Or Coma?* – and

I draw in a deep breath, saying instead, 'Wow... Jessica Parks.'

'I hope you're not going to be all gooey-eyed and starstruck,' Honey says, and laughs again. 'Jessica has more than enough fans fawning over her.' She sobers for a moment, opening her mouth as if she wants to say something more before she abruptly closes it again and changes the subject. 'Gosh, look at the time. We've been at it for hours, and I said I would meet Leonard for dinner.'

'Oh, shall I...' I flounder, not sure what exactly to do. This morning I was only meant to be in this room for a matter of minutes, and now... now I don't know what I am meant to be doing, where I'm meant to be going.

'Why don't you go to the bar, get a drink and something to eat. Whatever you need, just charge it to your room. I've arranged for Jean to leave you a few things upstairs and she'll meet you on set in the morning,' Honey says. 'My PA – you, now – has the room one floor up, so you're nearby if I need you.' She pauses. 'And I don't need you right now, so...'

And just like that, I am dismissed.

–

Although my room is decidedly smaller than Honey's, it's still the most luxurious place I've ever stayed in, although I would have slept in a box if I'd had to. I had envisaged creeping back into the laundry room to sleep among the fancy gowns and furs, so relief poured over me like water when Honey mentioned the room upstairs. Someone – Jean, presumably – has left a package on the huge king-sized bed in my room, containing more clothes, a neat set of heeled pumps that are ever so slightly too tight, and a set of hair rollers. As I shake the package, a lipstick falls out, a Cashmere Bouquet lipstick in a bright, vivid red, the tiny sticker on the bottom telling me it cost twenty-nine cents. Standing in front of the mirror, I slick a layer onto my mouth, the greasy feel and the waxy scent that rises as I smack my lips together reminding me that this is really happening. I really am here, in the Beverly Hills Hotel, in 1949.

Come on Lil, you've got this. Taking a deep breath, I recap the lipstick, and step out into the corridor. Everything feels fresh and new inside the hotel, as well as out on the street. When I walked this corridor this morning it was by no means shabby, but there was no mistaking the feeling that the hotel was old and carried a lifetime of secrets and history, whispers and murmurs that called out as you walked the hushed hallways. Now, the wallpaper is the same, the carpet the same luxurious style I walked on only hours before, but everything feels… newer. Brighter. Filled with promise and expectation as opposed to the mystery of what has gone before.

The doors to the Polo Lounge are heavier than I expected as I push them open and step inside. *Wow. This place is incredible.* Leather-seated booths line the perimeter of the restaurant, with tables in the centre set at discreet distances from each other, ensuring diner privacy, while a bar runs along the left-hand side of the room. Large flower displays are dotted throughout the restaurant area and piano music tinkles in the background, lending an air of sophistication to the room. When I peer round a column, I see there is an actual man, sitting at an actual piano, playing for the few guests that sit in the dining area, soft lighting reflecting the room back onto the glass doors out on to the patio. The air is full and heavy, filled with the murmur of muted conversation and fragrant with heavy perfumes – Chanel No. 5 and L'Air du Temps – and the sweet scent of cigar smoke, casting a slight haze over the heads of the diners. I don't think I've ever been in a room this posh in my life.

'Do you have a reservation?' a softly spoken hostess asks, as I snap my gawping mouth closed.

'No. Just a drink, please.' The hostess smiles graciously and ushers me towards the wood-panelled bar, where I slide onto a stool and wait for the barman to notice me.

'What can I get you?' Green eyes meet mine, and I open my mouth, but for a moment no words come out.

'Umm... I don't know. A... martini?' I sit up straighter. I don't think there's much chance of getting a hard seltzer or a CBD cocktail around here. 'Yes. A martini please.' I've never had a martini in my life, but if I'm going to be stuck in 1949 Hollywood I might as well embrace it.

'Sure. Dirty?'

'Yes?' I nod, trying to look decisive – and as if I have any idea what he means. 'Dirty. Why not?'

He mixes it expertly as I watch. There is something familiar about him, only I can't put my finger on it. No doubt he's been in a movie – or will be in a movie – that I will watch in the twenty-first century. Maybe.

'Thanks.' I lift the glass he slides in front of me, resisting the urge to wrinkle my nose at the sight of an olive on a cocktail stick resting on the side of the glass. 'Cheers.'

'Cheers.' He watches me with an amused smile as I raise the glass to my lips and take the first sip.

'Oh *shit*,' I gasp, coughing as the fiery alcohol hits my throat. 'That's *strong*.' Tentatively I take another mouthful, wincing as it goes down.

He raises his eyebrows, a smile twitching at his lips. 'Here.' The barman slides me another glass and when I take a sip it's just plain old orange juice.

'Thanks.' I give him a sheepish grin. 'I guess I made it obvious that I'm not really a martini drinker.'

'You could say that.' He lets out a peal of laughter that sends goosebumps sprouting all over my arms it's so familiar. 'Are you enjoying your stay at the hotel?'

'Umm… kind of.' I don't elaborate, not sure what to say. 'It's… very nice.'

'You're not from these parts, are you?' he says with a curious glance. 'That sounds like a British accent to me.'

'London,' I say, 'but I've been here a while. In LA, I mean. What about you? Have you worked here long?' The alcohol seems to have loosened my tongue. Or maybe it's the fact that I am in a hotel in Hollywood, forty-five years before I have even been born. 'I'm Lily, by the way.'

'A couple of years. Louis.' The barman looks down at the hand I offer, pausing before he shakes it. 'So, Lily, what brings you to the Beverly Hills Hotel?'

'Work,' I say, and it's not as though I'm lying. 'I'm working as a PA. Speaking of which…' Honey crosses the entrance to the bar, a tall, handsome man with salt-and-pepper hair standing next to her, her arm linked through his. 'That's my boss.'

Honey gives a small, gracious smile and inclines her head towards me in recognition, as the man, presumably Leonard, frowns in my direction before mimicking Honey's nod in greeting and they pass on by, on their way out to dinner.

'He's your boss, huh?' Louis says, his towel flying in and out of the glass in his hand as he polishes it. 'Mr Langford is here a lot, especially when he's working on a movie.'

'*She* is my boss,' I say, ignoring his raised eyebrow and returning to the martini. Despite the burn of liquor, it's weirdly delicious. 'You must meet some incredible people. Is this what you want to do? Or are you hoping to get into the movies?' I still think I know him from somewhere.

'No, no movies for me,' he laughs. 'I've seen too many miserable people sitting at this bar to want to get into the movies. If I can make people happy by pouring them a drink, then that's good enough for me.'

'Really?' I sit up straighter on the stool. 'Miserable people, huh? You'd think working in the movies would be a dream job, but I suppose it is just a job like any other and if a drink at the end of the day works...'

He frowns, reaching for another glass to polish. 'A drink and a friendly ear. Sometimes all they need is someone to talk to. And I don't repeat what they say... you're not really a reporter, are you?'

'Ha. No.' *Are there many female reporters in 1949?* The booze has definitely gone to my head on an empty stomach, and I change the subject before I say something that could get me in trouble. 'Do you ever try to help them? Like... I don't know... advise them. Or get them to make some changes?'

'No, but maybe I shoulda done.' He winks and moves off to the other end of the bar to serve a couple that have just entered, the girl clutching the man's arm as if already tipsy.

I sip slowly at the rest of the martini, interspersing it with sips of orange juice, and wonder if Buck's Fizz has been invented yet, before pulling the newspaper that sits at the end of the bar towards me. It's the same copy of the *LA Times* that sits on the table in Honey's suite. When Louis comes to stand in front of me again, I push the newspaper in his direction, tapping at the front page.

'Is this from today, this newspaper?'

He peers in, turning the newspaper so it's the right way up. 'Uh-huh. Saturday eleventh of June 1949. That's today.' He gives me a quizzical look as I push the martini glass towards him and ignore the paper. In exactly two weeks' time Honey Black will be murdered in the Paul Williams Suite of the Beverly Hills Hotel. I press my fingers to my mouth, the salty taste of olive brine still on my lips. What if that's the reason I'm here? What if I'm here to save Honey Black?

Chapter Four

My head throbs as I grope for the glass of water I always leave beside my bed, but it isn't there. Groaning, I roll over, tiny hammers knocking at the inside of my skull. *Whose idea was it to drink so much? Eric's?* Slowly, my eyes inch open, expecting to see the cramped, untidy bedroom of my dingy apartment, but I'm greeted with the sight of calming taupe walls, heavy cream drapes at my window, and everything comes back with a bang. *I'm still here.* I blink, tears pricking. I never thought I'd wake up longing for my depressing, lumpy single bed, and yet here I am, waking up in the most luxurious hotel in the world, wishing I was at home in my crappy apartment.

I swallow down my nausea as I recall the events of yesterday. I ended up sampling several of Louis's cocktails last night, each one at least as strong as his martini. He is fun, easy to talk to and – I feel the heat rising up my cheeks – easy on the eye, with his green eyes, lightly tanned skin, and dark hair that curls where it is ever so slightly too long. I slump back down onto the thick, bouncy pillows, unable to stop myself stretching along the Egyptian cotton sheets. A night at the Beverly Hills Hotel is every bit as comfortable as I imagined it would be. The only problem is… I force myself back into a sitting position, my skin feeling clammy. I shouldn't really be here.

Everything is a little hazy this morning, if I'm honest. After I had seen Honey leaving for her dinner, and the thought struck me that maybe she was the reason I was here, that I was meant to save her, I had sipped cocktails as I worked up the courage to ask Louis what he knew about her. Thinking back now, I hold my hands over my eyes, trying my hardest to remember what was said.

–

'What's this?' I ask Louis as he slides another glass in front of me.

'French 75,' he says with a grin. 'Gin and champagne. What do you think?'

I take a cautious sip, worried it will blow my head off like the martini, but it's surprisingly nice. 'Oh, that's delicious. Much tamer than the martini.' I press my lips together, my pulse rising as I get ready to ask about Honey. 'So, Louis, I know you said you don't discuss your clientele, but what do you know about Honey Black? I mean, I'm going to be working for her, and I just wondered if there was anything I should know.'

'Anything you should know? Like what?'

'Hmmm, I don't know…' I run my finger idly round the rim of the cocktail glass. 'Any enemies? Any… problems?' Damn. I'm not being terribly subtle.

'Enemies?' Louis lets out a laugh. 'As far as I know she's just a sweet girl from a small town who got lucky. She hasn't had time to make any enemies. Lily, I might be overstepping the mark here, but is everything OK?'

'Yes. Yes, of course.' I sip my drink to hide the flaming hot flush that creeps up my neck. 'I just… wondered, that's all. I wasn't expecting to be working for her.'

'You must have applied for the job – didn't you think you would get it?'

'Something like that,' I say, gloomily. I'm not sure how to process everything that's happened, and the alcohol isn't helping. Despite that, I gesture to my glass for a top-up. The thought of being stuck, away from everything I know and love, even if life isn't perfect in 2019, makes me go cold. 'I thought I'd be working as a chambermaid, not a PA to a movie star. I've never done anything like this before.'

Louis frowns as if not quite sure what to make of me. 'It's a good thing though… right?' He hands me a fresh cocktail.

'I don't know,' I sigh, suddenly overwhelmed. How am I supposed to save Honey from a horrible fate when I barely know a thing about her? Sure, I know all the things you can find on her Wikipedia page – I know she is an incredible actress, and that if she had lived it's likely she would have been a huge star – but nothing about her private life. How am I supposed to stop a murder with just two short weeks to do it, when all the details were hushed up? I don't even know who the main suspects were. The rumour was that the director had something to do with it, but Leonard didn't look like a killer as he passed through the hotel. But then, neither did Ted Bundy, I suppose. I have nothing to go on and while I'm the first to admit that I love true crime documentaries on Netflix, that doesn't make me a detective.

'If I'd known this was going to happen, I would at least have looked her up on the internet, got some idea about what I'm supposed to be doing.' I fold my arms on the bar and rest my head on them.

'Internet? What's internet? That something you have back home in England?'

Shit. 'Errr... something like that.' I raise my head. 'So, you don't know much about Honey?'

'Nope, sorry. I wish I could help but I probably know as much as you do.'

Oh no, Louis, you really don't.

Louis shrugs and leans in close, so close I can smell whatever cologne he's using. 'To tell you the truth, I haven't even really spoken to her. She's only been at the hotel since yesterday, and I believe they started filming today, but then you know that anyway.' He pats my hand. 'You'll be fine. Just keep your eyes and ears open and you'll learn whatever it is you need to know easy enough.'

–

As the sun creeps over the horizon, the short drive over to the set feels like an out of body experience. Honey has already gone on ahead to get her hair and make-up done, and I sit alone in the back of the studio car, the leather cool against the back of my legs, watching as I ride the familiar-yet-not streets towards the studio. Gone are some of the most recognisable sights – the Walgreens on the corner of Sunset and Vine has been replaced by a coffee shop named Norms, the red-and-white canopy that stretches over the sidewalk fresh and vivid. Instead of buildings crammed cheek by jowl, there are gaps between them, small stretches of scrubby grass punctuated by billboards advertising Wonder Bread and Camel cigarettes (More Doctors Smoke Camels Than Any Other Cigarette!). At the corner of Sunset and La Brea, we pass a drive-in restaurant, an unlit neon sign naming it 'Tiny Naylor's', the middle of the parking lot decorated with a circular planter, a feeble palm tree spouting from the centre. A lone Ford sedan, its edges soft and undeniably vintage (to my eyes, at least) is parked up, the outline of a man's profile visible in the driver's seat.

As we glide seamlessly, without the constant stop-start of the traffic, along the Sunset Strip before turning on to Santa Monica Boulevard, I press my face against the window, not wanting to miss a thing. The roads are quiet at this early hour, but a few people bustle along the side-walk, already busy, and I stare enviously at the dresses the women wear, the way the bodices fit snugly against their bodies, as the skirts flare slightly to the knee. I would pay a fortune for a dress like that in a thrift store, I think to myself, before I glance down at my own outfit, stroking the hem of my skirt as I realise I don't need to be envious. Not now. The men are pretty dapper, too. Some wear suits, others wear trousers and shirts, with braces over their shoulders as they hurry to their next destination. Although there is still that sense of hustle that I felt in LA in my own time, here everything feels a little jazzier and more exciting than I imagined it would, and I remember with a slight shudder that these people walking the streets, unaware of my gaze on them, are only four years out of World War Two.

'You OK back there, miss?' The driver glances in the rear-view mirror and I drag my eyes reluctantly from the window and give him a weak smile.

'Yes, fine. Thank you.' I look back out of the window, to the people going about their day, with no clue that for me, they've already lived their lives.

Fifteen minutes later, I arrive at the lot, sign in and head over to where Honey stands, already in full make-up and poised to begin her first scene. Excitement fizzes in my veins, despite feeling so wildly out of time and place, and slightly unsure about exactly what I'm supposed to be doing. The set is oddly familiar; it looks just the way I imagined it to. The cameras, the wires, the lights, and the people milling about are all just as you would find on any movie set in the twenty-first century, but I have to stop myself from gawping at the intricate hand-painted backdrops, so at odds with the green screens I would have expected to see. A runner points to a slight woman standing a little off to one side when I ask for Jean Lawrence, and as I make my way towards her, I hear a shout.

'No. *No*. This is *exactly* what I was talking about.' Leonard, the director, shouts in the face of a runner, shoving a clipboard at him before throwing his hands up in the air. '*How many times, people?* How many times do I have to tell you what I want? Are you all *idiots?*'

I pause, shock rooting my feet to the floor. I've never heard anyone speak so harshly to colleagues before, but then… maybe this is how it is on a movie set? I creep further to the perimeter of the set, not wanting to catch Leonard's eye.

'You. You, there.' Leonard grasps the arm of a girl as she tries to skirt past, a heavy, tiered dress in her hands. 'Get rid of that,' he wrenches the dress from her hands, dropping it to the floor, 'and get *him*,' he jerks a thumb in the direction of a good-looking actor in his twenties, 'another goddamn copy of the script. *Now*. Jesus Christ, it's like working with imbeciles.' Leonard throws his clip-board at the actor, clipping him on the side of the head as the girl scurries away, rubbing at the spot on her arm where Leonard grabbed her. Honey saunters over, her eyes big and a sweet smile on her lips as she begins to talk quietly to a seething Leonard.

'Hey. I'm Lily, Honey's new PA,' I whisper to Jean, holding out a hand, even as my eyes wander back to Honey and Leonard. 'So, that's Leonard?' I am still trying to process Leonard's behaviour, the way he casually threw the clipboard, not caring that he hit the young man, and listening to him now, it's not hard to see why people thought he might have had something to do with Honey's death. Leonard stands alone now, the violent red of his cheeks fading, but the air still rings with his harsh words.

'Of course that's Leonard.' Jean's tone is brusque, but when she turns to me, she smiles and I realise that she is only about my age, maybe a year or two older. 'The lipstick suits you.'

'Thank you so much for the package in my room, and for meeting me this morning. I'm not sure what I'm supposed to be doing, if I'm honest. As Honey's assistant.'

'Nothing too difficult. Some fetching and carrying, keeping Honey's diary, ensuring she doesn't miss any events or appearances. Keep on top of her correspondence, that sort of thing. Make sure she's on set when required, prepared for the day's scenes.' She gives me a curious once-over, her eyes lingering on my face, my hair. I reach up to pat down my damp curls. 'You must tell me if you'll require an advance on your wages. I understand things all happened rather quickly? Although Leonard should have told you he'd be expecting you to stay with Honey. She's very precious to him.' Her tone flattens again.

'Oh?' My interest is piqued. *Precious how, exactly?* Maybe Jean will let slip something that might help me figure out how to stop what is going to happen to Honey.

'Yes.' Jean smiles again, and I think maybe I imagined the off tone to her voice. 'He says she's going to make this movie a hit – and make him a lot of money. Watch.'

Honey is walking – although maybe sashaying is a better word – across the lot to where her love interest, a man who looks remarkably like Clark Gable, is waiting for her. The scene begins and once again I am struck by Honey's talent, the way she becomes her character so completely.

'Is that Clark Gable?' I whisper to Jean, as the two actors come together in a passionate kiss.

'No, that's Billy Walters. He styles himself on Clark, though.' Jean rolls her eyes. 'There's only one Clark.'

'True. I loved him in *Gone with the Wind*,' I say, glad to be able to speak honestly on one thing at least.

'We all loved Clark in that movie,' a voice says in my ear, and I turn to see a tall, blonde woman in a fur that belies the early morning California heat. 'Although I've stopped telling him that now, his head is getting too big.' Her lips twitch, and there is a mischievous glint in her eye. 'Jean, fetch me some water, would you?'

Jean hurries away on her skyscraper heels without a word and the blonde woman holds out a hand for me to shake. 'You must be Honey's new PA.'

'Yes, that's me. Lily.' I shake her hand, surprised by her strong grip. I am quite sure who the woman is, only I can't quite believe she is standing in front of me.

The woman arches a perfectly groomed eyebrow. 'Jessica. Jessica Parks.'

'Ms Parks, it's such a pleasure to meet you. I'm a big fan.'

'Really?' She smiles and I bite my lip. I forgot that so far, in 1949, Jessica Parks has only made two movies, even

46

if she did smash the box office with both of them. 'Why, you're too kind. How is Honey getting along?' She turns her attention to the scene playing out in front of us.

'Oh, she's amazing. So talented.'

'Isn't she just?' Jessica drops the smile, her lipsticked mouth covering her perfect white Hollywood teeth, as she watches Honey and Billy. 'I hope Leonard appreciates what he has in Honey, and he doesn't let that wicked temper of his get in the way. I was the original casting for Sofia, did you know that?'

'Err... no, I didn't.'

Jessica inclines her head in a gracious nod, never taking her eyes from Honey. 'I was. And then I worked with Honey on *Kentucky Queen*, and I realised – this part was made for her. I told Leonard straight away, "You must cast this girl as Sofia immediately! She's going to be a star!" And of course, Leonard did. We have a very close relationship – strictly professional, of course.'

'Oh, of course,' I say. I already know that Jessica will go on to make several more movies with Leonard at the helm, the ultimate dream team, winning Oscar after Oscar. 'And it looks as if your instincts were right – Honey is fantastic. Even if she doesn't seem to know that herself yet.'

'She is such a sweet girl.' Jessica's eyes go back to where Honey and Billy are laughing together, the scene finished. Billy says something and Honey swats him on the arm before she catches sight of us standing in the shadows. 'If you can't do something generous for your best friend, then who can you do it for? And of course, I have the kudos of being the one who discovered her! Hon, you were fabulous!'

I wait as Jessica steps forward, embracing Honey, who is grinning madly, her cheeks flushed a rosy pink. Although

Jessica is very nice, I have to admit to being a tiny bit disappointed that she doesn't have the star quality I always imagined she would have. Honey is the real star, bright and shimmering with charisma.

'Did you watch, Lily?' Honey squeezes my hand. 'What did you think? Was I good?'

Before I can respond, Jessica wraps an arm around Honey's shoulders, guiding her towards the Winnebago on the other side of the set. 'Honey, sweetie, you don't have long. Leonard will want you back on set in a few minutes, so you don't have much time.' She turns and looks over her shoulder at me. 'Could you bring us some coffee?'

And with that I am reminded that I am here to work – not as Honey's friend.

—

The day is long and tiring, although it is fascinating to watch Honey at work in between fetching cups of coffee and hunting out lost scripts, and even more fascinating to watch the way other people interact around her, hoping for some small clue to come to light. There's some waiting around, as lighting is adjusted, and Leonard screams for props, for costume, for make-up, never quite satisfied with what plays out before him. There is something almost magical in the way he makes tiny adjustments, bringing new life to each scene, a hint of genius among the bursts of fiery temper. I hand Honey tiny bites of cracker when she stops for a touch-up to her make-up, while she gazes longingly at the plates of cookies left out for the crew, and then I wince as she is packed tightly into a corseted dress, her face crumpling as the laces are pulled tight, her waist almost impossibly tiny. She looks frail and fragile as Leonard runs the scene with her before moving aside and shouting for silence, the camera beginning to roll again.

Jessica only has one scene today, and keeps her distance, spending most of the afternoon in her trailer until it's time for her to shoot her scene before the light goes. She is a pro, getting the shot in the can in one take, unlike Honey, who still manages to fluff her lines. By the time I get back to the hotel I am exhausted, dehydrated from a hangover and the heat of the sun, and my feet are killing me from running things backwards and forwards to Honey's trailer, but I wouldn't change a thing.

A housekeeping cart is in the corridor as I arrive at my room and I am reminded of Eric. Sinking onto the bed and kicking my heels off, I wonder what he is doing. Is he wondering where I am? Has *anyone* even noticed that I've disappeared? The months I've spent in LA so far have mostly been spent applying for production jobs and I haven't really made an effort to make any proper friends. I close my eyes, feeling my heart turn over at the thought of home. If I can just save Honey, then maybe I can get back. And when I do, I think, lying back on the soft pillows, I'll surround myself with new friends, and I'll definitely go to the movies with Eric... and then I am asleep before I can form the thought fully.

Chapter Five

The shrill ring of the telephone jolts me from sleep, and I gasp as my eyes fly open, my heart racing in my chest.

'Hello?'

'Lily, where are you?' Honey's voice is sharp, and it takes me a moment to place who's calling. 'Come to the suite and have drinks with me. I don't want to sit here alone all evening.'

Squinting in the dim light I peer at the clock. The hands show a little after eight o'clock and my stomach gives a growl, reminding me that I haven't eaten since the remains of Honey's crackers at lunchtime. 'I'm sorry, I was asleep. Let me get changed and freshen up and I'll be there.'

'Hurry up… we'll get room service.' Honey hangs up before I can respond. Resisting the urge to roll over and go back to sleep until morning, I force myself off the bed, the soles of my feet still sore from all the hours I spent in heels today. I wash my face, tie my hair into a ponytail and slide my Converse onto my feet before heading for the elevator down to Honey's suite.

'What were you doing sleeping? It's only early.' Honey stands to one side of the door to let me in. 'Let's order. I don't want to wait any longer for dinner, I'm starving.' I head into the lounge area, noting the open bottle of champagne from the bar on the table. Honey has a petulant look on her face, an empty champagne glass dangling from one hand.

'Honey, is everything OK?' Whatever – or whoever – has upset her, I guess it's my job to try and make it better. I think.

'Oh, sure, everything is just *swell*.' She sits on the chaise and reaches for the champagne bottle to refill her glass.

'It's just… you seem kind of… upset?' I take the glass she offers me, even as my temples let out a thud of protest at the thought of more alcohol. I've only just shaken off the hangover from last night's cocktails.

'Ugh.' She takes a healthy slug of champagne, and her eyes fill with tears that I think are genuine, but then she blinks, and I don't know if I imagined them. 'I was supposed to be going out for dinner with Leonard, but he blew me off – some financial meeting. He's got to keep the money men happy. I didn't do my best today, and I know I need to make it up to him.'

I'm not entirely sure what she means by that, but there's no mistaking the grit in her voice. 'I don't mind eating dinner with you. I would have eaten lunch with you too, if we'd actually taken a lunch break.' I take a sip of the champagne and miraculously my headache clears.

'Really? You would? Huh.' Her lips curve with the beginnings of a smile, the pout disappearing. 'I hate eating alone, but no one ever seems to want to sit with me.'

I think of the way Jessica had brushed me off earlier, and I wonder if it's more that people think they aren't allowed to approach Honey – seeing as she is the star of the movie – than that they don't *want* to approach her.

'Let's just order a salad and another bottle of champagne,' Honey is saying. 'I can't have anything too heavy.'

'What about the Waldorf salad? That looks good.'

'Oh no, Lily. Not the Waldorf. It has nuts in it, I can't eat nuts. Let's get the McCarthy salad.' Honey passes me the telephone so I can call down to room service. 'They say it's so good, it'll be world famous one day.'

I bite my lip, wishing I could tell Honey that one day the Polo Lounge will be known for it. Instead, I just nod, and ring through the order.

'So, I was supposed to meet Leonard, but he said he had a meeting that would run late… otherwise I wouldn't have bothered you.' Honey's tone is completely different now, and I realise that her shortness on the telephone was her playing the part of who she thinks Honey Black should be.

'Really Honey, I don't mind. I was only having a nap, and let's be honest, you did all the work today, not me.' I am rewarded with a bright smile, as Honey settles back on the chaise.

'I did good today, right?'

'You were brilliant. I don't know how you don't know it,' I say, meaning it.

'Nobody ever told me. You can perform in as many high-school shows as you want, but if you can't farm, you're nobody where I come from.' Honey shrugs, her cheeks flushing. 'Luckily for me, Leonard came along. That man changed my life. And Jessica, of course. Isn't she a doll? It was so kind of her to put me forward for the part of Sofia.'

'Shall we go through your lines before dinner, or do you want to rest?'

'Lines, I guess.' A cloud crosses Honey's features. 'That's the only thing I struggle with sometimes, getting

52

those pesky lines right. But if you want to make it, you have to put the work in, right?'

I walk over to the table and start rifling through the fresh pile of newspapers, avoiding looking at the date as I do so, but there is no script.

'It's not here,' I say. 'I left it on the table when I went upstairs last night.'

'I was practising in bed last night after dinner,' Honey says, walking into the bedroom and pulling back the bed covers. She shuffles through the pile of magazines next to the bed. 'It's not here either. You didn't bring it to the set?'

'No.' I shake my head. 'I woke up a little late and just headed straight out to the lot.'

'Oh no,' Honey wails. 'We have to find it! Leonard will be furious if I don't get my lines perfect tomorrow!'

'Listen,' I say quickly, as Honey flushes a deeper red and a tear threatens to spill its way down her cheek. 'It's no problem, I'll just speak to Jean and ask her to get another copy. Let me call her room now, and she can have it here for the morning.'

A sharp rap at the door stops us both in our tracks. 'That might even be her now,' I say, 'you might have left the script in the trailer, and she's brought it over.' But when I open the door, it's a waiter with a trolley carrying two silver domed plates and another bottle of champagne.

'I'm not hungry anymore,' Honey says, picking the bottle off the tray and turning her back.

'Leave it, please,' I say to the waiter before he can back out of the room taking the food with him, my stomach growling. 'Come on, you need to eat.' I place the salads on the table and Honey reluctantly picks up her knife and fork. 'I'll call up to Jean and get a copy of the script, but you need food before you can even attempt to learn any lines.'

—

The McCarthy salad is every bit as good as they said it would be, and I can understand why the hotel's clientele has raved about it for seventy years. Honey dabs at her mouth with a napkin and places it next to her plate, which still carries half the salad.

'That's me done,' she says, as she eyes the food. 'I can't afford to put on any more weight. I'd kill for a bar of chocolate, but this diet I'm on, I can only have a thousand calories a day.'

'You look perfect to me,' I say, but lay my knife and fork down in solidarity, even though I would have happily finished mine, the taste of avocado, cheese, tomato and bacon still dancing on my tongue. 'So, Honey, as we can't go over the lines right now, how about you tell me about you?'

'About me?' She looks doubtful and sips at her champagne, reaching one hand up to check her hair.

'Yeah, about you. Tell me about where you grew up, how you got your big break, about your family.' I need to collect as much information on Honey as I can, if I'm going to stop her from being hurt, and it's not like I have Google on my side.

Honey's face lights up. 'No one ever asks me that,' she says, 'well, not unless they want to put me in the newspaper.' Her glance flicks towards the pile on the table and I shift a little in my seat to shield her view. 'You're not goin' to do that, are you?'

'Of course not.'

'OK, well… where shall I start?'

'At the beginning?' I say. 'Tell me about your family.'

'I grew up in a small town in Kentucky, with my mom and my dad and my three older brothers. My dad has a farm, so we all work on it. I mean, I used to, until I got offered a part in my first movie.' Honey drops the smile and places her champagne glass on the table as if she has lost the taste. 'I used to help my mom in the garden – she grew all kinds of vegetables. And chickens. The chickens were my responsibility.' She pokes at the chopped egg left in her salad bowl. 'You can't beat a fresh egg in the morning.'

'Do you miss it?'

'No.' Her face is set, her mouth a hard line. 'I don't miss it at all.' But she looks away, blinking. 'My dad wasn't very happy when I left to go into the movies, and he was even more angry when I married Magnus. It wasn't what he wanted for me at all.'

'You've been married?' I'm shocked, although I'm not sure why. I know people used to get married a lot younger than we do in the twenty-first century, but Honey isn't even twenty-one yet.

'Sure. You didn't know? That's why I was so angry with Annabel – she let him on set.' Honey looks up at me, as if pleased to be able to tell her story to someone who hasn't read it in the newspapers a hundred times already. 'I married Magnus Michel the day I turned eighteen. I met him on the set of my first movie and it was a whirlwind romance – love at first clapperboard, that's what the newspapers said about us. He's older than me, and he swept me off my feet… We were married in Las Vegas, just us and two witnesses off the street.' Her smile fades and she reaches out to top up her glass, her tone brisk. 'It didn't work out though. I don't really want to talk about him.'

'I'm sorry, Honey.' Intrigue flares, and I have to bite my tongue to resist asking her what happened between them. 'I've heard of Magnus, but I didn't realise the two of you had been married.' Magnus Michel is a star of old Hollywood, linked to at least three major actresses of his time, including a brief marriage to Jessica Parks in the early Fifties. There is no mention of Honey in the articles I read about him though, it's as if she never existed.

Honey's voice thickens as her soft, Southern twang leeches through. 'Don't y'all believe everything you read about that man,' she says, her face darkening as she takes a gulp of champagne, failing to hide her grimace as she swallows. 'Why don't you tell me about you, Lily. Tell me about England.'

I feel a pang of homesickness as I think of the busy London streets, tube hanging on the way into work, the parks, cold lager, Scampi Fries, a filthy doner kebab on the way home from a night out. 'I miss it, I guess. I miss silly things, but I had to come here. All I ever wanted since I was a child was to come to Hollywood and be part of the movies.' Blinking, I sniff back hot tears at the thought of my mum, before she got sick, sitting in our little flat in south London. My mum, *who hasn't even been born yet.*

'What's it like in London? Is it still all rubble? I hope they didn't hit the Ivy, I always wanted to go there, ever since Laurence took Vivien Leigh.'

'Rubble?' I frown, unsure how to answer before I twig what Honey means. *Rubble. World War Two only ended four years ago.* Goosebumps rise on my arms, and I take a hasty swig of lukewarm champagne. 'Oh no, not really, not now.' Truth, but not quite. 'The Ivy is fine, I think.'

'I'm glad all of that is over, aren't you?' Honey sighs. 'I was seventeen when the war ended, and it felt like it had gone on forever. I thought I was going to be stuck in Little Creek for the rest of my life. We lost so many boys, too, in our little town. My mama was so relieved my brothers all came home. Did you lose anyone?'

I swallow, thinking of my mum, but that's totally different to the fear and heartbreak Honey is talking about. 'Um, no. I was lucky. I didn't lose anyone in the war.' It feels crazy to be talking about something that I learned about in history class as if it only happened a little while ago. Which, of course, for Honey, it did.

'And what about a guy? You got a guy back home?' Honey leans forward, as if anticipating juicy gossip.

'Ermmm, no,' I say, laughing at her exaggerated look of disappointment, but also relieved at the change of subject. 'There was a guy here though.'

'Ooh, tell me about him.'

'Well, he turned out to be a total shit, so it wasn't great.'

'Lily!' Honey presses a hand to her mouth, suppressing a wicked grin. 'Well, I suppose most of them are.'

'I caught him cheating, threw a drink over him and never saw him again.'

Honey stares at me, her eyes wide in admiration. 'You threw a drink over him? Remind me never to cross you. He sounds like he got exactly what was coming to him.' She leans in conspiratorially. 'I could have done with you on my side when Magnus was around.'

I catch my breath, hoping she'll elaborate, but she says, 'So, no one now? I hope you're not going to let that boy break your heart and hold you back. No man is worth that, Lily.'

'There is someone I think is kind of cute.' I think of Louis's dark hair, falling over one eye as he shakes a cocktail maker and feel the start of a blush creeping up my neck.

'The bartender I saw you talking to last night?' Honey raises an eyebrow and smirks – clearly, I don't have Honey's acting skills. The telephone shrieks into life and Honey jumps up to answer it.

Louis *is* cute, I think as Honey murmurs into the receiver, so quietly I can't make out her words, but I can't let myself get involved in anything romantic – I don't belong here, and it's only a matter of time… less than two weeks if my theory is correct, and then I'll be back in my own time, making beds for a living.

'That was Jessica,' Honey says, reaching for her handbag and pulling out her lipstick. 'I have to meet her for drinks, I'm afraid.'

'Oh. Of course.' I get to my feet, feeling strangely disappointed that our evening has been cut short. I had hoped that Honey would open up to me about Magnus, shedding some light on things. 'I'll get out of your hair. I hope Jessica is all right.'

'She just needs a bit of girl time. I think she's got boy trouble, and we need our girlfriends when that happens right? I would ask you to join us but I'm not sure she'll want an audience.' Honey smiles, but she is already ushering me towards the door, and I step out into the corridor promising I'll be on set by seven o'clock the following morning.

Checking my watch, I see it's still early, and after talking about Louis to Honey I decide one drink before bed won't hurt. Heading down the corridor and into the lobby, the doors to the Polo Lounge stand open and my heart skips a beat as I catch sight of him at the bar, laughing with Billy Walters. Quickly, I swipe my finger over my teeth and check there's no lipstick on them, giving my curls a volumising scrunch before stepping towards the bar. As I approach, there is movement at the rear entrance to the lobby from the path that leads to the gardens. The doors to the gardens are at a right angle to the Polo Lounge, and I find myself sliding into the alcove beside the lounge, peering round the corner into the darkness outside. Leonard and Jessica stand in the shadows of the manicured hedges that line the garden path, believing themselves to be out of sight. Jessica presses one hand to her mouth, shaking her head as Leonard gesticulates towards her. Are they *arguing*? I want to step out, but I can't risk being seen.

'*Enough*, Jessica.' Leonard's hushed tones are a whisper on the night breeze, and I watch transfixed as Jessica reaches out and snatches at his sleeve. I can't make out Leonard's response, but he grabs her wrist, pulling her arm up high, away from his jacket. Jessica glares at him for a moment, and then with a sob, she tugs herself free and marches towards the lobby without a backward glance.

She hurries inside, head lowered and hair falling in a curtain as if to shield her face from view. Still concealed in the entrance to the Polo Lounge, my breath coming loud in my ears, I watch as Jessica reaches the corridor that leads to the Paul Williams suite, her arms folded across her body. The rear doors are whisked open again, and I swivel to see Leonard striding into the lobby, headed to the elevator just as Jessica disappears from view. I'm not sure, but it looks as if she has been crying.

'Hey stranger.' Warm breath and low tones in my ear make me jump and I turn to see Louis standing behind me, green eyes sparkling. 'What are you doing lurking here? You coming in for a drink? I'll make you something special.'

'Sure.' I paste on a smile and follow him through into the bar, turning back to see Leonard standing at the closed elevator doors, his face like granite. Was Leonard really meeting Jessica instead of the money men he told Honey he was seeing this evening? If so, why would he lie to Honey about it? Although they entered the hotel separately, I got the feeling that they had spent the evening together... and it sounded as though they had argued – Jessica certainly seemed upset. I think of the way Leonard reached out and grasped Jessica's wrist, the way her face had crumpled in pain. Could Leonard and his wicked temper play a part in Honey's demise, just like the rumours said?

Chapter Six

'What's your poison?' Louis stands to one side to show off the bottles on the bar, but I shake my head, the buzz from the champagne I drank with Honey already fading to leave me with the vague beginnings of a hangover.

'Just orange juice, please,' I say, as the piano guy tinkles away behind me. 'And some advice, if you're willing to offer it.'

'Sure.' Louis serves the other customers at the bar before coming back to me, a frosted tumbler of juice in his hand. 'So, what's the problem?'

'You ever have a friend that might... I don't know, be mixed up with the wrong guy?' I ask, thinking of the way Leonard had twisted Jessica's arm away from him. If he could behave that way with Jessica, an already established movie star, there's nothing to stop him getting physical with Honey.

'The wrong girl... sure. We're not talking about you, are we?' Louis's face clouds with concern and I shake my head

'Hell, no. I got rid of my wrong guy... ages ago.' I don't know why I said that so vehemently – it's almost as if I want Louis to know I'm available. Which is ridiculous, because I belong seventy years from now, in a world of online dating and reality TV shows, of iPhones and 5G and the world at my fingertips via the internet. I definitely don't belong in 1949, in the Beverly Hills Hotel, working as a PA for a movie star who is about to be murdered. There is a sharp pang somewhere around my ribcage and I take a hasty swig of orange juice, the cold, sweet liquid sliding down my throat. 'What did you do? Did you warn them? Tell them that perhaps the guy or girl they thought was so great might actually… not be?'

'No. Definitely not.'

'No? Not even if you knew something bad would… *might* happen?'

'Maybe if I knew for sure that something bad was going to happen, but then the chances are I wouldn't be able to stop things anyway.'

He's got a point. But this is *murder*.

Louis fixes his deep green eyes on me. 'Sometimes warning people off can make things worse. You might have whatever it is all wrong, and then what happens?' He blows out a long breath. 'But on the other hand, you have to do what feels right.'

What feels right is to warn Honey, to tell her everything, even as my throat closes over at the thought of telling her that she's in danger from *someone* – but I can't tell her who, because I don't know. What if I tell her and she thinks I'm crazy? Because let's be honest, that's exactly what I thought myself, not that long ago. She could fire me, and then I would blow any chance of finding out who is going to try and kill her – even if she *doesn't* fire me, there's still a chance that she could end up dead if I can't find the right person in time. 'Maybe I should give it a little more time. Just to be sure.'

Louis takes my now empty glass from me, his fingers brushing mine and sending a bolt of electricity through me. I think he felt it too, as his eyes meet mine and a smile lifts his mouth into a curve. 'Maybe you should have another drink.'

–

The next day the car picks me up and I spend the journey to the lot with my face pressed against the window, only today my mind is full of Honey and what is going to happen to her, and I barely pay any attention to the changed landscape outside. She clammed up last night after she mentioned her marriage to Magnus, and I got the distinct impression that she didn't want – or wasn't allowed – to talk about it, and it's got me feeling uneasy. There are so many rumours in the twenty-first century about the so-called Golden Age of cinema that Honey's reluctance to talk about Magnus, and the way Jessica lowered her head as she scurried away from Leonard last night, have got my mind whirring. Lots of things will come to light in the decades to come – Clark Gable's illegitimate daughter, the product of a rumoured date rape, with Loretta Young, Errol Flynn's alleged taste for underage girls, right through to Harvey Weinstein's appalling behaviour that led to the #MeToo movement – but I'm sure there are plenty of other secrets hidden beneath Hollywood's golden veneer. I scrub my hands over my skirt, the thoughts making me feel grubby, and leaving a sour taste in my mouth. I don't want Honey to be a secret, brushed under the red carpet.

'Miss?' The driver's voice cuts into my thoughts. 'We're here.'

I raise my head, and blink. 'Thank you.' Sliding from the car I see a crowd of people at the gates, shouting and waving as one of the assistants approaches. They are there hoping to be chosen as extras, and as I battle my way around the edge of the crowd towards the entrance booth, I can't help but watch as the men and women desperately try to gain attention, dying to get onto the big screen.

Honey is in her Winnebago with Jean when I arrive, her hair tightly wrapped in rollers.

'Morning sugar, how are you?' The air in the trailer is stiflingly hot and Honey smiles at me from beneath the make-up girl's brushes as Jean gives me a brisk nod, but there is an unspoken tension in the air, as though I have interrupted something.

'Good. Thanks.' I hope the worry I feel over Honey doesn't show on my face. 'Where do you need me today?'

Jean steps forward. 'I have some things for you to do this morning, Lily, I'm sure Honey won't mind me borrowing you.'

I glance back at Honey as Jean grips my arm and leads me from the trailer. Honey's eyes are fixed on Jean, but she waves a hand in my direction. 'Go on sweetheart, I'm all set here.'

When Jean slams the trailer door behind her I'm not sure if it's entirely accidental.

Jean has me running around for most of the morning, searching out replacement glasses for a scene inside the saloon, when Leonard decides he's not happy with the existing ones. Tempers flare, and more than one glass is broken, leaving my nerves jangling when not one, but two of the male extras think it's OK to pinch my bottom as I scurry past with glasses piled high. My teeth clamp down hard on my tongue as I bite back the urge to tell them exactly what they can do with their grasping hands.

Eventually Honey and Billy shoot their next scene together, but I find it hard to concentrate despite the magnetism between them. There is some tension when

Honey forgets her lines again, Leonard throwing the script to the ground, and marching towards Honey and Billy, causing my pulse to rocket. In addition to this, I watch Jessica as closely as I can, looking for a sign that perhaps she and Leonard are involved together, that he was the reason for her tears last night. Leonard is harder to watch after his outburst, as he stalks furiously to the sidelines of the set, shouting directions, his voice coming in angry waves. I bump into him during the afternoon break, as I hurry towards Honey's trailer with a salad, Leonard's eyes on a sheet of airmail paper that flutters to the ground as we collide.

'Oh God, sorry,' I gasp. 'I mean… here, let me…' Awkwardly I stoop down, snagging the letter between finger and thumb. I hold it out to Leonard, and as I run my eyes discreetly over the scrawled penmanship I make out Honey's name, and the X of a kiss scratched into the bottom of the page.

Leonard snatches the letter out of my hands, irritation grazing his features. 'Listen sweetheart, you wanna make it in this town? You should probably watch where you're going.'

I stare back at him, swallowing down the urge to tell him perhaps *he* should watch where *he* is going. He raises his eyebrows at me, before stalking off, leaving me wondering if he has it in him to stab Honey to death.

–

Back at the hotel, I am lying on my bed, thinking about the letter Leonard was reading (was it a love letter? Did Honey write it, or did someone write to him *about* Honey?), when there is a brisk knock and then Honey pushes her way into my room, not caring that I am in my robe as she sits on the end of the bed and grins at me.

'Come on,' she says. 'Get dressed.'

'Why?' I pull my robe tighter around me, smoothing one hand over my curls.

'We're going out.'

'Out? Now? Where?' Half of me is intrigued, excited by the thought of a night on the tiles with Honey Black in 1949, the other half is exhausted from a day on the lot. Thank goodness Jean pressed an envelope containing a wage advance into my hands as I left the set earlier.

Honey has her head in my wardrobe and pulls out a green swing dress that makes me think of Betty Grable. 'Just get dressed. Lily, I thought you were a kindred spirit. I'm getting shades of Annabel here.'

Oh God, no. 'I am. A kindred spirit, I mean.' I tug the dress on, pausing to look in the full-length mirror. It fits perfectly, hugging my curves and making my waist seem much smaller than it really is.

'Very pretty,' Honey says, with a wink. 'You know what you're missing though? A little smoky eye.'

'Oh, I don't—' All I have is the lipstick Jean left me. I would never dream of going out with just lipstick in my own time; I would have spent hours on my face, but looking at Honey now, I see all she wears is lipstick, a little mascara, a faint blush of rouge and some powder, her skin flawlessly matte.

Honey pulls a small tin from her purse. 'Here.' She wets the tiny brush inside and mixes it with what I realise is a solid cake of black mascara. 'Close your eyes.' The brush gently strokes my lashes, and when I open my eyes I look more like me, the 2019 version.

I slick on a little of the Cashmere Bouquet lipstick, and let Honey take me by the hand and lead me downstairs and out onto the sidewalk, shrugging off the strain of my day on set. I feel that odd spinning sensation again, as though this is all something unreal, flinching when I surreptitiously pinch my own thigh and realise, once again, that this is definitely not a dream.

'Where are we going?' I ask, as she leads me towards a sleek black Lincoln Town Car, surprising me by getting behind the wheel herself.

'The Palomino. You heard of it?' She grins at me as I slide into the passenger seat, the white leather sticking to my legs in the evening summer heat.

'The Palomino?' The only Palomino I can think of is the Palomino Club in North Hollywood, but that shut down years ago. 'I'm not sure.'

She guns the engine and screeches out onto the street. 'It's new, it just opened a few months back. It's where all the hipsters go. I hope you like it.'

Of course, it didn't shut down… it only just opened. 'Wait… hipsters?' Visions of man buns, plaid shirts and beards dance through my head.

Honey rolls her eyes. 'Honestly Lily, I think you live in another world sometimes. I mean all the cool cats go there. I wanted to get you out of the hotel for a while. Have some fun.'

It's a twenty-minute drive from the hotel to the club, and Honey drives too fast and talks non-stop. She seems more relaxed away from the set, just the two of us, and I spend most of the drive trying to summon up the courage to ask her about Magnus, and her relationship with Leonard.

'So,' I say when she finally takes a breath. 'You and Leonard get along well, huh?'

'Sure,' she shrugs, 'he's a real swell guy.'

'You don't think he can be a little…'

'A little what?' She takes her eyes off the road to look at me and a worm of fear squirms in my belly. She has a lead foot and a short attention span. 'A little intense, sure. He likes everything to be perfect on set, but that's why he's so good.'

I was going to say aggressive, but I just nod. 'And what about Magnus? How come he showed up on set? You seemed really upset with Annabel over it.'

'Well, yeah.' Honey snorts, but her face is like granite. 'I was upset, and I really don't think anyone could blame me. He's—' She swings the car off the road, into a small parking lot. 'Here we are.'

It really is the Palomino Club, the famous LA club that closed in the mid-Nineties – but as I stand in front of it now, it is very much open, the neon sign out the front proclaiming, 'NEW LIVE ACT TONITE' with names I don't recognise underneath. The front of the building looks like a Wild West corral, and as the door swings open the strains of Hank Williams reach my ears.

'Oh my gosh, Honey, this is incredible!'

'I knew you'd love it.' Honey grabs my hand and pulls me towards the door, and as she pushes it open, I am assaulted by a wave of heat from the bodies in the club, the twang of guitars and the scent of hops and cigarette smoke on the air. 'This way.' She pulls me towards a booth before spinning on her heel and heading to the bar, weaving her way between dancing bodies. A trickle of sweat runs down my spine as I wait, the heat of the room thick and sultry.

The place is packed, the air a hazy blue with smoke from the cigarettes everyone seems to be holding, the tickle of tobacco an almost refreshing change from the sweet scent of vape fumes that I'm more used to. A tall guy who is not Hank Williams but sings just like him is on stage, with a band behind him. Everywhere I look people are dancing, drinking, laughing and I find my feet beneath the table are tapping in time to the beat, eager to get up on the dance floor. I look for Honey, but there is no sign of her, so I push my way between the throngs of people dancing and drinking, until I get to the bar.

'Just a beer, please,' I say to the bartender, as I catch a flash of blonde hair in a darkened corner. Honey is leaning over a table, one hand against the wall, talking to someone I can't see. I feel a pang of disappointment that she brought me here only to abandon me before we even got a drink, but I guess when people know your face everyone wants to say hi.

'Fancy seeing you here,' a voice breathes in my ear, and I jump, beer spilling over the sleeve of my dress.

'Louis!' I grin at him, a warmth spreading through me at the sight of his familiar face. 'What are you doing here?'

'Same as you – drinking, dancing.' He holds his beer bottle aloft. 'Who are you here with?'

'Honey brought me, but she kind of got side-tracked.' I look over to the corner, but she is gone again. 'How about you?'

Louis shrugs. 'Just a few friends, no one important.'

The song changes to something upbeat and jazzy, and I feel a spark of recognition at the first few notes that play. 'My gran loved this song!' I exclaim.

'I'm sorry,' Louis says soberly, as he stands rooted to the spot. 'You must have lost her very recently.'

'Oh.' I realise I have once again forgotten where – when – I am. 'I meant to say loves, not loved. She's… very cool. I didn't have you down as a jazz fan.'

'I didn't think I was until I started coming here, but music is music, right?' He places his empty bottle on the bar and holds out his hand. 'Do you want to dance?'

I cast a glance over the dance floor. Everyone seems to be engaging in some *very* energetic swing dancing, something I can't say I've ever tried before. 'What about your friends?'

Louis turns towards a bunch of rowdy lads at one of the far tables. 'They'll be fine. Come on, Honey's done a disappearing act, and you don't want to dance alone, do you?' He grabs my hand and pulls me onto the dance floor. 'Interesting footwear.'

I look down at my Converse. 'I'm not really a heels kind of girl. Oh!' Louis spins me out of his arms, twisting and twirling me until I am breathless and giddy, and completely ignorant of my two left feet. Watching the other girls on the dance floor, I try to mimic the swing of their hips as I am whirled around, and I must be doing something right, as a man cuts in, slipping my hand from Louis's into his.

'Relax doll, I'll show you how it's done.' Leering at me, his breath is as ripe as his armpits, and I am relieved when Louis cuts back in. I've never been so blatantly man-handled before, and I can't say as I enjoy it.

As we return to stand together at the bar, Louis's arm rests against my shoulder and I feel a zing deep in my belly before I move away slightly, raising my arm to attract the bartender's attention. It's not that I don't want him close to me, more that I am worried about what will happen if I let him know that I do. The bartender brings the drinks and Louis holds out a dollar bill, but I wave him away, paying the bill myself.

'My round!' I shout, clinking glasses with Louis, before taking a sip of icy cold beer. If this was at home, in my time, I would have taken a dozen photos, making sure we had just the right angle before posting them on my Snapchat story, along with a Boomerang of our clinking glasses. Instead, tonight, I am just living in the moment.

'I've never met anyone like you before,' Louis says, his eyes never leaving my face as he sips at his own drink. 'No girl I know would pay for her own drinks… is that how they do it in England?'

Loosened by the alcohol I laugh. 'Something like that.' We take our drinks to a vacant booth, and I sigh as I get to rest my poor, aching toes.

'So, did you sort out whatever it was that was bothering you last night?' Louis asks, and my smile drops. I shouldn't be having fun with Louis; I should be trying to track down whoever is going to kill Honey.

'Not really,' I say, picking at the label on my beer bottle. 'It's hard to sort it out when I don't even know where to begin. I'm sorry, I know I'm being vague. I wish I could tell you more.'

'I'm good at keeping secrets.' Louis clinks his beer bottle against mine.

I'm not worried Louis won't keep my secret; I'm worried he'll think I'm bonkers. 'How do you know if someone is a good person?' I ask instead, thinking perhaps he'll have a foolproof way of recognising a shit thanks to all his hours behind the bar.

'I guess you don't,' Louis says after a long pause. 'I guess you just have to trust your instincts – until they prove themselves unreliable.' Not very helpful if I'm honest. I don't have time to sit back and wait to see if Leonard loses his temper at Honey, or an obsessed fan goes crazy, and it's not even as though I have any instincts about either scenario.

'But what if you don't have time...' My voice trails off as a flash of blonde whirls past me on the dance floor. At first I think I'm imagining her but when she whirls past again, laughter lighting up her face, I realise she's real. I had forgotten all about Honey. 'Shit.'

'What is it?' Louis leans in close as I lower my voice and I can smell the beer on his breath. It's not unpleasant and for a moment I imagine pressing my mouth to his before I shake the image away.

'It's Honey.' I discreetly lift a finger in the general direction of where she is now slipping into a booth, a dark-haired man following her with his hand dangerously low on her waist. 'She's over there, with a guy. I should have been keeping an eye on her.'

Louis glances to where Honey is now leaning forward, smiling flirtatiously as the guy leans in, his elbow resting on the table. 'She's an adult, Lil. You're her PA, not her minder.'

'Is that who I think it is?' I say, unable to tear my eyes away. You can almost feel the air crackle between the two of them, and there was me putting it down to their acting skills.

'Yeah,' Louis breathes. 'Billy Walters. I hope Honey knows what she's doing.'

'What? Why?' I drag my eyes away, focusing on Louis's face instead. 'They're colleagues – they can go for a drink after work, can't they?' But even as I say the words, I think that I'm not fooling myself... or Louis.

Louis raises his eyebrows. 'She's playing with fire,' he says. 'If America's sweetheart could be a man, Billy would be it. Happily married to Cynthia Lake, America's *other* sweetheart.'

'Oh. Of course. I remember,' I breathe. I wish, not for the first time, that my phone worked, that I had access to that little Google icon that could tell me anything I need to know. 'He has affair after affair, a recipe for disaster, right?' Louis gives me a quizzical look as Billy reaches for Honey's hand, their fingers interlocking briefly before Honey looks over her shoulder and tugs it away. 'Do you think I should go over there? Tell her that we should leave? I don't want her getting into any trouble.'

'No,' Louis says and flicks his wrist to glance at his watch. 'It's closing time soon, so hopefully people will start to leave, and no one will notice them. The press would have a field day seeing them here together. It's best if we don't draw attention to them. I can give you a ride home.'

'I should say goodbye, at least.' I slip over to the booth, waving discreetly to attract Honey's attention. I gesture to tell her I'm leaving, and she waves me away before she turns her attention back to Billy. I follow Louis out to his car, a battered old Cadillac, its bodywork a faded blue spotted with rust.

'This is your car?' I run my hand over the spotlessly clean dash. It might be old and in need of some TLC but it's still a beautiful car.

'Sure is. I saved all my money from every odd job I ever had to buy her. She's not the prettiest, but I'm saving to do the repairs.'

'I think she's lovely,' I say, wondering what Louis would think if I told him that seventy years from now people will be prepared to pay thousands of dollars for a car like this, rust spots and all.

We talk the entire way back to the hotel. I learn that Louis is really a musician, his first love being the guitar and the piano, and that although he loves working the bar at the Beverly Hills, his dream is to become a performer.

'What's your dream, Lil?' he asks, keeping his eyes on the road.

I think for a minute. 'This, I guess,' I say eventually. 'Working with Honey, working in the movies. It's all I ever wanted. I guess you could say I'm living my dream right now.' Biting my lip, I have to look out of the window and blink rapidly to get rid of the tears that sting my eyes. It's true that I am living my dream, it's just that I should be living it in the twenty-first century. And if what Eric told me in the Paul Williams Suite is true, I'm only going to be living it for two weeks before everything goes horribly wrong.

I change the subject. 'So, you live with your parents?'

'Nah, I share an apartment with a coupla guys over on Vine. Too crowded at home – there's a lot of us. You have to meet my sister, Tilda. You'll love her. She's kind of… wild, I guess – sometimes I think she doesn't belong here, she belongs to a different time – but…' He glances over at me. 'I think she's your kinda gal.'

'I can't wait to meet her,' I say, unease prickling my scalp. In any other circumstances I would love to meet Louis's sister, but meeting her, liking her, and maybe wanting to become friends with her feels strangely terrifying. 'And what about…' I swallow, my mouth suddenly dry, 'girlfriends and stuff? Do you—'

'Here we are.' Louis comes to an abrupt halt outside the hotel. 'Sorry Lil, I have to get home, but I had fun tonight. See you tomorrow, maybe? And don't worry about Honey, I'm sure she'll be fine.'

That's easy for Louis to say, I think as I wave goodbye and make my way inside. Have I made a mistake leaving Honey at the Palomino on her own? What if it isn't Leonard and his fiery temper that I should be watching after all? What if I should be protecting Honey from Billy Walters? It's a question that keeps me awake for hours, until I eventually drop off around four o'clock in the morning, with no idea that things are about to get a whole lot worse.

Chapter Seven

A loud pounding drags me from sleep, my heart racing as I struggle my way into consciousness. Blearily, I glance at the clock, registering that it is six o'clock and I'm going to be functioning today on two hours' sleep, before the hammering starts again, my name filtering through the door.

'All right,' I shout, dragging the complimentary robe from the back of the chair and shrugging it on. 'I'm coming.'

Jean pushes her way inside as I pull the door open, a pile of newspapers in her arms. 'Where's the fire?' I say grumpily. 'You could have at least brought some coffee, or a Red Bull.'

Jean looks at me oddly before shaking her head. 'You need to go and see Honey,' she says, shortly. She is dressed in a cream Chanel blouse with a contrasting black pussy bow – one that I would have snatched right off the rail in a Goodwill store – and a pair of high-waisted navy blue trousers with a wide leg. Her hair is twisted into a sleek chignon, her face is immaculately made up, and I can smell the powder she uses. By contrast, I look like I've spent the night in the gutter, my curls tangled into corkscrews sticking out all over my head, a smear of last night's mascara leaving a black streak under my eyes. Surreptitiously, I lick the fabric of my sleeve and rub it under my eyes as Jean walks to the small table, kicking my Converse out of the way.

'Have you seen this?' Jean holds up today's *LA Times* and jabs a finger at the front page.

'Jean, it's six o'clock in the morning. I opened my eyes to you hammering on the door. I haven't seen anything.' *Tea*, I think, *what I wouldn't give for a cup of tea. None of that wimpy Lipton stuff either. A proper cup of PG Tips, brewed for three minutes, so strong you can stand the spoon up in it.* I settle for swigging water out of the glass next to the bed, before I take the paper that Jean is still thrusting in my direction.

'Oh, bollocks.' Ignoring Jean's shocked gasp, I run my eyes over the headline. *BLACK AND WALTERS GET CLOSE AT PONY CLUB.* Not very original, I think, or witty. The picture accompanying the headline makes it seem even worse. Honey and Billy are leaving the club, clearly the worse for wear. Honey is grasping Billy by the hand, leaning into him as more flesh than is acceptable in 1949 spills out from her blouse. Billy is looking down, his arm around her waist and dangerously close to her bottom. 'Oh yikes… who else has seen this?'

Jean shrugs. 'Who knows? Everyone, or at least it will be everyone by lunchtime. They have all the newspapers on set.' She presses a hand to her mouth. 'Leonard receives the newspaper with his morning coffee. He's probably already seen it.'

'Couldn't we get rid of them?' I start pacing, thinking hard. The shit is really going to hit the fan, and it's my job as Honey's PA to sort it out, isn't it? What if this article is the catalyst that pushes Honey's killer over the edge? I knew I shouldn't have left her there last night.

'Well, we can remove them from set, but won't everyone just go and buy one – or send us out to buy more if they want to read them?'

This is a nightmare. Although I suppose I should be thankful that I don't have to worry about TMZ and Page Six. Imagining the Twitter storm a story like this would create in 2019, I thank my lucky stars it's *only* print. I scan through the article, fury igniting in my veins. It says Billy and Honey were seen together at the Palomino, referring to Honey as a 'starlet' in 'revealing' clothes, seen 'throwing herself' at Billy. Billy is only referred to as a happily married 'up and coming movie star'. *What will Cynthia Lake make of this?* is the final line of the article.

'This is rubbish,' I say, throwing the paper back on to the pile. Every other paper carries the same picture, with some similar version of the headline.

Jean raises her eyebrows, pursing her lips into a prim bow. 'Lily, I know you like Honey, but honestly, I don't know how you can say this is rubbish. Look at the photograph, obviously the two of them were… enjoying themselves… on what clearly seems to be a date. And Billy a married man, too. Honey has to understand that she can't just swoop in on any man she pleases.'

'No, Jean, I mean this is absolute rubbish. And you can take that look of disappointment off your face.' I shrug off my robe and reach for some clean underwear and yesterday's dress. Jean sniffs and turns her back as I start to get dressed, eager to see Honey and get this mess sorted out. 'I was there last night, with Honey. She took me out for drinks and dancing, but I lost track of her. I was dancing with Louis, and Honey was talking to other people.'

'You were there? With... the barman?' Jean turns around, her mouth open, seemingly not bothered now about seeing me in my knickers.

'Yes. And his name is Louis, not "the barman".' I sniff the fabric of the dress, relieved to find it smells only of perfume, with a lingering hint of cigarette smoke. 'Honey sort of abandoned me – we saw Honey and Billy in a booth just before we left, and Louis offered me a ride home.'

'So, they *were* there,' Jean breathes. 'Poor Cynthia.'

'No, it wasn't like that,' I say, thinking of Honey tugging her hand away. 'They were there together, but not *together*. They were just dancing, drinking, having fun. I never saw anything... untoward.'

'But look at the photo – Honey is all over him.'

'No, she wasn't.' The more I think about it, the more I think Honey was just drunk, rather than flirting. The way she had leaned across the table to hear Billy talk seemed sloppy, as though she was propping herself up. And she had tugged her hand away, hadn't she? If she was having an affair with Billy, why pull away from him? She would have been too drunk to think about pictures being taken.

'You should have told her to leave, you must have known how it would have looked.' Jean turns her disapproval on me. 'Didn't you see the press waiting?'

'No.' I shake my head. 'We left before her. Louis said not to go over and tell her to leave in case we drew attention to them both. We left and he dropped me off here.'

'Oh, Louis did, did he?'

'What's that supposed to mean?'

'Did he make you leave straight away?'

'Yes, but I don't see…'

'He probably called the newspapers!' Jean tuts, throwing her hands in the air. 'Lily, you silly girl. He probably rushed you back to the hotel so he could go home and call the newspapers himself, so they could get there before Honey and Billy left.'

'No. Louis wouldn't do that. He wanted to leave without speaking to them so we could protect them. The last thing he would do is call the papers and tip them off.' *At least, I don't think he would.*

'Oh Lily, you have so much to learn,' Jean sighs. 'Wouldn't he call the papers? How well do you really know him?'

'Well enough,' I snap, snatching up my bag and wishing more than anything that I had a mobile phone that worked, that I could text Louis and ask him right now to show Jean that I'm right. 'He works at the Beverly Hills Hotel, Jean; he sees famous people all the time. Why would he tip them off to Honey and Billy?'

'Barmen don't get paid an awful lot, Lily.' Jean stands next to me, her head on one side in a poor attempt at sympathy. 'He could have been tempted by the money they would pay – it's a hell of a scoop.'

He wouldn't, would he? I pause, thinking back to the previous evening. I had been hoping that we would stop for a drink somewhere quieter on the way home, or even that Louis might have come to my room – just for a drink – but he had seemed absurdly keen to drop me off and leave.

'Regardless of who tipped them off,' Jean continues, 'I dread to think how Leonard is going to react when he sees this.'

Shit. I had forgotten about Leonard. 'Will he be furious?' I ask, already knowing the answer. 'After all, there's no such thing as bad publicity, right?'

'I don't know about that.' Jean frowns, her forehead wrinkling. 'This is a big budget movie – he can't afford to lose the audience because of Honey's scandalous behaviour. There are other stars who would gladly step into Honey's role.'

'Honey's...' I am stunned. 'Billy is the one who is married! Honey hasn't done anything wrong.'

'Tell that to Cynthia.' Jean looks at her watch and snatches up her pile of newspapers, all business again. 'Honestly Lily, everyone knows it's always the other woman's fault. Look, you go and see Honey – she needs to know what's happened. You'll need to prepare her for more bad press, particularly once Cynthia gets wind of it, if she hasn't already. She might be America's sweetheart, but she takes no prisoners. I'll go and try to diffuse the situation with Leonard before... well, I'll just go and calm Leonard down.' And she is gone in a cloud of Chanel No. 5, leaving me the copy of the *LA Times* to take to Honey.

The newspaper leaves an inky stain on my damp palms as I make my way down to Honey's suite. Could I have caused all of this by agreeing to dance with Louis last night? If I had just made more of an effort to keep an eye on Honey, maybe I could have prevented this from happening. The idea that Louis could have called the newspapers to tip them off makes my blood run cold before I shake the thought away. No, I trust Louis. *Don't I?* There is something so kind and familiar about him that makes it difficult for me to believe he would ever betray that trust. A feeling that I have known him before, maybe in another life. And then there's Leonard. What if this article ruins his plans for the movie? Could it push him over the edge into hurting Honey? After all, if the tears on Jessica's face the other night are anything to go by, he's not always the amazing guy that Honey seems to think he is, and there's no doubt that when it comes to the movie, he's got a fiery temper. Either way, I have to do my best to diffuse the situation – as it stands things look really bad for Honey.

I step out of the elevator, and as I pass Jessica's room, one of the housekeeping staff lays today's newspaper down so that it just peeps under her door, the do not disturb sign still swinging from the handle. Waiting until she disappears around the corner, I double back and snatch up the paper. *One down, who knows however many more to go.*

It's not until I am almost at the door to Honey's suite that I hear raised voices coming from within. I slow to a stop, standing as close to the door as I dare, pressing my ear to the wood. Honey's voice, shrill and high-pitched, filters through, her Southern twang more pronounced than usual.

'Honey… humiliate me… you'll regret this.' A man's voice, gruff and raw with anger. *Please don't tell me Leonard got to Honey before Jean got to Leonard.* Flinching at the sound of smashing glass from within, I raise my hand to try the handle, but before I can connect with the door it flies open, and I have to take a hurried step to one side as a tall man, easily over six feet tall, with a head of inky black hair marches past me with a face like thunder. I wait a moment as he punches at the elevator button before I step into Honey's suite.

'Honey? It's me, Lily. Are you OK?'

Honey looks up from where she sits on the chaise, her head in her hands, the remains of the champagne glasses glittering on the carpet in front of her. 'Lily. I see you've met my ex-husband.'

Chapter Eight

Magnus Michel, Honey's ex-husband. I hadn't recognised him as he stormed past me, his face purple and ugly with rage. When Honey had mentioned him earlier, I had pictured him as he will look in around twenty years' time, at the height of his career – lightly suntanned (probably from a bottle, now that I think of it), with a neatly trimmed moustache and thick silvery hair – forgetting that it is 1949 and Magnus is barely thirty.

'That was Magnus?' I turn to look behind me, past the open door and out into the corridor, but it's empty, the dial on the elevator showing that Magnus is already on his way upstairs. 'He was… *is* my mum's favourite, after Clark Gable.'

'He is?' At first, I think Honey is upset, but as she raises a pink-cheeked face, her mascara smudged into black swirls under her eyes, I realise she is furious. 'I didn't know the movie was released in London yet. He'll be so pleased, I'm sure.'

Shit. I forgot that the movie that made Magnus into an international star hasn't even made it across the Atlantic yet. I wish, not for the first time, that I had stopped and thought before I opened my mouth. I move across the thick carpet to where Honey sits on the chaise and perch next to her. 'He's really mad, huh?'

'Really, really mad.'

'Why is he here? I mean, I know you were married, but you're not together anymore, right?' I place a hand on her arm, feeling the vibrations of her anger as she shakes her head.

'He saw the newspaper,' Honey says, swiping a finger under her eyes, her fingertip coming away black with make-up. 'Not that it's anything to do with Magnus – you're right, we're separated. He's no one to me, not now...' She sighs. 'There was a headline this morning, a photograph of me and Billy.'

'I saw it,' I say. 'Jean showed it to me first thing this morning.'

'Oh *no*. Oh, no, no, *no*.' Honey gets to her feet, letting out a shriek of frustration so loud that I fully expect security to burst through the door. 'Leonard is going to be furious!'

'One angry male at a time,' I say, still wondering how Magnus got here so quickly as I watch Honey pace the suite. Her tiny fists are clenched as she marches back and forth, and I feel my own blood spark in response. 'Was Magnus still in town? He seems to have arrived while the news was still hot off the press,' I say, as her pacing slows, and her fists begin to relax.

'He's here for a promotional thing, for his new movie.' *Right, the movie that is going to take him transatlantic.* 'But he has contacts at all the newspapers... someone would have tipped him off. He was here before the sun was even up, ranting and raving at me.' She blinks as her eyes fill with tears. 'And I know he's going to go straight to Leonard, show him the newspaper if Jean hasn't already. What if he kicks me off the set? I'll be ruined.'

'He won't.'

If there's one thing I do know for certain, it's that Leonard won't kick Honey off the set... *at least, I don't think he will.*

'How can you be so sure?'

'I just... know,' I say. 'Listen Honey, I think the best thing we can do is get you to set early, so you can talk everything through with Leonard. You didn't do anything wrong, OK?'

'I shouldn't have gone to the Palomino... I definitely shouldn't have drunk Tom Collins all night with Billy.'

'But you did – and you didn't do anything wrong!' I say, exasperation making my voice rise. 'Billy is married – not you. You're the innocent party in all this – even if you did go on a date with Billy, he's the one in a relationship. I know you didn't do anything. I was there, remember?'

Honey gives me an odd look. '*Innocent?* You know they'll all blame me, Lily. That's how it is. I'll be the scarlet woman – just ask Magnus.' She pauses, drawing her brows into a deep V. 'I'm sorry I left you alone last night, Lily. I really did want to take you out, but then I saw Billy and he bought me a drink and then... well, you can see for yourself how it went.'

'Honey, it's OK. Louis was there too, and we saw you guys dancing together. Dancing. That's all, nothing else, and certainly nothing like the newspapers are alluding to. I'll tell Leonard that myself if I have to.'

'You would?' Honey stops pacing, a smile beginning to twitch at the corners of her mouth.

'Of course, I would – what kind of friend would I be if I let Leonard believe something that wasn't true?' Even as I say the words, I gulp down the nerves that flutter in my ribcage at the idea of facing down Leonard.

'Lily, you are such a good friend, you know that? When I first met you, I just knew you had a kind heart. I knew you would become someone special to me.' Honey reaches out and squeezes my hand. 'Let me go and wash my face and then we'll head to the set. I want you to come in my car with me today.' She scurries away, skipping around the shattered glass on the carpet.

Such a good friend. I'm trying to be, I think, as I get to my knees and start collecting up the fractured shards of the champagne saucers.

'Lil?' Honey peers out from the bathroom as I throw the glass shards into the waste bin, a wicked grin across her face. 'I looked good in the pictures though, right?'

–

I feel the atmosphere on set the moment Honey and I step out of her car. I can't even tell you what a treat it is, to be chauffeured into a Hollywood studio in a huge black Chrysler, when you're used to commuting on a hot, stinky bus every morning, but I can't enjoy it, not today. Not while Honey is gazing out of the window, silent, her hand going to her mouth every five minutes as she nibbles on her nails. She may present a tough face to the rest of the world, but I'm learning that the real Honey Black is far more vulnerable than she lets on. Now, we are here, and there is a definite air of *something* on set.

We cross the lot, me following Honey as she walks briskly to her trailer, the morning sun warm on my shoulders already. As we approach, Billy steps out of the trailer next to hers. Honey's steps falter and I wait for him to acknowledge her, but he doesn't. He looks away, more interested in his feet, and I think if we were in my time he'd have his eyes on his smartphone, so he didn't have to make eye contact with her.

'Morning Billy,' Honey says quietly, her face dropping as he passes by without speaking.

'It's OK,' I whisper, 'he might just feel a bit weird.'

'Maybe.' Honey gazes past me to where Billy is headed to the refreshment trailer, her cheeks flushing pink. 'I was hoping that nothing would have changed between us, you know? We're friends. At least, I thought we were.'

'Give it a day or so to blow over,' I say. 'Oh…' Looking over Honey's shoulder I see Jean step out from Honey's trailer. 'Hi Jean.'

'Hello, Lily.' Jean gives me a brisk smile, before her attention turns to Honey. 'Honey, I was looking for you. Leonard would like to see you in his trailer please. Immediately.'

Honey lifts her chin and gives a slight nod, any trace of vulnerability slipping away. 'Yes. OK. I'll be there in just a minute.'

Jean swishes past us and I give Honey's hand a reassuring squeeze. 'Go on, before he gets pissed off waiting for you. I promise, Honey, it's going to be all right.'

–

Honey is in Leonard's trailer for the best part of an hour and when she comes out, she is pale and quiet, tucking her hair behind her ears and avoiding eye contact with everyone as she climbs the small steps to her trailer. If you didn't know better, you might just think she has a hangover, but of course, thanks to the newspaper everybody does know better, not that anyone says a word. Not until Jessica arrives.

'Lily.' Jessica appears beside me, the polar opposite of Honey this morning. Even though she isn't needed on set today she is perfectly made up, flaunting her figure in a Claire McCardell dress, the halter top a creamy white with a cinched-in waist, a full blue-and-white striped skirt below. 'I saw the papers,' Jessica says, her voice low. 'Is Honey all right?'

'Sort of,' I whisper back. Honey and Billy have both appeared from their respective trailers as Leonard begins to shout instructions and the extras begin to take their places, with a murmur of excited chatter. 'She was more furious than upset. Leonard had her in his trailer for over an hour when we arrived, but she's not letting it affect her performance today.' If anything, Honey has been on top form.

'Oh, poor Honey. She should never have gone out with Billy last night.'

A flicker of irritation buzzes over my skin. It's hard to reconcile the way women are so easily blamed for everything here in 1949. I never really considered myself a feminist, but the way even Jessica, her best friend, seems to be blaming Honey makes my blood boil.

'It's not Honey's fault,' I say sharply. 'And she didn't *go out* with Billy, she went out with me. They were just dancing, having a few drinks; she didn't do anything wrong.'

'Tell that to Cynthia Lake.' Jessica lights a cigarette, wafting the smoke in my direction. The smell makes my stomach turn and I resist the urge to cough as she offers me one. I shake my head.

'Jean said Cynthia takes no prisoners.' My eyes wander to where Billy and Honey are now locked in an intimate embrace. Or, it would be, if there weren't so many cameras on them. There is nothing sexy about a sex scene when a million eyes are watching.

'*That* is an understatement.' Jessica follows my gaze. 'Cynthia is the absolute definition of jealousy, not that Billy hasn't given her things to be jealous over before.'

'But she's a huge star,' I say. 'Why on earth would Billy leave her? She's beautiful, successful, talented. She has it all.'

'Billy has always been a flirt. I mean, look at him.' Jessica gestures to where Billy is talking to a runner, the scene on a break for a moment. She's holding a clipboard and he is leaning in, a smile playing about his lips. 'He can't help himself. It drives Cynthia crazy.'

'Has he ever actually cheated on her?'

'Not officially, but there was this one girl…' Jessica leans in, and I can smell the waxy scent of the lipstick she uses, cut with tobacco smoke. 'Cynthia was convinced something went on between them, after a similar thing happened. The papers shared a picture of Billy coming out of a club with a fan – you must have seen it? It was just last year.'

'I… err… I wasn't in LA then,' I mumble, but Jessica is still talking.

'Cynthia found out where the girl lived and turned up there out of the blue.' Jessica pauses for dramatic effect. She's not an actress for nothing. 'She tipped a can of paint over the girl's car and slashed her tyres. She did it in the dead of night, the girl woke up and came outside to see her car vandalised and Cynthia there, screwdriver in her hand, all wild-eyed and panting.'

'Wow.' I let out a breath. 'She sounds… kind of crazy.'

'Oh, she is.' Jessica nods. 'The studio hushed it all up, gave the girl a thousand dollars to keep her mouth shut.

Not that they needed to really, I don't think Billy would have the balls to cheat on Cynthia, not properly. Cynthia went to Florida "for a break".' Jessica catches Leonard's eye as he strides across the set, blowing him a kiss, before turning back to me. 'Listen Lily, let's talk properly later. I'd like to get to know you better.' She eyes me carefully, a slight smile on her lips before she turns and dashes after Leonard, her cute pumps racing across the grubby tarmac of the lot.

My mind reeling from the fact that Jessica Parks wants to get to know me, I turn back to watch the scene Honey and Billy have almost finished filming. Billy has his arms around Honey, tilting her back slightly so he can look deep into her eyes. It's convincing, I'll say that. Despite the cameras there is still a crackle in the air around the two of them, the chemistry almost visible, and I don't think I could ever get bored of watching them together. That's why I have to save Honey. It's not Billy creating the chemistry, it's her. She's destined to be a superstar.

'Let me through,' a voice shouts behind me, and I turn, along with Jean and several others standing on the edge of the set. 'You, there. Get this brute away from me. Don't you know who I am?'

A woman with immaculate red hair that falls perfectly over one eye, in heels that would cripple me if I even looked at them, pushes her way past security and on to the set. Her eyes flick over me before she almost visibly dismisses me, searching the lot until she pauses dramatically on the edge of the set, pressing one hand to her heart.

Leonard steps forward, just as Billy raises his eyes, his arms loosening around Honey, causing her to stumble backwards and almost fall.

'Darling, I wondered if we would see you. Break, everyone!' Leonard calls out, one arm reaching out to encircle the woman, drawing her close.

'Leonard.' The woman sags against him slightly, before she catches sight of Billy and Honey stood frozen together on the tarmac. '*You*.' She shoves Leonard off, and strides towards Honey, her face like thunder. Cynthia Lake is here, and she's not happy.

Chapter Nine

'Cynthia. How wonderful to see you.' There is a hushed silence as Honey steps forward, her arms outstretched. Even Jean is speechless.

'*You.*' Cynthia hisses, knocking Honey's arm to one side. '*Get away from me.* And get away from my husband.'

Honey lets out a trill of laughter that hangs in the dusty, dry air. 'Cynthia, darling. Bless your heart. I'm assuming you're all het up about this nonsense in the newspaper this morning?'

Billy steps forward, his mouth open to speak, but Cynthia glares at him. 'You listen to me, you…' she pauses, eyeing Honey up and down, 'you… *hussy…*'

'Cuts up a rug pretty good, huh?' Honey winks in Billy's direction, and I close my eyes, my heart sinking. 'Who knew Billy Walters was such a ducky shincracker?'

'Stop!' Cynthia shrieks. 'You stay away from him, you understand?' Her face is an ugly shade of crimson, as her hand flies back and connects with Honey's cheek in a resounding slap. 'How dare you try and humiliate me like this? You're making a fool of yourself, you know that?' She leans in, spittle flying from her perfectly made-up lips. 'Billy is *devoted* to me, he *adores* me, don't you, Billy?'

Billy, the wimp, tugs ineffectually at Cynthia's arm. 'Cyn, come on, hon. Calm down.'

Honey smiles, a slow, dangerous smile, as the imprint of Cynthia's palm stains her cheek an angry red. 'Well, if Billy adores you, then you really don't have anything to worry about, do you? Maybe you should sit back and enjoy the publicity... you don't seem to have had much of your own lately.' Honey turns to Leonard, who shakes his head, his lips pursed. 'Leonard, I'm guessing that's a wrap for today?'

–

Honey is silent in the car as we speed away from the set. I still expect her to pull her phone from her pocket and start scrolling – it's such a habit for me that it feels odd to not be surrounded by technology, to not have all the information that I need at my fingertips. Instead, I am inching my way through 1949, *baby stepping*, trying my hardest not to mess things up.

'Are you OK?' I ask Honey eventually, the silence in the car too much to bear. Ever the professional, Honey pastes on a smile.

'Sure am, sugar. Don't you worry about me.' She looks frighteningly young in the dying light, Cynthia's palm print fading to a rosy pink on her pale cheek.

'That was pretty brave of you back there,' I say, thinking of the exasperation on Leonard's face and the rage on Cynthia's. Leonard might be fiery, but he's got nothing on Cynthia and her unhinged fury. Maybe she's the one I need to protect Honey from – her perform-ance today has certainly put her in the running for prime suspect.

'She's a bully,' Honey says simply, her gaze going to the darkened windows. 'I don't want to talk about it anymore, Lily. Can we please can it?'

'Just one thing.'

'*What?*'

'What in the name of God is a ducky shincracker?'

Honey turns to face me, a smirk on her lips. 'It means he's a good dancer, Lil. Where the hell have you been? Under a rock?'

'London,' I say simply, spreading my hands wide in a shrug, relieved when Honey lets out a gulp of laughter, killing off the last vestiges of tension.

We pull up to the hotel, the building glowing a faint pink from the outside lighting. A pack of reporters huddle to one side of the entrance, pressed against the hedges to avoid hotel security, their notepads and the huge cameras around their necks a dead giveaway.

'Wait a moment,' I say, laying a hand on Honey's arm. She looks exhausted, and I don't want her to have to run the gauntlet in order to get to her room. I slide out of the car and sashay over to the huddle, wishing I had thought to put on the heels Jean brought me. It's very, very difficult to sashay in Converse trainers.

'Hello there, chaps.' I emphasise my British accent, in the hope of dazzling them into forgetting why they are here. 'Who are you waiting for? Ingrid?'

'Honey Black.' One of the men with the cameras says, looking me up and down. 'You know, the actress?'

I resist the urge to glance back towards the car, where Honey is hidden from view. 'Is that so? No one has ever *really* heard of her though, have they? I mean, I know she has a movie coming out and there was something about Billy Walters in the papers this morning but… anyway, I heard she moved hotels.'

'You work here, honey?' another guy asks, lighting a cigarette.

'Uh… yeah. Yes, I do.' I shrug. 'You guys can wait here all you want, but Honey Black isn't staying here anymore. I thought you guys were here for Ingrid Bergman. Only if you *were* waiting for Ingrid, I would tell you to go around the back. She always goes in by the back door.'

They glance at each other and then back to me. 'Really?' one of them says, a sceptical look on his face.

'Sure.' I force a smile. 'Every time she stays here. Don't say that I told you, though.'

With a buzz of conversation, the reporters move on, lugging their cameras and notepads around the corner. *If I could tell them that one day everything they do could be done on a tiny screen, I wonder what they would say?* Heart pounding, I wave Honey inside.

–

Once inside Honey's suite, I head straight for the windows to close the drapes. There is a small scrum of people milling around on the street outside the hotel, growing larger by the minute. A huge man in a suit appears, looking like someone from a Ray Winstone movie, barging his way through the crowd as a small woman, tiny compared to his stature, follows behind him. Her hair is neatly curled, and large sunglasses sit on her face, despite the fact that it is almost dark outside. *Yikes. Sorry, Ingrid.* I whisk the curtains closed and turn back to Honey. She has slipped her shoes off, her bag by her bare feet, but she hasn't moved.

'Honey? Is everything all right?'

'I don't know.' She cocks her head on one side and scans the room, her eyes flicking past me. 'It feels as though… it feels like someone has been in here.'

'Really?' I copy her movements, scanning the room, but nothing seems out of place. 'Jean, maybe? She left the set before us, if Leonard had something he wanted her to drop off, maybe she swung by here and let herself in?' But there is nothing on the table, no script, no note.

'Maybe.' Honey moves to the bar, popping the cork on the champagne. 'It just feels… different in here, that's all.'

'Housekeeping,' I say. 'They replaced the champagne and the saucers.' There is no sign of the remnants of shattered glass from this morning after Magnus's visit.

'Yes,' Honey says distractedly, her eyes still roaming the room as she takes her now full champagne saucer and goes to sit on the chaise. 'That's probably it. Lil, you can go now. I think I'm going to take a bath and get to bed early, after dinner with Jessica. It's been a hell of a day.'

'Of course.' It really has been a hell of a day. I wouldn't say no to a Red Bull right now, and I wonder briefly what the 1949 equivalent is. Probably something highly illegal. 'Call me if you need anything.'

I leave Honey to her bath, planning on going back to my room for a quick shower and to re-pin my curls before heading downstairs to the bar, to see if Louis has seen the newspapers and get his take on things. I have been in my room for five minutes, just enough time to slide out of my trainers and let my dress drop to the floor, when the phone rings, the shrill single ring of a room to room call.

'Hello?' I try to keep the sigh from my voice.

'Lily, it's me, Honey. Please, you have to come back to the room… I told you someone had been in here!'

-

'Lily!' Honey yanks me inside the room, before slamming the door and sliding the gold chain across. She wears a robe, and her face is smothered in cold cream. 'I told you, didn't I? I knew it, I knew someone had been here.'

'What do you mean? How do you know?'

'Can you smell that? It smells like… cigarette smoke.' She sniffs the air, and I discreetly inhale, thinking that maybe there is the tiniest hint of smoke on the air, underneath the peachy scent of Honey's bubble bath. The sound of water thundering from the taps echoes from the open bathroom door. 'Let me turn the bath off.'

Honey follows me into the bathroom, her hand shaking as she points to the small shelf where the bottle of expensive bubbles sits. 'There.'

I look, but I'm not sure what at. There's just an empty space next to the bottle. 'What am I looking at?'

'It's gone!' Honey lets out a sob. 'My snow globe. It's gone. Someone has taken it!'

A snow globe? I don't remember seeing it, but the last time I was in this bathroom I wasn't sure what year it was, and I hadn't long cracked my head on the bathtub.

'Are you sure? Why would someone take that?'

'It's precious to me,' Honey hiccups, tears making tracks in her face cream. 'My mother gave it to me – it's a scene of our town at Christmas. She gave it to me to remind me of Kentucky, to remind me of her. It's the only thing I have from home!'

'But I still don't understand why someone would want to take it?'

'To upset me!' Honey wails. 'Lily, you don't understand… when I miss my mother, I shake the globe and then I'm back there.'

I hand her a tissue as she sniffles, then dabs at her eyes. I miss my own mother more than words, and the thought of staying here in 1949, never able to see a photograph of her, or hold the few things she left to me, makes me want to cry too. 'Maybe it got broken. Maybe the housekeeper didn't want to tell you, or maybe she thought that it was just a trinket, that it wasn't important.' The lies taste salty on my tongue, as if tainted with Honey's tears.

'You think?' Honey raises her eyes to mine, and I nod, reassuringly.

'Of course. That's all it is. Nothing to worry about. Can we get your mum to send you another one?' I lead Honey from the bathroom and steer her back towards the bedroom, closing the bathroom door firmly behind me. 'Here. Drink this.' I hand her the glass of now lukewarm champagne and then move across the room to switch on the wireless. 'Put your feet up and listen to some music, relax before you go for dinner with Jessica.'

–

I hurry back to my room, once again, my mind whirling. I might have talked Honey down, but honestly, I think she is right. I think someone was in her room, and they did take her snow globe, and I think the lingering scent of cigarette smoke in the bathroom is a clanger of a clue. The only thing I can't figure out is why? Why would someone break into Honey's room purely to steal something that isn't even valuable? To unsettle her? Or is this just a precursor to what's going to happen in two weeks' time?

As I unlock my door I find myself holding my breath, senses on red alert in case someone has been in my room too, but everything seems undisturbed. Locking the door behind me, I perch on the end of the bed and run my fingers through my hair, before pressing my hands over my eyes. Someone is going to kill Honey in less than two weeks, and I need to figure out who. The snow globe may or may not be related, but even if it's not, someone was still in Honey's room. Someone who probably oughtn't have been. The cigarette smoke might be nothing, but I don't have much else to go on right now.

Standing, I start to pace, the thick carpet luxurious beneath my aching feet. Everyone in this town seems to smoke, and if that's my clue then I'll have no end of suspects. Leonard smokes, I'm sure I've seen him with a cigarette on set. He's directing the movie she's starring in, and although there has been some *unsavoury* publicity in the press, surely it's not worth killing her over… Unless there's more going on between them than meets the eye. I think again about the letter he dropped, Honey's name standing out in the raft of scrawled handwriting. I have no idea if Honey wrote it, or if she is the subject of it. I'd love to get my hands on the letter and read it properly, to see if it offers up any clues to their relationship. Jessica definitely smokes – she's rarely without a cigarette between scenes – but she's Honey's best friend, and she's the one who put Honey forward for the role of Sofia in the first place. Why would she do that if she wanted to hurt Honey? And then there's Jean. I'm not sure if Jean smokes, but she seems incredibly disapproving of Honey.

I screw my face up, rubbing at my temples as the start of a headache begins to pulse. If I'm honest, there are three people far more likely to want to get Honey out of the picture. Billy Walters for one. Although in 2019 he might have trended on Twitter for a couple of days, and perhaps been the subject of a few entertainment podcasts, in 1949 the scandal stakes are higher. Is he worried she could ruin his marriage *and* his career? His wife, Cynthia Lake, would be glad to see the back of Honey too – according to Jessica her jealousy knows no bounds, and she has a reputation for not being... I hate to say stable, but I can't think of a more suitable word. I imagine that Honey's reaction to her appearance on set won't have helped. And then there's Magnus, Honey's ex. Why was he even at the hotel this morning? He may have already been in town for some promo work, but to beat Honey's door down at the crack of dawn over some newspaper pictures? It seems like a strong reaction to something that doesn't really concern him. Is he jealous of Honey's success? Or is he jealous that she has moved on without him, even though he allegedly left her? The skin on my scalp prickles with the unsettling instinct that there may be something more to the break-up than Honey is letting on.

Sighing, I throw myself down on the bed and slump back against the pillows. I thought that an addiction to true crime shows on Netflix would have primed me for this a little better, but I'm finding it harder than I expected to figure out exactly who would have a clear motive to harm Honey. All I've succeeded in doing is muddying the waters for myself. I roll over and bury my face in the pillow. Right now, I think skint and single in twenty-first-century LA would be a damn sight easier than life here in 1949, and not just because of the lack of Wi-Fi. I need a drink.

Chapter Ten

Cynthia Lake is sitting alone in a booth as I walk through the restaurant, her eyes on the menu in front of her. Keeping my gaze dead ahead, I sidle past and make my way to the bar, frowning when I see that's not Louis behind the bar, but someone else.

'Can I get you something?' The bartender smiles at me, and I peer past him as if expecting Louis to magically appear.

'I was looking for Louis.'

'He's not here right now,' he says, a faint hint of a Mexican accent reaching my ears. 'Can I get you a drink?'

'No, thank you. Is he here tonight? Or is he not working?'

'No, no, he's in.' The bartender jerks his head in the direction of the doorway. 'He just had a little business to attend to. He'll be back soon.'

'Thanks.' I turn to leave, before I pause. 'Could you just tell him Lily was asking for him?'

The bartender gives me a nod and turns to the pretty blonde at the other end of the bar. *Business to attend to?* That sounds kind of serious. Jean's words filter back to me, accusing Louis of calling the press on Honey, and a stone settles in my stomach. I wander out of the bar, through the doors at the back of the lobby and out into the gardens. The scent of jasmine fills the air, and while the sky overhead is clear and dotted with stars, the air is warm and there is a soft orange glow coming from the lighting at the pool area. I inhale, letting the calm, quiet night air wash over me, and I wonder what Eric is doing now. Is he out on the tiles in WeHo? Has he even noticed I'm gone, or does he think I couldn't hack the cleaning job anymore and I've blocked his number? *I'd rather be here than there.* The thought flits across my mind and I realise it's true. Movement catches my eye and I look up to see Louis walking briskly towards the other side of the building, past the ballroom. I open my mouth to call his name, but something about the way he moves stops my voice in my throat, and instead I push away from the wall I'm leaning against and follow him, keeping my eyes on him as he disappears from view.

'Seriously?!' A voice floats on the night breeze from around the corner, followed by a hasty hushing sound. The voice is high-pitched, female, and I feel my pulse pick up as I creep closer on sneakered feet, curiosity mounting. Muted conversation comes again, and I peer around the corner.

Louis stands with a young woman, his shoulder almost touching hers, obscuring her face from my view, both of them huddled close to the immaculately kept shrubs that surround the pool area, away from the puddles of apricot light cast by the cabana lighting. Louis shifts, taking a small step back, and I catch a glimpse of her face. She's young, maybe a couple of years younger than me, so twenty-two or -three? She has a heart-shaped face, with blonde hair pulled back from her forehead with an Alice band. She looks wholesome and pretty, but she looks up at him now with a sceptical look on her face that diminishes the wholesomeness. Whatever Louis has just said to her, she doesn't seem impressed. Louis leans down, his voice barely audible as the crash of my pulse in my ears drowns everything else out. The girl frowns as Louis gestures as if to say that's all he's got, and then fumbles in her purse for a pen, before starting to scribble notes in the pad she's holding.

There is a crushing sensation in my chest as I pull back around the corner out of sight. *Notepad, pen, muted conversation. Jean was right.* The girl looks like a journalist – the notepad is a dead giveaway – and Louis must have been the one to tell her that Honey was in the bar with Billy last night. The closeness of their bodies tells me that he knows her, and I wonder what story he's giving her, and what the consequences may be. More bad press could be a motive for Honey's murder, given what happened today. The bridge of my nose begins to fizz as my eyes sting.

I risk another peek around the corner, just as the woman glances in my direction, her hand reaching out to tap Louis on the arm. Pulling out of sight, I turn on my heel, hurrying as quickly as I can towards the hotel, my heart in my mouth. Clearly I was wrong about Louis, but no man is worth losing your shit over. My feet slow as I reach the entrance to the bar and see Cynthia still sitting in the same booth. Now I just need to go back in there and tell her the same thing.

–

'A martini. Dirty, and make it snappy,' Cynthia barks at the waiter who hovers nervously as I approach the booth.

'I'll have the same, please,' I say. My stomach rolls, but I am not sure if it is the thought of another martini (I mean, who knew they drank so much in the olden days? I'd give my right arm for a bottle of kombucha), or the thought of sitting down next to Cynthia Lake.

'Cynthia?'

Cynthia looks up as I advance towards her, and I pray she can't hear my heart hammering in my chest. 'May I sit down?' I find myself exaggerating my British accent, the way my mum used to when she was on an important telephone call.

Cynthia frowns, but she doesn't say no, the menu still laid on the table in front of her.

'My name is Lily; I work for Honey Black.' I slide into the booth opposite her before she can change her mind.

'I have nothing to say to you.' Cynthia's voice is low and smooth, but there is no hiding the fury that lurks there.

'Please, Ms Lake, just hear me out.' I lay a hand flat over the menu that she is still pretending to read. 'Someone needs to explain to you what really happened last night.'

'It's perfectly clear what happened last night,' she hisses at me. 'The photographs are there for all to see!'

'Ladies, drinks on the house, courtesy of the Beverly Hills Hotel.' I smile gratefully at the waiter, only to look up and see Louis as he rests two martinis on the table in front of us. 'Enjoy.'

I look away without speaking, as Cynthia takes a huge gulp, grimacing slightly as the burn of the alcohol reaches her throat.

'Cynthia, I know you're angry,' I say calmly, once Louis is safely back behind the bar, 'but I promise what you saw in the newspapers wasn't how it was. I know, I was there.'

'I'm sure you were,' Cynthia says acidly, 'encouraging the little trollop, no doubt. What better way to grab her some publicity than to be seen with *my* husband?'

I shake my head. 'Honey is mortified. The last thing she would ever want is to cause trouble between you and Billy. Billy is – was – her friend, they had drinks and went dancing, that's all. Honey had too much to drink and Billy was taking her home.' Yikes, maybe not the best choice of words.

'I can see he was *taking her home*,' Cynthia says. 'The whole of America could see that this morning. Listen Lola—'

'Lily.'

'Whatever. Listen to me, do you think this is the first time I've had to deal with some little girl trying to get her hooks into Billy? It *isn't*. He's handsome, he's rich, he's famous – they all want a piece of him, but he belongs to *me*.' She slams her hand down on the table, making me jump. Louis looks up from where he is polishing the bar with a raised eyebrow, and I shake my head slightly. Cynthia lowers her voice. 'Do you have any idea how humiliating it is for me, to see my husband plastered all over the newspapers with some… some… *floozy* draped over him? And as for Honey's little performance this morning… Don't you know *who I am*?'

'I understand,' I say, feeling a smattering of sympathy for Cynthia. 'I really do. I had a boyfriend who cheated on me, and I know exactly how you're feeling…'

'Cheated?' Cynthia squawks. 'Billy doesn't *cheat* on me! These little tarts are all over him, trying to steal him away from me, and I'm telling you it won't ever happen! I won't let it.'

Jessica wasn't wrong about Cynthia's state of mind. Her voice gets louder and higher, as her cheeks flush an ever brighter shade of scarlet. Billy is the one I've seen being flirty on set, not Honey. A bubble of anger pops low in my belly and any hint of sympathy for Cynthia dissipates.

'Hey now, wait just a minute,' I say. 'How dare you call Honey names? How dare you accuse her of being the one to lead Billy astray? Honey's done nothing wrong. Billy's the one who's married, so perhaps you should be having this conversation with him?'

Cynthia gets to her feet, a five-foot-four-inch bundle of rage, and I do the same, sliding out of the booth. 'How dare you?' she shrieks. 'How dare you speak to me like that? What are you – a PA? A runner? Some nobody, that's for sure. You can tell Honey Black from me that she needs to stay as far away as humanly possible from my husband, or so help me God, I will deal with her myself.' And she sweeps out of the bar, oblivious to the stares of the other drinkers.

–

I sink back into the booth, hoping it will shield me from the stares, but judging by the buzz of gossip it's too late. I press my hand against the hot skin on my cheek. *Some nobody*. Cynthia's right. I am nobody – why would a nobody like me be able to save Honey Black? When my mother came home and told me the lump in her breast was serious, that the cancer had gone to her bones and her time was limited, I thought my world had ended. But my mum was stubborn, and she wouldn't give in without a fight. She made me finish my degree at the London Film Academy, she made me promise that I wouldn't let myself wallow after she was gone. She made me promise to go to Hollywood and live the dream I'd had since I was eight years old. And now I'm here, and my mum is gone, and

I'm really trying, but if I can't save Honey then what do I do? I'll be nobody, still.

'Here. You might need this.' Louis appears by the booth with yet another drink. Bourbon, straight. 'She was really mad. Are you OK?'

'I'm fine.' I knock back the drink, coughing as it scorches my throat. 'I don't think I helped Honey though.'

'Stick around? I'm getting off in an hour or so. You can tell me all about it.'

The thought of sitting here, or worse, at the bar in full view of everyone isn't remotely appealing. 'You know what? I think I'll give it a miss.' The image of him standing with the reporter outside in the gardens ignites a fiery ball in my stomach, fanned by the flames of Cynthia's words. *I'm not going to be a nobody. I'm going to save Honey Black.* 'I don't think you and I have anything to talk about.'

Pushing past Louis I stride from the room, ignoring him calling my name as I blink furiously. I'm almost at the exit when I bump into someone standing in the doorway.

'Sorry.' I hold up my hands, and then see who it is. 'Honey! Are you…?' I peer behind her, suddenly worried that Cynthia is still around.

'I heard what just happened,' she says, biting her lower lip. 'We were about to come in for a drink when we heard the raised voices.' I glance towards the elevator where Jessica stands. She offers me a tiny smile, but there is concern etched across her features. 'Gosh Lily, no one has ever stuck up for me like that before. You were wonderful.'

'Well,' I feel my cheeks warm with the beginning of a blush. 'Where I come from, we don't let women slut shame other women.'

'She called me a slut?' Honey's mouth drops open. 'I am *not* a slut.'

'No, she didn't say that. I mean... I wouldn't let her blame you for what happened with Billy last night.'

'I guess I should probably stay away from Billy for a little while off set,' Honey says. 'You wanna have a drink with me and Jessica?'

'Not tonight,' I say, suddenly exhausted, and aware of Louis standing at the bar watching us. The stress of finding that Louis had gone to the papers, followed by the showdown with Cynthia, has left me tired and drained. 'I'm going to go to my room.'

'You want me to come with you? Jessica won't mind if you want company. She really likes you.' Honey glances towards the open doors to the Polo Lounge. 'And Cynthia was *horrible* to you.'

'No, you go ahead. I'll be fine.'

'OK.' Honey reaches up a hand and presses it to my face. 'You're a real swell friend, Lil. Thank you.'

Jessica approaches, her brows drawn together. 'You're sure you're all right, Lily? That was utterly magnificent, by the way.'

'Honestly, I'm fine. Please, go and enjoy your night.' I just want to be alone.

With a reassuring smile, Honey steps past me into the bar, followed by Jessica, and I take Jessica's place beside the elevator, trying to blink away the tears that prick my eyes. Honey may put on a tough façade on set — her handling of Cynthia this morning was bitchily fantastic — but away from the public eye she is one of the kindest, sweetest people I have ever met. As the elevator doors close behind me, I lean back and close my eyes, thinking of the fury on Cynthia's face as she called Honey those awful names. I hoped that by speaking to her I could resolve things and maybe even persuade her that she didn't need to be here for Billy's filming schedule, thereby getting her out of the picture completely. I remember what I heard about her slashing the other woman's tyres and tipping paint over her car. How much of a leap is it from criminal damage and vandalism to murder? A cold fist clenches around my heart. I hope I haven't made things worse for Honey.

Chapter Eleven

Tension fills the air on set the following day, as I stand in the shadows, trying to keep out of sight. Jean stands on the edge of the set, clipboard in hand, with her hair pulled back tightly into what we would call a Croydon facelift at home, as Honey and Billy prepare to shoot their next scene. The scene has had to be reshot several times and Leonard's furious tones are harsh and jagged as he calls for retake after retake, screaming at the actors, the runners, the extras. Everybody's nerves are frayed. Now we watch the actors intently, desperate for them to get it in the can, and I feel a flicker of alarm as Billy sends Honey a charming grin. Does the guy never learn? Honey doesn't return the smile, keeping her features blank as she stares coolly past him. I give her a thumbs up, pushing a reassuring smile onto my own face as Cynthia Lake stalks on to the set. She comes to stand alongside Jean, who throws me a sideways glance as she turns to greet Cynthia, giving her a sympathetic smile as she rests her manicured hand on Cynthia's arm.

How well does Jean know Cynthia? They must have worked together before, as Cynthia was the star of one of Leonard's previous movies. Could Jean be the one who tipped off the press, and then tried to blame it on Louis to cover her tracks? If I hadn't seen Louis and the reporter with my own eyes, I could well have believed it. The thought makes me feel vaguely nauseous.

Billy and Honey finally shoot their scene – not a love scene this morning, thank God – and when Leonard calls cut, the relief is palpable. Honey hurries towards her trailer, her head down. Louis might not be who I thought he was, but he was right about one thing, Honey is simply a sweet girl from a small town, and she doesn't deserve this. Billy makes a break for his own trailer, and Cynthia scurries after him. I pretend not to notice how he pulls away from her slightly as she thrusts her arm through his, and I gather my clipboard and pen, reaching automatically to feel for my phone in my pocket before my hand drops away.

'Lily. Great scene this morning,' Jean says, as I pass by her. 'Shame there wasn't as much chemistry between Honey and Billy as usual.'

Am I imagining it, or is there something self-satisfied in Jean's tone? 'Is it any wonder there wasn't much chemistry?' I say tartly. 'After what happened? And the fact that Cynthia is on set watching Honey's every move… well, it's bound to create problems.'

'Perhaps Honey shouldn't have behaved the way she did,' Jean sniffs.

'Are you fucking kidding me?' The words erupt before I have a chance to even think about it. 'Why are you all blaming Honey for what happened? She's separated from Magnus – Billy is the one who should think about the way he behaves. And as for Leonard shouting at Honey, Billy was in that scene too! Maybe the fact that his witch of a wife was watching meant that *he* couldn't perform properly, not Honey.' My breath catches in my throat, heat burning in my cheeks. 'I wouldn't be at all surprised, Jean, if *you* were the one who tipped off the press.' I almost enjoy watching her face fall at my words.

Jean pales, her mouth opening and closing like a drowning fish. 'Well,' she says eventually, 'there's no need for *language*, Lily. I have *never* been spoken to this way in my *life*.' She glares at me, and I eye her coolly, not budging an inch. I've had enough arguments in Wetherspoons late on a Saturday night to be able to stand my ground.

'How dare you insinuate that I was behind the press taking those photos?' Jean sniffs again, righteous and indignant. 'I am extremely loyal to Leonard; I would never dream of doing anything to jeopardise his work.'

'And what about Honey? Would you be happy to do something that might jeopardise her position?' It's on the tip of my tongue to tell Jean that I've seen the way she looks at Leonard, and that nothing would surprise me about her.

'You don't seem to be too bothered about jeopardising your own position,' Jean snipes. 'You seem to be going out of your way to defend Honey, even if it means upsetting the wrong people. You simply don't speak to people that way, Lily. To myself...' she glances sidewards towards Billy's trailer, 'or Ms Lake.'

'Honey has done nothing wrong,' I mutter, knowing that Jean is expecting an apology. An apology she isn't going to get.

'Honestly, Lily.' Jean gives a bitter laugh. 'You think Honey Black is Miss Perfect? Let me assure you, she isn't. After all, Billy might be married, but Honey is too.'

I watch, deflated, as Jean stalks away towards the catering trailer. Of course, Honey is married – although she and Magnus are separated, they aren't divorced yet. Now Jean has reminded me, I get that sinking feeling once again that by trying to put in a good word for Honey, I have potentially made things worse.

Leonard marches across the lot, and as he enters the catering truck I realise I have been given a golden opportunity to get my hands on the letter he dropped. *His trailer is empty.* Picking up my clipboard, I walk briskly towards it as if headed to a meeting, only glancing around when I reach the door. I press down on the handle and the door springs open, and I slide inside, my heart beating a frantic tattoo in my chest. Even if the letter doesn't drop any hints, if Leonard *does* have something to do with Honey's death, maybe there's something here that can point me in the right direction.

The trailer is cluttered, the table littered with papers. A spare jacket, a shirt and two pairs of trousers hang on a hook beside the door, and the air in here is stiflingly hot. Aware I don't have much time, I rifle through the papers, searching for the pale blue airmail letter that carried Honey's name, but all I find are memos from the studio, a letter from his daughter, a receipt for a meal at a diner in West Hollywood. There is a small room at the back of the trailer, with a couch that appears to double as a bed. Sweat trickles down my spine as I slip inside, pulling the door closed behind me, wondering if this is it, this is where I find the clue. Digging beneath the folds of the blanket on the cushions, my fingers encounter cold, slippery fabric. A bra. *Ugh.* I throw it down, but not before checking if it's Honey's size. It's not, and I wonder if this doubles as Leonard's casting couch. The thought makes me feel grubby and I scrub my hands over my skirt, wishing for a bucket of hand sanitiser. I am about to open a set of drawers when the sound of Leonard's voice reaches me, thunderous and white hot with rage, and the trailer door bangs shut. I freeze, pressing my hands over my mouth as a squeak threatens to erupt. If Leonard finds me here, I'm done for. Fired, at the very least.

'Honey… unacceptable… business…' I catch a word or two, and it's not hard to decipher that Leonard is bawling Honey out over her performance today. 'Everything… done for you…' Knees creaking, I tiptoe to the door, pressing my face to the gap where the hinges meet. Leonard is pacing backwards and forwards, gesticulating wildly, as Honey sits perched on the end of the sofa, her face in her hands. The trailer is dimly lit, but her shoulders shift up and down as if she is crying. *Poor Honey.* I hold my breath, panic fluttering in my chest as I remember the rumours that will spread about Leonard.

Silence stretches out like toffee, and unable to bear the suspense, I peep out again. Leonard is standing with Honey locked in his arms. He strokes her hair, her face resting against his chest, and as I watch he drops a kiss on her blonde head. It feels oddly intimate, and my heart pounds in my chest. What is going on? Is there something between Leonard and Honey, something more than actress and director? Is that why he's so furious about the pictures of her and Billy – is it about them personally, rather than the scandal of their potential affair hurting the movie?

Turning, I size up the small window behind the sofa. I'm not sure I'll fit, but the longer I'm in here, the more chance there is I'll be discovered. Stealthily, I climb onto the back of the sofa, and ease the window wide open, before sliding one leg out, then the other. I balance on the edge for a moment, suddenly sure my bum will get stuck, the ledge digging into my stomach. I breathe in as deeply as I can, and push myself hard away from the back of the sofa, falling to the dusty ground below like a cork from a bottle. Brushing myself off, I lean against the side of the trailer for a moment, trying to catch my breath. *Could* Leonard be the one to kill Honey? After all, he obviously feels a lot for her, so could jealousy cause him to lose his temper and kill her in her hotel room? Hollywood did such a good job of hushing up any information connected to Honey's murder that despite my prior knowledge, I feel woefully underprepared. I've never felt the lack of a Google search so much in my life – along with the lack of boba tea, good face serum, and the caffeine jolt of a can of Monster. I scrub my hands over my face, suddenly overwhelmed. Everywhere I look I seem to find more and more people who have reason to harm Honey, and I don't seem to be any closer to finding answers.

'Lily? What are you doing?' I jump as Jessica's voice reaches me and I look up to see her standing at the steps to Leonard's trailer.

'Jessica, hi!' *Busted.* 'I was just… waiting. For Honey.' I gesture towards the trailer. 'She's… uh… she's in there with Leonard.'

'Oh. Of course.' Jessica runs her eyes over my dusty skirt. There are no raised voices now, just that long, still silence. I hope Honey isn't doing something she's going to regret. 'Actually Lily, I wanted to talk to you anyway, so I'm glad Honey isn't around.'

'Oh?' I let Jessica slide her arm through mine – Jessica Parks! Walking with me! Like we're friends! I feel a pang of homesickness as I imagine what my mum would say if I could have told her. 'What did you want to talk about?'

'I don't know if you know,' Jessica lowers her voice conspiratorially as she leads me towards her own, smaller, trailer. 'It's Honey's birthday on the twenty-sixth of June –

she'll turn twenty-one.' *Of course. Honey Black was murdered the night before her twenty-first birthday.* The thought of it sends a shiver down my spine. 'How about we throw her a surprise party the night before?'

'A party?' No, no, no. There is no way I want to throw a party for Honey the night before her birthday, no way I'll be able to keep her safe if hundreds of people have access to her on the last night of her life.

'Yes – don't you think that might take the edge off everything she's been through this week? She can't go home to be with her family because of shooting, but I thought we could all celebrate her here.'

'It's a great idea,' I say, a spark of inspiration igniting. 'Only, do you think we could do it a little earlier? The week before perhaps?' I stumble over the words, hurriedly trying to assemble my idea.

'The week before? But that's... this weekend. Will there be enough time?'

'Yes, absolutely enough time.' Enough time to pull a party together, but hopefully not enough time for the killer to pull their plan together.

'But surely it makes more sense to have it on her birthday?' Jessica frowns.

'I think the shooting schedule is pretty heavy the following week – Honey has a ton of scenes, so I'm not sure she'll be up for a party. Plus, her mother said she might visit, and if she does Honey will want to spend time with her.' I cross my fingers at the white lie.

'OK...' Jessica gives a slow nod. 'Maybe it could work. I mean, you'll have to organise it all, I'll be far too busy learning my lines for the movie, so I don't have time to put things together, but I'm sure you will.'

'Of course.' I give her a wobbly smile.

'Well, that's swell then.' Jessica smiles back, and I notice a tiny graze of red lipstick on her teeth. 'How about we meet tonight to talk things over, make some plans? Could you get away?'

I feel a flutter of anxiety at the thought of pulling together a huge birthday party, in secret, in the space of a few days, but I remind myself that I took care of my mum, wrote my dissertation, and worked evening shifts in the local supermarket all at the same time. I've juggled stuff before, and I can do it again. *Without the use of the internet? While trying to stop a murder before it happens? Good luck, Lil.*

'Lily?'

'Yes. Tonight. No problem.'

'Meet me in the hotel lobby at seven,' Jessica says. 'I know somewhere we can talk privately, without anyone listening in to spoil the surprise.'

As Jessica climbs the steps to her trailer, I feel an overwhelming urge to tell her what's going to happen – that I have less than two weeks to discover who is going to kill Honey. I open my mouth, but as she steps into the trailer, a blast of stuffy air wafting from inside, I close it again. I'm on my own with this one. But what better way to figure out who has it in for Honey than to have everyone in the same room, at the same party, at the same time?

Chapter Twelve

Honey slides into the back seat of the Chrysler beside me and pulls off her sunglasses. Her eyes are still slightly rimmed with pink. 'It's been a long day, Lil.'

My mouth feels dry, but I ask the question anyway. 'How did things go with Leonard?' I can't get the image of his arms around her out of my mind.

'I don't want to talk about it.' Honey leans back and closes her eyes. 'It's been awful on set, and it didn't help that Cynthia was there, shooting daggers at me all day. No wonder my performance was affected.' She sniffs. 'Maybe I made a mistake coming to Hollywood. Maybe my daddy was right.'

My stomach sinks and I reach out a hand and place it on Honey's arm. 'It's just a bad day. My mum used to say, "it's tomorrow's fish and chip paper".'

Honey smiles weakly and opens her eyes. 'Your mom sounds great.'

'She was.'

'And she's probably right. But it felt so difficult today. When Leonard offered me the part, I didn't even think about things like this happening. I just thought about the acting, about being in a movie. I didn't think about everything that goes with it.'

'You never told me how it all happened, not properly.'

'I didn't?' Honey's mouth twitches in a tiny half smile, her spirits lifting. 'It was all I ever wanted; you know? To be in the movies. It was my dream; from the first time I saw Cary Grant and Katharine Hepburn in *Holiday* when I was twelve years old. I couldn't believe it when Leonard came to town to shoot *Kentucky Queen* – I wasn't long out of high school, and I was working the farm with Mama and Daddy – and they were filming right across from the town hall. I saw Jessica filming her scene as I ran to the store, and I had to stay and watch. She was just mesmerising, and I thought, *I want to be her.* I made every excuse I could to run out to the store every day after that and I guess I wasn't very subtle about things. After a few days, I was picking up ice cream we didn't need, when Jessica approached me. She said she'd seen me watching and asked if I wanted to be an extra, so of course I said yes.'

'Of course you did.' I can just imagine Honey, in denim cut-offs and a plaid shirt, a lifetime of chicken shit ahead of her, watching enthralled as Jessica delivered her lines. It must have seemed exotic and glamorous to a girl who grew up on a farm.

'So, I did a couple of scenes in the background, and then one evening Jessica introduced me to Leonard. The girl who was meant to play Alison got sick and he needed someone to replace her, so I auditioned for him. Jessica helped me learn my lines and gave me advice on hitting my marks and which are the most flattering camera angles. She told me what a call time is, and what Leonard means when he says it's the 'magic hour'. After we finished shooting, I told Leonard I wanted more. I heard Leonard and Jessica talking about *Goodtime Gal* and I knew Sophia was the perfect part for me – Sophia is a sassy go-getter, who knows what she wants, and that was *me*, Lil. I went to see Leonard… I thought he'd take some convincing, but I read for him and then he offered me the part.' She pauses for breath. 'All I ever wanted was to be somebody.' Honey turns a serious gaze on me, and I see myself reflected back. Isn't that what I wanted? To escape from the rundown estate I grew up on to the bright lights of Hollywood, to *be somebody*?

'And then there was Magnus – he played Jessica's love interest – he was so charming, so handsome… so different to the boys I'd grown up with. He tried to turn me down, saying I was too young, but I was persistent.' Honey gazes out of the window, her face clouded with memories. 'It started with a drink after shooting finished for the evening, then he took me out for dinner… it got very intense, very quickly. I couldn't say no to him.' Her fingers twist together in her lap. 'It seemed like the natural thing to do to get married when we went on a location scouting trip to Vegas – the perfect stepping stone to what I wanted my life to be. Jessica did ask me if I was sure, but I knew it was exactly what I needed. And besides, my father was already furious.' Her voice hardens and she stares down at her hands as she picks at her nail polish. 'He said he only agreed to me working as an extra to get it out of my system, and that I belong on the farm, not in Hollywood.'

'Will you go back?' I ask.

'One day,' Honey says, turning to me with a cat-like grin. 'With my Oscar in my hand. Best Actress. That's what I'll win.'

I can't help but return the smile, even as my stomach does a slow roll. 'I would put money on that.'

'Did you see Jane Wyman won Best Actress this year for *Johnny Belinda*? Can you imagine walking up on stage as they call your name, and Laurence Olivier handing you that statue?' Honey leans back and sighs. 'That would make it all worth it, Lil.'

We travel the rest of the short journey in silence as I try to put her words out of my mind. I don't think I imagined the steely determination in her voice as she recounted her road to fame, and I think Honey is tougher than she looks. Estranged from her family, with a broken marriage behind her before she's even turned twenty-one, all Honey wants is to win the most prestigious award an actor can win. To *be somebody*. That would make up for all of it, and maybe even reunite her with her family. If I can just keep her alive.

–

Loitering in the lobby, I wait for Jessica, my heart skipping a beat as Leonard steps off the elevator, his eyes narrowing as he catches sight of me.

'*You.* I've been looking for you.' He marches towards me, and my limbs turn to jelly. *Does he know I was in his trailer?* I hadn't pushed the window closed after I tumbled out, hadn't even *thought* of it until now. *He must know.* My mouth is suddenly sandpaper dry.

'Leonard. Was there something the matter?' My words come out wavery and wimpy.

'You tell me,' he hisses, grasping my elbow and tugging me away from the prying eyes at the reception desk. 'What in *God's name* were you thinking?'

He pushes his face close to mine, and I can smell onions on his breath. 'I'm sorry,' I say quietly, 'I was just looking out for Honey.' Crossing my fingers behind my back, I hope he doesn't ask me to elaborate.

'Honey's a big girl, she can take care of herself,' he says tightly. 'Jesus Christ, don't you know who she is? What repercussions this can have? For me? For the freaking studio?'

'Who… who is?' I drop the crossed digits as I realise that perhaps Leonard and I are talking at cross purposes. He's not making any sense.

'Cynthia goddamn Lake, who else?'

Oh. 'Leonard, let me explain, I didn't—'

'I don't want to hear it. I've had Cynthia in my office, complaining about you, saying you verbally attacked her in the lounge.' Leonard sucks in a deep breath through his nose. 'You do not *ever* speak to Cynthia that way again, do you hear me? And you certainly don't insinuate that Billy Walters cheats on her. I don't need her getting all crazy on *my* set, because of some nonsense you've been spouting at her, understand?'

I nod meekly, flinching as his words rain down on me like bullets. 'I understand.'

Leonard closes his eyes and lets out a breath. 'Stay out of trouble and keep your mouth shut, or I'll make sure your ass is run out of this *state*, not just this town.'

–

Fifteen minutes later, I have finally stopped shaking, the colour slowly coming back into my cheeks. I can't believe Cynthia ran to Leonard – I only told her the truth. I never meant to upset her; I just wanted her to back off Honey. Jessica enters the lobby from the corridor that leads to the first-floor suites. She smooths over her light blue blouse, pressing her lipsticked lips together, before lifting her hand in a small wave in my direction. The bellboy gawps at her as he manoeuvres a luggage cage across the lobby, but I'm not sure if it's that he thinks her outfit, with its clinging capri trousers, is risqué, or if it's just the fact that it's Jessica.

'Lily.' She leans over to air kiss both cheeks, and I get a whiff of Chanel No. 5. 'Let's go, shall we? Follow me.'

Feeling mildly dazed, the world taking on that slightly dream-like state again, I get to my feet and hurry after her as she clicks her fingers at the valet, and he scurries away for her car. We stand in an awkward silence on the red carpet that leads into the hotel, and I offer up a shy smile as she turns to look at me. She opens her mouth to speak as the valet pulls up but my name on the air is much deeper than I was expecting.

'Lily!' Louis emerges from the side of the building, the soles of his shoes slapping the sidewalk as he hurries towards me. 'Lily, could you wait a second?'

Jessica arches an eyebrow at me as she takes the keys from the valet, and slides into the driver's seat of the Cadillac. It's a fiery red, with whitewall tyres and white trim, and it looks a hundred times livelier than Louis's beat-up banger.

'What do you want?' I hiss at Louis as he approaches, breathless and panting.

He frowns, glancing towards Jessica and then back to me. 'I wanted to see if you were OK after your run-in with Cynthia.'

'I'm fine,' I say shortly, cutting around the trunk of the car to the passenger door.

'Really? Lil, what is it? What did I do?'

'Honestly, Louis? Did you think I wouldn't find out?' I yank the door open and Jessica peers out, intrigued.

'Find out what?' Louis takes hold of the door frame. 'What, Lily? At least tell me what I did.'

'Why? So you can report that back, too? I *saw you*, Louis. I saw you huddled up with that reporter yesterday evening.' I push his hand away and slam the door, frantic-ally winding the window up. 'I know it was you who sold the story of Honey and Billy at the Palomino.'

Jessica's eyes widen and she guns the engine, filling the night air with a throaty roar.

'Honey and Billy?' Louis takes a step back, his cheeks flushing. 'Lily, I—'

But I don't hear what he says as Jessica takes her foot off the brake, and we roar away into the night.

—

'Wasn't that the cute bartender?' Jessica asks as we pull out onto Sunset Boulevard. The Strip is livelier than it is in the morning, and it almost feels familiar as neon signs light up bars and restaurants along the way.

'Yes,' I sigh, 'it was.'

'You two got a thing?' Jessica glances at me, her face illuminated with a soft yellow glow from the streetlights outside.

'No,' I say glumly. 'I thought he was a nice guy, but I think he's the one who sold the story of Honey and Billy.'

Jessica shakes her head. 'You can't trust anyone, sweetie. Not in Hollywood.' She pulls off the road and I realise where we are.

'Hey! We're at the set.' I lean forward in my seat, peering out on to what is usually a busy lot. Now it is deserted, not a soul around.

'I thought you might like to see it when it's a little quieter.' Jessica gets out, and sliding a key out of her pocket, unlocks the gate. 'Don't tell Leonard.'

Inside the gates, the set is as familiar as ever, but there is an almost ghostly hush about the place. This part of the set is outside, far from the entrance to the trailers and the crowds at the gate, and the night sky above us is prickled with stars. It's the exterior of the Western town where the movie is set, and usually it would be swarming with extras in Stetsons and cowboy boots, looking on as Honey and Billy film their high-octane scenes. Where usually the cameraman, the lighting guy and the props manager would be huddled at the edge of the set, there is no one. No yelling of directions, no glaring white lights that heat the set to unbearable temperatures, no crowds of extras loitering. I wish I could say I prefer it, but it feels a little eerie. One of Honey's costumes – a huge, ruffled affair – hangs on a rail looking empty and deflated, and without the lighting the painted backdrop looks tired and jaded. Goosebumps prickle along the backs of my arms as the word *ghost town* floats into my mind.

'Did you know David O. Selznick filmed the burning of Atlanta before they'd even cast Vivien as Scarlett O'Hara?' Jessica's voice makes me jump.

'No, I didn't know that.'

'She wasn't cast until the last minute.' Jessica hops up on the stoop of a saloon, setting the doors behind her swinging gently. 'How are you enjoying your time on set, Lily?'

'It's… incredible,' I say, coming to sit beside her. 'Like nothing I ever imagined.' I certainly never imagined sitting with Jessica Parks, discussing a birthday party for Honey Black.

'And working with Honey? You enjoy it?'

'I love it. She's amazingly talented. She brings every scene to life.'

'She is. More than expected, I think.'

'She's ambitious,' I say slowly, thinking over my conversation in the car with Honey earlier. 'Dedicated. She's worked hard already to get where she is. Honey wants to be the best she can possibly be, but I don't think she's realised yet how incredible she actually is.'

'She's certainly determined.' Jessica lets a small smile tug at her lips. 'She turned up on the set of *Kentucky Queen* so often I think Leonard thought she was going to become one of the props if he didn't find her a part. She was just a kid – you would have thought all her Christmases came at once, the day I gave her Sophia.' Jessica keeps her attention on the dirt below as she sketches a circle with the toe of her pump. 'How did she take the newspaper pictures?'

'Pretty hard. It was a shock enough to see her own face plastered across the papers, but then Magnus showed up and yelled at her, and she got chewed out by Leonard for a poor performance, even though it really wasn't her fault.'

'Magnus? What do you mean Magnus showed up?'

I turn to look at Jessica. 'She never said? Magnus showed up at her suite and started yelling and smashing glasses.'

Jessica presses her lips together and her eyes darken. 'That asshole,' she mutters under her breath, pulling a packet of cigarettes from her pocket. She offers them to me, and I shake my head. 'He was a fathead when he was with her, treating her like dirt, and worse when they broke up. I stayed with her for weeks after it happened.' She breathes out a long stream of smoke into the night air.

'She's stronger than people think.'

'She hasn't said anything about going home?' Jessica asks, not looking at me.

'No. We talked about home, but she's not going back. She won't let people like Cynthia Lake chase her away. Like I said, she's stronger than people think. You're her best friend, you must know that.'

Jessica smiles, stubbing her cigarette out. 'She sure is. I was worried that it was all getting too much for her and she would run away. It wouldn't be the first time a rising star couldn't handle things, but our Honey is made of stronger stuff, huh?'

'Yeah.' I nod. Jessica is so much more approachable, so easy to talk to once she's off set and away from Leonard. That's what makes her a star, I guess, the ability to maintain her professional persona even when things are kicking off.

'…birthday.' Jessica is saying, but I haven't heard a word.

'Sorry? I didn't catch that.'

A fleeting wrinkle of Jessica's nose belies her irritation, but her tone is pleasant as she says, 'I said after all of this, Honey deserves something really special for her birthday.'

'She does,' I say, 'but I really do think we need to do it this weekend.'

'You think you can pull it off?'

'Oh yeah, sure.' I flap a hand, nonchalantly. 'All I need is for you to help with the guest list.'

Jessica takes me on a tour of the rest of the set at night, while we talk over plans for Honey's birthday guest list – Jessica puts forward Clark Gable, Olivia de Havilland and Barbara Stanwyck while my palms get sweaty just thinking about sending them an invite. I feel exhausted, in a good way, as we pull into the hotel, and butterflies of excitement pitch in my stomach at the idea of organising the party and potentially getting a step closer to discovering who is responsible for Honey's death.

'Oh dear.' Jessica sighs as she pulls up to the valet and gestures to the shrubs alongside the building. 'It looks as if you have company.'

Louis steps out of the shadows, his hands held up in a gesture of peace. 'Lil, can we talk?'

'No,' I say shortly. 'Thanks for a lovely evening, Jessica. I'll see you tomorrow.'

Jessica flashes a look between me and Louis as if reluctant to leave, before she hurries up the red carpet into the lobby.

'You could at least let me explain.' Louis's voice is low and filled with something I can't identify. Regret, I hope. 'Please?'

'I don't want to talk to you,' I say, 'but you owe Honey an apology, and you definitely owe me an explanation.'

'It wasn't what you thought.'

'Not now.' I hold up a hand. 'Meet me tomorrow, when I get back from the lot, and I'll talk to you then. But you better have something worth listening to.'

Chapter Thirteen

I wonder if I should have spoken with Louis last night instead of giving him extra time to think up excuses for his behaviour, when at seven p.m. sharp the following evening there is a rap on the door. Louis stands there, his hair swept back off his forehead, looking smart in tan trousers that are slightly too big for him secured with a black belt, and a crisp white shirt. My heart turns over and butterflies swarm in my stomach.

'Hey.' The word hangs frostily in the air as I tug the skirt of my candy-pink and white striped dress free of the door as I pull it closed behind me. I have no idea where the dress came from, but it was hanging in the wardrobe, alongside the green Betty Grable dress, so I guessed either Jean or Honey had left it for me.

'You look pretty,' Louis says, his eyes resting on my face.

I don't say a word until we step into the elevator and the doors close. 'I would have been happy to meet you in the lobby. Or did you come up for some other reason?'

'Like what?' Louis frowns, and I look away, preferring to look at his reflection in the mirror.

'I don't know. To see if you could dig up any more dirt on Honey, maybe?' I keep my eyes on the reflection, watching for his reaction.

He scrubs a hand over his clean-shaven chin, pressing his lips together. 'I swear to you, Lily—' The elevator doors ping open, and he pauses as we step out. Jessica is crossing the lobby to the bar, and she slows almost to a stop, giving me a questioning look. I shake my head and walk ahead of Louis, out towards the main entrance to the hotel. 'Lily, wait. Please.'

I stop on the red carpet. 'What? I only want the truth, Louis. Don't lie to me. I saw you with that reporter.'

'Then let me explain!' Louis throws his hands up in exasperation as the valet watches us intently. I grab his arm and tug him around the corner out of sight.

'Explain then,' I hiss, 'but this had better be good! Honey was destroyed by those photos in the newspapers. You don't know the consequences of something like this.'

'I do,' Louis says quietly. 'I've seen it all before. I've kept my mouth shut about things you wouldn't believe.'

'I already know about Spencer Tracy's affair with Katharine Hepburn. And Loretta Young's daughter with Clark Gable. And Elizabeth Taylor's affair with Eddie Fisher – even though he was married to Debbie Reynolds, who was her *best friend*.'

'What? Elizabeth Taylor…'

Shit. The Taylor/Fisher scandal doesn't happen until the Fifties. 'Forget about it. You were going to explain.'

'Lil, that girl you saw me with. She's not a reporter, I swear. I would never, ever tell anything to the newspapers. It's more than my job's worth… I like you, Lily. And I like Honey. I wouldn't want to hurt either of you.' His green eyes fix on me. 'Please, Lily, you have to believe me.'

'I…' I swallow. I want to believe him. I *really* want to believe him, because if I can't trust him, then I don't have anyone I can talk to about Honey. 'She had a notepad and a pen. She was writing down what you were saying.'

Louis nods. 'She was. But I swear, it wasn't anything to do with the newspapers. My sister is supposed to be getting married and we were talking about venues... look, can we go somewhere? Somewhere fun? I've spent the last couple of days feeling like a heel thinking I'd upset you. Let me make it up to you.'

'Your sister?' I hesitate, wanting to believe him but still full of nagging doubt. Still, I feel as if there is something he might be keeping from me.

'Please, Lil?'

I glance up at the hotel, at the darkened window to Honey's room. 'OK.'

'Come on then, Christine's waiting.'

'Christine?'

'The car.' Louis grins, and I don't have the heart to tell him that Christine is not the best name for a car. In fact, I'm not sure I want to get in her again if that's her name. Thanks, Stephen King. I follow Louis out to the car park, pausing momentarily as he unlocks Christine's passenger door, before sliding in beside him.

'So where are we going?' I ask as he heads out towards Sunset, before turning onto Beverly Boulevard.

'Somewhere ace.' He flashes me a grin, his hands light on the steering wheel as the sunset behind us gives his treacle-coloured hair a fiery glow. The atmosphere between us has lightened and the knot in my stomach has eased somewhat, although I haven't shaken off my suspicions entirely. 'Somewhere really ace. Much, much more exciting than film sets, or star-filled hotels.'

'Wow, it must be somewhere super special.' A laugh bubbles up in my throat despite myself. 'Come on, you can't leave me hanging. The beach?' *Wrong direction, Lil.* 'To see a band?'

'Even better.'

'Louis! Come on!' He indicates to come off the highway, past a billboard advertising toothpaste, and I feel a flicker of recognition.

'Here we are.' He pulls smoothly into a parking space outside a row of buildings, one with a lit neon sign outside.

'Oh my gosh, Louis, bowling?' I fumble for the handle, my fingers slipping as it sticks for a moment. 'Wait,' I say, my eyes roving over the building ahead of me. 'I've been here before.'

'You have?' There is a trace of disappointment in Louis's voice. 'Damn. I didn't think you would have made it this far out of town.'

But I barely hear him. The Highland Park Bowl looks completely different to the last time I saw it, on a Christmas night out with some of the other staff from the hotel. Then, the façade was a mess of peeling white paint, the name written in faded black letters.

'Lily? Are you OK?'

'Yeah, I'm fine… just…' I shake my head again. 'This is brilliant, I love bowling. I have to warn you though, I am pretty amazing at it. Like a… shark. A bowling shark.'

Relief washes over Louis's face as we walk towards the pristine building, the paint now a fresh and brilliant white. 'A shark, eh? I'm more of a tiger, myself. We'll see though, huh?'

Inside the bowling alley, it feels weirdly familiar and yet not. The space is as I remember it, but the décor is obviously different. The lighting is dimmer, and I see the pinsetter is on the lane, not in the ceiling as part of the lighting fixtures as it was the last time I was here. But the bar is the same, and the wooden flooring under our feet is too, as we grab our bowling shoes and set up our lane.

We drink milkshakes and play two games, the conversation between us flowing more easily now. It's hard to stay mad at Louis, and deep down, I desperately want to believe him. I push the thoughts – and doubts – out of my mind and let myself enjoy the evening. We laugh as I slip over on the shiny floor, crashing in a candy-striped heap, and laugh harder when Louis does it too, when it's his turn to bowl. He buys me a chocolate shake, and I buy him a malt, then finally we bowl our last balls.

'A bowling tiger? Are you having a laugh?' I giggle, as the scores are shown. I have smashed Louis's scores to smithereens.

'I love it when you say stuff like that,' Louis says with a grin. 'You sound so… British.'

'Don't change the subject,' I say, 'give me the rightful recognition I deserve as the queen of the bowling alley.'

'Your majesty.' Louis swoops into a deep bow.

'I'm sorry,' I say, the smile dropping from my face. 'For thinking you sold the story about Honey to the papers.'

'Forget about it.' Louis gives an awkward shrug, and holds out a hand. 'Will you allow me to escort you to the diner on the next block?'

I pretend to think about it. 'Will there be fries?'

'Anything your heart desires, my lady.' And as Louis straightens up, our eyes meet and something crackles on the air between us, ready to ignite a spark on dry timber.

–

'Tell me about your family.' Louis snags a French fry and eyes me closely.

'What do you want to know?' My pulse speeds up at the thought of talking about home, and I realise that I have barely thought about Honey all evening.

'Everything.' Louis pauses. 'Do you have brothers or sisters? What are your parents like? Do you miss them? Do you miss England?'

'Woah, one at a time!' I laugh, shifting in my seat and hoping that Louis can't tell that I feel kind of weird. 'In answer to your first question – no, I don't have brothers and sisters. It's just me and my mum. At least, it was. Now it's just me.' A lump forms in my throat and for a moment I can't catch my breath.

'I'm sorry. You don't have to talk about this if you'd rather—'

'No.' I shake my head, taking the napkin Louis hands to me. 'I want to. It was just us… she died two years ago from cancer. She was my best friend.' I haven't spoken about my mother since she passed. I haven't had anyone to speak about her to. 'My mum was the one who got me into the movies – she loved all the old stars, the black-and-white films. We'd watch them every Sunday.' I smile at the memory. 'I was hooked from the first time we watched *Gone with the Wind* together. She was so excited when I got into the London Film Academy, but then she got sick the year I graduated. I put everything on hold to take care of her.' I can still feel it, the exhaustion that weighed me down as I walked home late at night from my job at the local supermarket, the fear as I put my key in the lock that she would have worsened in my absence. The movies were an escape for both of us, the romance of *Gone with the Wind*, the unbearable tension of *Gaslight*, the light-hearted banter between Katharine Hepburn and Spencer Tracy the perfect antidote to the reality we were facing.

'She loved the movies too? I bet she would be happy you made it to Hollywood.'

'She would have been over the moon.' A sob chokes its way out, my voice thick. 'The night before she died, she made me promise that I would follow my dream, go to Hollywood, and make something of myself.' It had been her dream too, but getting pregnant at nineteen and raising me single-handedly after my dad did a runner before I was even born meant that she never got to do it. 'She left me some money in her will, just enough to get to Hollywood and give myself enough time to find a job.' She left a note too. *Don't let me down, Lily*, the letter had said. *Go to Hollywood, follow your dream, and live it for the both of us.* The tears stream down my face, and Louis hands me another napkin, squeezing my hand.

'She sounds incredible,' he says. 'She'd be so proud of you. You came to Hollywood, you're PA to a movie star! You made it, Lil.'

'I had to clean a few toilets before I got here.' I choke out a laugh, ignoring Louis's quizzical look. 'I was terrified when I got on that... when I left.' *Nice save Lil – who knows how common commercial flights were in 1949?* 'I had no idea whether things would work out, and I had nothing to come home to if it all went wrong, but sometimes you have to do what feels right, you know?' Although, at this particular moment, I have no idea if I've done the right thing. The pickle I've found myself in is like nothing anyone could ever imagine and the only plan I have for getting myself out of it is to save Honey, and I have no idea how I'm going to do that. *And I have no idea if it'll even work – if I'll even be able to get back home.*

'You're an amazing woman, Lily.' Louis reaches out and rests his hand on the table, his little finger pressing lightly against mine. 'You graduated from college – I don't think any girl I know has gone to college. And I certainly don't know many women who would travel halfway across the world to chase a dream. Especially on their own. My sister couldn't do it, and she's incredible.'

Turning the conversation to him gives me some breathing space. 'You have one sister?'

'Three sisters, two brothers.'

'Wow.' I sit back, unable to comprehend the idea of so many kids in one family. 'Are you the oldest?'

'Nah, I'm in the middle. Two brothers above, three sisters below. I'm the difficult middle child.' Louis gives a wry smile. 'Nate and Scott are both married, and Tilda, the sister below me, is waiting on Reg for a ring – he's unofficially asked her, and they're saving for the wedding. Aimee and Scarlett are both in high school.'

Tilda must be the sister he met at the hotel. 'And your mum and dad? What are they like?' Suddenly I am hungry for information, I want to know every little detail about him.

'Mom stays home and takes care of us all. She's amazing. Her pot roast is legendary.' He smiles at the thought of it. 'She used to be an actress, before. She was pretty successful, made a little money, but then she met my dad and got pregnant with Nate. She didn't want to go back to it. My dad works in a garage, he's a mechanic. They're good honest people. They live out in Santa Monica.'

I imagine a house full of people, all talking over each other, laughing, telling stories. It's what I always wanted when I was growing up, but there's only so much noise you can make with two of you.

'Do you see them a lot?'

'Yeah, I guess you could say that. Mom likes me to come for dinner every week. They think I'm living all fancy over here, so Mom likes me to come home so she can bring me back down to earth.'

'She sounds wonderful.' Part of me wishes I could meet her; the other part prays I don't. It's going to be hard enough to leave Louis as it is when the time comes.

'She is.' His hand brushes against mine as he reaches for the last of his milkshake, and the warmth of his skin makes my breath catch in my throat. I get that overwhelming sense again that I know him, that we've met before all of this, even though I know it's impossible. 'She kind of reminds me of you.'

Unsure how to respond, I excuse myself and head for the ladies' room, grateful for the cool air that wafts in through the open window. What's going on? I can't let myself have feelings for Louis – we're not meant to be together. I'm here to stop Honey from being murdered – I can't think of any other reason why I would have woken up in 1949 – and then somehow, I'll be catapulted back to the future, where I'll be back to cleaning the bathrooms of the Beverly Hills Hotel, and mildly flirting with Eric. I lean over the sink and splash cold water on my face. When I think about it like that, there's no reason whatsoever for me to want to go back to my own time.

But you have to save Honey. You're the only one who knows what's going to happen to her – therefore you're the only one who can stop it. And if that means you go back, then you don't have a choice.

I dry my face on a paper towel and smooth back the dark curls that have frizzed around my face, before slipping the lipstick Jean gave me out of my pocket. I pass it over my mouth and press my lips together, pushing a smile onto my face. Yes, I have to save Honey, but first I have to arrange a surprise birthday party for her, with no contacts and no access to the internet. I'm going to need some help.

Chapter Fourteen

'I need your help.' I blurt the words out to a surprised Louis as we walk back to Christine. He wouldn't let me pay the bill, not even go Dutch.

'Yeah? With what?' Our feet hit the sidewalk in unison, our footfalls echoing satisfyingly in the still night air. 'Is everything OK with Honey? You know, after the photos... I mean it, Lily, I didn't talk to any reporter.'

His words give me pause. Nothing is going to be OK with Honey in two weeks' time if I don't figure out what's going on. 'I know, Louis. I'm sorry I didn't give you a chance to explain before.' I feel prickly with shame at jumping to conclusions.

'So, what can I help you with?'

'It's her birthday on the twenty-sixth of June.' Just mentioning Honey's birthday makes a lump form in my throat. 'Jessica asked if I would arrange a birthday party for her, but I have no idea where to start. I mean, I'm new in town.' *Sort of.* 'The party is happening on Saturday, and I don't have any contacts.' *Or access to Google, or social media where I can do a shout-out for recommendations.*

'Yikes. Saturday?' Louis slows and turns to face me. 'But you said her birthday isn't until the twenty-sixth?'

'Yeah,' I say.

'Well, sure, I'll help if I can.' Louis grins and I feel an overwhelming urge to kiss him. 'You could speak to the hotel manager and see if the Crystal Ballroom is free? That would be the perfect location to host a party and once he knows it's for Honey, and that Leonard will be invited, he'll bend over backwards to keep him happy.'

'Really?'

'Leonard is a big deal in Hollywood, Lil. I'm sure he'd be happy to give you the ballroom. There's a bar in there too – on Saturday, you say?'

Excitement bubbles in my veins. Maybe I *can* pull this off. 'Yes, on Saturday.'

'It's my night off… but I'll offer to work the party if you'd like? It would be kinda cool to be at the party of the century. The hotel can probably help with decorations.'

'Louis, you are an absolute diamond. Thank you so much.' I reach up and kiss him on the cheek, trying to ignore the spark that flies between us, the electricity that crackles when my lips meet his skin.

'Aw shucks.' His cheeks redden and he pulls away, drawing the car key from his pocket. Christine gleams in the moonlight ahead of us, and Louis opens the passenger door for me, the leather cool on the back of my thighs as I slide in. He jumps in the driver's seat but doesn't put the key in the ignition. 'Lil, if it's Honey's birthday on the twenty-sixth then why are you planning the party for Saturday? Surely having an extra week to plan it would take the pressure off you a little?'

I open my mouth, the lie about Honey's heavy filming schedule and the imaginary visit from her mother ready to roll off my tongue, but I can't do it. I can't lie to Louis. Even though I am trying my hardest to deny it, I really like him. Like, *like him*, like him.

'This is going to sound really weird. Insane, probably, but I need you to listen to me.' I look at Louis, at his green eyes fixed on mine, at the way the moonlight slants in through the car window onto his dark hair.

'Um… OK?'

I take a deep breath. 'I think something really bad is going to happen to Honey the night before her birthday.'

Louis opens and closes his mouth a couple of times. 'Bad how? Why do you think something is going to happen to her?'

'It's complicated,' I say, my pulse spiking. Maybe this was the wrong idea. Maybe I should have just kept my mouth shut.

'Is she mixed up with… I don't know, criminals, or the mob? Did someone threaten her?'

'Not exactly.'

'Then how… Lil, are you a psychic or something? Because my mom is into all that kind of stuff, and—'

I reach out and touch the back of his hand with one finger. 'It's really complicated, and I can't explain it.' I pause and take a breath. 'I just know that something awful is going to happen to Honey the night before she turns twenty-one. I thought that having a party that night would be a bad idea, because there would be so many people, and I wouldn't be able to keep an eye on everyone.'

'So…' Louis frowns, 'you know something bad is going to happen, but you don't know who is going to do it?'

'Yes. Exactly that.' Relief washes over me – perhaps Louis doesn't think I'm crazy, perhaps he might actually be able to help me. 'I figured that the party would be the perfect place for someone to hurt Honey on the night but—'

'But if you hold the party the week before, it gives you a chance to scope out anyone who looks a little sketchy.

And reduces the number of people around Honey on the night that you think it's really going to happen.'

'*Yes.*' I could cry with relief. 'Louis, that's exactly what I mean. But I can't tell Jessica or anyone else, they'll think I'm crazy.'

'I never said I didn't think that.' Louis's lips curve up into a smile and I find myself returning it.

'I need to spend the party watching, observing, trying to see if there is anyone who potentially wants to harm Honey. To see if there is anyone there who shouldn't be. Basically, I have to spend the next few days being Magnum P.I. to try and stop this before it happens.'

'P.I.?' Louis says, puzzled. 'As in private investigator? Lil, if you know a private investigator then let's speak to him and get him to investigate! It sounds too dangerous for you to settle this on your own.'

Oh boy. I don't even know if Tom Selleck has been born yet. 'It's kind of a figure of speech, where I'm from. I don't actually know a P.I.'

'Oh.' Louis lets out an awkward laugh, and in the moonlight, it looks as though he is blushing.

'But if I did…' I grin. 'I would definitely get him on the case.'

'I'll be happy to help you,' Louis says. 'With the party, and with… the other stuff.' He looks at me closely, and I feel a blush rise on my own cheeks. 'You're quite a gal, Lily.'

–

When Louis pulls up to the hotel, I dither over saying goodbye, wondering whether he'll make an attempt to kiss me. He doesn't.

'Thanks for a swell night, Lil.' He holds the car door open as I step out onto the red carpet, not sure whether I feel relieved or disappointed not to have been kissed. 'And don't worry, I'll help you with Honey, however I can.'

I lift a hand as Louis drives away, leaning against one of the iconic pink columns in the entrance. The night is still and warm, the sound of cicadas renting the air. Have I made a huge mistake opening up to Louis? Is he on his way to Santa Monica to tell his mum that he's met a madwoman? Tears prick the back of my eyes. Everything here seems so complicated, I feel like a fish out of water. Everything I say, everything I do, it all takes so much effort to think it through to make sure I don't make a mistake. I'm too different – and it's not just because I'm a woman, or because I'm British. I think back to a few days ago, to cleaning the Paul Williams Suite with Eric, and I realise that despite everything I don't miss it. I miss gossiping with Eric as we clean the hotel rooms (though I don't miss the cleaning), I miss my mum, I miss London, I miss crime documentaries on Sky (although I wish they'd done one on Honey Black to give me a heads-up), I miss TikTok and Instagram. I miss sushi, and my phone, and that squidgy curl cream that smells of coconuts and makes my hair look frizz-free and swishy. But I don't miss feeling lonely and alone, in the busy hustle of modern-day LA.

I push myself away from the pink column I've been resting on with a new sense of resolve. I might have to watch what I say here, but I am making a difference. When I do go back to my own time, hopefully Honey will still be here, making a ton of movies and winning her Best Actress Oscar, and Louis will always remember me, even if it is as a mad British girl who might have been a psychic. Something chimes in the back of my mind, but I shake it away and head into the hotel lobby. Whatever happens later, right now I am here, in 1949, and I have a job to do.

The lobby is empty when I make my way to the elevator by the first-floor suites, and I lean against the wall as I wait for it to arrive, closing my eyes briefly. There is no elevator guy at this time of night, and I am grateful that I don't have to make conversation, as plans for the party tick through my mind. I realise I have no idea about the budget. Do I even have a budget? And how am I supposed to pay for anything? I really hope Jessica doesn't want me to pay for things up front, because 2019 Lily only has fourteen dollars in her bank account and 1949 Lily doesn't even *have* a bank account.

The ping of the elevator forces my eyes open, and I move forward to step into the car, but as I do, I see movement at the end of the corridor, outside the door to Honey's room. Slamming my hand on the button to hold the elevator, I watch to see if it's Honey – maybe we can grab a nightcap together – before I realise the figure is far too tall to be Honey, and looks like a man.

Oh no. I peer cautiously around the door of the elevator, my hand still pressed to the hold button. Maybe she invited someone back for a drink? If I didn't know what was going to happen to Honey in just under two weeks' time, I wouldn't necessarily be anxious, but I do know, and I am. Holding my breath, I squint in the dim hallway lighting, trying to see who it is. He has his back to me, but it looks as though he is trying the door to Honey's room. He wears a black shirt, and his hair is covered by a hat, but without seeing his face I have no idea who he is. I think he's too short to be Leonard, but measurements have never been my strong point. Magnus, maybe? He turns, and I slip back inside the elevator and frantically hammer my hand on the button to go up, letting out my breath in a whoosh of relief as the door closes and the elevator ascends.

Once back inside my own room, I lean against the door and try to slow my frantic pulse. It could be nothing, I tell myself. Someone lost in the hotel, a fan who thought they might be able to see Honey, room service. Maybe Honey had entertained him in her room, and he was trying to get in because he forgot something. Feeling as if I am clutching at straws and knowing I won't sleep tonight until I know she's OK, I reach for the telephone next to the bed and dial Honey's room.

'Hello?' After six rings she picks up, her voice blurred with sleep.

'Honey? It's Lily.'

'Lily? What time is it?'

'A little before one. Sorry, I woke you up. I was just checking you were OK.'

'I'm *fine*. I was sleeping.' She tuts, her tone petulant. 'I had a headache after dinner, so I was asleep by ten.'

'Well, OK. I hope you feel better in the morning. I'm sorry to disturb you.'

'Hmmm. See you in the morning.'

I hang up and sink slowly onto the bed, suddenly overwhelmingly exhausted. So, Honey was asleep by ten o'clock this evening, meaning that she definitely hadn't been entertaining whoever it was outside her room. So, the question remains, who was it? And what did he want?

Chapter Fifteen

Jessica is waiting for me at her table in the Polo Lounge the following afternoon, after calling and asking me to meet her for lunch. She is immaculate, her blonde hair pulled up into a neat chignon, her skin clear and her lipstick a bright brick red. I, on the other hand, feel as though I have been dragged through a hedge backwards. I wasn't needed on set today, but despite no alarm clock chiming in my ear this morning I have been awake for hours. After speaking to Honey last night, I couldn't get the image of the man at her door out of my mind, and I tossed and turned all night, wishing I had been brave enough to confront him.

I skirt through the bar towards the booths at the back of the restaurant, throwing a shy smile in Louis's direction as I do. His sister, the blonde girl I saw him with outside, is tucked onto a stool at the far end of the bar, and she gives me an icy stare as I hurry past. I hope he's not asking her to help with the party, because judging by her expression she doesn't seem the party type.

'Lily!' Jessica waves a hand in my direction, leaning across the table to do the Beverly Hills double air kiss as I reach her. 'It's wonderful to see you.'

'You, too.' I feel wrong-footed. I am the girl who fetches coffee and stands in the midday heat, with aching calves and a dehydration headache, waiting for the stars to need me. I don't lunch in the Polo Lounge with a world-famous actress.

'I took the liberty of ordering the salad for both of us, I hope you don't mind.'

I shake my head. 'Not at all. That would be lovely.'

'And some wine?' Without waiting for my response Jessica pours us both a glass of cold, crisp white wine. I doubt I could afford it on my 2019 wage even in 1949. 'Lily, are you OK? You look a little tired.'

I take the wine glass and sigh. 'I didn't sleep well.'

'No?' Jessica frowns, leaning in and lowering her voice. 'Lily, what is it? Is something wrong?'

I pause, not sure what to say. *Everything* is wrong – but it's not as if I can tell Jessica anything. She'll definitely think I'm bonkers, and if she tells Leonard and he fires me as Honey's PA, then I'll lose all access to her, to the set, to everything I need to stop her murder from happening. 'It's probably nothing. I saw a man in the corridor outside Honey's suite last night, and I was a little concerned, but the more I think about it the more I think it must have been Leonard, or Magnus.' *Who else could it have been?*

'A man? Outside Honey's room?'

'It *must* have been Magnus, or Leonard. Right?' The uneasy gnawing starts up again in my stomach. 'Maybe checking in on her?'

'I'm sure it was,' Jessica says. 'If you're worried you could always call in extra security? Although…' she taps a manicured nail against her chin, 'if it turned out to be nothing, Leonard would be furious at the extra cost.'

I shake my head, not wanting to further incur the wrath of Leonard. 'No, it's OK. I'm sure it was nothing. Honey thought someone had been in her room the other day, and I guess I was on high alert.'

'Honey thought someone was in her room? What... they broke in?'

I had assumed that Honey would have mentioned it to Jessica, seeing as they're best friends. 'She thought so. Her snow globe was gone – you know the one she brought from home? And it smelled of cigarettes in her room.'

'Gosh, how frightening.' Jessica frowns and reaches for her wine glass. 'Did you call security? Does Leonard know?'

I shake my head. 'Honey didn't want me to say anything. Maybe housekeeping broke the globe and were worried about getting fired.'

'Maybe.' Jessica doesn't sound too convinced. 'Is Honey OK? I know how scary it can be when something like this happens. I have a few... extreme fans.' She gives a wry smile.

'She's fine. A trooper, you know.'

Jessica smiles and presses her palm against the back of my hand. 'I know I kind of sprung the birthday party idea on you, but I wondered how things were going?'

'Good.' I smile, the wine dancing on my tongue. 'I have the venue sorted I think, and Louis is working on the bar side of things. I was going to ask the catering truck if they could help with the food.'

'Really?' Jessica's nose wrinkles. 'The catering truck? Honestly, Lily, I think we can do a little better than that. Honey is going to be twenty one after all. And this is *Hollywood.*'

'Oh. Well, of course we can. I wasn't too sure... I haven't been in town long and...'

'Don't worry about the money.' Jessica flaps a hand. 'This is all on Leonard's tab. Just drop his name wherever you're ordering from, and they can bill him. For the food, go to Musso and Frank, their food is divine, and they'll deliver to the hotel if it's for Leonard.'

'OK, no problem.' Luckily, I know where Musso and Frank is on Hollywood Boulevard, as it's still there in 2019. I feel a flicker of excitement at the thought of seeing the well-known restaurant seventy years earlier. 'I can go over there today after lunch.'

'Excellent.' Jessica leans back in her seat. She hasn't touched the salad in front of her, so I haven't touched mine yet, and my stomach gives a low growl that I hope she doesn't hear. 'Lily... the reason I asked you here wasn't about the party so much as... Honey.'

'Honey?'

'How is she, truly? Does she really seem all right to you?' Jessica's brow furrows. 'What you've told me today about someone getting into her room has me even more worried about her.'

I push at the leaves on my plate in an attempt to stall for time. Eventually I say, 'She's OK. I mean, the Billy Walters thing upset her a lot, I know that. But she's tougher than everyone thinks.'

'Hmmm.' Jessica taps her chin with one long, red, fingernail thoughtfully. 'That's just it, I'm not sure she is. She seems a little, I don't know... off? I expected her to bounce right back after the photos appeared in the newspapers – I almost expected her to laugh about it, I guess – but she's not her usual self.'

Laugh about it? I'm not sure I could ever laugh about it if something like that happened to me, but then I'm not used to being in the spotlight.

'She's tired from shooting too.' I think about the missing script, the snow globe that disappeared from her room and the incriminating scent of cigarette smoke in

150

the bathroom. Leonard, shouting at her, before pulling her into his arms. The figure outside her hotel room last night. I don't want people to gossip about Honey and I have no idea who I can trust. 'It's her first major role, I guess it's a big thing to get used to. Deep down she's still that small-town girl.'

'Well, of course.' Jessica smiles and turns to gesture to the waiter for more wine. 'And seeing Magnus must have upset her too.'

I give up any pretence that we're going to eat and take another sip of wine that goes straight to my head. 'It was a shock, seeing him, I think. And she was pretty upset when he left.' I don't say that I suspect Magnus hit Honey while they were together. That she is well rid of him.

'Of course she would be. Just because you're not with someone it doesn't mean that you stop caring for them.' Something drifts across Jessica's features, an emotion that I can't read. 'Will you be inviting Magnus to the party?'

I had thought about it but decided against it. If Honey saw him there it would upset her, even though it would be a shame to miss out on seeing how he behaves around her. 'I wasn't going to.'

Jessica lifts one slim, white shoulder in a half shrug. 'He is her husband. Technically they're still married.'

'But they're separated. I don't want to upset Honey.' *Especially not when it might be her last birthday.* 'Remember Annabel? Honey was furious when she let him on set that day, so I think Magnus appearing at her party would wreak all kinds of havoc. It's a terrible idea.'

'I don't think you quite understand, Lily. You have to invite him,' Jessica says gently. 'It's the way Hollywood works, I'm afraid. He's out of town at the moment so he more than likely won't come, but at least you've invited him. If you don't, he'll be offended and accuse Honey of shutting him out, and it'll be worse in the long run, believe me.'

–

I take a cab over to Hollywood Boulevard, my forehead pressed to the cold glass of the window. We stop at a red light outside Grauman's Chinese Theatre and my heart skips in my chest as I see the poster outside.

JESSICA PARKS IS CARLA IN
LEONARD LANGFORD'S
KENTUCKY QUEEN!
Introducing Honey Black as Alison.

I close my eyes, drawing in a deep breath before opening them. The poster is still there, showing Jessica's wide-eyed gaze and swishy blonde hair, the edges of it just starting to curl. Running my eyes over the space outside the theatre I note the empty gaps between the foot and handprints, gaps that will be filled in by the likes of Bruce Willis, Robert de Niro and Melissa McCarthy in years to come. There is an Alice sensation to the whole scene – an absurd feeling that I have fallen down some kind of rabbit hole into another dimension, tumbling over and over myself until I no longer know what is real and what isn't.

I lean back against the headrest, Jessica's words reverberating in my mind. If Magnus is out of town, then maybe it's not him and I can confirm he's out of the picture. If it is him, then will inviting him to the party give him the reason he needs to come back and hurt Honey? *And if he's out of town… then it couldn't have been him I saw in the corridor last night.* My temples pulse with a dull ache, and I am beginning to understand why the butterfly effect is such a big deal.

Musso and Frank looks almost identical to how it did – will do – when I walked past almost every day on my way to work at the Beverly Hills Hotel. The sign overhead proclaiming it 'Hollywood's Oldest Restaurant' is the only thing missing – which is understandable, I guess. Other than that the green frontage is the same, with the blinds half closed against the windows for privacy, and when I step inside, the private booths and the bar running the length of the restaurant are all as I remember from the one time I came here for dinner. It helps to shake off the weird feeling I've been carrying around all day, and I paste on a smile as the maître d' approaches.

Joseph, the proprietor at Musso's, is delighted when I tell him about Honey's party and I leave the restaurant a short while later feeling as though maybe, *just maybe*, I can pull this whole thing off. Buzzing with anticip-ation, I decide to take a slow walk back to the hotel, instead of jumping in a cab. It's a long walk, but I don't know whether I'll get the chance again to wander through Hollywood seventy years earlier than I ever have before, so I head on to Sunset Boulevard and start to stroll, enjoying the warmth of the sun on my back. The last few days have been a whirlwind, so it's a joy to wander in the summer sun, a spare pair of Honey's sunglasses fixed to my face. It's warm. Too warm, almost. A bead of sweat trickles between my shoulder blades, followed by another, and I feel the thump of a headache sharpen at my temples. *The wine*, I think, *I shouldn't have drunk the wine at lunch.* Thirst tickles at the back of my throat, and I am relieved to see a diner sign ahead of me, next to a pharmacy. Slowing my steps, it takes me a moment to get my bearings. I'm at

8100 Sunset, only instead of the signs for Starbucks, CVS and Trader Joe's I'm used to seeing, there is a diner, a neon sign on the window announcing burgers and thick shakes. Relief is cool and swift as I picture an ice-cold vanilla milkshake, and maybe a portion of fries before I carry on back to the hotel. I place a hand on the door, ready to push my way inside when I pause, my stomach giving a horrifying lurch. At a table in the far corner of the diner is Leonard, sitting opposite Jean, who glances up at him coyly.

Yikes. I pull back, and peer around the window frame. Yes, it is definitely Leonard and Jean. It's just a lunch meeting, I tell myself, they're probably discussing something about the movie. *So why not meet at the Polo Lounge? Or somewhere else more… fancy? And what about Honey?* My hand goes to my mouth. *Could Leonard be seeing both women?* The diner – Googie's is the name above the door – is cute, but it isn't really the kind of place for a business meeting. Leonard reaches across the table for Jean's hand, when a body crashes against me from behind.

'Sorry ma'am, I'm so sorry.' A boy in his late teens holds up a hand in apology. 'I thought you were going inside. Can I get the door for you?'

'No, no thank you.' My cheeks flush and I step to one side. I can't go in there and risk Leonard and Jean seeing me if it isn't a business meeting. The boy – man, I guess, he must be eighteen or so – flashes me a grin, and I gawp as he passes through the door into the cool of the diner. He looks like a slightly younger version of James Dean. I peep inside, as he makes his way to the counter. It *is* a slightly younger James Dean. A James Dean who just got into town and is about to embark on his acting career, becoming one of the most famous actors of all time.

I look away, feeling slightly sick at the knowledge that this vibrant man, with a charming smile and impeccable manners, is just six years away from killing himself in his Porsche.

On wobbly legs, I peel myself away from the window, just as Leonard gets to his feet and helps Jean with her thin cardigan before they make their way towards the door, Leonard's hand on Jean's back. *Shit.* I hurry along the boulevard before they exit the diner. The whole experience has left me feeling off-kilter. Finally, satisfied I am far enough away to go unnoticed, I resume my slow walk towards the hotel. Passing by the dark windows of the Last Call nightclub, I feel that shudder of intuition again. This is the place which will become the Viper Room where, in 1993, River Phoenix will take a drug overdose and die, and his brother Joaquin will call the paramedics to try and save him. Where Johnny Depp will leave the stage and rush outside to find his best friend being loaded into an ambulance. I can feel the ghosts of people who haven't even been born yet, their fate already written. Can I change Honey's fate and save her? With aching feet and my damp dress sticking to me, I toss over the suspects in my mind. Is Leonard even more of a suspect now? I thought maybe he was having an affair with Honey, but is he with Jean, too? I've felt the long arm of Leonard's powerful temper first hand, and not just on set. It's clear how Jean feels about Leonard – could she be responsible for Honey's death? Jealousy is a powerful emotion. And what about Cynthia Lake? She believes Honey is after Billy, and she already has a reputation for being wildly unstable. And then there's Magnus. Already furious with Honey over the scandal with Billy, anything could tip him over the edge. The party is the best chance I have to observe all of these people in one place.

I reach the hotel, grateful for the shade of the trees as I skip round the back to dip my feet into the pool. I am less happy to see the figure that skirts past me, head down, rushing from the back entrance of the hotel towards the car park. A figure that looks suspiciously like Magnus Michel. Magnus Michel, who is supposedly out of town.

Chapter Sixteen

It's the night of the party. I have managed to get through the rest of the week without giving the game away and have somehow pulled everything together. The food has been delivered to the Crystal Ballroom – including a huge three-tiered chocolate cake, that I know Honey will be powerless to resist given her terrible sweet tooth – the room has been decorated and Louis has set up the bar, while I worked on Honey's lines with her in an effort to keep things as normal as possible. It looks fantastic, the gold and silver balloons contrasting with the heavy cream drapes at the windows, the scent of jasmine and honeysuckle floating in from the garden through the open French doors. The chandeliers that hang from the ceiling sparkle, lighting the room with a soft, warm glow, and luxurious displays of roses, gladioli and lilies surround the dance floor. It's the perfect night for a party, and I feel quietly confident that tonight I'm going to uncover *something*. Now, I knock lightly on Honey's door and wait for her to open up.

'Lily, come in.' She grabs my arm and pulls me inside, a frown creasing her brow.

'Is something wrong?'

Honey stands in front of me, biting her bottom lip. She wears a simple white cotton shift dress with gold sandals, her hair styled in loose curls Marilyn style. She's Marilyn, before Marilyn is even a thing. Her face is dusted with powder, her eyes smoky, but her lips are missing what I now think of as her trademark coral red lipstick.

'You haven't seen my lipstick, have you?' She turns and heads towards the bathroom, rifling through the make-up bag on the shelf. 'I can't find it anywhere. I had it this morning...' Her voice is muffled as she delves deeper into the bag, her back to me.

'I haven't,' I say, pulling my own lipstick out of the small clutch I'm carrying. It's not the right shade and Honey dismisses it, pulling out a different lipstick in a more vibrant red. It contrasts strikingly with her blonde hair, making her seem even more glamorous than before.

'And my scent?' After lining her lips and smacking them together, Honey holds up a half empty bottle of perfume, the faint familiar waft of L'Air du Temps rising as she waves it in front of me. 'Look! This was a new bottle and now it's half empty.'

'I haven't used your scent, Honey.' I move towards her, taking the glass bottle from her hand as she blinks rapidly. 'Are you OK? What's going on?'

'Nothing.' Honey shakes her head and turns back to the mirror, her eyes meeting mine in the glass. 'I wasn't *accusing* you, Lily. I just thought maybe...'

'Honey, do you think someone has been using your things? Do you think someone has been in here again?' Alarm makes my pulse rise as I think of the figure I saw outside her bedroom door a few nights earlier.

'Oh, I don't know.' Honey narrows her eyes, capping the lipstick and shoving it deep into the make-up bag. 'No, it's nothing. I'm a little tired, that's all. You look pretty.'

I'm wearing a long-sleeved, pale blue satin dress, with a V neckline, a row of tiny buttons dotting the fabric from the neckline to mid-thigh. Fitted at the waist, the satin clings to my skin before flaring out over my hips and falling gracefully to my knees. Thanks to Jean, I've ditched the Converse in favour of a pair of sparkly, low heeled shoes in rose gold. I feel like a million dollars and thank my lucky stars that while Jean might not seem to like me very much, she doesn't dislike me enough to send me to a party in my work clothes.

'Aren't you a little over dressed for dinner? I thought we were going to grab a salad somewhere quiet together? Although I suppose I should be grateful you're not wearing those darned sneakers.'

'I...' I realise I hadn't actually thought about what Honey would say when she saw me dolled up to the nines. 'I thought we could try for a table at Musso's?' I mean, Honey will be eating food from Musso's tonight, it just won't be at the restaurant. 'And then I thought we could go on somewhere else. Dancing, perhaps? Just the two of us. Properly, this time.'

'Oh, I don't know, Lily...' Honey looks doubtful. 'I've had a long week, and things haven't gone so great, you know, after the Billy thing? Leonard was furious, and if he finds out I'm out dancing again tonight... the newspapers... I dread to think how he'd react if he sees me on the front page again.' She presses her lips together, the idea of hitting the front page not wholly distasteful to her.

I am already flipping through the clothes in Honey's wardrobe, searching for the perfect outfit for the party. I can't let her back out on me now, not when half of Holly-wood is waiting to celebrate her downstairs. 'Honey, you are not staying home tonight. Having a shit week is the perfect excuse to get dressed up and go for dinner and dancing. Come on, let's dress you up – you can't let me go out like this on my own.' I ignore her raised eyebrows, pulling out the perfect dress.

'No need to speak like an anchor-clanker, Lily.' Honey's eyes slide to the floor-length oyster silk gown I'm holding. It's Grecian style, fitted in all the right places, and I know she's going to look fantastic in it. 'Maybe if we don't stay out too late...'

'That's my girl.' I shove the gown in her direction.

'I'm going to need a girdle with that one.'

'A...? Blimey, OK.' I take the girdle as she shucks off the linen shift and holds her arms above her head so I can help her on with the undergarment. 'I can't believe I ever complained about Spanx.'

'Sometimes, Lily, I have no idea what you're talking about,' Honey gasps, as she yanks the hook and eye fasteners closed, and I slip the silk over her head.

'There. You look beautiful.' I glance at the clock on the nightstand. I told Louis I'd bring Honey down at seven o'clock and it's a few minutes to. 'We should go. Musso's gets pretty booked.'

In the lobby I pause, before pulling Honey towards the staircase that leads down to the Crystal Ballroom. Not having a working mobile phone, I wasn't able to text Louis or Jean and give them the heads-up that we were on our way, and I hope people are quiet as we approach the stairs. I can't hear any music and I let out a breath.

'Lily? Why are you heading for the ballroom? I thought you wanted to get to the restaurant?'

'Just a sec, Honey. I need to pass a message to Louis.' Ignoring her protestations about finding Louis at the bar, I grab her hand and pull her towards the staircase. As we descend there is a hush, the room beyond in darkness, and suddenly the chandeliers fill the room with light.

'What?' Honey presses her hands to her mouth as a room full of Hollywood's finest chorus, 'SURPRISE!' She turns to me, her hands still over her mouth, but I can see the grin on her face. 'Lily, what on earth…? Did you do all of this? For me?'

'Well,' I shrug as Jessica approaches and leans in to kiss Honey. 'It was Jessica's idea to throw you a party. I just arranged a few things, with some help from Louis.'

'But…' Honey gazes around the room, at the extravagant balloon displays, the tables heaving with Musso's food, at the familiar faces dancing, talking, and laughing, all decked out in their best party clothes. Her eyes settle on the giant birthday banner, the number twenty-one blazing out in gold glitter. 'It's not my birthday until next week!'

'Lily didn't want to spoil your visit with your mom next weekend, so we bumped it up a little.' Jessica lays her arm around Honey's shoulder. 'Happy early birthday sweetie!' A passing waiter stops and Jessica grabs two glasses of a lethal-looking cocktail, handing one to Honey. 'Cheers.'

'My visit with my mom…?' Honey looks at me, confused, her glass halfway to her lips.

'Drink up,' I say, spying Louis behind the makeshift bar. 'Have fun, Honey. I'm going to grab a drink.' Before she can question me about her mother's imaginary visit, I slip past Esther Williams, wave a hand at Jean who is sipping primly on a drink in the corner, and squint as I pass the piano, not 100 per cent sure if it really is Bing Crosby who sits at the keys bashing out 'Why Can't You Behave?' before finally reaching the safety of Louis and his cocktail shaker.

'Hey Lil, you really did it.' Louis grins as he hands me a drink and I take a healthy swig.

'Bloody hell Louis, what in God's name is in this?' I turn the glass in my hands, the alcohol still scorching my throat.

Louis tries to hide the grin that curves his mouth upwards. 'Well, Miss Potty Mouth, it's called a between the sheets.' He drops his eyes and I feel my cheeks grow warm. 'It's like a sidecar... but then it gets a little jazzy. It's rum and cognac.'

'No wonder it blew my socks off.' I grin back at him and enjoy the way he looks me over as if seeing me for the first time.

'Wow,' he says, 'you look incredible. I can't believe you pulled this off... the look on Honey's face was priceless.' He leans in and lowers his voice. 'So, you think whoever has it in for Honey is here tonight?'

'I don't know.' I scan the room, but there is no neon arrow over anyone's head, pointing them out as the killer. 'It's not impossible.' The thought makes me shiver.

'Hey. Hey you. Bartender.' A voice calls from further along the bar and I look over to see Cynthia Lake waving her empty glass in Louis's direction. A subdued Billy Walters stands beside her, looking as if he wishes he could be anywhere else. 'Another drink over here.' Cynthia catches my eye, and a sneer rises on her face.

'You serve her,' I say quietly. 'I was hoping she wouldn't come but I guess wherever Billy goes, she goes, especially if Honey is involved.'

'I don't know what he sees in her,' Louis says, before smiling and holding up a finger in her direction in a 'one minute' gesture.

'Keep her sweet,' I say, 'I'm going to scope out the rest of the guests and see if there's anyone here that shouldn't be and keep an eye on those who should.' I look behind me, to where Honey is dancing, another full glass in her hand. 'And to keep an eye on Honey, too.'

Chapter Seventeen

Hours later, the party is still going strong, and Bing has been replaced by a live band, some musician friends of Louis's.

'Penny for them?' Jessica comes to stand beside me, still remarkably sober considering how she's been putting the drinks away. Both she and Honey have had full glasses in their hands every time I've seen them, but where Honey is getting sloppy, stumbling over her partner's feet on the dance floor and laughing a little too loudly, Jessica is still her usual poised self.

'Just enjoying the party,' I say, clinking my glass against hers. It feels surreal to be in the same room as people who are either Hollywood royalty already, or will be in a few short years. Ingrid Bergman is in the corner, deep in conversation with Clark Gable. He is impossibly handsome in real life, and despite the rumours about him having terrible breath, I think I would still kiss him. For the brief moment that Billy has been allowed out of Cynthia's sight he has necked two beers and is trying to convince a young woman who may or may not be Elizabeth Taylor to dance with him. I dread to think what Cynthia will say when she comes back from the ladies' room.

'Do you think Honey's enjoying herself?'

'Absolutely,' I say firmly, and I'm glad she is, especially if I can't stop what is going to happen. 'She's certainly enjoying the cocktails.' I smile, but keep my eyes on Honey, who is dancing with Lee Dubois, Billy's sidekick on the movie. 'I can't believe so many stars came out for Honey's birthday. This is her first major role; I didn't think half of these people would show.' I can't help but feel completely starstruck – the room is filled with millions of dollars' worth of acting talent.

'It sounds awful, but they came for Leonard more than Honey,' Jessica says, nodding at Lana Turner as she dances past. 'They know if they turn up here, Len will remember them the next time he has a part they want. Playing nice goes a long way in Hollywood.'

I open my mouth, on the brink of asking Jessica if that's why she's been so kind to Honey, when she says, 'Oh no. Seriously?'

I follow her gaze to where Magnus rests on the bar, a smirk on his face and a short glass of something strong in his hand as he leans in close to talk to Celia Johnson. 'Damn. I was hoping he wouldn't come.'

'I thought he was out of town,' Jessica says, her tone chilly. 'Let's hope Honey doesn't realise he's here.' She turns to face me, her voice softening. 'You did a good job tonight, Lily. Honey will remember this night for the rest of her life.' She gives me a tight smile and then, raising a hand to someone across the room, she excuses herself.

The rest of her life. The words take away the small buzz I have from Louis's cocktail, and I suddenly feel remarkably sober. Remembering that my job tonight is not to have fun, but to protect Honey, I walk a lap of the ballroom, watching everyone as I go. Vaguely familiar faces fill the room, but I have no idea if I recognise them from the set, or from old movies. Ingrid Bergman is now dancing with a small man with slicked–back hair, as Leonard talks animatedly with Olivia de Havilland, a fat cigar wiggling at the corner of his mouth. A man stands in the corner, half hidden behind the drapes, dark blond hair curling over his forehead, his eyes fixed on Honey. I don't recognise him, but there is something about him that seems familiar. There is no sign of Jessica, but I spot Jean leaning against the wall, a half empty glass in one hand. She is watching Leonard with a miserable look on her face.

'Jean? Can I get you another drink?'

Jean jumps at the sound of my voice over the music. 'Oh, Lily. You look very pretty. No, I don't think I want another.' She glances in Leonard's direction. 'I might head up to my room soon.'

'Really? It's only early.' I follow her gaze to Leonard and raise my eyebrows. 'I haven't seen you dancing yet… there are some cute guys here.'

'Oh no, I couldn't. I'm not… I'm not *modern* like you, Lily.' Jean shakes her head and blushes, before reaching out a hand to a passing waiter who carries a tray of canapés, snatching one. 'Thank you, Jimmy.'

'Pleasure, ma'am.' The voice is familiar as the waiter walks away; I realise it is the man who crashed into me outside the diner.

'You know that guy?' I ask, watching as she crams the canapé into her mouth, eating her feelings.

'Jimmy? Sure I do. He's just arrived in town, but I've known his mom for years. He's at college, but he wants to act. He wants to be in the movies, so I said I'd introduce him to Leonard. There's something about him, you know? I think the kid could go far.'

'I think you could be right,' I say sadly, watching as James Dean earns a few extra dollars waiting on the crowd he so desperately wants to join. I am half tempted to tell Jean to keep him away from fast cars, but I have enough on my hands trying to keep Honey safe.

I leave Jean stuffing canapés and trying not to cry as I circle the room, watching the guests intently. Honey has moved on and is dancing with Clark Gable, something I know will make her heart almost burst out of her chest, and I notice that once again, her glass is full. As I pass by the dance floor, a hand shoots out and grabs me by the wrist, and I find myself face to face with Magnus Michel.

'How about it, sugar?' He leers at me, his dark hair breaking free from its Brylcreem prison and falling over his forehead.

'How about what?' I go rigid, as he tightens his grip.

'A dance, what else?'

Honey whirls past me in Clark Gable's arms, giving me a sloppy thumbs up as she does. She hasn't seen Magnus yet. 'Uh… sure.'

He slides his arms around my waist, and my pulse increases, frantic and twitchy. This is a hundred times worse than any bottom-pinching, or casual 'doll's or 'sweetheart's thrown my way on set. Under the stale scent of alcohol that seeps from his pores there is the scent of something else, something… dangerous. Something that could be mistaken for charm if Honey hadn't insinuated things about him. Magnus's hands slide down and cup my bum and I reach round and yank them back to my waist. He pulls me tighter, and I can smell the overpowering scent of sandalwood, along with old booze and sweat.

'Relax honey, you're all uptight.'

Double ugh. Magnus whirls me around the room, until I am nauseous. The nausea only intensifies when his hands slide down to my bum again.

'Don't.' I yank his hands back up.

'Oh, come on sugar, don't play hard to get. Don't you know who I am?' He leans in close, his mouth tickling my ear. 'I'm Magnus Michel. I always get what I want.' His eyes slide in Honey's direction. '*Always.*'

'Couldn't keep her though, could you?' The words fly out of my mouth without warning, fear slicing through my veins like lightning, my breath coming short as Magnus squeezes my ribcage, hard.

'Think you're smart, huh?' Magnus hisses in my ear, as the pressure on my ribs makes it hard to breathe. 'Think you're funny? Cleverer than me? So did she.' He flashes a grin in Honey's direction, and I press my hands against his chest, but it's like pressing against rock.

'You don't scare me,' I whisper, hoping that he can't feel the panic beginning to vibrate through my body.

'No?' Magnus smirks. 'You should be afraid, little girl. You don't know what I'm capable of.' His hands slide straight down to my backside again, this time adding in a squeeze as they do.

'I said *don't.*' Without thinking my hand flies through the air and cracks him across the cheek.

'Lily!' Honey cries, her hands flying to her mouth as Magnus pulls away from me, muttering *bitch* under his breath. 'Oh no. *Oh no.*'

'What the hell just happened?' Leonard's voice is loud, the band faltering as everyone turns to look in our direction.

'She hit me.' Magnus glares at me, a brilliant red stripe across his face where my hand made contact.

'You *groped* me,' I say, bubbles of anger bursting in my chest. 'I don't care who you are, you can't behave like that.'

Magnus laughs, spiteful and bitter. 'As if I'd touch someone like *you*. I could have any woman in here.' He turns to Leonard. 'Leonard, come on. You can't let her do this to me.'

Leonard looks at me and back to Magnus. 'Magnus, I hear you pal, but I think it's time you left. Things are winding up anyway.'

Magnus wipes a hand over his forehead as he glares at me, and then Honey. 'You'll regret this,' he growls, before he turns towards the cloakroom, and I feel Leonard turn his gaze on me.

'What the hell is wrong with you? Get out of here,' he hisses as he marches after Magnus, the band resuming their play.

Honey flutters towards me, her uncoordinated movements betraying how much she's had to drink. 'Lily, that was *bad*. You shouldn't have hit him.' She shakes her head blurrily. 'Why did you do that? You don't know what he's like – he's going to be so *angry*.' Her hands tremble anxiously at her sides, coming up to press against her mouth. 'You know he'll tell Leonard he was just having some fun.'

It wasn't 'fun', it was a form of assault, but the thought of trying to explain it that way to Honey, when in seventy years' time women will still have to justify why they won't accept this behaviour from men, is far too exhausting. I sigh, my palm still tingling. 'Sorry Honey, guess I didn't realise. I'll smooth it over with Magnus tomorrow.' Honey blinks up at me, fear lacing her features despite the amount of alcohol she's consumed. 'You don't need to worry about him, OK? Look, that guy is waiting to dance with you. Is it… is that Gary Cooper? Go on, don't keep him waiting.'

Still wobbly from my encounter with Magnus, I wait until I am sure he is gone before I allow myself some fresh air. Figuring Honey is safe enough in the arms of Gary Cooper, I step out through the French doors to the patio, my shoulders relaxing as the warm night air hits me. *Magnus could be the one. He's angry and arrogant, and I think he has the capacity for violence.* I can still feel the imprint of his fingers digging into the skin on my ribcage.

Thinking I am alone, I let out a long breath, before low voices carry over from the honeysuckle bower at the far end of the garden. They are too quiet for me to make out their words but in the dim glow of the garden lighting I can just make out Jessica, sitting in the bower next to a man. *Magnus. He was supposed to have left the party.* I pull back against the wall, not wanting them to spot me, as Jessica gets to her feet and stands over Magnus, her arms waving frantically. Intrigued, I try to inch closer, but the light falls in such a way that to step further along would leave me exposed.

'Unacceptable… agreed that you…' Jessica's voice rises, as she jabs her finger in Magnus's face. I wonder if she is angry at him for showing up at the party, or whether she witnessed our exchange on the dance floor. Politics meant I had to invite him, but she was convinced that he was out of town and wouldn't show… and she wouldn't want him to show up, knowing it would upset Honey. Magnus lights a cigarette, his movements quick and furious, his voice an angry hiss.

Another, louder, even more furious voice erupts from inside the ballroom. Recognising the angry squeal, I reluctantly turn away from Jessica and Magnus, hurrying back inside only to find the very thing I was dreading. Cynthia is standing in the centre of the ballroom, shrieking at Honey, who is flushed a violent red and swaying on her feet. Billy stands to one side, tugging uselessly at Cynthia's arm as she bawls at Honey.

'You're a *disgrace*,' Cynthia hisses as Honey blinks drunkenly. 'Hanging off other people's husbands all night. I warned you before, when those photos were leaked, and I won't warn you again. The next time I find you near Billy, you'll regret it, because it'll be the last thing you ever do.'

Billy grasps Cynthia more firmly, pulling her towards the open door into the lobby. 'That's enough Cynthia, we're leaving.'

But it's too late. The band has stopped playing, someone has raised the lights in the ballroom, and those who aren't standing around to gawp at Cynthia's rage have started to drift away on a fog of martini and gin and tonic.

'Come on Cynthia, we'll talk tomorrow.' Leonard has her by the other arm and he and Billy remove a cursing Cynthia from the ballroom. I turn back to Honey, but she is gone.

'Lil,' Louis calls from the bar, and points towards the open French doors. 'She went that way.'

Jesus, out into the garden to bump straight into a still furious Magnus. Ignoring my aching feet, I hurry outside, where Honey stands with her back to me, her shoulders heaving and her hands over her face.

'Honey? Are you OK?' I wrap my arm around her shoulder and glance towards the bower at the bottom of the garden. *Empty, thank goodness.*

'She just started… *shouting*.' Honey's voice is slurred, and I wonder exactly how many cocktails she's drunk tonight. 'Why is she so awful? I'm not as awful as her, am I, Lily? I know I've hurt people, done things I shouldn't, but I did it because I *had to*. I just wanted to be a movie star; I didn't ask for any of *this*.'

Part of me wants to let Honey ramble, to see if she'll expand on exactly what these terrible things are, but I am conscious of the lack of privacy out here. 'Honey, you're not awful, I promise you.' *Determined and ambitious, yes, but not awful.*

'I didn't even do anything tonight… Billy asked me to dance, and they said it would be a good idea…'

'Who said it would be a good idea?'

'And then she was shouting and shouting and Lily… it was *horrible*.' Honey sobs louder and I pat her back protectively, sure I hear rustling in the bushes behind us.

'It's OK now, Billy's taken her home, and I guess the party is over anyway. Come on.' I guide her towards the French doors. 'Let's get you up to your room.' As we walk away, I hear it again, a rustling in the bushes as though Honey and I aren't alone out there.

–

'Fresh air hit her good,' Louis whispers as we lead Honey towards her suite, Honey stopping to lean against the wall with her eyes closed, small hiccups erupting every now and again.

'No shit,' I whisper back, stone cold sober. Louis's eyes widen briefly, and I remember I shouldn't curse so much, not here, not in 1949. 'How much did she drink?'

'No idea,' he shrugs, 'the bar was crazy busy all night, but I never served Honey once. People must have been getting drinks for her… I guess they would, being the birthday girl and all.'

'I guess.' I've seen Honey drunk before, that night at the Palomino, but she's barely touched a drop in public since – she's been so careful, aware of her image and her growing sense of being in the public eye. Something sharp and uneasy prickles between my shoulder blades.

We grab an arm each and hustle Honey along the empty corridor. Honey yelps as we pass Jessica's room, tripping over her own feet, and I shush her as we approach the door of her suite, handing Louis the key. We manage to get her onto the bed, and I slide her shoes off and tuck a blanket over her, as a light snore erupts from her lips.

'Yikes,' Louis laughs gently as I place a glass of water next to the bed. 'Someone's going to have a hell of a headache in the morning.'

'Let's hope Leonard doesn't give her too much of a hard time.' With one last look at Honey's sleeping face, we slip away, closing the door gently behind us.

'Lily!' Jessica hurries along the corridor towards us, her hair slipping from its perfect up-do. She stumbles slightly on her heels, placing a hand on the wall to right herself. 'Is Honey all right? I looked for her in the ballroom, but someone said she'd left.'

'She's… a little worse for wear,' I say, 'but nothing that can't be cured by a bacon sandwich and a couple of Advil in the morning.'

'Oh gosh, I think we all had a little too much.' Jessica stifles a hiccup. 'And you, Lily… are you all right? I heard about… well, about what happened with Magnus.'

My cheeks grow warm, and I look down. 'I'm fine. I'm sorry it happened… I didn't mean to ruin the party.'

'You didn't ruin anything; in fact I think you were quite impressive.' Jessica looks past me to Honey's closed hotel suite door. 'Honey had a whale of a time. Well done, Lily.'

She clasps my hand tightly. 'I'll let you get to bed.' And she turns and walks – a little more steadily now – back down the hushed corridor towards her own suite.

'I'll walk you to your room.' Louis falls into step with me, as I bypass the elevator and head for the stairs. As we push open the door to the staircase, I catch a flash of movement, as if someone is sprinting up the stairs ahead of us.

'Did you see that? It looked like someone rushing up the stairs, but I didn't see anyone in the corridor just now, did you?' The unease spreads to the base of my spine as I recall the dark figure outside Honey's room previously. Could it be the same person?

'Could be someone who got the wrong floor maybe?' But Louis looks doubtful, even as he says it.

'Listen, I'm going to stay in Honey's room tonight, just in case.'

'You don't think—'

'No,' I say quickly, 'I don't think anything will happen tonight, but I want to keep an eye on her.'

'I don't know, Lily, maybe you should stay in your own room. I mean, Honey's out for the count...'

'I want to stay with her. Just in case.'

'You still think something bad is going to happen to her?'

I don't think, I *know*. 'Yeah, I do. And I have to stop it. I know it sounds crazy but... you just have to trust me.' We are back outside Honey's door, and I slip the key in the lock. 'Thank you, Louis, for everything. I'll talk to you tomorrow?'

I watch him head back towards the lobby and close Honey's door, leaning against it as I watch her chest rise and fall with every breath, her face calm and peaceful.

Tonight has been more stressful than I thought it would be and despite spending the evening feeling as if I were stalking every guest at the party, I'm still no closer to knowing who wants to kill Honey Black.

Chapter Eighteen

Dragging myself into wakefulness, I blink, my eyes dry and gritty as I find every part of my body hurts. Forcing myself into an upright position, I recognise the dimly lit room as Honey's suite, and the reason for my aching back and twisted shoulders is the fact that I spent the entire night squashed on Honey's chaise.

A hangover thuds at my temples, and I swallow dryly. Bloody Louis and his killer cocktails – I only had a couple. I swear when I get back, I'm going teetotal. Ignoring the twist in my chest at the thought of my own time, I glance across to Honey's bedroom. The door is open, and I can just make out the rise and fall of her shoulders, hear the slight snore as her breath whistles in and out. She's going to have an even worse hangover than me when she wakes up. At the thought of Honey's hangover, memories of last night come flooding back. Magnus, a vivid red handprint on his cheek, my palm stinging. Jessica, her voice ripe with anger as she hissed at the silhouette in the bower. Cynthia Lake making yet another scene as Billy tried to drag her away. Where was Leonard while all this was happening? I rest my forehead on my knees, recalling the way he hissed into my ear as he marched a furious Magnus from the room. *What a mess.*

Peering between the drapes to the street below, I see the sun is already starting to climb high in the sky. Honey isn't shooting until this afternoon, but when I check the clock, I realise this afternoon is going to come around sooner than expected. Collecting up my shoes, I tiptoe towards the door, barefoot, planning on heading to my room for a quick shower before coming back down to wake Honey. Then I see it.

A slip of white paper peeps out from under the hotel room door. Glancing towards the bedroom where Honey still sleeps soundly, I reach down, tug it free and slowly open it.

Go bACk TO wHeRe YOu CamE fRom
tHis iS YOuR lASt waRNinG

The words have been cut from a newspaper, the sheet of white paper crinkly with glue, and for a moment I have to resist the urge to snigger at the haphazard letters, the sheer cliché of it all. Letters cut from a newspaper, formed to make a threatening note? It doesn't feel very original. And then I read the second sentence again.

tHis iS YOuR lASt waRNinG

Does this mean that Honey has received more of these? Forgetting all thoughts of a restorative shower, I walk into Honey's room and shake her gently. She doesn't move. I shake her again, but no response.

'Honey?' Shoving her shoulder hard, I feel a twinge of panic. 'Honey, wake up!'

'Huh?' Finally, she blinks groggily, her mascaraed eyelashes half glued together. The remains of last night's lipstick casts a pink smear across her chin, and she couldn't look less like a movie star if she tried. 'Lil? What's going on? Did I oversleep?' She pushes her way up the bed, holding her head in one hand. 'Jeez Louise, I think I overdid it on the cocktails. Do you feel all right, Lily?'

'Fine,' I lie. 'Honey, I need to talk to you.' But she is pushing the duvet back, swinging her legs out of the bed and scurrying towards the bathroom. I wait impatiently as I hear the toilet flush, and then the sound of teeth being brushed in the bathroom.

'What's a girl got to do to get a cup of coffee around here?' Honey appears in the doorway, lipstick removed from her chin. 'I feel like something died in my mouth.' She climbs back into bed and leans against the propped-up pillows, closing her eyes. She does look pale, her cheeks an off-white, while dark circles ring her eyes.

'Ugh,' she sighs, 'what was I drinking? Honestly Lil, I don't know if I can get to the set today. I feel like I'm dying.' Her eyes ping open. 'Wait... how did I get back here last night?'

'I brought you back, with Louis.'

'Oh. Thank you. Was I awful? Magnus always says...' She trails off.

Bloody Magnus. 'No Honey, you weren't awful at all, I just didn't want you coming back here on your own, and Louis is a gentleman, he wouldn't let either of us go home alone.' I pause for a moment, a horrible thought scratching at the back of my mind. 'Honey. What *do* you remember about last night?'

'Hmm, not a lot.' She gives a wan smile, before pulling a face. 'Drinking cocktails. Dancing... dancing *a lot*. I think I danced with Clark.' Honey gives me a coy smile and I nod. 'Not much else though. I guess I drank way too much.' She reaches for my hand. 'But honestly Lily, I had the most wonderful time. I just don't feel so good now. Oh!'

'What? What is it?'

'You…' Honey stares at me, open-mouthed, before she presses her hands to her lips. 'You hit Magnus!'

Heat creeps up my neck, warming my face. 'Yeah. I did.'

'Oh my gosh Lily, you are going to be in such trouble when Leonard hears about this.' Honey shakes her head, before clutching her temples dramatically.

'He already knows, so I think that ship has sailed. I'll probably be fired.' I shift on the edge of the bed, my back still aching from my night on the chaise. 'Although it should be Magnus in trouble, not me. I didn't do anything wrong.'

'Lily, you hit him!'

'He deserved it!' I draw in a deep breath. 'Honey, he groped me last night. Put his hands all over me. I told him to stop, and he didn't. That isn't acceptable behaviour and there's no reason why either of us should put up with it.' I feel sick at the memory of his hands on my ribcage, persistent and invasive, his hissed threat into my ear.

'He's going to be so angry.' A dark cloud passes over Honey's features, and she looks younger than her almost twenty-one years. 'You don't know what he's like.'

I have a fair idea of what kind of guy Magnus Michel is. 'He's a bully, Honey.'

'But…'

'No buts.' I shake my head firmly as Honey looks at me, her face pale. 'You don't have to put up with it – if you hold these men to account for what they're doing then perhaps they'll change. Most likely they won't, but at least you've made a stand against them. It's not right, Honey, and that's why I reacted the way I did.'

'It was pretty magnificent. And satisfying too, I bet.' Honey gives me a small smile. 'I've never met anyone quite like you before, Lily.'

I return the smile — it was bloody satisfying actually — and then I remember the reason I woke her up.

'Honey,' I say, fingering the slip of paper in my hand. 'I have to show you something. Look at this.' I pass her the note and watch her face for a reaction as she scans the words.

'It's just a note,' she shrugs, and goes to screw up the paper.

'Don't screw it up!' I lean over and snatch it from her hands. 'This is evidence.'

'Evidence? Of what?' Honey looks at me in amusement. 'Don't be ridiculous. It's just a silly note, Lily, it's nothing to be worried about. Ugh, my head is pounding. Are you going to fetch me some coffee or not?'

'Honey, this is not just a note, this is serious.' *More serious than she realises.* 'Do you have any idea who could have sent it? Someone wants you gone.'

'Oh Lil, I've had lots of those letters. Nothing has happened to me yet.'

'Wait a minute.' I shake my head, feeling my brows knit together, an action that exacerbates the thud at my temples. 'What do you mean, you've had lots of them? Where? Delivered here?'

'Sure, delivered here.' Honey gets back out of bed, picking up her empty water glass as she moves towards the bathroom. 'I had one not long after you first arrived.' She reappears in the doorway, glass now full. 'That's why I freaked out, I guess, when my snow globe went missing. I received a letter like this — the same cut-out letters, the same message – and then I thought someone had been in my room and taken my snow globe.'

'Why didn't you tell me?' *Could it have been from Magnus? Trying to frighten Honey back into his arms?*

'I did.' Honey moves to her wardrobe, shucking off her robe as she goes. She scoops up her dress from last night and hands it to me before standing in front of the rail in just her underwear.

'Wait…' Honey's right. She did tell me. About the snow globe going missing anyway, and I told her it was probably the maid who broke it, even though I knew what was going to happen to her in two weeks' time. 'You never told me about the letter.'

'I told Jean,' she says, 'and she told me that that's what happens when you become a star. You get letters, and some are nice, and some are nasty, you just have to roll with it. So that's what I'm doing.' Honey gives me a grin despite the green tinge to her face and walks back towards the bathroom with her clothes over her arm. 'I'm rolling with it.'

I shake my head as Honey closes the door and reach for a hanger for the oyster silk she wore last night. I'm not sure how I'll convince her that these letters might be something we should be concerned about, but I am certain whoever sent them will have something to do with what will happen in a few days' time. I slide the hanger inside the dress and reach to hang it up, freezing as I do. On the bodice of the dress, just where the silk would sit against Honey's ribcage, is a black smudge. It looks suspiciously like newsprint.

–

After managing to persuade Honey that skipping filming today would lead to a fate worse than death (dodgy choice of words, I know), I am glad when Honey leans back in the car and closes her eyes, avoiding any possibility of small talk. The smudge on her dress made the blood freeze in my veins – I'm certain that whoever pushed that note under the door must have been at the party last night, and they came into close contact with Honey. The only problem is, Honey danced the night away with several different people, so the process of elimination is going to be difficult. I need something more, something concrete.

As soon as we arrive on set, I know something has happened. The air is subdued, Cynthia lounges against one of the walls, a smug look on her face, and Billy is avoiding my eye, Honey's eye, and that of anyone else who dares look in his direction.

'Are we late?' Honey whispers to me, as we walk on to the lot, picking up on the strange atmosphere. Jean marches towards us, her mouth set.

'Honey. Leonard wants to see you. In his trailer. Now, please.'

Honey shoots me a panicked look, her face still pale and sickly.

'Go,' I say, 'I'll be there in two minutes.' I watch as Honey scurries away towards Leonard's trailer, Jean's voice like needles in my hungover ears.

'Where were you this morning, Lily? I came to your room but there was no answer.'

'I stayed with Honey in her room last night.'

Jean looks unconvinced.

'Honey had a little too much to drink, so I stayed to keep an eye on her.' The image of the dark figure running up the stairs, away from Honey's floor, suddenly looms bright in my mind and I have to swallow hard. *Was it him?* Did the guy I saw running away come back and put the note under Honey's door? Was he hanging around, waiting until the corridor was clear? The very idea of it – of him creeping around outside the room while Honey and I were sleeping – makes me feel nauseous.

'I should think Leonard will want to speak with you as well, Lily, after your behaviour last night.'

'As long as he speaks to Magnus, too.'

Jean shakes her head, her mouth twisting. 'What *is* your problem, Lily? Why do you insist on behaving like… like an animal? Is that the way women do things in London? Because in Hollywood we show *respect* for other people, we don't speak to them like trash.'

'Why did you tell Honey it was normal to receive threatening letters?' I say now to Jean, ignoring her words and the pinched expression on her face.

'What? I never…' Jean blusters. 'I just meant… if you want to be famous, you have to understand that not every letter you receive is going to be pleasant. Not everyone is going to love you,' she says snippily.

'Did she show you the letter she received?'

'Well no, but…' Jean shrugs. 'Jessica handles it much better than Honey. You don't hear her complaining about fan mail.'

Biting my lip so hard I taste the metallic tang of blood on my tongue, I shake my head and walk away, towards Leonard's trailer. Jean calls after me but I ignore her, too pissed off to listen anymore. Honey could be in danger – Honey *is* in danger – but it seems that no one will take it seriously. Before I have the chance to ponder Jean's involvement in Honey's demise, shouting erupts from the trailer.

'Unacceptable!' Leonard shouts. 'This is the second time in a week, Honey!'

Tapping lightly on the door, I don't wait for a response and let myself in, catching Leonard mid rant. Honey sits on the small sofa, her head down, as Leonard looms over her.

'What do you want? I thought I fired you last night?'

'Not quite. Honey,' I say, ignoring Leonard's furious tone, 'are you OK?' Leonard holds a newspaper in his hand, and as I catch sight of the front page my heart sinks. 'Oh no. Really?' I glance at Leonard, at the red spots that dance on his cheeks, at his clenched jaw. 'May I?' With a resigned shrug he hands me the *LA Times*.

A photo of Honey crying in the garden last night graces the front page, as I stand with one hand on her shoulder, looking eerily ghostly in the black-and-white photo. A smaller photo lower down shows Cynthia Lake leaving the party, one hand raised in front of her face. As I run my eyes over the article, the gist of it is that Honey had a party, disgraced herself (again), poor Cynthia, Honey is a scarlet woman. They reference her dancing with Billy, with Clark Gable and others, while 'poor husband, Magnus' left the party in despair.

'This is bullshit.' I throw the newspaper down on the table and meet Leonard's eye.

'I beg your pardon? How dare you speak to me like that? Let me remind you—'

'Why are you shouting at Honey?' My knees tremble as I force myself not to look away, aware that I might be confronting the person who is going to kill Honey in less than a week's time. 'How is this her fault?'

'Lily, don't…' Honey looks up at me, mascara weaving its way down her cheeks. Her face is a sickly creamy white and I catch a faint whiff of old booze as she reaches a hand towards me.

'Honey is disgracing this picture,' Leonard says, his voice white hot. 'This is the second time she has appeared in the newspaper for scandalous behaviour.' He glares down at her. 'I wanted you for this part because you were perfect for it, but if this continues to happen then I'll have no option but to give your role to someone more deserving.'

'Oh Leonard, please…' Honey wails. 'Lily, please don't argue with him.'

'No, Honey. Let me explain what happened last night.' I turn back to him, as he watches me grimly. 'Honey was upset at the party because Cynthia went off at her again. Honey danced with Billy — which in hindsight was probably a mistake — but Honey had had far too much to drink. She went outside for some fresh air, as you can see in this photo, Leonard, and I went out to comfort her. There was someone in the bushes,' I say. 'And judging by this—' I gesture to the newspapers, 'I would say that someone knew *something* would happen at the party. Someone knew to send the press to hide in the bushes, waiting for some ideal moment.' I look at Honey, then to Leonard. 'Someone wants you to throw Honey off this movie.'

Chapter Nineteen

'This is outrageous,' Leonard fumes. 'Honey, I think it's time you got yourself a new PA. One who knows how to conduct herself in public.'

'Wait, Leonard, listen to me, please…'

'You're fired!' Leonard roars, as Honey winces, pressing her hands over her ears. 'It's your responsibility to make sure Honey isn't misrepresented in any way. It's your responsibility to make sure everything runs smoothly when it comes to the star of *my* movie – but since you arrived all that's happened is complete chaos. Get your things and leave.'

Oh no. This can't be happening. 'Mr Langford, I'm sorry.'

'Leonard, please,' Honey stands, her blue eyes filled with tears. 'Please don't fire Lily.'

Leonard glares at us both, his nostrils flaring and his jaw set. He's like a coiled spring, and as Honey reaches out, sliding her hand through his arm, I half expect him to knock her away. She presses herself close to him, tears spilling over as she lifts her face. 'Please? I'd be lost without her, Leonard. I know things haven't gone so well lately, with the bad press, but it's not Lily's fault. All she's done is look out for me and try to make sure that I'm all right. She loves movies. She loves *your* movies.'

'Really?' Leonard pauses, then shakes his head. 'No. Absolutely not. Lily, get out. You're fired.'

Casting a panicked glance at Honey, I give a slow nod, and step back towards the door. 'I'll go and get my things.' I'm glad my voice comes out calm and steady, as inside I am a crashing tidal wave of panic and fear. *What will I do now? How will I save Honey if I'm not allowed anywhere near her? And how will I ever get back home?*

'Lily, stay where you are.' Honey pulls away from Leonard, her voice like steel. 'If she goes, I go.'

Oh, blimey.

'What?' Leonard's tone is a flashing blade, the single word carving the air as he looks from Honey to me, and back again. 'Honey, don't be ridiculous.'

'I'm not the one being ridiculous.' She lifts her chin, and I feel a surge of admiration. 'Lily stays, or I leave. I mean it, Leonard.'

Leonard's gaze flickers in my direction and I keep my features blank, as my heart races in my chest.

'Well?' Honey demands. 'You know I'm the star of this picture, and while I'm grateful for every opportunity you've given me, you know I'm in demand now. Everyone loved me in *Kentucky Queen*. We could be the dream team, Leonard, you and me, but I need Lily.'

'I'm sorry about what happened with Magnus last night, but I felt... compromised. I shouldn't have hit him.' I keep my eyes on Leonard and cross my fingers behind my back. 'And I really do love every movie you've ever made. I've seen *Kentucky Queen* fourteen times.'

Leonard eyes me closely and I think I see a tiny bit of his anger leaching away. 'It was an overreaction, the way you behaved, and in public too. But I can see why... perhaps...' He lifts his chin and I uncross my fingers.

'Mr Langford, you need to use this to your advantage. The movie is called *Goodtime Gal*, isn't it?'

'Ye-es.'

'Honey is a perfect example of a *Goodtime Gal*,' I say. 'Look at her! She's beautiful, funny, confident... she's a single girl, who likes to go out and have fun. A small-town girl who's making the most of the opportunities life – *you* – have given her. She's relatable for thousands of women, and that's why she'll be a superstar, not just because of her incredible talent. She's the epitome of a modern woman, and I think you'd be surprised at how many women wish they could live the way she does.'

'Now, I don't think so...'

'Yes, you would, Leonard.' Another voice comes from the doorway, and I turn to see Jean standing at the entrance to the trailer. 'The war changed everything for us. Women aren't docile little creatures to be looked after anymore, and there are more modern-thinking women out there than you realise. You're being too harsh on Honey.'

Wonders will never cease. I throw her a smile of solidarity, but Jean doesn't return it, her eyes never leaving Leonard's face. Honey stays silent.

After a moment, Leonard scrubs his hands over his face and then says, 'Fine. Jesus. Honey, get over to make-up and sort your face out. You're due on set in less than twenty minutes.' He looks at me. 'You can go with her; I don't want to see you in here again today. Jean, come in here and shut the door.'

Honey hurries towards me, squeezing Jean's arm as she passes. I don't breathe until I get outside, the sun harsh and bright as we step out on to the lot.

'Oh my gosh, Lily you were magnificent in there!' Honey throws her arms around me and hugs me hard. 'The way you stood up to him! And do you really think women think like that? Do you really think I could be a role model for other girls?'

'Sure do. And it was *you* who was magnificent, not me,' I say with a forced grin. 'Go on, get over there and sort your face out. And by the way… I'm not sorry at all about hitting Magnus Michel.' Honey lets out a yelp of laughter and runs towards the make-up trailer, as I feel my smile drop. Honey could be a role model to women, if I can just keep her alive long enough.

–

Honey acts her socks off throughout the afternoon. She and Billy are electric together, the air crackling around them as they gallop through their lines, and even Leonard can't be cross with her anymore as they wrap the final scene of the day. He throws an arm around her shoulders and pulls her close as they finish, but my breath still sticks in my throat until he lets her go. Leonard might be happy with Honey's performance today, but that doesn't mean something won't happen between now and Saturday that means he'll lose his temper again.

Honey seems much happier when we arrive back at the hotel, brushing aside my suggestion of dinner. 'I'm going to meet Jessica,' she says, 'I want to tell her what happened today.'

'Oh, sure.' Hiding my disappointment, I say goodbye. I had half hoped that Honey would have dinner with me, and we could have relived the way we both stood up to Leonard, solidarity in sisterhood. 'See you tomorrow.'

Now, a light tapping comes at the door, and I wonder if Honey has had a change of plans. She never likes to eat alone. But it isn't Honey who stands there.

'Louis! I thought you were working.'

'I was.' He smells like limes and sunshine and there is a fluttering in my belly that feels suspiciously like butterflies. 'I just got off. I'm going to meet Tilda at Googie's diner, so I wondered if maybe you wanted to meet her... if you're not too busy...'

'I'd love to.' The echo of loneliness that had followed me to my room after Honey left for dinner with Jessica dissipates, and I follow Louis out to Christine with a renewed spring in my step.

There is no sign of Tilda when we arrive at the diner – the same diner I saw Leonard sitting in with Jean – so Louis and I order milkshakes, our fingers touching as we both reach for a straw at the same time. My skin buzzes, as if shot through with electricity, and I shove the straw into my drink, avoiding Louis's eye.

'So how was Honey when she woke up this morning? She was kind of buzzed last night.' There is a flush across Louis's tanned cheeks, and I wonder if he felt it too.

'Yep, she felt pretty gross. Those cocktails were strong enough to fell a horse.'

'Really?' He grins at me over his shake. 'I didn't think they were so bad.'

'I don't know how many she drank...' I tail off, as the thought that has been niggling at the back of my mind all day fully forms. 'Louis, I think someone was out to get Honey wasted last night.'

'Well, it was a party.'

'No, I mean, seriously wasted.' I sit up straighter, real-isation sitting hard and sharp under my ribs. 'I think they wanted her to get drunk because they knew something would happen. Something that would get into the papers and cause a scandal. Everyone on set knew how furious

Leonard was last time.' *Could someone have slipped something into her drink? I don't even know if GHB was invented in the Forties.* I tell Louis about the newspaper, the photo, and how Leonard went crazy at Honey today, how I was almost fired. *How did Billy and Honey end up dancing together?* Honey, if she had been sober, would have known that was a terrible idea. 'They knew if photos of Honey appeared in the newspapers today, drunk, that Leonard would be furious. I think someone wants her out of the picture.' *Quite literally.*

'Wow.' Louis sits back heavily, his eyebrows raised. 'Who, though?'

'I don't know. I thought maybe Jean… I think she's jealous of Honey. Magnus was at the party, and I already found him in Honey's room, making her cry. There's something not right between them. They've split, but Honey can't – or won't – talk about why.' I pause for a moment, the words feeling too big for my mouth. 'I got the feeling that perhaps… Magnus isn't the perfect gent he portrays on the screen. That maybe he gets a little…' I raise my hands in two fists. 'He's so arrogant and entitled… I can imagine that he would be incandescent if he thought something was going on between Honey and Billy.'

'That's awful.' Louis leans forward, lowering his voice. 'Lily, you said something is going to happen to Honey… do you think Magnus could be behind it?'

I think of the way Honey shrank away from him, the way he had gripped my middle tightly as he hissed into my ear… of the dark figure running down the corridor away from her room. 'It's possible. There was a threatening note slipped under her door, and apparently it's not the first one.'

'Louis! Did you even think to get your sister a shake?' Tilda's voice is loud over the murmur of voices and the jukebox in the diner as she makes her way towards our table. 'Oh, I'm not interrupting anything, am I?'

'No,' Louis rolls his eyes, 'and you want a shake? Maybe you should try being on time.' But he gets up and goes to the counter to order.

I turn my head to watch Tilda approach, but the girl walking towards our table isn't the girl I saw Louis with outside the hotel, and again in the bar. This girl is petite, with vibrant red hair and a wide, toothy grin on her freckled face. She is nothing like the sour-faced blonde I saw with Louis.

'Lily, right? I'm Tilda, Louis's sister. It's so nice to finally meet you.' The girl slides into the seat opposite me as I try to find the words to speak.

'Tilda? You're Tilda?'

'Yeah.' Tilda looks at me with a frown. 'You were expecting someone else?'

'I thought you were blonde… and taller. I saw Louis with a girl, and I thought she was a reporter… and he said she was his sister. But it wasn't you.'

Tilda frowns for a moment, before rolling her eyes. 'Blonde? Kinda grouchy looking? Nah, she's not a reporter. That's Evelyn. That's his girlfriend.'

Louis approaches the table, smiling in that open way he has, but I don't hear what he says as I get to my feet, my pulse roaring in my ears. He slides a milkshake across the table to his sister and I catch sight of a dark bruise-like smear on his wrist.

'Lily?'

'Sorry.' I hold up a hand to Tilda, ignoring Louis's puzzled expression. 'I'm so sorry, I just realised. I have to go.' And I hurry out of the diner into the warm night air.

–

Did he actually say she was his sister? Hurrying away from the diner I round the corner and slow my pace, my breath hitching in my chest. He did, I'm sure he did. I asked if she was a reporter and then he said his sister was getting married, they were making plans, that's why she had the notepad. Hot tears spring to my eyes and I swipe them away angrily. *So what if he has a girlfriend?* There can never be anything between us, and I barely know him, so I don't know why I'm so upset. We've never been on a date – not officially – and Louis has never tried to kiss me, but I feel as though he lied to me. He never mentioned Evelyn, or said he had a girlfriend, and I was so relieved to have met someone who genuinely seemed to be a nice guy that I never even thought to question it when he said she was his sister. I trusted him – enough to confide some of my suspicions about what will happen to Honey. I thought guys were different in 1949, but what with Magnus and his wandering hands, and now Louis letting me think there was something – a spark at least – between us, it turns out men are arseholes whatever decade, *whatever century,* you're in.

He lied to me. I picture Louis's face as he realised what Tilda was telling me. Did he look upset? Or guilty? Or totally confused as he slid the milkshake onto the table? I stop, my breath catching in my throat. *The bruise.* As he slid the milkshake to Tilda, I saw a dark smudge of a bruise on his wrist. But now that I think about it, it was too dark to be a bruise. It looked more like newsprint. I swallow, suddenly feeling sick. If Louis lied about Evelyn being his sister, what else could he have lied about?

Chapter Twenty

I roll over on the bed, my eyes hot and puffy, as a fist raps on my door. I came straight to the hotel after I left the diner, holding back the tears forcing their way through the lump in my throat until I got back to my room. The knocking comes again, more insistent this time, and I groan.

'Lily?' someone hisses through the door. 'Open up!' It's not Louis's voice, so I slide off the bed and fumble for the door catch. Honey stands on the other side, a neat Chanel clutch in one hand, a bottle of vodka in the other.

'I saw you rush through the lobby and into the elevator.' Honey steps inside, carefully placing her bag on the chair before twisting the lid on the bottle. 'You looked upset, so I fetched some supplies and came straight up.' She holds up the vodka. 'You got glasses?'

I give her a weak smile and grab two water glasses from the bathroom, watching as she pours a generous shot into each.

'So, you wanna tell me what happened? It wasn't Magnus again, was it?'

'No, it wasn't Magnus.'

Another tap comes at the door, and I glance at Honey before crossing the room and pulling the door open. The last person I am expecting to see stands on the other side.

'Jessica?'

She sweeps past me into the room as I blink, staring out into the empty corridor before slowly closing the door. Two Hollywood movie stars are in my hotel room. My mum's favourite actress is *in my hotel room*. The floor tilts beneath my feet and I squeeze my eyes shut briefly, gripping the door frame to steady myself before turning.

'Honey saw you were upset and rushed straight to the bar. When she didn't come back, I guessed she came to you.' Jessica pats my arm. 'Is everything OK, Lily?'

'Tell us what happened, Lil.' Honey pushes my glass back into my hand and I take a tentative sip. 'Was it a boy?'

Jessica leans forward from where she's perched on the end of the bed. 'It's all right Lily, we're your friends. Us girls have got to stick together.'

I sigh, the lump back in my throat. 'I feel like an idiot.'

'Oh, sweetie.' Honey shuffles up the bed, so we are both sitting against the pillows, and Jessica slides off her red heels and curls up at the end of the bed. It's like some sort of weird slumber party.

'Louis... you know, the bartender?'

Jessica nods, taking a gulp of Honey's vodka. 'I knew it,' she says, 'I knew he was going to cause you trouble ever since he accosted you outside the other night.'

'I thought he was the one who sold the story of Honey and Billy at the Palomino to the papers; I thought I saw him talking to a reporter.' Honey lets out a gasp, but I carry on. 'He told me the girl was his sister... but it wasn't. It was his *girlfriend*.' My voice cracks.

'What an asshole.' Honey knocks back her drink, grimacing at the burn of alcohol.

'It's me who's the asshole,' I say gloomily. 'He never told me he had a girlfriend, but then he never actually asked me on a date or kissed me. I just liked him. And I thought he was different.'

'All men are the same,' Jessica says, with a hint of bitterness. 'Say one thing, mean something else. Make promises they don't keep.'

I do another shot of vodka, grabbing a glass for Jessica too. The overwhelming feeling of having two movie stars in my hotel room has dispersed like smoke, and it feels more like three girlfriends, hashing over life. It feels real, for the first time since I found myself here. 'I think he might have lied about other things too.'

'Really? Like what?' Honey slides her hand into her purse and pulls out a forbidden Hershey bar.

'A moment on the lips, Honey,' Jessica says, lighting a cigarette. I half expect the fire alarm to go off, until I remember in 1949 it's odder *not* to smoke. 'All men do it. Lie and manipulate us, just to get what they want.'

I realise I can't confess my suspicions about Louis without giving away the fact that something terrible is going to happen to Honey. 'Oh, I don't know. Lots of things, I guess. It's hard to trust someone when you don't feel they've been honest with you.'

'Amen to that.' Honey raises her glass. 'Magnus lies through his back teeth.'

Jessica reaches forward and clinks her glass against Honey's and then against mine.

'Do you ever...' The words trip over my tongue, tangled and twisted. 'What would you do if you knew something was going to happen and you wanted to stop it?'

Jessica stills, her cigarette halfway to her mouth. 'What do you mean?'

I shrug, wishing I hadn't said anything. The vodka has made me reckless, but I honestly feel as if I am getting nowhere with trying to find a way to stop Honey getting hurt. 'I don't know, just a feeling, I guess. Ignore me, I'm a little drunk and heartsore tonight.'

'Aren't we all?' Jessica's tone is wry. 'Things could be worse; you could be Magnus Michel, expelled from a party in front of all of Hollywood.'

I gape at her as Honey's face freezes momentarily before she splutters out a laugh. 'Jessica!'

'What?' Jessica smirks. 'It's true, the guy is a wrong number. I guarantee you he'll still be the same old entitled, arrogant Magnus, doing whatever he pleases without a single thought for anyone else. Leonard won't have dealt with him at all.'

The conversation slides into other men in the golden age of Hollywood and the rumours that circle them, Jessica confirming some and dismissing others as Honey and I shriek with shocked laughter. None of us hear the knock at the door at first, until it comes hard and fast. We fall silent, glancing at each other.

'It's probably Jean, telling us all to go to sleep,' Jessica says with a smirk as I slide off the bed and head towards the door.

Cracking the door open an inch, I see Louis's face peering back at me. 'Oh. What do you want?' I am aware of Honey and Jessica, peering over my shoulder to get a look at him.

Louis glances past me to where the women stare at him from the bed. 'I, uh… I just wanted to make sure you were all right. You rushed off pretty quickly earlier.'

'I'm fine,' I say primly.

'She's totally fine,' Jessica calls from behind me.

'Did I…' Louis runs a hand through his hair in a way that gives me goosebumps. 'Did I do something wrong? Only I thought we were friends, and you kind of… well, I feel as if you're mad at me.'

I look down, feeling decidedly shitty. In all fairness, he didn't really do anything wrong. It was my own interpretation of events that made everything go tits up. But then I see the dark stain on his wrist, so clearly newsprint, and fire flares in my belly again. It's not about Evelyn, or me, it's about Honey. 'You know what you did,' I hiss at him, half closing the door. 'You tried to convince me to stay in my own room last night, so you could slide that note under Honey's door.' A gasp from behind me makes me turn, and Jessica's eyes are on us, watching intently. 'I can't believe I confided in you,' I whisper, trying to keep my voice low. 'I believed I could trust you – but then you go and do that! You won't get away with it, I'll make sure of it.'

Louis seems speechless for a moment. 'Lily, stop. You're not making any sense. I'm sorry I didn't tell you about Evelyn, I just… I like you; I think you're really cool and different and the way you look at life… it's so refreshing. *You're* refreshing.'

'OK, that's enough, buster.' The door is wrenched open and Honey glares at Louis, her cheeks flushed a hot pink. I'm not sure if she's tipsy, furious, or tipsy *and* furious. 'I don't know who you think you are, but you are *not* about to break Lily's heart.'

Oh, bloody hell, Honey. 'Your behaviour is despicable, and we…' Honey sweeps her arm to encompass myself and Jessica, 'we are *not taking it anymore*. So, take your girlfriend and your lies and your… your… *swishy hair* and just. Buzz. Off.' And she slams the door in his face.

Jessica claps and whoops, coming to the door to high five Honey and me. 'Honey, that was incredible!'

Honey grins at me, slightly breathless. 'It's true what you said, Lil, about not having to put up with men and their bad behaviour. You were right – it is liberating.' She throws her arms around me and hiccups.

I try to smile back, but I can't help but feel as if something still isn't right, only I can't put my finger on it. I don't know what it is, but something in my gut is telling me I still don't have a handle on what is going to happen to Honey. Suddenly I feel hot and stifled, desperate for some fresh air.

'Sorry ladies, do you mind if we call it a night? I'm exhausted.'

'Of course.' Jessica gives me a hug and passes Honey her bag. 'I have an early call tomorrow anyway...' She waits as Honey steps out into the corridor, then lowers her voice. 'Lily, I know there's more to this than just the bartender having a girlfriend.'

Something wriggles in my belly, uneasy and sour. 'No, there's nothing else, I promise.' I don't know how I hold her gaze, but I do, as she gives me a long, hard look.

'You know you can talk to me? If there's anything you're worried about in relation to...' Jessica glances over her shoulder where Honey is jabbing at the elevator call button.

'Of course.' I think of the note, the thick black newsprint that smudged the white page.

Jessica waits a moment, as if she wants to say more, but Honey calls her name, and she gives me a brief nod. '*Anything*, I mean it. See you tomorrow, Lily.'

–

The pool area is silent as I slide out of the rear doors, hurrying past the Polo Lounge and across the paved footpath to the cabanas. The gate creaks slightly as I enter, the empty pink-and-white cabanas a ghostly pale in the moonlight. Perching on the edge of the tiles, the night air is thick and warm, and I slip my shoes off, sighing as my hot feet enter the cool water. I don't know what to think about Louis, as I close my eyes and let the water lap gently at my ankles. He had newsprint on his wrist – and the smudge on Honey's dress perfectly matches where his hand would have rested as he guided her back to her room last night. He was keen for me to go back to my own room – but was that because he wanted me to be safe, or so the coast was clear for him to slide the note under Honey's door? And Honey was wasted – Louis was the bartender. He said he never served her, but how would I know any different? He could have been slipping her extra shots. *Why, though?* Money? That's the only reason I can think of. Bartenders don't make a lot, and music is his first love. Honey's a hot ticket at the moment, maybe he's bumping up his wages by selling stories. Despite all of this, none of it sits right. In my gut, I still feel Louis could be a good guy – although is it just my hormones talking? I'd love nothing more than to talk it all over with Jessica, but I can't get the image of her and Magnus arguing in the gardens out of my mind. I let out a long sigh, the scent of jasmine thick and heavy on the stifling night air.

'Big sigh. Sounds like you've got a lot going on.'

I open my eyes to see Tilda, Louis's sister, sliding into place next to me. She shirks off her sneakers and sighs as she dunks her feet next to mine.

'You all right? You hurried out of the diner pretty fast.'

'Uh, yeah. Sorry. That was rude of me.'

Tilda shrugs. 'Who cares about stuff like that? I thought you were upset, so I made Louis come back to the hotel. You saw him, right?'

'I saw him.' I look at the water, not at her.

'He's a good guy,' she says. I can feel her eyes on me, but I don't look up, keeping my focus on the dark water ahead. 'But he should have told you about Evelyn. She's one cold fish by the way. If he marries her, I'll die.'

I can't stop the grin that pulls at my lips. 'She kinda looked like a cold fish,' I say. 'I was sort of glad it wasn't her that showed up to the diner.'

Tilda laughs, bright and loud in the still air. 'Trust me, I would rather die than be anything like Evelyn. Nothing is ever good enough for her, and my God, does she like to let everyone know about it.'

Louis appears at the edge of the cabana area. 'Tilda? You out here?'

Tilda glances at me, and I reluctantly nod. 'Here. By the pool.'

'You're not meant to be out here; you'll get me fired. It's for guests only... Oh.' Louis rounds the pool area, pulling up short when he sees me. 'Lily. I didn't know you were here.'

'I should go.' I pull my feet out of the water, but Tilda rests a hand on my arm.

'No,' she says. 'I think you two need to talk things out. Investigate where things have gone wrong between you.'

Louis gives a wry smile. 'Tilda's good at investigating. She's got a big nose that she likes to poke into other people's business... if you wanted another point of view on... *that other thing.*'

'I take an interest,' Tilda says, her red hair flying as she shakes her head. 'I *do not* poke my nose in. I wanted to be a reporter but then I met Reg.'

'Why would meeting Reg stop you?'

Tilda looks at me askance. 'Because soon I'll be a *wife*, Lily. Raising babies and dishing up mac and cheese every Wednesday night.'

Oh. Of course.

'What *other thing* are you two talking about anyway?' Tilda asks.

Louis looks at me and then says, 'Lily thinks something bad is going to happen to Honey Black.'

'Honey Black? The actress?' Tilda looks from me to Louis and back again.

'I don't think,' I say, narrowing my eyes in Louis's direction. 'I *know*. Just don't ask me how. The only thing I don't know is who is going to do it. And I only have until Saturday to figure it out.' I give Louis a hard stare. 'There was a note shoved under her door, in letters cut out of newspaper.' I do get up now, my feet leaving damp prints across the tiles as I approach him. Grasping his wrist, I shove back his sleeve, revealing the smudge of print, a faint grey now. 'Newsprint, like this.'

'What?' Louis pulls back. 'You really do think I did it? You're not just accusing me because of Evelyn?'

'Why else would you have newsprint on your wrist? You could have sneaked back there and shoved it under her door when I went to my room.'

Louis pushes his sleeve up, revealing the smudge in full. 'Lily, I lay out the newspapers on the bar every morning and every evening. That's why I have newsprint on my wrist. If I'd sent the notes, don't you think I would have washed it off?'

'Someone wanted her drunk last night, so they could call the papers on her and get her in trouble with Leonard. You were the bartender; it would have been easy for you to give her doubles instead of singles.'

Louis shakes his head. 'I don't have to stand here and defend myself to you, Lily. Since you've been here, all I've done is try and be your friend, because I genuinely like you. I might not have mentioned Evelyn,' at this Tilda lets out a snort, 'but that's only because I thought you might not want to get to know me if you knew about her. Nice girls don't want to hang out with guys who have girlfriends.' He fixes his eyes on me, and I have to force myself not to look away.

'That's ridiculous. I can hang out with whoever I want, no one's going to think badly...' I trail off, remembering where – when – I am. People probably *would* think badly of me. Look at how Cynthia responds to Billy and Honey's friendship. 'If Evelyn isn't your sister, then why did she have a notepad? She was writing down everything you said... how do I know you're not lying to me about telling her things about Honey?'

Louis sighs, a deep, long breath full of frustration and hurt. 'Because Tilda's getting married. Evelyn has appointed herself as unofficial – although probably official in her mind, sorry Til – maid of honour, and she was asking me about ideas for wedding venues. That's why she had a notepad.'

'Venues?' Tilda squawks. 'We haven't even set a date!'

Louis steps closer to me, and I can smell his aftershave on the air, my stomach flipping. 'Just ask yourself this, Lily. Why?'

'Why?'

'Why would I want to hurt Honey Black? What do I have to gain from it? Surely it makes more sense that someone close to Honey would be more likely to be responsible? I don't even know her.' Louis's eyes darken. 'In fact, we only have your word for it that anything is even going to happen to Honey.'

I open my mouth, but nothing comes out. It *is* more likely that it's someone close to Honey, and he does only have my word for it that anything will happen at all. He might think I'm 'refreshing', but he might also think I'm bonkers. In fact, he definitely will if I tell him *how* I know something will happen to Honey.

'I'm sorry,' I whisper, my chest tight. 'I don't know what to think anymore… something really is going to happen to Honey, and I'm so desperate to help her that I guess I'm clutching at straws.'

Louis's expression remains hard, until Tilda gets to her feet and nudges him. 'Apology accepted,' he says grudgingly, 'but this is the second time you've accused me of something I haven't done, Lil. I know I make mistakes—'

'Like Evelyn,' Tilda pipes up, and Louis glares at her.

'But I swear, I do not have it in for Honey Black.' He finally softens, and a warmth spreads through me as I give him a wobbly smile.

'We should probably help you figure out who does though,' Tilda says. 'I mean, you've told us about it now, right? And three heads have to be better than one.'

'The guy,' Louis says suddenly. 'There was a guy in the stairwell last night… you think he was going after Honey?'

'I don't know, but something about it felt off.' Tilda's right, three heads are better than one, and I feel a glimmer of hope that maybe I might actually be able to do this.

'It's getting late,' Tilda says, getting to her feet, splashing water across the still warm tiles. 'I have to shoot – Reg was supposed to get home from work hours ago and I said I'd meet him.' She casts a sly glance in Louis's direction. 'Why don't you come for dinner with Lou tomorrow, Lily, and we can talk about this properly? He's promised Mom he'd be home and she's making her special meatloaf.'

'I… err…' I look to Louis for guidance, just in time to catch him pulling a face at Tilda that roughly translates as 'I'm going to kill you.'

'Mom would love to meet you,' Tilda grins. 'We've all heard a lot about you.'

Louis groans and it's my turn to grin. 'In that case, I'd love to come.'

'Great. We can talk more then. Don't worry, Lily, I'll be right beside you when you crack this case.'

–

Louis apologises as I walk back to his car with him. 'I'm sorry, Lil, she's a force of nature.'

'She's like no one I've ever met before,' I say. 'So… honest, and likeable. She's actually pretty charming. Reg is lucky to have her.' And he really is, considering Tilda is giving up her dream of being a reporter to be with him.

'So, you'll come for dinner tomorrow? I don't want you to think that I didn't want you to,' Louis says, toying with his car key.

His cheeks turn a subtle shade of pink in the light of the streetlamp outside, the air around us crackles, static with electricity, and I think for one dizzying moment that he's going to kiss me.

'Will Evelyn be there?' I ask, breaking the tension between us. 'I mean, I should probably meet her properly...'

'Listen, the thing with Evelyn and me, it's not—' But before he can finish speaking, Louis gives a shout and pulls away, leaving me breathless with anticipation. 'There he is, Lil! That's the guy!'

I turn to where Louis points behind me, before he sprints across the car park.

'Louis, wait! It might be Magnus!' I follow him, my feet hitting the tarmac running, as Louis gives chase to the shadowy figure that has emerged from the back of the hotel. 'Louis!'

As I round the corner, I find Louis on the ground, a dark figure struggling beneath him. A wave of anxiety breaks over me at the thought that Louis might have just floored a paying guest of the hotel, but that vanishes when I see a crumpled mass of oyster silk on the tarmac beside me. I pick it up, the fabric falling like water through my fingers as Louis turns the guy face up and I finally get to see who has been lurking in the corridor to Honey's room.

Chapter Twenty-One

'Who are you?' Louis loosens his grip, and the man struggles into a sitting position, rubbing his forehead with one hand.

'You're not Magnus,' I say dumbly, feeling a rush of relief at the realisation Louis hasn't just rugby tackled Hollywood's leading man to the ground. The relief soon fades as the man takes advantage of Louis's loosened grip to try and squirm away.

'No you don't, pal.' Louis tightens his hold, and the man gives up easily, his body becoming slack under Louis's weight. 'I asked you a question – who are you?'

'And what are you doing with this?' I hold up Honey's party dress, watching his face as his eyes go from Louis, to me, to the dress before he lets out a breath and closes his eyes.

'Can y'all let me up? I'll tell you everything if y'all just let me up off this sidewalk.' The man looks up at Louis, who glances at me. I nod. There is a familiar twang to his voice as he struggles to his feet, dusting his old Levi's down.

'So, you gonna answer me?' Louis asks, slightly breathless with effort.

The man sighs, suddenly looking overwhelmingly weary. 'My name is Joe. Joe Faulks.'

'That doesn't really tell us much,' I say, as I look him over properly. He is maybe six feet tall, with a mop of dirty blond hair and piercing blue eyes, and defined arm muscles that move distractingly as he brushes his hands over his white T-shirt. If I were going to cast this guy in a movie, he would definitely get the part of *vulnerable cowboy.* 'What are you doing here, Joe Faulks? And why do you have Honey Black's dress?'

'It ain't what you think.' He has the good grace to blush. 'I wanted to see her is all.'

'Lots of people want to see her,' Louis says, his tone softer than I was expecting. 'What gives you the right to see her over anyone else? Have you been creeping about in the corridor, sneaking up to her room?' I've a feeling I might have seen him at the party last night as well, lurking in the drapes.

'I can explain it all, but can we go somewhere a little more private? Only Honey isn't here, and I don't want her seein' me until I'm ready.'

I want to protest, but Louis already has Joe by the arm and is leading him through the gardens towards the bower at the back of the hotel. Joe perches on the edge of the seat, in the same spot where Magnus sat the previous evening, his long legs stretched out in front of him. He looks young and gangly, as if he doesn't fit with his surroundings. I know only too well how that feels.

'OK, explain,' I say, crossing my arms and staring at him, the way I would with the kids on the estate back home when they asked me to buy them fags.

Joe picks at the skin around his fingernails, not meeting my eye. 'It was me,' he confesses, 'in the corridor last night, and the other night too. I went to Honey's room, but I couldn't knock on the door. I tried, I really did, but

I couldn't get my nerve up. I could hear her through the door, talkin' on the telephone.'

That must have been the night I called her to see if she'd had a visitor. Joe must have snuck back there after I went to my room. 'Go on,' I say, my tone losing its hard edge. He just looks so... *sad*.

'We go way back,' Joe says quietly. 'We grew up together. I just wanted to see her, to make sure this was what she really wanted. I wanted her to know that her daddy wouldn't be angry if she wanted to come back. To come home. To me.'

'To you?' Louis frowns, but I hold up a hand to shush him before sliding around to come and sit beside Joe in the bower.

'Joe,' I say gently, 'why don't you tell us everything, right from the very beginning.'

'Her name ain't Honey, you know,' Joe says as he looks up at us, tucking his hands under his denim clad thighs. 'When we met back in the first grade, she was just plain old Betty Sue. It took me until I was fourteen to be brave enough to ask her if she wanted to go get a milkshake.' He gives a rueful laugh and shakes his head. 'She told me she didn't know what took me so long.'

'So, you guys were dating?'

'She was my girl. My daddy knew her daddy, her mama knew my mama... it was perfect. I asked her to marry me on the night of her sixteenth birthday, under the stars. I'd asked her daddy for permission, and then I took her out to the honeysuckle, and she said yes.'

'Oh, Joe.' His shoulders round and I can almost feel the hopelessness emanating from his every pore.

'I loved her,' Joe says, his voice catching. 'I would have done anything for Betty Sue, but it wasn't enough.'

I swallow down the lump in my throat, as Louis places a warm hand on my shoulder. 'So, what happened? How did Honey end up here without you?'

'The movie people happened.' Joe shrugs, but it seems like it's an effort. 'They came into town, shooting a new movie, and they asked if they could make use of her daddy's fields. Betty Sue was always fascinated by the movies, so she went out to watch one morning. He saw her and it was all over for me.'

'Who?' I ask, but I have a sneaky feeling that I know. 'Who saw her?'

'Magnus Michel.' Joe almost spits the name at me. 'He saw her, and he decided he wanted her, wasn't nothing going to stop him. Betty Sue came home talking about Magnus this and Magnus that, and I knew right then that somethin' was going to happen.' Joe swipes his hand under his nose, and blinks hard. There is a tightness in my chest – Joe's version differs slightly to the one Honey told me. She's not quite as innocent as everyone believes her to be. *She* was the one to set her cap at Magnus, not the other way round. *He tried to turn me down, saying I was too young, but I was persistent.*

Joe goes on, 'Magnus was starring in the picture with Jessica Parks, and one day Betty Sue came over and told me that they'd offered her a part in a movie. She was leavin' me. She tried to tell me that it wasn't anything to do with Magnus, that she just wanted to act, but I knew that wasn't the truth.'

'Did you try to change her mind?' Louis glances at me as he asks, and I wonder what he's thinking.

'Tried to,' Joe shrugs again, 'but she had her heart set on it. Her daddy was furious, told her not to bother comin' back, and her mama was weepin' and wailin' all over, but she just packed up her things and caught a ride out of town with Magnus.'

'Did you try to contact her before now?' What he's told me fits with what Honey told me about her father's reaction to her leaving to star in the movies, but even without that I get the feeling that Joe is telling the truth.

'I did, ma'am. It was in the newspaper that she and Magnus had got married – gosh, didn't that just about break my heart – so I wrote to her. She never replied, and after three letters I took a trip out to California to see her, but she wasn't home, and Magnus answered the door.'

'You wrote and she didn't reply?' I glance up at Louis, wondering if he's thinking the same thing I am.

Joe shakes his head. 'I never got to see her either, Magnus made sure of that. Well, Magnus and two broken fingers.' Joe gives a mournful smile at my gasp of surprise. 'Let's just say Magnus didn't want me on his property. He's not a nice man, you know, and I worried about her from the moment she left the farm until the moment I heard he was leavin' her.'

'Joe...' I say cautiously, 'you didn't ever... write any other letters to Honey, did you? Here, at the hotel?' I pause for a moment. 'Nothing... threatening?'

'Threatening?' Joe gets to his feet, and as he stands over me, I regret mentioning it. His eyes are wide as he shakes his head. 'No ma'am, I'd never... I *love* Betty Sue. I'd never threaten her or do anything to upset her.' He freezes for a moment, a fierce blush creeping up the side of his neck. 'I did do one thing awful though.'

Louis has thrown his arm over my shoulder, and I like the feeling of his weight leaning against me, as if protecting me, but even so I pull away. Evelyn is between us, even if she's not physically here. Evelyn, and seventy years.

'What do you mean you did something awful?' Louis says. 'Joe, you need to tell us if you did something to Honey. It's important.'

'I broke into her room,' Joe says, the blush that stains his cheeks growing ever brighter. He shifts on the balls of his feet, and I feel Louis tense.

'That was you?'

'I just wanted to feel as if she was close by. I went in the bathroom and sprayed a little of her perfume, and then I saw that stupid snow globe her mama gave her, and I thought...' Joe coughs and then blinks, his eyes growing red. 'I know she loved it, it reminded her of home. I thought if I took it, it might make her call home, that maybe she might call me if she was too afraid to call her daddy and then I could get the chance to tell her for myself that she could come back. But she didn't call. Once I'd been in her room, I couldn't stop myself from going back when I knew she wasn't there.' He fumbles in his pocket and pulls out Honey's missing lipstick. 'I guess you should give that back to her. I took her party dress too, it smelled of her perfume.'

I take the lipstick from him and run my finger thoughtfully over the capped end. 'Or...' I say slowly, 'you could give it to her yourself?'

Louis raises his eyebrows at me. 'Is that a good idea?'

'Joe,' I say, 'is that all you did? Went into her room and took her snow globe and lipstick? Nothing else? Not a script? And you didn't send her any other letters other than the ones you sent to the house she shared with Magnus?'

'No ma'am, I swear on my mama's life. I wouldn't do anything to hurt her acting. I want her to come home because she wants to, not because she has to.'

213

I lead Joe towards the back entrance to the hotel. The heels of his cowboy boots ring out an echoey click on the tarmac as we walk, and he smells of hay and something earthy. 'Honey has had a rough day today. This might backfire on me, but maybe a visit from home is just what she needs right now.' I don't think Joe is a threat to Honey – I think he is a gentle giant who loved her too much – and the knowledge that if I can't stop what is due to happen on Saturday Joe will never see her again is unbearable.

The three of us walk along the hallway to Honey's suite and as Joe steps ahead, Louis reaches out to grab my arm. 'Lil, are you sure this is a good idea? What if Honey doesn't want to see him? What if Magnus is there?'

'Louis, this might be the last time Joe ever gets to see Honey. I have to give both of them this opportunity.'

Honey takes so long to answer the door that at first I think maybe she went out after she left my hotel room. I am about to apologise to Joe, when the door flies open and Honey stands there, her feet bare and her face free of make-up. She looks about fifteen.

'Lily! What are you doing here? I thought you were sleeping.'

There is a fluttering in my chest, a brief moment of panic that I might have done the wrong thing. 'I have someone here to see you. An old friend.'

'Oh no,' she says. 'I can't see anyone; I don't have any make-up... oh.' Her hands fly to her mouth as Joe steps out from behind Louis, a shy smile on his face. 'Joe? Joe, is that really you?'

Before Joe can reply Honey flies towards him, throwing her arms around his waist. I shoot Louis a secret grin, feeling wobbly with relief. 'Let's get you two inside, before anyone sees.'

'Joe, I can't believe you're here, it's been so long.' Honey gazes at him as he takes a seat on the chaise next to her. 'Wait… what are y'all doin' here? You didn't come to take me back to Kentucky, did you?'

'Joe just wanted to see you,' I say, smiling at the way she's slipped into her natural Southern drawl. 'He's missed you.'

'Oh,' Honey says, her cheeks flushing pink as an unreadable emotion crosses her face. 'Lily, I've known Joe for over half my life.'

'Joe told me,' I say gently. 'Louis, I think we should head out of here, let these two catch up. Honey, I'll see you on set tomorrow?'

'Hmmm?' Honey turns from where she is gazing at Joe, and I realise that Magnus might have turned her head, but her heart still belongs to Joe. 'OK, sugar. Lemme see you out.'

At the door Louis discreetly slides out first, and Honey presses her face close to mine. 'Can you believe he's here?' she whispers. 'I loved him from the moment he walked into the classroom.' Her face clouds over and she looks at her bare feet, at the vivid red polish on her toenails. 'Do you think he'll ever forgive me for leaving him, Lil? I never wanted to hurt him – or anybody else – but I needed Magnus.'

'I think you guys will be good.'

'And Leonard can't be mad about it, right? I mean, the newspapers love a story about love – and a childhood sweetheart is even better!'

'I guess… I hadn't… thought about it that way,' I say, pulling out her lipstick from my pocket. 'Here, this is yours. Now go on, go and catch up.'

Chapter Twenty-Two

'So, you solved the mystery of who broke into Honey's room,' Louis says, as Honey's door closes. He gives me a smile as the elevator arrives, my stomach flip-flopping as we travel to the floor above.

'She was happy to see him, right? I hope it wasn't a mistake letting him go up there.'

'I think he's genuine,' Louis says, 'and you can see he really loves her. Maybe this was what needed to happen – maybe Honey will decide it's Joe she really wants and pack up and move back to Kentucky. She'll live a long and happy life; they'll have six kids, and the eldest girl will be named Lily after you.'

I laugh, as the elevator pings and we step off together, walking slowly towards my room. 'Thank you,' I say. 'For everything tonight... the shake, the advice. Rugby tackling a Kentucky cowboy.'

'Any time,' Louis says with a grin, but his tone is deadly serious. My mind has gone completely blank, the only thing I can think is how much I want him to kiss me, and for Evelyn to fall down a well and never be seen again.

'I'm sorry.' The words come out as a whisper. 'For... you know. Thinking you were the one to want to hurt Honey.'

'I'm sorry too, Lil. I should have told you the truth about Evelyn. It was a dumb thing to lie about.'

My heart cracks a little at his words, but I shake my head, as if shaking them free. 'Friends?'

Louis grins, wide and genuine, and I realise I've missed it. 'Friends. Good night, Lily.'

'Good night,' I whisper, my pulse hammering in my ears as he gives me a wave and turns to the elevator. I slip inside the door, unable to resist peeking out as he walks along the corridor. He doesn't notice me as he jabs at the call button and starts to whistle.

Once inside my room I close the door and press my fingers over my eyes. As much as I know I shouldn't want Louis to kiss me, shouldn't let myself have feelings for someone when I'm leaving in a few days, it feels impossible. Louis may not have been entirely truthful about Evelyn, but I haven't exactly been up front and honest with him about my own situation. Before, I've always ended up with shallow, pretty boys – good-looking, charming men who know exactly what they can get away with, just like Magnus with Honey. Louis is so different; I can't help but wish I'd met him in my own time.

My foot slips as I step towards the bed, my heart stopping as I glance down at the carpet. A single white square, neatly folded, identical to the one Honey received, has been pushed under my door. My skin prickles, and my hand goes to my throat. *It could be anything. A room service menu. A telephone message.* Slowly, I reach out with icy fingers and pick it up, unfolding it before I can change my mind. The words – cut from newsprint – leap off the page and my stomach rolls, even as my palms grow clammy.

I'M wAtcHiNg yOU
mInD YouR BUsiNeSs
tHis IS yOuR lASt WaRnInG

Everything feels too loud, too bright, and I squeeze my eyes closed, panic lodging like a stone in my chest. They know. Whoever wants to harm Honey, they know that I suspect something. Now it's not just Honey I have to save, it's myself too.

—

My fingers are stained grey with newsprint when I eventually emerge from a groggy, fitful sleep, the note shoved under my pillow. After I had read it what felt like a hundred times last night, I had hovered over the phone, debating whether to call Honey, before discarding it as a bad idea. Instead, I had sat at the window, looking out on to the mostly silent hotel entrance, afraid to close my eyes. Jean returned in the early hours in a cab, a smile pressing at her lips as she hurried inside. A small man let a tiny dog pee against the hedge, ignoring the glare of the valet, and then as the sun had started to make its way over the horizon, Magnus stomped his way onto the red carpet at the entrance, and I had pulled away from the window, my heart in my mouth.

Jean is in the lobby when I make my way downstairs. She's taken a leaf out of Jessica's style book this morning, with baby blue capri pants and a white shirt that's a little more fitted than usual, her hair softly waved. I try to sidle around her, not wanting to get an earful about something else either Honey or I have done wrong, but as I slink past, she shoots out a hand and grips my arm.

'Lily,' she says. 'I've been waiting for you.'

'You… have?' My eyes go to the clock on the wall behind the reception desk. 'Won't you be late? I'm sorry, I'm running behind. Honey will already be on set; they're filming the car scene today.' It's a big day for Honey, the first major action scene she's ever done.

'Then I'll walk and talk with you.' Jean falls into step beside me. 'You can come in the car with me this morning.'

I give her a curious sidelong glance as Leonard's Lincoln town car pulls up outside and the valet tosses her the keys. It's sleek and silver, and as I slide in beside her, I feel as if I am the movie star. 'Wow,' I breathe, 'this is incredible.'

'Just keep your feet on the floor and nowhere near the seats,' Jean snaps as she pulls smoothly out on to Sunset Boulevard.

I stroke the soft grey interior, marvelling at Jean's driving skills. The car is so long I have no idea how I would drive it through the streets of London, and as for parking it... no chance.

'I wanted to speak to you about yesterday,' Jean says, her eyes never leaving the road. 'About what you said... about modern women.'

'Right.' I say no more, my brain foggy with exhaustion.

'I've never heard anyone say the things you said before – about modern women wanting something more,' Jean says, her tone less abrupt. 'It was quite refreshing.'

'Thanks.' I feel an absurd sense of pride. Jean approves of me! 'Where I come from it's kind of the norm. Women are... *almost* equal to men in some respects.'

'I suppose all that running around in ambulances and making bullets rubs off on you. You know, keeping it all together while the men were fighting a war.'

'Errrm... yeah. Something like that.' Jean doesn't need to know that the only war I have ever fought is with a duvet cover.

'While I don't disagree with you – I wasn't lying when I said I think a lot of women think that way – I do need to warn you that that kind of behaviour won't be tolerated by Leonard.' She glances at me quickly before returning her gaze to the almost empty road ahead.

'What do you mean?'

'I mean, Honey needs to watch herself. Leonard has given her a real opportunity by choosing her as the star of this movie – she can't embarrass him, or she'll be off the picture. I don't think she understands quite how... old-fashioned Leonard can be. All this turning up at his trailer and being... *emotional* needs to stop.'

Wow. I'm starting to think that my initial impressions of Jean's feelings for Leonard were right.

'I mean it, Lily.' Jean's voice rises, shrill and pitchy. 'You need to rein her in, or I can't even begin to imagine what will happen to her. If she's not careful being thrown off the picture will be the least of her problems.'

'What's that supposed to mean?' I am too tired and anxious to deal with Jean's passive-aggressive bullshit today.

Jean turns on to a winding dirt track, off the main highway, dust flying and obscuring her vision as she fails to answer me.

'Jean!'

She slows to a stop and as the dust clears, I see we have arrived at the location for Honey's car chase scene. People are milling about in the dust, the wind whipping it into tiny tornadoes. I see Leonard, scowling at a clipboard, as Jessica adjusts her oversized sunglasses, trying to keep her hair out of her face. Billy Walters stands with Cynthia Lake, a miserable look on his face, and there is no sign of Honey.

'Jean, what did you mean about Honey? That losing the picture will be the least of her worries?'

Jean looks out of the windscreen at Leonard. 'Exactly that. Not everyone on this movie thinks Honey is the bee's knees. As I said, Leonard is very old-fashioned, lots of people on set are despite the rumours you might have heard, and it'll be easy for Honey to make enemies if she carries on the way she is.' Jean pulls the keys from the ignition. 'It's different in Hollywood, Lily. Men behave any way they please. Women – *good* women – don't.'

'Leonard is married, isn't he?'

'Yes. Well, in name. I believe they live very separate lives.' Jean's voice holds a note of longing as she watches Leonard clap Billy on the back and look over his shoulder as if searching for someone. 'Not that it's any of your business. You really need to work on that attitude of yours, Lily.'

If we were in a cartoon, a lightbulb would have gone off over my head. 'You're lucky Leonard lets you drive his car. He must think a lot of you. I can't imagine my ex ever letting me drive his.'

'My daddy was a mechanic. I grew up driving bigger things than this. Now, get out of the car. We're late.'

I watch as Jean hurries over to Leonard, a smile rippling across her face as he greets her. If I'm not mistaken, Jean seems to be warning me to keep Honey away from Leonard. I think of the way Leonard had screamed at Honey then pulled her close, wrapping his arms around her and kissing the top of her head, the confusion I felt over whether their relationship was strictly professional. If Jean believes Honey is having a relationship with Leonard, it would be the perfect motive for her to want to remove Honey from the picture completely.

'Lily!' Jessica hurries awkwardly over the rough, uneven dirt path towards me in scarlet high heels. 'Where the hell is she?'

'Who?' A gust of wind whips the red–brown dust up and grit crunches between my teeth.

'Honey, of course,' Jessica hisses, glancing over her shoulder to where Leonard paces and Jean appears to be offering soothing platitudes. 'She was meant to be here over an hour ago. Did you see her again last night? She told me she was going straight to bed.'

Shit. It never occurred to me to check on Honey this morning – she had seemed so happy when I left her the previous evening – and the letter through my door knocked me for six.

'I need to go back to the hotel,' I say, trying to mask the panic that filters into my voice. Did I make a horrible mistake leaving Honey with Joe? Is he the one I should be watching, sweet, sad, heartbroken Joe? What I wouldn't give for a working mobile phone right now – to be able to dash off a quick text, to make a brief phone call confirming Honey is OK.

'You think she overslept?' Jessica frowns. 'Sure, that'll be it. She's probably on her way now, by the time you get there she'll be here, and it'll be a waste of time.' She glances over her shoulder again. 'Leonard isn't happy though. Honey is on her last warning with him.'

'No, Jessica, you don't understand, I need to—'

'I'm sorry,' a voice calls out and I turn to see Honey getting out of her car, the driver holding the door for her. She stumbles slightly as her feet hit the dirt and as she rights herself, it looks as though she's been crying. 'I'm so sorry, Leonard, please don't be angry.'

'I need to get this scene in the can, Honey, while the light is right.' Leonard's voice is a low growl, and he shoots me a sour look. 'Shouldn't you be making coffee, or something?'

Honey heads towards the chairs set out under a large canopy, in the absence of a make-up trailer, as Jessica gives me a tight smile and turns to follow Leonard, an expression I can't read crossing her features. Worry? Or fear, perhaps? It seems even Jessica is worried that Honey will push Leonard too far.

—

'Honey? What's wrong? Did something happen with Joe?' I crouch at Honey's feet, not minding the dust that stains the bottom of my skirt. She sits in a director's chair, her face pale and blank as the hair stylist fusses with her curls.

'No,' she says eventually, looking down at me. Her eyes are dark and rimmed with pink. 'Joe was… lovely, he was everything I remembered him to be. Better, actually.' She swallows hard. 'I should never have left him. I should never have come here.'

'What? Honey, don't say that. You're going to be a star; you're following a dream. You're going to be a role model for all the girls out there who wish they could but are too scared to try.' I reach out and take her hand, her fingers cold against my palm. 'If I knew it was going to upset you, I would never have brought Joe to your room.'

'I told you; it wasn't Joe.' Honey sighs and waves a hand at the stylist still fussing with her hair, brushing her away. 'Joe left early this morning – we talked all night, Lily. I told him how sorry I was for leaving the way I did. After he left there was a knock on the door. I thought maybe he forgot something, or he'd changed his mind about leaving without kissing me goodbye. I even thought maybe it was you, checkin' up on me.'

Honey twists her arm, so that her hand lies palm up in mine, shoving the sleeve of her blouse up with the other hand and I draw in a sharp breath at the ugly purple bruise that rings her wrist. 'Jesus, Honey, what happened?'

'Magnus,' she says thickly. 'It was Magnus at the door. He was drunk, and furious. He told me that he'd seen Joe leaving my room. I tried to push him away and close the door, but he grabbed me and pushed me inside. We rowed, for hours.' A tear slides down her cheek and drops off her chin. 'He called me the most awful names, Lily, he said he'd ruin me, that he'd make sure I was out of Hollywood for good. That I was nothing without him, and that if it wasn't for him, I wouldn't even be here, I'd just be left rotting in that old hick town.'

'Oh, Honey.' I want to pull her close for a hug, but there are too many people milling around and I don't want to draw attention to the fact that Honey is upset. 'What happened between you two? Why did you really split?'

Honey raises her eyes to mine, tired and drained. 'I made such a terrible mistake, Lily. Magnus… I never really wanted him; I just wanted that next step.'

I don't speak, but something horrible is dawning on me.

'I needed Magnus, Lily, you understand? How could I be taken seriously after one small part, without Magnus on my arm? I wanted to be a star, and I knew that having Magnus as my husband would speed it all up.'

'Oh, Honey.'

'He knew, I'm sure of it. It didn't take long before it backfired on me. He hit me, Lil. He hit me once and promised he'd never do it again, but it did happen again, and it kept on happening. He'd get drunk and find something wrong with me – what I was wearing, I looked at a man for too long, I drank too much – and I had to forgive him because I had nothing and no one else. I never even told Jessica what was really going on. I told her he left me. The same as he told the newspapers – that *he* was leaving *me*.'

I wonder if Jessica will leave Magnus in years to come for the same reason. I wonder if I should warn her somehow.

'And then,' Honey goes on, 'Leonard offered me this role in *Goodtime Gal*, and the money was enough that I didn't need to rely on Magnus. I thought he'd get over me easily, there were always girls chasing him, but it's like he still hates me.'

'Five minutes!' A yell comes from the other side of the track, where Honey's car for the scene is waiting.

'Shoot.' Honey sits back and gives in to the stylist, closing her eyes as the make-up artist brushes over her eyelids. 'You can't tell anyone, Lil.'

'I won't, I promise. But we could call the police… I think you should. Call the police and tell them that Magnus assaulted you.'

'What?' Honey gasps, her lips a pinched white. 'No, I can't do that, not to Magnus. It would make things worse. Please, Lily, promise me you won't say anything.'

I begrudgingly assent, but I am already thinking about how this could affect what is going to happen on Saturday. Could Magnus's jealousy rage out of control? *He said he'd ruin me, that he'd make sure I was out of Hollywood for good.* It doesn't feel impossible. Before I can warn Honey that she needs to be careful she is up and out of the chair, running across the dusty track to where Leonard directs her into the waiting car.

Chapter Twenty-Three

'I'll get you for this, you see if I don't!' Jessica shrieks at Billy as he walks away from her, the final part of their scene in the can as Leonard yells cut.

Jessica smiles and shakes out her hair, before winking in Leonard's direction and sashaying over to me. 'What did you think? Was I good?'

'Errrm... you were great?' I say warily. I only caught the final part of their scene after dealing with Honey. 'Really great. Excellent.'

'Did you speak to Honey? Was everything all right?' Jessica pulls out a compact and rings her mouth in a vivid red. 'I'm a little worried Leonard will ask me to step into Honey's role if she doesn't sort her behaviour out. I mean, I would be the natural replacement but it's a lot of work.' Jessica checks her teeth for lipstick and pulls a face. 'I hope Honey has a good explanation for her tardiness.'

'She... does,' I falter, not sure what to say. Honey has sworn me to secrecy, but I feel as if Jessica should have some idea, she is Honey's best friend after all. 'Magnus went to see her.'

'*Magnus?*' Jessica's eyes widen, and she presses her lips together.

'Please don't tell her I told you—'

'Of course. I wouldn't say anything,' Jessica tuts. 'What did he want?'

'He, errr… just to talk about some things. He wasn't too happy with… I don't really know to be honest.' Heat creeps up my neck, and my toes curl in my sneakers. I don't want to break Honey's confidence, but it's very difficult to lie to Jessica when I feel her gaze pinning me like a rare butterfly.

'Well,' Jessica says, an uncertain note to her voice, 'the divorce isn't final yet, so they probably had things to discuss. I just hope he wasn't angry with her for what happened between the two of *you*.' She eyes me coolly. 'As long as she's all right, that's all that matters. Lily, I need to run some lines with Billy, but can we chat about this later?'

'Billy?' I look behind me in confusion. Billy is stepping into the car, and I can just make out the back of Honey's head as she sits in the driver's seat. 'But Billy's in this scene with Honey.'

'Huh?' Jessica peers past me, pressing her fingers to her collarbone. 'Oh… my mistake. I thought this was Honey's scene. The one where she leaves Billy and screeches away, and gets chased by the cops?'

I shrug. 'There must have been a change of plan.'

Jessica looks down at her wrist, checking the time. 'I need a quick word with Leonard, and then I'm going to go and get a glass of water, sit down for a moment. I'm still exhausted from the party and I've been on set since the early hours. We probably shouldn't have drunk so much last night.' She smiles and rests her hand on my arm. 'Will you excuse me?'

She does look pale, and as she hurries towards Leonard I press my hand to my cheek, exhaustion pulling at my bones, wondering if I look as drained and tired as the two actresses. The clapperboard sounds and Honey pulls away, her tyres kicking up dust.

–

There's something wrong. The car careers around the corner, headed for the next bend in the road. As she flies past, I catch a glimpse of Honey's face, white and fearful, and as the car speeds by, dust flying, I don't see any sign of brake lights.

'Wait.' I look around for Jean, for Leonard or Jessica, for anyone who might listen. 'There's something wrong,' I shout. 'The brakes, there's something wrong with the car!'

But it's too late; as I start to run after the car, it screams around the next bend in the dusty track, disappearing from sight. There is the rip of tyres on gravel, followed by a horrendous bang.

'Honey!' I shriek, grateful that I sacked off heeled pumps in favour of my trusty Converse this morning, as I force my legs to work harder. Leonard's face is rigid and pale as he runs past, gesturing for others to follow suit. Jessica stands immobile at the edge of the track, her shoes and the hem of her trouser suit covered in red dust as she blinks. I can't stop to see if she's OK, I have to get to Honey, but as I round the corner, I pull up hard. It's not just the short run that stops my breath in my throat. The car, a beautiful sleek Cadillac not five minutes ago, lies to one side of the track, the hood crushed against a tree. Crumpled and concertinaed. Smoke rises from the mangled metal, and there is a roaring in my ears. Everything seems to slow down, the world muted, as I watch Leonard run to the car, yanking the door open with difficulty. Cynthia runs past me, her mouth opening in a silent wail. I feel the heat of the sun beating down on top of my head, the grit between my teeth and in my eyes, the dryness in my throat as I try to swallow, frozen to the spot, and then Leonard is pulling Honey free and my feet can move again.

'Let me help.' I run to Honey as Leonard drags her from the car, pulling her out of danger and cradling her head gently as he lays her on the ground. 'Honey? Can you hear me?' Her eyelids flutter but they stay closed, a huge lump forming just below her hairline, a thin trickle of maroon marring her pale skin.

'Lily, stand back.' Jessica's voice is quiet in my ear over Cynthia's wailing. 'The emergency services are on their way; they need room to get to her.'

Leonard tilts Honey's head back slightly, checking her breathing and pressing his fingers to her neck to feel for a pulse. 'She's breathing.'

Oh, thank God. 'Honey, please, please wake up.' I lean in, smoothing her blonde hair away from her face. *She has to be OK.* It's not meant to happen today, I'm supposed to have a few more days to try and stop this. 'You have to, you have too much left to do. Think about Joe, you only just found each other again. Honey, please…' There is a damp splash on Honey's white blouse, then another, and I swipe my hand over my cheeks.

'Excuse me ma'am, let me get to the patient please.' A hand lands on my shoulder and I look up to see Jessica, as she leads me out of the way to allow the paramedics in.

'She's in safe hands, Lily.' Jessica's blouse is streaked with dust, her usually immaculate hair whipping across her face in the desert breeze, her face a bone white. 'Come on, we need to let them take her to the hospital.'

I watch, dry-eyed now, as they load Honey onto a stretcher and into the waiting ambulance. Her eyes remain closed, and her hands look tiny and white, as if they're made of porcelain as they lie on her belly, on the blanket keeping her warm. Further along a second ambulance waits, and as they close the doors on Honey I see Billy on a stretcher. He lets out a moan, and Cynthia sobs as she climbs into the ambulance with him, Jean helping her up the small steps into the back. Beyond them, Leonard stands angled away from me, arms folded across his body as he stares out at the mangled ruin of the car. I can't see his face, and I wonder what he is thinking.

'Come on.' Jessica threads her arm through mine. 'I'll take you to the hospital.'

–

The hospital is quieter than I am used to, without the ringing shouts of drunks, and the gangster mumble of teenage Londoners I experienced the last time I was in A&E. The smell of sickness and disinfectant is the same, though, making me think of my mum and all the time she spent having treatment, and my stomach churns.

I don't know how long we've been here waiting for Honey to wake up, but it's long enough for my bum to go numb on the plastic chairs, and for darkness to fall outside. Every time a doctor walks past I prick up my ears, hoping for news, but so far, all they'll tell me is that she's stable.

Leonard marches back and forth in the corridor, Jean wringing her hands as he frequently stops to hiss at her. I hold my breath trying to hear over the murmur of voices from the nurses' station.

'…should *never* have happened… waiting… the press.' Leonard's voice is tight with fury, and Jean's eyes widen.

'…only since… Lily…' Catching my name on Jean's lips, I move to where Leonard now stands beside her, a frown on his face.

'Lily, what?' I ask.

Jean looks down, shaking her head before she raises her eyes to mine. 'I just said, all of this… trouble, it's only started since you arrived on the scene, Lily. Everything has gone horribly wrong since you showed up.'

It's like she's kicked me in the stomach. 'What?'

Leonard watches me closely, his eyes dark. 'Jean has a point, Lily. Things seem to have taken a turn since you started working for Honey. How exactly did that come about anyway?'

'You can't think… I would never…' My heart is in my mouth as I frantically search for the right words to say. How can I tell them, *I'm from seventy years from now, and I know Honey will be murdered in a few days' time?* My pulse thuds, staccato and jarring in my ears. *Am I going to become a suspect myself?* 'I've nothing to do with it,' I croak, 'I've not spoken to the press, and I would never—'

'Is there any news?' I've never been so pleased to see Jessica. She's been back to the hotel and changed into clean clothes, but there is a deep line between her eyebrows that I'm sure wasn't there this morning.

'She's still asleep,' I say, aware that I am still filthy with dust, my face grimy and sweaty. Leonard and Jean haven't taken their eyes off me. 'Excuse me. I really need to go and wash my face.'

'I'll call you if the doctor comes.' Jessica seems unaware of the atmosphere as I stumble towards the restroom.

Closing the door behind me, I allow myself a brief moment to close my eyes and breathe deeply. Today has left me in no doubt that Honey's murder will happen on

Saturday, just as it had originally, and I am the only one, apart from the culprit, who knows it is going to happen. *Do Leonard and Jean really think I was involved, or are they detracting suspicion from themselves?* I rerun the images of the car, racing past with Honey's terrified face behind the wheel. The way it hadn't slowed as she approached the bend, the distinct lack of taillights. This was deliberate – someone tampered with the brakes, knowing Honey would be filming her car chase scene today. Did they hope that that would be all it took? The idea of it makes me nauseous and I reach over and turn on the cold tap, splashing my face with water, before sticking my head under and taking a quick mouthful.

Feeling if not restored, then at least less grubby, I slip back out into the emergency room, my heart skipping a beat as I see an empty corridor. I am about to go to the nurses' station when I see Jessica, leaning against the wall on the other side of the ER. Magnus stands in front of her, his broad back to me, as he presses one hand on the wall on either side of her, trapping her in place.

Her face is turned up to his, and it looks as though he is questioning her, as she first nods, then shakes her head. I can't see her face completely as Magnus's arm blocks my view, but she doesn't seem upset. She seems more… angry. I sneak closer, trying to hear what they are saying.

'She's… wife…' Magnus is saying, but I can only catch every other word or so. '…don't… try again!' Jessica pushes his arm away and I realise she is furious. Magnus turns, his mouth set in a grim line, and I still as his gaze lands on me.

'*You.*' His eyes widen, his lip curling, and I take a step back, fighting the instinct to flee. 'I should have known you would be here, interfering. Hasn't anyone told you to mind your business?'

'Nurse!' Jessica calls out. 'Can you ask this man to leave? My friend is very sick, and I don't want her waking to up to find… *him* here.'

'There's no need,' Magnus snarls, his face changing to the familiar scowl I'm more used to. 'I'm leaving anyway.'

Rubbing my hands over my arms, suddenly cold, I have an odd sense of déjà vu as Magnus storms his way out of the hospital. 'What was all that about?'

Jessica's jaw is clenched. 'Honey doesn't need to see him when she wakes up.' She looks me over. 'Are you all right? You're very pale.'

'Yes,' I lie. A chill tickles its way down my spine, raising goosebumps on my arms at Magnus's words. *Mind your business.* I can see the jagged edges of cut newsprint against the stark white of the note in my mind's eye.

As if on cue, a doctor appears in the doorway, scanning the ER until his gaze lands on me. 'Are you Lily?' he asks. 'Miss Black is awake and asking for you.'

Chapter Twenty-Four

'Hi.' Honey looks like a little doll tucked up in her hospital bed, but she smiles weakly when I walk in. Leonard stands on the other side of the bed, and I can't help but glance down at the sheets, where his hand rests on hers.

'I'll leave you two to it,' Leonard says gruffly. 'Don't keep her too long, Lily, Honey needs to rest.'

'Of course.' I wait until he has left the room before I lean over and peck Honey on the cheek. She is pale and a large white bandage covers her temple. A bruise shadows her left cheekbone, but I can't be sure that it wasn't there this morning after her run-in with Magnus. 'How are you feeling?'

'Sore.' Honey winces as she pushes herself up the pillows. 'But the doctor says I'll be OK. Just a bit bruised and battered.' Panic flits across her face. 'What about Billy? Is Billy all right?'

'Shhhh.' I plump the pillow behind her, gently pushing her back against it. 'He's fine. He has a bit of a concussion and a broken ankle, but apart from that he'll be fine. You're very lucky, both of you.' I pause for a moment. 'What happened, Honey?'

She frowns, her mouth twisting in pain as the skin around her bruised temple moves. 'I don't know... I remember putting my foot down like Leonard told me to and feeling scared at how fast we were going for just a second and then...' she pauses, gesturing for the glass of water next to the bed, 'there was a bend... I pressed the brake, and nothing happened. I remember thinking maybe I'd pressed the wrong pedal for a moment, and then that was it. I woke up here.'

I was right. Someone had tampered with the brakes. 'It's OK,' I soothe, as my mind frantically turns over what Honey has just told me. 'I'm so relieved you both came out of it all right.'

Honey takes a sip of water and leans against the pillow, her eyes drooping. 'I'm sorry, Lily, I don't remember anything else.' Her eyelids droop, and within seconds she is asleep.

I tuck the blanket up to her chin and refill her water glass, almost jumping out of my skin as Jessica appears in the doorway.

'Hey,' she whispers. 'How is she?'

'Tired and bruised,' I say, matching her low tone. 'We should probably leave her now.' I too am exhausted, a heavy weariness that makes me unsuccessfully attempt to fight the yawn at the back of my throat. 'Listen, you didn't see anything... suspicious this morning, did you?'

Jessica gives me a sharp look. 'Suspicious? Like what exactly?'

'I don't know... someone lurking around who looked like they shouldn't be there. Hanging around the car, maybe?'

'Lily, it was an accident. Unless... do you think this was deliberate?' Jessica's voice takes an icy tone. 'That's quite a strong accusation.'

'I'm not accusing anyone.' I blink rapidly, aware of the stinging behind my eyes. I don't want to argue with Jessica, if anything I want reassurance that my gut instinct is wrong. 'I just… I don't know how this could happen, and I wondered if you'd seen anything unusual.'

'No, nothing.' The sharpness is gone from her tone, and she rubs a hand over her face. 'Sorry, Lily, I didn't mean to snap. I'm exhausted, and I can't imagine anyone wanting to hurt Honey. When you all work together on a movie you become like family. There were plenty of people around this morning but no one…' She stops, her hand going to her throat.

'Jessica? What is it?'

She turns to me, her hand still clutching the delicate gold chain around her neck. 'I did see something… I saw Jean. She was,' she frowns as if trying to recall, 'she was there early, I'm sure she was. Before Leonard arrived, before I arrived. She came out of the shed where the car was being kept when I was walking over to get my make-up done.'

Jean was there. Jean, who told Leonard things have only gone wrong since I arrived. Numbly I say goodbye to Jessica and stumble my way out to the parking lot, before realising I have no idea how I am going to get back to the Beverly Hills. The thought of walking, even in my Converse, makes me want to cry.

'Lily? Hey, Lily! Over here!' Louis waves at me from across the parking lot, where he leans against Christine. The sight of him is like a tall glass of water on a hot day and I hurry across the still warm tarmac, forgetting all about my aching feet.

'What are you doing here? How did you know?'

'Miss Parks came back to the hotel – she was covered in dust, and she looked upset – so the duty manager brought her into the bar for a glass of champagne. She knocked it back in one gulp and then just came out with it – she told us Honey had been in an accident. I knew you'd be here, and I knew you'd probably not have a way of getting home.'

'Oh, Louis.' The lump in my throat is back and I don't think this time I'll be able to swallow it down.

'She isn't going home.' Tilda slides out of the car, her red hair tied back in a neat ponytail, and her face clean and fresh without make-up. I run my hands over my wild, tangled curls, in a vain attempt to smooth them down. 'She's coming back with us.'

'Oh no, I couldn't possibly...' I flap a hand, my voice thick with unshed tears and exhaustion.

'Tilda, Lily might not feel up to it,' Louis says, glancing at me.

'Nonsense,' Tilda replies, in the worst fake British accent I've ever heard. 'When has Mom's meatloaf ever *not* solved a problem? Remember when you wanted to ask Jenny Miller to the prom, and she said she wanted to go with Tommy Fradenburgh? Mom's meatloaf fixed your crying that night.'

As if on cue, my stomach gives a noisy growl, as Louis scowls in Tilda's direction. 'That settles it,' she says. 'Get in the car, Lil.'

Half an hour later we pull up alongside a modest single-storey house in one of the quieter areas of Santa Monica. It feels calm and restful after the rush of Hollywood and as I step out of the car I marvel at the peace and quiet, inhaling the soft scent of salt on the sea breeze. The roads are silent, the trees that line Fourth Street cast shadows over the sidewalk, and every house looks buttoned up tight for the evening.

'This way.' Louis takes my elbow and leads me through a gate in the cute picket fence that surrounds the garden.

The house is painted a pale mint green, and as I follow Louis up the steps to the wrap-around porch, the outside lamps glowing a soft yellow, I feel as if I am in a movie. *It's a Wonderful Life*, maybe. Or *Back to the Future*. The first one obviously, because everyone knows that sequels never quite match up, unless it's *The Empire Strikes Back*. 'Don't be nervous,' he whispers as he taps once on the front door before pushing it open. From the way he wipes his palm over the fabric of his trousers, I could be mistaken for thinking that perhaps he is more nervous than I am.

'Lou, finally you're home.' A slim woman with the same fiery red hair as Tilda and a hint of a Brooklyn accent bustles into the hallway, wiping her hands on an apron tied loosely about her waist. 'You must be Lily. I'm Louis's mom. Call me Debbie.'

'Hi. It's nice to meet you.'

'You've had a heck of a day,' she says, wrapping me in a hug. She smells floral, with buttery undertones, like my mum when she'd been baking. 'Tilda told me what happened. You poor thing. Are you all right? And Miss Black?'

'She will be,' I say as she leads me into a cosy kitchen-dining area, where a table has already been set. The smell of meatloaf is on the air and my stomach growls again.

'Ma, Lily's starving and exhausted,' Tilda says. 'Can we do the questions later?'

'It's fine,' I say as Louis ushers me into a chair. 'She's going to be OK, thank goodness.'

'Well, ain't that a blessing for us all.' A man sweeps into the room, tall and regal, with a face that I imagine Louis's will match perfectly in twenty-five years' time. 'You must be Lily. I'm Andy, Louis's father.'

'Nice to meet you.' I shove my chair back to stand and shake his hand, but he rests his hand on my shoulder, gently pressing me back into my seat.

'No, you stay there. No need for all that.' He looks at Louis. 'Son, you make sure Lily has everything she needs tonight.'

'I'm already on it, Pa.'

'Tilda made up the spare bed for you before she left for the hospital,' Debbie says, as she leans across the table and lays a heaped plate of meatloaf and mashed potatoes in front of me. 'It's the other bed in Tilda's room, if you don't mind sharing?'

'Oh no, honestly, I'll go back to the hotel. I couldn't possibly impose on you.' My accent has veered into parent-meeting-headteacher, posh telephone voice territory.

'It's not *imposing*,' Tilda says as she slides into a chair with her own plate of food. 'Louis doesn't want you going back to the hotel alone after the day you've had, and I want you to stay. We have things to *discuss*.' As she forks a piece of meatloaf into her mouth, she winks.

'Well, OK, if you're sure?' Warmth floods my veins as they all take their seats at the table, Aimee and Scarlett, Louis's younger sisters, rushing in from upstairs, and everyone starts to eat. They talk over one another, laugh, argue, and tease each other as I sit and observe, basking in their hospitality.

This was how I wish it had been at home. Mum did her best, but it was always just the two of us, the house always slightly too quiet. Don't get me wrong, we had a lot of good times, but they faded once she got sick and every mealtime was something to be navigated carefully.

Now the good times have been drowned out by the tough times.

'You will, won't you Lily? Evelyn *never* wants to do it,' Aimee is saying as I shake away thoughts of my mum.

'Hmmm? Yes, of course.' Aimee grins at me, and I turn to Louis. 'What have I just agreed to?'

'Having your hair braided by Aimee before bed.'

'Oh, thank God. I can think of far worse things I might have said yes to.'

–

After dinner, Louis's parents and the younger children beat a hasty retreat, leaving me, Tilda, and Louis alone at the table.

'So.' Tilda leans in, her face solemn. 'What's the real deal with what happened today? There's no way for a minute I believe what happened to Honey was an accident.'

Relief makes my scalp prickle. 'I don't think it was an accident.'

'What actually happened?'

'I don't know,' I say, the image of the speeding car flashing through my mind. 'Honey was driving – it was a chase scene, and Leonard had told her to put her foot down. She roared past me, and she looked terrified... then as she took the corner she didn't slow down, and a moment later she came off the road.' Nausea swirls in my belly just talking about it.

'It sounds awful,' Louis says quietly, reaching out to squeeze my hand.

'Her brakes didn't work,' I say thickly. 'When she zoomed past me, there were no taillights. Honey wouldn't have deliberately not touched the brakes, and she told me when she woke up that nothing happened when she tried to slow down.'

'Someone tampered with the brakes,' Tilda says, her voice barely above a whisper.

'I think so, yes.'

Louis frowns. 'But who?'

'Wait, let me get a notepad.' Tilda jumps up, returning a few moments later with a legal pad and a pencil. 'We need to write a definitive list of suspects. Lily, we don't have much time – if what you say is true, we only have a couple of days to find out who has it in for Honey.'

'We?' Louis's voice is tinged with sarcasm, but I feel touched by Tilda's willingness to help.

'Yes, *we*. So, Lily, who first?'

'Errmmm… Leonard, I guess?' His was the name that cropped up in the book I read all those years ago, the prime suspect until it was all hushed up.

'The director, right?' Tilda scratches his name down on to the yellow paper. 'Why him?'

'He loses his temper ever so easily, especially when it comes to the movie,' I say. 'He told Honey any more bad press and she's out – he really went nuclear on her. But then I saw him hugging her in his trailer. They'd been arguing and… it just didn't feel like a normal director-actor relationship. It felt… closer, I suppose.'

'You think maybe they're having an affair?' Louis asks.

'It's possible… what if he loses his temper with her on Saturday and he lashes out? How many times is murder down to a crime of passion?'

'Woah. *Woah*. Hold on a second – murder?' Tilda looks from me to Louis, her eyes wide. 'Is that what you think is gonna happen?'

'You think someone is going to *murder* Honey?' Louis's face pales as he scrubs a hand over his chin.

Shit. I had forgotten that I hadn't actually told anyone what I knew was going to happen. 'I... yeah. I know I said something bad, well, that's it. Murder. I believe someone is going to try to murder Honey Black.'

'*Murder.*' Tilda lets out a shaky breath. 'You can't get much worse than that, right?'

'What makes you think it's going to be murder?' Louis frowns. 'When you said *something bad* I figured she would be fired... not *murdered.*'

Oh blimey. 'I just... *know.* It's hard to explain, but you just have to trust me. Look at what's happened to Honey already. She had threatening notes through her door, warning her to go back to where she came from, and now today, the brakes being cut on the car... well, isn't that proof enough that someone wants to kill her?'

'Someone definitely doesn't want her around, and they are escalating things, that's for sure,' Tilda says. 'Murder doesn't seem unbelievable.'

'I'm sorry I didn't tell you before. I completely understand if you don't want to help. This is serious. Dangerous, even. I wouldn't blame you at all for not wanting to be involved.'

'We're still helping.' Tilda's voice is firm. 'Right, Lou?'

Louis sits up in his chair, pushing his hands through his hair. 'Uh... yeah. I guess.' He flinches as Tilda's foot makes contact with his shin under the table. 'Of course, we'll still help, Lily. It's just... it's *murder.*'

'We're *still in.*' Glaring at Louis, Tilda taps her pen on the legal pad. 'So, Leonard. He can't keep his temper, especially about the movie, and especially around Honey.'

Louis looks concerned, shifting in his chair as if still not 100 per cent convinced all of this is a good idea. 'He's the one who told her to put her foot down. Maybe I can keep an eye on him on Saturday. He often comes into the bar.'

'Who else?' Tilda raises an eyebrow.

'Jean,' I say, feeling more confident. 'She is awfully jealous of Honey – I would even go so far as to say I felt she was telling me to warn Honey off Leonard this morning.'

'Why would she do that?'

'Jeez, Lou.' Tilda rolls her eyes. 'Because Jean is in love with Leonard, you dummy.'

'She is?'

I confirm with a brisk nod. 'She was also at the scene of the car chase this morning, before I arrived on set.'

'I thought she gave you a ride to location?' Louis says.

'She did,' I say, tapping a finger on Tilda's yellow pad. 'Write this down, Til. Jean was on location this morning, before she thought anyone else was on set. Jessica told me she saw her when she arrived. Why would Jean leave the hotel to go to the location of the car, then back to the hotel to fetch me? Why would she go to the set at all that early in the morning?' I gasp as I think of something significant. 'Jean told me this morning that her dad was a mechanic! She would know how to tamper with the brakes.'

'*Jean.*' Tilda writes her name and underlines it in heavy lead. 'Definitely a top candidate. Nothing like a woman scorned.'

'Magnus,' Louis says, 'he's the next one on the list.'

'Magnus Michel?' Tilda yelps. 'But he's… he's famous! And handsome… and…'

'And also told Jessica he'd be out of town, before showing up unexpectedly at the party,' I say darkly. 'I saw him arguing with Jessica in the bower after Leonard told him to leave that night, while everyone was inside dancing. She didn't sound very happy with him, but I haven't seen her alone to ask her what they were arguing about. He was only invited because of Hollywood politics, and I think he might have been behind tipping off the press in the bushes... There's also the fact that Magnus and I had a... slight altercation that night.'

'Slimy creep,' Tilda tuts, her opinion veering wildly. 'Maybe he's jealous and wants Honey back?'

'Maybe,' I say. 'Definitely put Magnus on there. There was something else too... something he said to me earlier at the hospital. It was the exact wording of a phrase on the note I received.' Louis shakes his head, his lips pressed into a thin, hard, angry line. 'Magnus also visited Honey in her hotel room this morning.'

'He did?' Tilda frowns and scrawls his name down. 'Do we know what he wanted?'

'Honey said he was drunk and angry when he saw Joe leaving her room,' I say. 'There was a bruise on her wrist this morning, from Magnus grabbing her. He's not what the public think he is – he's not charming and sophisticated, he's a violent, jealous bully. Honey left him for hitting her, and he doesn't want to let her go.'

'If he can't have her, no one can,' Louis says under his breath, 'and if Honey were to tell the newspapers what he was really like, maybe that would be the end of him, too.'

'Two reasons for Magnus,' Tilda says. 'Anyone else?'

'What about Joe?' Louis says, but even as he speaks, he looks uncertain.

I shake my head. 'I don't think Joe would hurt Honey. He loves her, and he wants her back, but from what I can gather she still feels the same way about him. It could work between them if they can figure out the logistics of it all. Look at Jon Bon Jovi – he married his childhood sweetheart and it all turned out OK.'

'Jon Bon…?' Tilda and Louis gape at me, their faces almost identical as they both knit their brows into a tight frown.

'Never mind. All I'm saying is I don't think it's Joe. But put him on the list anyway, we could still do with knowing where he is on Saturday.'

We add Cynthia Lake to the list, and although Tilda wants to discount Billy, who has never shown any dislike towards Honey, I point out that he could blame her for inciting Cynthia. 'What about Jessica Parks?' Tilda asks, as she runs her pencil down the list. 'Was she on set this morning too? Could she be jealous of Honey?'

'Jessica?' I frown. 'I don't know. They're best friends. Jessica has so much more than Honey already – she's more famous, she has a great reputation in the business – I'm not sure what else she could gain. She was the one who got Honey the role in the movie in the first place. That aside, she strikes me as a girls' girl, you know? She's very supportive of other women.' I shake my head. 'She was on set, but she was working on her scene with Billy before Honey started shooting. I think we need to try and find a way to keep eyes on all of these people in the run-up to Saturday.'

Tilda nods. 'That gives us a few people who potentially don't want her around. So, how are we going to make sure we keep Honey safe from them?'

We spend another hour trying to figure out a way of protecting Honey, until finally I can't stop yawning and Louis pushes back his chair, just as the doorbell chimes.

Tilda frowns and goes to answer it, her scowl even more pronounced when she comes back into the kitchen. Standing behind her is a pouting Evelyn. 'It's for you, Lou.' Tilda throws herself back into her chair without looking at him.

'Louis!' Evelyn goes to him, putting her arms around his neck. My cheeks warm and I shift in my seat, not sure where to look. Evelyn turns, her eyes narrowing. 'And who is *this*?'

'Umm, Ev, this is Lily.' Louis disentangles himself, looking as uncomfortable as I feel.

'Lily, huh.' She runs her gaze over my face and my scalp prickles. 'Friend of yours, Tilda?'

'She is now, aren't you, Lil?' She casts a mischievous look in Louis's direction. 'But she was Lou's friend first. What?' she demands as Louis shakes his head. 'It's true, isn't it, Lily? You were friends with Louis before you were friends with me.'

Oh boy. 'Kind of?' I say, getting to my feet. I hold out a hand. 'Hi Evelyn, I'm Lily. A friend of Tilda's *and* Louis's.'

Evelyn sniffs and doesn't shake my hand. 'I've seen you,' she says, 'at the hotel. You're that sad, lonely girl who sits at the bar on her own.'

Well, that stung. Evelyn lets out a laugh, high and tinkly, and I catch Tilda's wince. I lower my hand and sit back down.

Louis hasn't moved. 'What are you doing here, Evelyn? We talked about this—'

'I wanted to surprise you, and you, Tilda.' She finally turns to face Tilda, who rolls her eyes and sighs.

'Surprise us with what? More wedding junk? I don't know why you're getting all excited over things – Reg and I haven't set a date, and I have *more important* things to think about at the moment.' Tilda raises her eyebrows in my direction.

'Nothing is more important than your wedding,' Evelyn says, 'although if I'd known you had *company* then I wouldn't have come over. I'm sorry, Lala—'

'Lily,' I say.

'Oops! *Lily*, I apologise, but this is family business.' Evelyn looks at me expectantly and the penny drops. I stand, pulling my thin sweater from the back of the chair and folding it over my arm.

'You're right,' I say. 'I'm sorry, of course I'm imposing. Louis, thank your mum for me. Her meatloaf was incredible. Tilda, I'll catch up with you later? And Evelyn,' I smile at her, meeting her icy blue eyes as she tilts her chin in the air. 'It was *such* a pleasure to meet you. I'm sure I'll see you again.'

Tilda shoves her chair back and grabs my forearm. 'What? No, Lily, you're staying over tonight! Remember?' She lowers her voice. 'I really don't think you should be on your own.'

'You're… staying over?' Evelyn purses her lips as Louis wraps an arm around her shoulder and begins to steer her gently towards the front door.

'Evelyn, it really isn't a good time. I thought we agreed you wouldn't do this.'

I try not to listen as Louis gently passes Evelyn her jacket and opens the front door, ushering her outside, but it's hard not to. 'Staying? Here? But Louis… who is she? You barely know her. Do you?'

Louis murmurs something I can't catch, and I wonder what he's saying in response. 'And *meatloaf*.' Evelyn's hissed words float into the house on the warm sea breeze. 'You said your mom only makes that on *special occasions*.'

Louis closes the door, cutting off the low rumble of his response, as Tilda splutters with laughter. 'Ugh, I told you she was a piece of work.'

'She seems… nice,' I lie, as Tilda raises an eyebrow at me again. 'OK… she seems high maintenance.'

'Understatement.' Tilda pulls a face. 'She's only trying to organise my wedding so she can show Louis what a great catch she'll be as a wife.' She sticks her fingers down her throat, and I force the smile to stay in place on my face. I really don't want to think about Louis and Evelyn getting married.

The front door snicks closed, and Louis reappears, his cheeks flushed pink, and his dark hair slightly ruffled. I scan his face for lipstick, wondering if he kissed Evelyn on the doorstep.

'Sorry Lil,' he says, pushing his hand through his hair, 'Evelyn, she's a…'

'Nuisance?' says Tilda.

Louis shoots her a look. 'I was going to say, she can be a lot. She doesn't handle rejection very well.'

'There's a reason she's never had Mom's meatloaf,' Tilda says with a smirk.

I want to laugh, bubbles of hysterical giggles welling up in my throat before it unexpectedly turns to tears. 'Oh gosh,' I gasp, as tears slide down my cheeks and a sob escapes. 'I'm sorry, I don't know—'

'You're exhausted and overwhelmed.' Louis hands me his handkerchief, the cotton soft in my fingers. 'It's been one heck of a day. Come on,' he says, holding out a hand. 'Time for you to go to bed.' I follow him along the corridor to a door that stands half open, a glimpse of pale yellow walls and the soft glow of a lamp emanating from inside. 'Here, this is you. I'll be just there,' he gestures across the hall to the door opposite. 'If you need me.'

'I'll have Tilda right next to me,' I say, my tears drying. 'I think I'll be OK.'

Louis holds my gaze, and my stomach does another of those huge swoops. *Damn you, Evelyn. Damn you Louis, for not being born in 1995.* 'I think you will be, Miss Lily.'

I smile, and crushing his handkerchief into my fist so he doesn't ask for it back, I step into Tilda's room. 'Good night.'

'Lil,' Louis whispers, just as I think he's going to leave. 'Will you tell me one day? Once all this is over? Will you tell me how you know that something awful is going to happen to Honey?'

–

'How did they end up together?' I ask, as Tilda settles into the bed across from me.

'Who? Louis and Evelyn?'

'Yeah. I don't want to speak out of turn, but I wouldn't have put Louis with someone like Evelyn.' I reach up and flick off the lamp beside my pillow, hiding the faint blush that heats my cheeks.

'That makes two of us,' Tilda says, her tone dry. 'Remember I said he asked Jenny Miller to the prom, and she said no? Well, he ended up going with Evelyn. He felt sorry for her because she moved from Connecticut in her senior year, and she didn't have a date.'

'He must want to be with her though? It's been how long? Six years?'

I think Tilda shrugs, but the room is dark, bar a faint silver glow at the edge of the window from the full moon outside. 'He didn't tell you? They're not together anymore. Louis told me this morning. Evelyn is stubborn, Lil. Louis told her it's over two nights ago, but she just won't listen.' There is a rustling as Tilda turns over in bed. 'She carries on as if nothing has changed. Only now, I think things have changed for Lou.'

I feel a shot of pity for Evelyn before I shake it away, remembering the expression that crossed her face as she looked me over. *What does Tilda mean, things have changed for Louis? Is it because of me?* I press my face into the pillow. *Does Louis feel the same way I do?* The impossibility of it all makes me want to cry, but I'm all out of tears.

'Maybe she'll get what she wants one day,' I say. After all, I won't be here to get in the way.

'Maybe Louis will get what he wants,' Tilda murmurs, 'and I don't think Evelyn will be a part of that. I hope not anyway.' She gives a sleepy snort of laughter.

I roll over, trying not to think of Louis and Evelyn together. I have no right to say what I really think, or feel – a few days, and I'll be home again, trying to resist the urge to google the public records to see if they ever did get married. My last thought before I fall asleep is that six years is a long time to never have been invited over for meatloaf.

Chapter Twenty-Five

The next few days are spent flitting between the hospital and the hotel, waiting for Honey to get the all-clear to come home and trying to squash the panic that surges every time I think about Louis's request for me to tell him how I know something bad is going to happen. I have caught a glimpse of Evelyn in the hotel bar once or twice, using her presence as an excuse not to be alone with Louis for long enough to allow him to probe me further on it. Finally, on Friday Louis drives me to the hospital for the last time, and I am light-headed with the knowledge that I only have twenty-four hours left to figure out who is going to try to kill Honey.

When he asked if I would tell him how I knew things, I had faltered, not sure how to respond. Who would believe that a little less than two weeks ago I was living in LA in 2019, that I carried a mobile phone, that there would have been two female prime ministers, a Black president? That we have access to hundreds of different TV channels, that special movie effects are done with CGI and computers. That we travel all over the world, easily and readily, to far-flung places that Louis can only dream of visiting. Who in 1949 would believe it? Louis will think I'm crazy if I tell him the truth – he'll probably want nothing more to do with me. When all this is done, I'll go back to my own time and when I do, I'll never see Louis again. I can't tell him. I can't ruin the little time we do have together.

Honey is sitting on the edge of her hospital bed when I arrive, Joe perched next to her holding her hand tightly.

'Hi Honey, how are you feeling?'

'I'm all right.' She nods, but she still looks pale.

'This place looks like a florist.' Huge bouquets fill the small hospital room, and I flick open the card on a particularly large bunch of yellow roses. 'Sending best get well wishes, Alfred.' I look at Honey. 'Alfred?'

She presses her lips together hard as if trying not to smile. 'He delivered them to me himself. Said he hopes I'm better soon, and when I'm able, he has a script he'd like to send over.'

'Alfred? Hitchcock?' No wonder Honey can't stop grinning. 'Alfred Hitchcock wants to send you a script? Honey, this is incredible.' *I knew it. I knew she would be a star.* Even the knowledge that Leonard won't be best pleased can't dampen my spirits.

'And Joan sent these.' Honey holds up a box of expensive liqueur chocolates. 'Can you imagine, Lily? Joan Crawford – *the* Joan Crawford – sent me chocolates! I didn't even know she knew who I was.'

'Everyone will know who you are soon,' I say. I just hope it's for the right reasons. Joe says nothing, his fingers fumbling awkwardly with Honey's overnight bag.

'The doctor said I can leave, and the studio have sent a car, so come with us?'

'Of course.' I pass over Honey's cardigan, waiting as Joe chivalrously helps her with it.

I peep in on Billy as we pass, but the room is empty, and I hope he has already been discharged. The last thing I want is for Honey to run into Cynthia on the way out. I'm pretty sure Cynthia will blame Honey for Billy's broken ankle and I feel another stir of anxiety at the thought of Saturday being only a day away.

The press line the street to the hotel as we pull in and Honey waves graciously from the open car window. Cameras flash and they call her name as she gets out of the car, Joe helping her as she stumbles slightly.

'Honey! Miss Black! Who's the guy?' a voice calls out, and Honey pauses, her arm linked through Joe's.

'This is Joe,' she says coyly, 'he's my—'

I suddenly have a sixth sense that I know exactly what she is about to say. 'No more pictures, thank you. Honey, inside *now*.'

The cameras go wild, Honey's name shouted over and over as she steps into the safety of the hotel lobby. 'Why didn't you let me tell them Joe and I are engaged?' Honey says, as we head towards the Paul Williams Suite.

Engaged. I had a feeling that was what she was going to say – I just wish she'd given me a bit of a heads–up. Magnus is going to go *mental*.

'When did this happen?'

'Oh Lil, don't look like that. Aren't you happy for me?' Honey pouts, as Joe starts to rearrange the gifts that have been brought to Honey's hotel room. Flowers, champagne, cakes and brownies line the bar area, with more dotted around the room, on top of the table and the piano.

'Well, of course I'm happy for you – for both of you,' I sigh. 'But have you even told Leonard? And what will Magnus say?' I whisper the last part, not wanting Joe to overhear. I don't know how much Honey has told him.

'Leonard will be fine. And it's none of Magnus's business.'

It kind of is, seeing as how their divorce isn't final yet, and knowing what I know I am finding it hard to batter down the frantic butterfly wings of panic I feel. And will Leonard be fine? I'm not so sure. This news has just given me a whole other thing to fret about. Magnus will most definitely *not* be fine.

'What about Joe?' I hiss. 'Has he thought this through? Does he know what it means if he marries you?' I think of the script Alfred Hitchcock wants to send over; the way Honey is beginning to make a name for herself among her peers as well as her fans. Does Joe realise that even if he marries Honey, if she gets another big movie part there's no way she'll go back to Kentucky?

Honey blinks, her eyes filling with tears. 'Lily, I thought we were friends.'

'Oh Honey,' I sigh. 'We are friends… that's why I want you to be sure. I don't want you to have any more trouble, like you did with Magnus.'

'Oh Lil, that won't ever happen!' Honey beams now, the tears drying up suspiciously quickly. 'Joe isn't like Magnus, *at all*.' I really hope he's not. 'He wants me to be a success. And I love him, Lily. So much.'

I can't rain on her parade anymore, even though something uneasy coils like a snake in my stomach. I can see Honey's engagement announcement ruffling feathers all over.

'Do you want me to call anyone? Your mom?' I ask, but Honey shakes her head.

'Joe already called home.' She smiles up at him, and I think that maybe, just maybe, if I can get her through Saturday still alive, then perhaps Honey has found her happy ever after.

'Maybe we should just keep this between us for now.'

'What do you mean? Why?'

'I think you two should enjoy it for a while before the press, Leonard and Magnus are made aware. Get used to being together before we make a really splashy announcement. Just for a few days. How about it?'

'If you think that's best, sure.' Honey gives Joe a besotted smirk. 'I'm going to spend some time here, with Joe, this afternoon.' She gives me a meaningful look and I grin, despite the heavy knot in my chest.

'OK, you kids have fun. I'll come and check on you later,' I whisper as she sees me to the door. 'Congratulations, Honey. Or should I call you Betty Sue?'

Honey laughs and swats me on the arm. 'Oh you! Get out of here, I'll see you later.'

I head to the bar, hoping to catch up with Louis and grab a bite to eat before I go and see Jessica. I'd thought she might have been at the hospital this morning, but I guess she must be more shaken up than I realised. I've only known Honey for a couple of weeks, but in that time, I've grown fond of her, even if she can be a bit obnoxious at times, and I found it traumatic.

Louis is wiping over the bar, and I don't see Evelyn until it's too late.

'Oh. Lily.' Evelyn gives me a fleeting look, one that conveys so much more than any words could. Self-consciously my hand goes to my hair, to the wild cork-screw curls that I haven't been able to tame this morning.

'Evelyn. What a surprise.' I slide onto a stool, refusing to let her icy glare freeze me out. 'Just a glass of water please, Louis.'

'Louis's just getting off, aren't you?' Evelyn reaches out and presses her fingers against his hand, proprietary and obvious. 'We're wedding venue hunting this afternoon.' Louis slides his hand away.

'Wedding venue…?' I raise my eyebrows, hiding the confusion I feel. Tilda did say they were broken up, didn't she?

'For Tilda and Reg,' Louis says, catching my eye. 'Although to be honest, Ev, I'm not sure it's a good idea. Tilda and Reg still haven't set the date and you know she's not really…'

'Two birds with one stone, Louis,' Evelyn says crisply. 'It's good to have a few in mind,' she gives a coy giggle.

Louis frowns. 'Evelyn, please, you know we're not—'

'Plenty of time for all that though,' Evelyn says, making sure she catches my gaze. 'What about you, Lily? Anyone special?'

I shake my head. 'Free as a bird, Evelyn, that's me.'

'Oh, you poor thing.' Evelyn cocks her head on one side, studying me as if I am some kind of exotic creature. 'It must be quite difficult for you,' she lowers her voice, '…you don't fit in one way or the other, do you?'

It takes me a moment, my first thought being, *How does she know? How does she know I'm not meant to be here, that I don't belong in 1949?* before she carries on, her eyes flicking down to the sneakers on my feet.

'I mean, look at you. You just… don't quite fit. Your… style, if one could call it that. The way you speak, the things you say. Louis often laughs about your funny turns of phrase.'

'I…' I feel myself tense, and I am afraid to look in Louis's direction, Evelyn's words slicing through me like a hot knife through butter.

'Evelyn, there's been a change of plans.' Louis's tone is cold enough to freeze lava. 'I can't make it this afternoon.'

'But Louis—' Evelyn protests, as Louis comes around from behind the bar and expertly slides her from the stool, walking her towards the hotel lobby.

'I'll see you later, Evelyn.'

Masking her undeniable fury, Evelyn pouts and with a hard look in my direction she flounces from the bar.

Louis turns to me, his cheeks flaming. 'I'm sorry, Lil. She should never have said that.'

'It's OK.' It's not though. Pushing off the stool, I turn to leave before pausing. 'I can't help the way I am, Louis.'

'I never said that about you, Lily.' Louis is earnest as he reaches for me. 'I swear to you – I never said anything about the way you look or the things you say.'

'I thought we were friends.' My voice cracks, and I feel my eyes begin to fill.

'We *are*. Evelyn is… she's difficult, Lily. Jealous. Stubborn. I like the way you are. The funny things you say. The way you cuss, and you don't even care if you shock people. You're cool and brave and… different. Please believe me.'

I look down at my feet, at the battered grey Converse that have taken me from tube hanging in London, to Uber trips in LA, to walking until my feet ache all the way back to the Paul Williams Suite. Evelyn is right, I don't fit in. 'I do believe you,' I manage to choke out.

'Listen, Lily, the thing is, me and Evelyn, things aren't what you think.' He reaches out, lifting my chin so I have to look at him.

No. Lily, you can't do this.

'There's been a development.' Pulling away, I am keen to change the subject. 'Honey is in her room with Joe… her *fiancé*.'

'Her… oh my gosh.' Dropping his hand, Louis shakes his head. 'I'm guessing that *he* doesn't know?' He nods towards a booth at the back of the bar, where Magnus sits, his head slumped over an untouched cup of coffee.

'Oh man.' I turn away before he can lift his head and make eye contact with me. 'Drunk?'

'Yep. I made him a coffee, but this is the second one he's let go cold in front of him. I kinda don't want to remind him of where he is just in case he asks for a whisky.'

'What are we going to do with him?'

'I'm not sure there's anything we can do.' Louis nods as Magnus lifts his head briefly. 'You're certain someone… something is going to happen to Honey tomorrow?'

'Pretty certain, yeah.' *Definitely certain. Wikipedia might not be that reliable, but it doesn't lie about things this big.* 'Magnus is going to be furious when he finds out about their engagement. I think I managed to get Honey inside before the tabloids realised the true nature of her relationship with Joe, but I should imagine there will be some speculation.'

'Do you think we could get Tilda to leak something? About how Honey is recovering well alone in her hotel room? It might not work, but it's worth a shot, if it means Magnus doesn't find out until after Saturday. That'll give us more time to break the news gently, if necessary.'

My gut twists at the realisation that it probably won't be me who deals with Magnus. That I'll be back in 2019, with unlimited traffic jams and the sweet cloying scent of vape smoke on the air, on my knees scrubbing out the tub that Honey Black once bathed in. 'Good idea. Do you mind speaking to Tilda? I'm going to see Jessica now; I need to let her know that Honey is back from the hospital.'

'She doesn't know?' Louis frowns.

'Not that I know of. She wasn't there this morning, but she was pretty upset and exhausted last time I saw her.' I'm keen to get out of the Polo Lounge before Magnus realises I'm here. 'Thank you, Louis, for everything.'

Louis takes my hand, linking my fingers through his and squeezing. I squeeze back, not trusting myself to speak, and then hurry towards Jessica's suite, my mind working overtime, trying to drown out my heart.

I pass Jean in the corridor, and she gives me a tight-lipped smile.

'How is Honey?' she asks. There is a note of something I can't quite put my finger on in her voice. Almost concern, but not quite. Something different.

'She's good,' I say, watching her face, but it's a blank mask, the same pleasant expression she puts on for everyone on set. The only time I've really seen Jean become anything other than bland or annoyed is when she's talking about Leonard. And Honey and Leonard together, in particular. An image of Jean, rummaging about in the garage on location, far before anyone else made it to the set looms in my mind. 'Honey's in her room. Alone.' I add, as an afterthought.

'Hmm. Good.' Jean nods. 'I can't stop, I have to be somewhere.'

'Jean?'

'Yes?'

'What are you doing tomorrow?'

'Tomorrow?'

'Yes, tomorrow. Saturday. We're not filming, because Leonard wants Honey to rest, so I wondered if you were busy.'

'Err...' Jean flushes a hot pink. 'I'm pretty busy. I'm going to take a long, hot bath and read my new novel, and maybe... maybe paint my nails.'

'Excellent. Sounds like you have your day all planned out.' It sounds terribly boring, and I wonder if she's lying to me – or if she thinks I was going to ask her to spend the day with me. That would probably be her worst nightmare.

Watching as she hurries away, I realise she must have come from Jessica's room. Honey's suite is on the same floor as Jessica's – Honey's at the far end, while Jessica's is closer to the elevator – while mine and Jean's rooms are on the floor above. I knock lightly on Jessica's door and wait a moment.

'Lily, darling. How are you?' Jessica opens the door looking much better than the last time I saw her. Her hair is curled into loose waves, and as we aren't filming today due to the accident, she wears a thin silk dressing gown, with a ruffled feather trim in a rich, yellowy cream. I think longingly of my worn marl grey Shein loungewear that I bought for twenty quid from a Facebook advert and wonder if this is the 1940s Hollywood equivalent. 'Do come in. What can I do for you?'

'Well.' I feel a bit wrong-footed. I thought that Jessica would have been waiting for news of Honey, but then I remember Jean scurrying away down the corridor. 'I just came to let you know that Honey is back from the hospital. She's a little shaken, but she's going to be fine.'

'Oh, that's wonderful news.' Jessica smiles. 'I was going to call the hospital but then Jean told me Honey was being discharged this morning. I wanted to go and see her...' Her voice cracks and she runs a finger under her eye. 'I just found it too difficult. Every time I think of Honey, I see the… the car, the way it…'

'I understand. It was very upsetting for everyone; it must have been awful for you.' I pass her a tissue from the box on the table. 'I saw Jean in the corridor.'

'Oh?' Jessica reaches for the teapot on the small coffee table and pours herself a cup, pouring one for me without asking. 'Yes, she popped by to see how I was.'

'That was good of her,' I say, but a spark of irritation flares. Jean hasn't been to see how Honey is.

'I'm so pleased Honey is home and resting well. She must be exhausted.'

'She's pretty tired,' I say. 'She was rather overwhelmed at the hospital. I've never seen so many flowers and gifts. She's a popular woman. She even had flowers from Alfred Hitchcock.'

'Alfred…?' Jessica says faintly. 'My goodness. How wonderful.'

'He has a script he wants to send over to her.' I feel absurdly proud.

'*Really?*' Jessica's eyes widen, her hands pressing to her mouth. 'Well, that really is wonderful news. Although, maybe keep it under wraps from Leonard for the time being. He doesn't want to lose his rising star just yet!' She raises her eyebrows. '*Alfred Hitchcock*. My goodness.' She reaches for her teacup, knocking the table holding the teapot, and I reach out to steady it before it can spill over the *Goodtime Gal* script on the table. Jessica hurriedly picks the script up.

'I thought I would use the extra time to work on my lines,' she says primly. Parts of the script are underlined, and I feel a little surprised that she was able to focus on learning her lines when Honey was still in the hospital.

I know I couldn't think about anything except Honey, but then, I know things Jessica doesn't. As if reading my mind, she sighs, hugging the script to her. 'I didn't get much done, I'm ashamed to say. It's all been terribly—' A choked sob escapes her before she shakes herself and smiles bravely.

'I know you're very upset. But I wanted you to know Honey is OK and she'll probably want to see you...'

'Oh of course, that goes without saying. I'll go and see her shortly. I'll bring her some champagne.'

'And I wondered if...' I swallow, not wanting to ask a favour of a woman who is a Hollywood household name, 'you would mind... not *looking after* Magnus, but keeping an eye on him?'

'Magnus?' Jessica freezes with her cup halfway to her lips, her eyes narrowing. 'Why on earth would I need to look after Magnus?'

'He's a little... upset too,' I say. 'He's been in the bar all night, and he's in a bit of a state. I'm worried about Honey – he seems completely unable to let her go, and I'm concerned that he'll... do something silly.'

'Really.' It's a statement, not a question, and her tone is as frosty as a November morning in London, as Jessica lowers her cup to the table and gets to her feet. 'Don't worry about Magnus, Lily. You leave him to me.'

Chapter Twenty-Six

'I did it.' Tilda is wriggling on the bench with excitement, dangerously close to knocking the newspaper next to her onto the path, as I enter Sunset Park, across from the hotel. 'I called the newspapers and leaked it that Honey was in her hotel room alone. I referred to myself as a "source close to the actress".' She sits back, unbelievably pleased with herself.

'Brilliant, you're a diamond.' I sink onto the bench next to her, enjoying the rays of sunlight that weave their way through the trees overhead. 'Fingers crossed this stops any news of Honey and Joe's engagement reaching Magnus's – or Leonard's – ears… for now, anyway.'

'Do you think one of them will try to kill Honey?'

I sigh. 'Honestly, I'm still not sure, but this information could be the one thing that tips Magnus, at least, over the edge. Louis said he's been drunk since last night, and he doesn't seem terribly stable.'

'Has Leonard said anything about the accident?' Tilda is serious, her eyes wide.

'I haven't had the courage to speak to him about it. He was furious at the hospital, while we were waiting to see Honey. He was pacing and hissing at Jean about how it shouldn't have happened.'

'The accident shouldn't have happened, or Honey shouldn't have walked away from it?' Tilda raises an eyebrow and nausea washes over me.

'I don't know. Jean brought me into it then – she said all this trouble with the press, and then the accident, has only happened since I arrived.'

'She said *what*?'

'It's such a mess.' I blink back tears. 'Part of me wishes I didn't know what was going to happen, and the other part of me wishes I knew more.' I wish there had been more than a cursory two paragraphs dedicated to her death in that trashy book of scandals. I wish someone had cared enough to refuse to allow Hollywood to hide what happened. When I think back to how Eric and I had discussed Honey in her suite, seventy years after it all happened, I wish I hadn't laughed it off as an old legend, a ghost story designed to spook the tourists. Now, I feel sick with the knowledge that I just dismissed her, another story to be forgotten in time.

'Sooo...' Tilda says slowly, 'tomorrow is the day. What's the plan? How are we going to keep Honey safe?'

'A stakeout.'

'Whaaat?' Tilda starts to bounce again, the bench creaking under her slight weight. 'Are you kidding me? Like, a real-life stakeout? Lily, this is just like being in the movies for real!'

'Real being the operative word.' I press a hand on her arm to still her. 'Til, I know this is exciting, but it is real life. Honey really is going to get hurt, and we're all in trouble if the killer finds out that we know, OK? We have to be cool.'

'OK, cool, I'm cool.' Tilda stops bouncing and looks a little sheepish. 'Sorry.'

'We have to stay focused. I spoke to Jessica earlier this morning and asked her to keep an eye on Magnus.'

'You did?!' Tilda presses her hands to her mouth. 'What did she say? I can't believe you asked a favour of a movie star.'

Neither can I. 'Well, her words were, "Leave Magnus to me". She didn't sound very happy – I think deep down Jessica knows what kind of person Magnus really is. It's not what you want for your best friend, is it?'

'Absolutely not.' Tilda shakes her head solemnly. 'What about Leonard and Jean?'

'Jean says she's planning on a pamper day in her room. Bath, reading her novel, painting her nails. She might have been bluffing – let's not forget that Jessica said she saw her leave the garage on set the morning the brakes failed on Honey's car – but she's on the same floor as me, so she should be easy to keep tabs on if she does leave the room. I have no idea where Leonard will be, which is where you guys come in.'

'What do you want me to do?'

'Can you be at the hotel early? I need you to stake out the lobby and if he leaves, follow him. I know that the murder will take place in Honey's hotel room, so the murderer will at some point obviously be in the hotel. That makes it difficult, as most of the suspects will all be there tomorrow at some point or another. If you can keep your eyes on Leonard, and let me know if he's in the hotel, that will help.'

'OK. And Billy and Cynthia?'

I pause for a moment, rubbing my hands over my eyes. 'Billy can't go far with a broken ankle, and I don't think he is a threat to Honey. Cynthia, on the other hand...'

'Especially when she sees this.' Tilda unfolds the newspaper that sits on the edge of the bench. The headline reads *BLACK AND WALTERS IN HORROR SMASH*, and the photo beneath a picture of the mangled car wreck is the revived one of Billy and Honey leaving the Palomino.

'Yikes.' I smooth a hand over the page, ink staining my fingertips. 'I think it's a good job you leaked it that Honey is recovering alone.' Louis must have seen the papers this morning to have suggested it.

'I have an idea to get rid of Cynthia tomorrow,' Tilda says. She gets to her feet and holds out an arm. 'Come on, walk with me.'

I follow Tilda out on to the footpath that meanders through the park, past the pond filled with large koi, ducks paddling frantically on top of the water.

'I'm going to call Cynthia tonight,' Tilda says in a low voice, the newspaper tucked under her arm, 'and invite her to an audition in Burbank – the Disney studios are located there, and since they've been so successful with the cartoons, I don't think she'll turn it down.'

'Cartoons? *Oh.*' It takes me a moment to understand, before I remember *Sleeping Beauty*, *Cinderella*. All the Disney animated movies that I grew up watching.

'Cynthia will definitely want to audition – apparently the studio is talking about making *Alice in Wonderland*. Cynthia is so vain she'd love to voice Alice.'

'I love...' *that movie* is on the tip of my tongue, '...that idea. Tilda, you're a genius.'

'She'll have to go all the way out to Burbank, and once she realises there is no audition, it'll be too late for her to come back and cause problems. And in any case, one of us will be waiting in the lobby to watch her return.'

Tilda blushes, her cheeks clashing with her red hair, as she brushes the tip of her sneaker along the concrete.

'You actually are brilliant.' I stop and grin at her. 'You've really researched this, haven't you? Finding out which movie Disney are looking at producing next, planning to leak stuff to the papers.'

'Maybe I could make a good investigative reporter after all.'

'You know what, Tilda? I reckon you probably would.'

–

Louis is leaning against Christine as I walk back into the hotel grounds, the sun starting to lower in the sky. There is no sign of Evelyn, thankfully, although I do give a half glance over my shoulder just in case she pops out of the shrubbery, and my heart speeds up at the sight of him. He looks tanned and relaxed, his hair ruffled in the breeze, and I can't help returning the grin that spreads across his face as he sees me.

'You see Tilda?' Louis grins, his face lighting up. 'She's something else, huh?'

'She's wonderful.' *And wasted sitting at home, married to Reg, popping out a baby a year for the next few years.* But I don't say that out loud. 'Is Magnus gone?' I glance towards the entrance to the hotel lobby, half expecting him to come stumbling out.

'Sure is. He staggered back to his room not long after you left, and I haven't seen him since.'

'Hopefully he'll sleep until tomorrow, and then Jessica said she would keep an eye on him.'

'What about Honey?' Louis asks.

'Honey?'

'You have everything else in place – Jessica and Magnus, Jean in her room, Tilda watching Leonard, but what about Honey? How are you going to keep an eye on her? She'll think it's odd if you follow her around all day on what is supposed to be your day off.'

I can't believe I didn't think about this earlier. I was so focused on making sure everyone else was covered that I forgot I need to watch Honey as well. 'I could try and get her out of the hotel for the day?' I say, feeling my brows knit together. 'Maybe Joe could take her somewhere?'

'There's a cute diner out on Highway 39 that my mom used to take us to as kids,' Louis says. 'It's far enough to keep them out for a while, and Honey shouldn't get pestered by the public. They do an amazing pie – boysenberry. You can't get it anywhere else.'

'Boysenberry... do you mean Knott's Berry Farm?'

'Yeah! That's the place! I can't believe you know about it.' Louis shakes his head. 'We should go for pie once all this is over.'

'We should,' I say, trying to keep the upbeat tone to my voice. Knott's Berry Farm isn't just a diner in 2019 – it's an amusement park, where you can still get the pie, and jam, and pan for gold. 'It sounds like the perfect place to keep Honey out of harm's way.'

'Lily.' Louis's face grows sombre, and the giddiness of having created a plan for tomorrow fades slightly. 'Have you ever thought that... maybe this won't work? That, while we may be able to keep Honey safe tomorrow, there's no guarantee that whoever it is who wants to hurt her won't try again another day?'

Louis has a point, and it's one that I've tossed around in my mind over and over again since I got here. 'Have you ever heard of the butterfly effect?' I have a vague idea that it won't be discovered until the 1960s, but in for a penny and all that.

'The butterfly effect? No, I haven't.'

'Basically, it's the idea that one tiny change could have a huge impact on future events. For example, a tiny butterfly flaps its wings, causing a shift in the atmosphere and creating a tornado further down the line.'

Louis frowns and says nothing.

'What I mean is, by us making this change tomorrow, it will hopefully change everything. Honey won't die, the killer will realise we know something is going to happen, the killer might run out of the hotel and get hit by a car—'

'That's a bit drastic.'

'—Honey will realise that Joe is what she wants and run away with him… any one of those things could happen, changing Honey's fate forever.' My voice echoes around the almost empty parking lot, and I glance around to make sure we are not overheard. 'Basically,' I whisper, 'if we can change this one thing, we could save Honey's life – change Honey's life – forever.'

The way Louis looks at me now, as I finish my speech, my chest rising and falling as the passion that sparked in my veins begins to ebb away, makes heat rise in all sorts of parts of my body.

'Lily, about what I was trying to tell you about Evelyn and me earlier…'

Before Louis can finish speaking there is a shout from an open window, a frantic cry overhead.

'Help! Someone call the police! Please, it's an emergency!'

Chapter Twenty-Seven

I twist my head, spying a tousled, dark blond head peering out of the window, waving at us.

'It's Joe...' I whisper, my brain struggling to put the pieces together. 'It's Joe! Louis, that's Honey's room...' I am already running, my pulse pounding in my ears as I yank open the doors to the rear entrance and sprint past the Polo Lounge. Did I get it wrong? Did I mix the dates up? How could I have been so stupid? Eric had definitely said the twenty-fifth of June, hadn't he? And today is definitely Friday... the thoughts tumble over one another as I race along the hallway, my breath coming hard and fast.

As I reach Honey's hotel room the door flies open and Joe appears, distraught and dishevelled. 'Where is she?' I demand. 'What's happened?'

'She's in there. Oh God, please... did you call the operator? Is there a doctor coming?' Joe runs his hand through his hair as I push past him to where Honey sits on the chaise, fighting for breath. Her lips are a horrible shade of blue as she gasps and chokes.

'Oh no.' I turn to Joe. 'What has she eaten?'

'Huh? What...?'

'For fuck's sake, Joe! What has she eaten?'

He stares at me for a moment. 'Brownies,' he says, gesturing with shaking hands to the open box on the table.

'We had a brownie... she had two bites and then she just started... coughing and... and choking.'

Of course, she wouldn't have been able to resist. 'Honey, listen to me.' I crouch down, taking her hand in mine, and she looks at me, her eyes wide with fright. 'Try to breathe... slowly... don't panic, you're going to be OK. Joe – the phone, there on the counter – call the operator, call down to reception, I don't care who you call, just call someone!'

Joe looks around wildly for the telephone, knocking it off the counter as he fumbles for the receiver, panic making him clumsy. Honey fights for breath, her lips going from blue to purple, and I feel panic scratching at my insides as her eyes begin to close. This is it. A fucking brownie. I tried so hard and all it took was a fucking brownie.

'Stay awake,' I plead, squeezing her hands tightly in my own. 'Just keep breathing, in and out, that's it. Come on, Honey.' Glancing up at Louis I see my own panic and fear reflected back at me.

'Move back!' What feels like a hundred years later, a voice comes from the open hotel room door. 'Miss, out of the way, please! Move back I said!'

I stand, reluctantly dropping Honey's hand as an older gentleman with a cloud of fluffy white hair pushes me to one side. He has a large black bag with him, and as he pulls out a syringe, I realise he's a doctor. Or at least, I hope he is.

'She ate a brownie,' I stutter. 'It... it must have had nuts in. She's allergic.'

An arm wraps tightly around my shoulder, and I smell the familiar scent of Louis's aftershave as he pulls me close. I turn away, resting my face against his chest as the doctor administers a shot to Honey, and suddenly, finally, the rasping in her chest stops. I can't look for a moment, fear that I have failed to save her metallic on my tongue.

'Louis?' I whisper, my face still pressed against the soft cotton of his shirt.

'She's breathing.' The words tumble out with his breath, and my limbs feel limp and soggy.

'There.' The doctor stands back, keeping a watchful eye on Honey until he is satisfied that her breathing is regular and strong before he turns to Louis. 'Anaphylactic shock is extremely dangerous. I've given her a shot of adrenaline and she should be OK now, but you need to keep an eye on her. Let her rest, and any sign of her losing consciousness or irregularity in her breathing, you call me. I'm in room 201 if you need my help again.'

Louis thanks him and walks him to the door, as I help a muted Joe lay Honey down on the chaise, her face pale, her lips finally turning their usual blush pink.

'Honey?' I stroke her hair away from her face, as Joe perches next to her, his face the colour of old milk. Honey opens her eyes, blinking slowly. 'Oh gosh, you scared us so badly.'

'Scared myself.' The words are Kentucky thick as she smiles tiredly, her eyes closing again briefly. 'They looked just like the brownies my mother used to make.' She gives a feeble laugh and I smile, pressing my lips to her forehead.

'Sleep now, you need the rest,' I say, waiting until her eyes are completely closed and her breathing slows before I turn to Joe. 'What happened? Where did the brownies come from?'

'Gifts.' Joe points to the expanse of flowers, wine and bakery boxes that still litter the suite. 'These things had already been delivered to the suite before Honey came home from the hospital.'

Louis is already at the small coffee table, turning the open brownie box over in his hands. 'This one?'

'Yeah. I fed her the brownie – I thought it would be romantic, you know?' Joe says. 'I didn't know she was allergic... how did I not know?' He looks bereft, turning his gaze to where Honey lies sleeping.

'I only know because we ate together when I first started working with her,' I say.

'Lil,' Louis's voice is low, and there is a sharp note to it that makes me look up. 'Look at this.'

I take the box from him and he reaches in, pushing the remaining brownies aside. Tucked beneath the crumbly, squidgy cake is a note, folded neatly in half, on lavender paper. It reads: *I TOLD YOU THIS WAS YOUR LAST WARNING.*

'Oh my God.' I press one hand to my mouth, holding the note in my other hand with my fingertips, not wanting to contaminate either myself or the page. I can almost feel the hatred oozing off the paper, the fierce warning slashed into the page in harsh black lines. 'This wasn't an accident, was it?'

'It doesn't look that way,' Louis says. 'Is it the same as the other notes?'

'Almost.' I turn the paper over, but the other side is blank. 'The same words but written, instead of cut out of newspaper. Someone else knows Honey is allergic to nuts. Someone sent these deliberately.'

'Why would someone want to do that?' Joe's accent is more pronounced the more upset he is, his words thick like taffy. 'Why would someone want to hurt Honey?'

274

'That's the million-dollar question,' Louis says grimly. 'It's time to involve the police, Lily. This has gone too far now.'

I nod wearily, my battery drained. I've tried my hardest to keep Honey safe, but Louis is right. It's time to let the police take over. 'Yes, you're right. Who do I call? The station?' I feel disconnected, as if this is all a dream and any moment now, I'll wake up like Dorothy, back in my own bed with my loved ones all looking on, concern etched onto their faces. *Only there aren't any loved ones left, not now my mum is gone.*

'No.' Her voice is barely above a whisper, but Honey's eyes fly open, and she struggles into a sitting position. 'No police.'

'Honey.' Joe rushes to her side, squeezing his large frame onto the edge of the chaise next to her. He takes one of her tiny hands in his and kisses her temple. 'You need to rest.'

There is a brisk knock on the door, and each of us freezes in place.

'I'll go,' Louis says, hurrying across the carpet as another sharp rap comes from outside. A moment later Jessica walks quickly across the carpet, steady on her skyscraper heels as she reaches out for Honey.

'How are you, sweetie?' she asks, almost pushing Joe out of the way to sit next to Honey. 'Are you feeling better? You look...' Jessica looks up, our silence heavy in the air. 'What is it? What's happened?'

'Honey had an allergic reaction,' I say. 'It was serious. She could have died.'

Jessica's face changes, the smile dropping from her perfect red lips. 'Allergic reaction?' She looks at Honey. 'To what?'

'Nuts, in the brownies,' Honey says, stronger now. 'My throat closed, and I couldn't breathe.'

'Oh Honey, you poor dear, that must have been terrifying.' Jessica runs her eyes over Honey's face, as if checking to make sure she really is breathing properly.

'It was,' I say. 'Utterly terrifying.'

'Close call,' Joe mutters, looking at the floor.

'But you're OK now?' Jessica asks Honey. 'You don't still feel ill?'

'I'm fine now,' Honey says, but she still looks washed out and clammy, the tiny tendrils of blonde at her temples damp with sweat as she shifts to make room on the chaise for Jessica. 'It was an accident.'

'Two accidents in a week!' Jessica looks horrified. 'This is too much, Honey. I'm going to call Leonard.'

'He don't need to know,' Honey says, fear sparking behind her eyes. 'I don't want him...' She looks down at her hands, not meeting Joe's eyes. 'I don't want him to send me home.'

Jessica looks at Joe as if just noticing him for the first time. 'Who's this guy?' she peers closely at him. 'You look kind of familiar. Did you have something to do with this? Lily, what are you doing letting a stranger in here?'

'Oh no, Joe is—'

'A friend of Honey's,' I butt in, still not sure that Joe's status as Honey's fiancé should be common knowledge just yet, not even to Jessica. 'Just visiting, that's all.'

'Well, this is shocking,' Jessica says, still clutching Honey's hand. 'You must rest, you poor darling. You need to take care what you eat, you know that. Leonard needs you to be fit and well for filming on Monday – it was hard enough to get him to agree to these few days off.'

'We need to call the police. This wasn't an accident.' I move towards the telephone on the counter.

'No police,' Honey repeats. 'Lily, please don't call them. I ate the brownies. It was my own fault; I should have checked. Whoever sent them wasn't to know I had an allergy.'

'They did though, Honey.' I hold up the note, so she can read the angry black scrawl. 'Someone did, and they deliberately sent you those brownies knowing you have a terrible sweet tooth. They knew you wouldn't be able to resist them.'

Her face drains of colour and she sinks back against the cushions of the chaise. Jessica's face is a similar shade, her usually creamy skin taking on a sickly wasabi green.

'Calling the police is the sensible thing to do,' Jessica says, her hand shaking as she raises it for quiet, 'but it might not be the best idea. Honey's already had so much negative press, if the newspapers find out about this then...' She tails off, looking at the carpet.

'Look,' I say, ignoring Jessica. 'They used the same wording as last time, on the newspaper notes. Honey, the brownies weren't an accident, and I don't think the car crash was an accident either. I think someone really does want to hurt you.'

'But why?' Joe interrupts. 'Why would someone want to hurt Betty... Honey?'

'I have no idea, but I'm going to find out. In the meantime, Honey, we need to make sure you're protected and that means—'

'No police,' she repeats again, her voice low. 'I know you mean well, Lily, but Jessica is right, I can't afford to have the police involved.'

'I really do think you need to respect Honey's wishes,' Jessica says.

'Honey...' Joe's voice holds a hint of desperation as he fumbles for her hand again, but she knocks him away and gets to her feet.

'No,' Honey says wheezily, as she starts to pace. 'It's my life – I get to decide, not you. Everyone always wants to tell me the best thing to do, and for once I want to do what *I* want. I want to finish this movie. I *am* Sophia, *I am the Goodtime Gal*. I want my name to be up in lights in the theatres, I want everyone in America to know my name. I want directors to beg me to star in their movies. I want to prove to everyone back home that I made the right decision, that I was *good* enough. That's what I want. And then after...' she turns to Joe, 'I want us to go home, and make things right with my family.'

'Oh, Honey. That's what I want too.' Joe's eyes take on a misty sheen, and I find I have to blink, too.

'But don't think we're stayin' there.' Honey is on a roll now. 'We're comin' back to Hollywood and we're going to take the world by storm. Joe, if you don't want to farm, you won't have to, and if you do want to... well then, I'll buy you a farm. And you, Lily, I'm gonna give you the biggest pay rise you've ever had.'

'Honey, you don't need to...'

'And that is why you can't call the police.' Breathless now, Honey sinks back down on to the chaise and gratefully accepts the glass of water that Jessica hands to her. 'I can't do any of that if you call the police, Lily.'

'Lily just wants you to be safe,' Louis says gently. 'That's all.'

'I do understand that.' Honey is meek now, her fire has almost run its course. 'But if you call the police Lily, all hell will break loose, and the newspapers will be outside the window before you can shake a stick. I can't risk it. I can't risk making Leonard mad. After all, he told me after the last run-in with the paparazzi that that was it – it was my last warning.'

Chapter Twenty-Eight

I look through the remaining gifts, carefully checking for anything else that may contain nuts, feeling oddly peaceful despite the drama of the day and what is to follow in twenty-four hours. Glancing up at the others, my heart twists in my chest. These people are my friends. How can I leave? How can I leave some of the most wonderful people I have ever met, to go back to a time when I felt so alone? Eric is my only friend in LA, and I disappeared on him without any kind of explanation, so who knows if he'll ever speak to me again? In London, my friends had fallen away when Mum got sick, and now Mum is gone too. I've never even met my dad.

'Lily – here.' Jessica hands me a hot cup of tea. 'Are you all right? Tonight has been shocking for everyone.' Despite her words the colour has come back into her cheeks, and she looks as poised as ever. 'Do you really think someone did this deliberately?'

'How do you explain the threatening notes?' I say, making sure to keep my voice down so Honey doesn't hear. 'On its own I probably could have rationalised it somehow… but the fact that the note was in the brownie box means someone meant to hurt Honey. They knew she wouldn't be able to resist eating those brownies; she's constantly starving on that stupid diet of hers and she has such a sweet tooth.'

'It all seems so unbelievable… like something out of a movie.' Jessica shakes her head. 'It's more likely a coincidence that the brownies contained nuts. And I already told you, the letters from oddballs come with the territory.'

'Not like these, though. I'm worried.' I nod in Honey's direction, where she sits with Joe. 'I know she can be demanding and thoughtless sometimes, but she's been so kind to me. I want to protect her from the awful things that could happen. Protect her from people like Leonard. Like Magnus.' I watch Jessica's face for a reaction to those names, but her expression is blank. 'Maybe I should call the police.'

'Don't worry about Magnus. I have him all in hand. Although,' Jessica gives me a sideways glance, 'I'm still not sure why you're so worried about him. He's just an egotistical asshole.'

'Call it women's intuition.'

Jessica gives me a long look, before hugging me and then Honey goodbye and heading to her room. Honey's eyelids are drooping, so I motion to Louis for us to leave too.

'*Her last warning,*' I say to Louis as he walks me to the elevator. I have the half empty box of brownies under my arm, having rescued them from the bin where Joe threw them out. 'That's what the note said.'

'You think Leonard could be behind it all?' Louis asks. 'But why? Why would he want to hurt Honey? I thought she was meant to be the star of this movie – she's going to make him a fortune. What would he gain?'

Because I read it in a book, seventy years from now. Instead, I say, 'I don't know – professionally nothing. But if their relationship has been personal, then maybe he's warning her not to mess him around. Perhaps he's worried that the papers will find out they've been seeing each other – that could be damaging to his reputation. He's a married man.'

'So, Honey being seen with Billy – another married man – doesn't help,' Louis thinks out loud. 'He's worried they'll be discovered.'

'And then there's Magnus… he's already proven himself to have a wicked temper, and I honestly think he believes Honey belongs to him.'

'Now Joe is on the scene…'

'And Magnus still doesn't know about their engagement – I'm dreading how he'll react to that news. It's all a complicated mess.'

Louis pauses as I jab at the button to call the elevator, shifting on the balls of his feet. 'Lily, listen…' The tips of his ears turn pink, and he looks down, linking his fingers in mine. 'I wanted to say… whatever happens tomorrow; however things turn out… I think you're amazing. You're probably the most incredible woman I've ever met. You're brave, and funny, and kind and… you buy drinks too.' He grins and I grin back, my chest filling with something unexplainable. Something light, and full, and *good*.

'I think you're pretty swell, too,' I manage to say.

'Well… that's *brilliant* then,' Louis says, mimicking my British accent, and then he brushes my curls away from my face and kisses me. *Really* kisses me.

As his mouth meets mine, I swear I can see sparks fly. He kisses me long and deep and my legs turn to jelly. I am breathless, my pulse roaring in my ears and I swear, if this was a movie, fireworks would be exploding all over the place. I have never in my life been kissed the way Louis is kissing me, and as he presses his forehead to mine, our lips parting for a moment, I have only one thought. That he is *the one*. With that thought I pull away, conflicted and confused.

'I'm sorry,' Louis says. 'I shouldn't have done that. Lily, I'm so, so sorry, I'm…'

'I should go,' I whisper, grateful for the ding of the elevator bell as I slip into the car before Louis can say another word.

Maybe that's why I don't notice anything out of the ordinary when I step along the corridor to my room, my fingers pressed to my lips, my head filled with stars, until a body slams into me. An arm tightens around my waist from behind as I am shoved against the wall, the banana-leaf wallpaper a green blur as my face presses against it. My mouth is covered with a sour-smelling palm as I shriek behind it, my cries lost as panic courses through me.

'You were… told…' a husky voice, the sound of dark alleyways and silent underpasses, of footsteps keeping time in the dark, hisses in my ear, '…to mind your own… damn business.'

Momentarily, I freeze. I'm not being mugged by a random stranger in the corridors of one of the world's greatest hotels. This is related to Honey.

'You'd better leave town, you little bitch. Or you'll regret it.' The body pressed against me is wiry and hard, my breath hitching in tiny gasps as I struggle to breathe. 'Next time, I won't be so friendly.' He snickers in my ear, the arm about my waist tightens, my ribs screaming.

I nod, before simultaneously biting down on the fleshy palm that fills my mouth and kicking back and up with my sneakered foot. I make contact and judging by the shriek and the way the palm is whipped away from my face, I hit the right spot.

'*Bitch.*' The word is spiky with venom. 'I mean it. Get the fuck outta town or else.' And then I hear the whoosh of the door to the stairs opening as I sag limply against the wall, my face still pressed to the wallpaper.

–

Now, early morning sun streaming in through my open curtains, I scrub my hands over my face and swing my legs out of bed, heading for the shower. As steam fills the bathroom, I play the scene back, as if I'm in the editing suite. How did I step out of the elevator without seeing him? *Who was he?* My ribs ache as I stand, and I push a palm to my forehead, where my head hit the wall. He was too short to be Leonard, and too wiry to be Magnus. *Get the fuck outta town.* Whoever he was, the message was very clear. Whoever wants to kill Honey knows that I suspect something, and they're not afraid to let me know.

I stand under the hot water, letting it pound on my scalp and the bruise that is forming on my forehead. I thought I was finally getting somewhere – I have a solid plan in place for protecting Honey today, and I just have to make it through the next twelve hours without any hiccups. Only now, in addition to being assaulted and trying to keep Honey alive, there is the *other thing*. Why had Louis kissed me? Whatever I feel for Louis would be a huge mistake, on my part and on his, and not just because of Evelyn. The truth is, I feel much the same as he does, and if things were different, I'd run straight into his open arms. Only I know that this time tomorrow I will be back in 2019, where he will be ninety-six years old, and will have lived a full life without me. Today isn't a day for pondering my love life though. Today is the day that I need to save Honey Black — without getting killed myself.

—

'I don't want to go out,' Honey pouts, as I try to persuade her that Knott's Berry Farm will be fun. 'It's too hot, and I still don't feel well.'

'But Honey, I'm trying to help you.'

'Lily, Honey said no.' Joe stands protectively next to her, and I feel frustratingly outnumbered. 'She almost died last night; you have to respect that.'

She's going to die today! I want to scream at him, but instead I say, 'Honey, are you really set on not going out today?'

She nods, finally losing the pout.

'Then in that case, don't go out. And when I say don't go out, I mean *don't leave this room.* Either of you. You got me?'

'I don't know who you think made you the boss, Lily,' Honey says, crab-apple sour.

'Do. You. Get. Me?'

'But Lily—'

'No buts. Stay here. I mean it.' I grasp her by her upper arms and look into her navy eyes. 'After what happened yesterday, I mean to keep you safe, no matter what happens. If you really won't go out, then promise me you'll stay here with Joe.' I need to stop for a moment, my throat closing and my nose tingling. 'You're something special, Honey Black. I know you're going to be this big movie star and I'm just a PA, but you're important to me. You're my friend, and I think the world of you.' If all this goes wrong, I have to let her know that I really

285

tried, and no matter what she thinks, she doesn't need movies or Leonard Langford to be somebody. She already is somebody. 'I have never met anyone quite like you before.'

'Back at'cha, Lily Jones.' Honey's eyes light up and her cheeks pinken as she pulls me into a hug. I breathe in her familiar scent, feeling the weight of her arms around me, and pray that she'll still be around to hug tomorrow.

'Right.' I pull away, all brisk and British. 'I have things to do. Stay safe, you two.'

–

In the hotel lobby Tilda sits in a red Chesterfield, her newspaper held in front of her face like something out of a badly written spy novel. I give her a brief nod as I pass, lifting a hand in greeting to Louis who stands at the bar, polishing a tray of glasses. He meets my eye and I feel my cheeks burn at the memory of what happened outside the elevator last night.

The Polo Lounge is uncharacteristically quiet, and I choose a booth tucked into the corner, scanning to see if anyone could be the guy who assaulted me last night. Jean sits across the room by the open doors to the patio, her novel in front of her as she picks at a plate of pineapple and watermelon. I order eggs over easy and a glass of orange juice and sit back to observe, my nerve endings tingling every time the door to the lounge opens.

Jean doesn't lift her eyes from her book as she forks fruit into her mouth. Perhaps she was telling the truth when she said she was going to have a pamper day in her room. I feel a twinge of guilt at thinking she had lied, but then I remember Jessica telling me that she'd seen Jean early on set the day of the car accident, and then Jean's voice telling me her daddy was a mechanic, and I'm not so sure.

In the opposite corner of the room, Billy Walters sits in front of a plate of steak and eggs, his mouth downturned. His hair is mussed and untidy, a five o'clock shadow dusting his cheeks and chin, as he sits in shorts, one leg in plaster stuck out in front of him. I have no idea how they are going to get around shooting Billy with a broken leg, and I wonder if Leonard will replace him. If so, that gives Billy a motive for getting rid of Honey, seeing as she crashed the car.

Cynthia sits opposite him, perfectly made up and wearing what looks like a very expensive Chanel suit. She is talking loudly about her 'important audition in Burbank' and I exhale with relief. At least one part of the plan is running to schedule. I toy with my eggs, realising I'm too keyed up to eat, focusing my attention on the others. There is no sign of Leonard. Butterflies swarm in my stomach and I find myself half wishing that today was over already, even if it does mean going back to 2019 and spending my time hustling for production jobs and scrubbing other people's toothpaste stains out of the sink.

Movement across the room catches my eye and I see both Jean and Cynthia getting to their feet. They nod politely at each other, then I hear Cynthia squawking to Jean about her 'audition' before they both make their way towards the exit. Checking that Billy is still engrossed in his cold steak and eggs, I slide out after them. Cynthia marches straight through the lobby and out to a waiting car, as Tilda lowers her newspaper and tips me a wink. Jean, however, stands dithering in the lobby, by the elevator. I pull back out of sight. Jean checks her watch and paces a couple of times, and I think perhaps she's waiting for the elevator, when she tucks her novel into her handbag and marches briskly out of the lobby, onto the street outside.

'Well, that was weird.' Tilda gets to her feet and joins me. 'I thought she said she was staying in her room all day.'

'She did.' I frown. 'She looked a bit cagey, didn't she?'

'Want me to follow her?'

'No...' I think for a moment. 'Do you mind staying here? In the lobby? Only I think whatever happens to Honey is going to happen in her room, so I need to see who comes in and out of the hotel. If Jean is out, she's less of a threat.'

'But I thought Honey was leaving for the day?'

'Change of plan.' I explain what happened the night before and how Honey doesn't feel well. 'If you stay here and watch the lobby, I'll wait on Honey's floor. If anyone tries to get to her room, I can apprehend them. I just don't know how you'll be able to let me know that someone is on their way.'

'Wait here.' Tilda hurries into the bar and I turn my attention back to the lobby, where Billy Walters leans on his crutches, waiting for the elevator. Watching the numbers rise after he steps in, I only look away once I see the elevator stop two floors above Honey's. Billy's own floor.

'Here.' Tilda is slightly out of breath as she hands me a walkie talkie. 'Take one of these.'

'They're all the rage.' Louis's voice comes from over her shoulder, and I look up to see him grinning down at me. My breath catches in my throat, and I feel hot all over, a heavy blush rising from my chest to cover my neck. 'The security guys use them here at the hotel.'

Tilda has the good grace to move back to her stakeout position and I wait until she is seated before I speak.

'Louis, about last night…'

'I'm sorry,' he says, 'I shouldn't have done it.'

'It's just… I can't…' I look away. 'It wouldn't be a good idea for you to get involved with me.' I blink, aware of the sting of tears behind my eyes. 'But we're friends, right?'

'Lily, I…'

'I have to go and watch Honey's room.' I meet his eyes, but I am unable to read the look on his face. 'Keep watching the lobby.'

'Wait, Lil…' he reaches out, smoothing my hair away from my forehead. 'What the hell? You have a bruise.'

'I… after you left… a man assaulted me outside my room.'

'*What?* Jeez Lil, what happened?'

I shake my head, wincing as the movement makes my temples thud. 'He grabbed me, told me to mind my business. Or else. It's fine, I'm OK.'

Louis reaches out and lifts my chin, turning my face one way then the other, examining me. I can feel his breath on my cheek, and I close my eyes. 'Lil, this is dangerous. I don't want—'

'I can't talk about it now. I have to go and check on Honey. Just follow the plan, OK?' I give him a wobbly smile and head for the first-floor suites, pretending I haven't seen Tilda watching our every move over the top of her newspaper.

Chapter Twenty-Nine

Tucked into an alcove in the corridor, somewhere between the Paul Williams Suite where Honey languishes with Joe, and Jessica's smaller suite, I keep my eyes on the corridor. The elevator is a few feet down from where I hide, meaning I have the advantage of seeing anyone who steps out or comes through the doors to the stairway before they can see me, and so far all is quiet. As I wait, I think about the man from last night, the way he had pressed me hard against the wall, hissing threats into my ear. *What if he comes back?* The thought of it makes the hairs on the back of my neck lift and my knees grow shaky. There is no sign of Leonard, or of Magnus, and I don't know if this is a good thing or a bad thing.

A little before twelve thirty, there is movement at the end of the hallway and my pulse rockets, but it's just a waiter with a room service cart. Stepping out of the alcove I try to seem nonchalant yet busy as I stride past him, before slinking into the alcove on the other side of the elevator to watch where he goes. He knocks lightly at Jessica's door, then steps inside, before leaving without the cart a few moments later. As he walks towards the elevator, I glance at Jessica's closed door. She said she would watch Magnus, but she hasn't left her room yet, and I have to trust that she knows what she's doing. Reaching Honey's door I give a light double tap, relieved when she opens the door herself.

'Everything OK?' I ask.

'Fine,' she whispers. 'It's actually been nice to have a day away from set, relaxing in my suite. I haven't seen anyone all day.' She looks coy. 'Apart from Joe. We're going to stay here and play some chess.' She winks.

'Well, let's try and keep it that way.' I'm glad she's relaxed because my stress levels are through the roof. I point down the hall. 'I'll be just down there if you need me.'

'I still think you're being a little over dramatic, Lil,' Honey says, and I can tell she's resisting the urge to roll her eyes at me.

'Humour me.'

I slip back into the alcove, just in time to make myself invisible before Jessica's door opens. The room service cart rolls out, and then she steps out, wearing another chic Claire McCardell dress – this one is a deep blue, in a heavy, silky rayon, the entire body made up of tiny pleats that flare as she walks – and cute matching pumps. She fixes her collar and pulls on a pair of light summer gloves before she marches towards the lobby. I pull back, not wanting her to see me, although I'm not sure why. She must be leaving now to go and meet Magnus. I wait until she disappears from view before I pull out the walkie talkie.

'Tilda?'

'Lil? Any news?' Static crackles, her voice patchy and fragmented.

'Jessica is on her way. I think she might be meeting Magnus. Keep watching.'

'Will do.'

The corridor is silent, so I tiptoe my way to the room service cart, my stomach rumbling. If there's one thing I've learned in Hollywood, it's that actresses barely eat, and I lift the silver dome over the plate, hoping Jessica didn't suddenly decide she was starving. The remains of a fillet steak lie congealing in a pool of jus and blood, and I wrinkle my nose despite the growling from my belly. Thankfully Jessica hasn't touched the small bowl of fries that accompany it, and I tuck in, not caring that they are cold. Groaning as I lick the salt from my greasy fingers, I hear the elevator ding and hurriedly shove the dome back over the plate. There is something about the tray that doesn't look right, but I can't put my finger on it, and I don't have time to ponder as the same waiter steps off the elevator and I have to hurriedly make my way back to the safety of my alcove.

Twenty minutes later, all hell breaks loose.

–

'We have a problem,' Tilda's voice crackles through the walkie talkie, jumpy and distorted. 'Lily, I think… need… come…'

'What?' I shake the walkie talkie frantically. 'Tilda, what did you say?' I press the machine to my ear.

'You need to get back here!' Tilda's voice blares into my ear, all trace of static gone. 'We have a *situation.*'

Shit. I glance between the stairs and the elevator, wondering if it's safe to leave my alcove. I could miss someone coming to Honey's room. The light on the elevator stays sitting at the floor above. I wait for a moment, Tilda's voice growing increasingly shrill, before I sprint along the corridor.

I hear the commotion before I reach the lobby, and my feet slow as I round the corner to find the reception area bustling with paparazzi. The hotel manager, a tall, thin man with a gaunt face and jet-black hair stands ahead of them, waving his hands and trying desperately to push them back outside.

Tilda appears from behind a column, shoving her walkie talkie into her purse as she battles her way towards me.

'What the hell is going on?' I ask her, scanning the crowd.

'News just broke that Honey's first movie – you know the one she filmed with Jessica before Leonard offered her the part of Sophia? – is a smash hit in London. Lily, that picture is the most watched movie in theatres across Europe right now, and everyone is talking about Honey. Leonard sure knew what he was getting when he signed her.'

'Wait... what do you mean?' My brain can't seem to keep up.

'The movie – *Kentucky Queen*, it's called – is getting rave reviews across Europe and it's not Jessica that they're talking about. They're saying Honey stole the show, that she's the next Rita Hayworth, or Elizabeth Taylor.'

'My mum loved that movie.' Fierce, hot tears spring to my eyes and I blink rapidly.

'Huh?' Tilda frowns. 'Anyway, they knew Honey was staying here and then... well, it seems that sometime in the last fifteen minutes someone let slip that Joe and Honey might be engaged and... well, things got crazy.'

'Oh my God.' This is the worst thing that could have happened, today of all days. 'Magnus – have you seen Magnus?'

'Nope, no sign of him, but… I did go to the ladies' room a little while ago.' She looks sheepish. 'I had to! And Louis was watching the lobby. Jessica left around twenty minutes ago.'

That fits. But where is Magnus? 'We need to check his room and see if he's still there. If he is there, I don't want him to come down and see… this, he needs to hear the news away from here, where he can't hurt Honey.' My heart is in my mouth, and I feel dizzy, as if I can't get enough oxygen. 'What if he doesn't answer the door?'

Tilda holds up a key, swinging it from her forefinger. 'We use this.'

'Where did you get that?'

'From behind the front desk.' She shrugs nonchalantly, as the increasingly frantic hotel manager desperately tries to call in security. 'It's a skeleton key. I lifted it when this all kicked off. No one saw, don't worry.'

I make a grab for the key, but she holds it out of reach. 'No,' she says. 'I'll go and check on Magnus, you tell these guys something – anything – to get them to leave. They know you're Honey's PA, they'll listen to you.' And she sprints towards the stairs.

I hesitantly make my way to the edge of the scrum, holding up my hands. 'Guys, guys, quiet please!'

A firm hand lands on my elbow and I turn to see Joe standing behind me. 'Joe! What are you doing here? You're supposed to be looking after Honey.'

'She sent me,' he says, raising his shoulders slightly in a half shrug. 'She saw the cameras and all and she wanted to know what was going on. You told her not to leave the room, so she sent me.'

Oh no.

'That's him!' one of the paparazzi shouts. 'That's the guy! Here, you, over here! Look this way!'

Joe looks bewildered, as he turns from left to right, not sure where to look or who to listen to.

'No, this isn't him,' I shout, battling to make my voice heard. 'Wrong guy, sorry! This is… Honey's agent. Yes, her agent.' I shove Joe towards the bar, where Louis comes out to escort him into the back area.

'I have to go,' I whisper. 'Honey is alone, and I don't know where Magnus or Leonard are. Today is the day, Louis, and Honey is on her own.'

'Let me stash Joe somewhere safe and I'll meet you.' Louis's face crumples slightly. 'I don't want you to go in there alone, Lily.'

'Tilda is alone at the moment, checking on Magnus.' I bounce on my toes, eager to make it back to the Paul Williams Suite to see Honey is safe for myself. 'I'll see you there.'

Battling my way past the scrum of photographers, I promise them a full interview with Honey Black as soon as she is available, shoving my way between them until they part and let me through to the corridor. The elevator still sits at the floor above Honey's, but I hear footsteps hurrying down the stairs from above, and then Tilda's fiery hair appears, her face pale and solemn.

'He's not in his room,' she gasps, holding the skeleton key aloft. 'I knocked and there was no answer, so I just let myself in.'

'And no sign of him? What did the room look like?' *Was he furious before he left?*

'No, no sign of him. But the room wasn't trashed if that's what you mean. It was untidy, but then he's a guy.'

Tilda shrugs. 'And it stank of aftershave, like he had just showered and left.'

Maybe he did go and meet Jessica after all. I feel my shoulders come down from somewhere around my ears. 'I need to check on Honey.' I hurry along the corridor, Tilda close on my heels. The room service cart is gone, and the hallway feels cold and echoey. As I lift a hand to rap on Honey's door, my fingertips feel strangely numb, and I suddenly find it hard to swallow.

'Honey?' I tap again, harder this time, a cloak of dread enveloping my shoulders. 'Honey, it's me, Lily. I left Joe in the lobby; you can open up.' There is silence from the other side of the door, and with shaking hands I gesture for Tilda to pass me the skeleton key.

'Should we wait for Louis?' Tilda whispers. Her eyes are overly bright, and I think she feels it too. The overwhelming sensation that something is wrong.

'No.' Gripping the key so tightly my knuckles are white I shove it into the lock and turn, pushing the door open.

'*No.*' The word escapes my lips, even as I press my hands to my mouth. I am too late. I knew what was going to happen today, and Honey was alone for a matter of moments, but none of it matters anymore. I was too late.

Chapter Thirty

'Oh no.' The voice comes from behind me, from Tilda, whose face is white with shock. 'Oh no, no.'

Honey lies on the chaise, her face still and pale. One hand lies delicately across her stomach, resting on her sweet, pale pink dress. The other hand falls to the floor, her fingers slightly curled into her palm. Her white peep-toe heels lie at the bottom of the chaise as if she has kicked them off, although before or after being stabbed I couldn't say. She looks as if she is asleep – and if I tried hard enough, I could almost believe it – if it wasn't for the circle of crimson over her left breast, staining the pink silk.

Nothing else in the room is disturbed. The open door to the bedroom shows the mussed covers of the bed, a half empty glass of water still on the nightstand. In the main suite, Honey's script lies on the coffee table, her parts underlined, champagne glasses sitting next to it, the coupes drained. A chessboard is set up on the other side of the table, a game half finished. There is no evidence of an argument or a fight, no smashed glasses or overturned chairs. Honey's body draped across the chaise is the only sign of anything untoward.

'Honey.' I cross the room on leaden feet, swallowing down the nausea that rises. 'Honey, please.' Swallowing hard, I press my fingers to her wrist, her hand limp in mine, and then to her neck, frantically searching for a pulse, but there is nothing. Honey Black is dead, stabbed to death in her hotel room, just like they said would happen. 'Oh God Honey, I'm so sorry.' My throat is thick, pressure building behind my eyes, and Tilda reaches for my hand, her own face blotchy as her eyes redden.

'Honey? Honey!' The door bounces on its hinges as Joe flies into the room, Louis following behind him. 'No, no, no, Honey! What happened to her?' Joe's voice is a frantic shriek, his eyes wild. Pushing me aside, he runs to her, crouching next to the chaise and trying to lift her into his arms.

'Joe.' I say it gently, resting my hand on his shoulder. 'Joe, please, we're too late. She's gone.'

'She can't be,' Joe weeps, pressing his face into her hair. 'I only just found her again.'

'I'm so, so sorry, Joe. Louis.' My eyes meet his and see my own devastation mirrored back at me. 'Can you call someone? The police? Get the hotel manager to seal off the hotel? I don't know...' I am trying to remember everything I ever learned about preserving a crime scene from the true crime documentaries I would devour on Netflix, in between researching flights to LA and scrolling job adverts on Glassdoor and LA 411. 'I'm not sure what we need to do.' I turn to Joe. 'Joe, I don't think you should touch her... the police need to see how she was found.' But Joe is too busy sobbing, running his hand over Honey's hair as if trying to wake her.

And then I hear it. Faint, like a whisper on the breeze under Joe's cries. A rasp, and then a cough.

'Joe. Move back.' Pushing his shoulder, I force my way to Honey's side, not sure if I'm imagining it. I'm not. Gazing down at Honey I see the slightest rise of her ribcage, and then the cough comes again. 'She's alive!

Louis, she's alive!' I tear off my sweater and press it tightly against the wound on Honey's chest, not caring about the warm, sticky claret that stains my fingers. 'Call 911, get someone here right now!'

'911?' Louis looks at me in confusion.

'I've called the operator,' Tilda says, her hands shaking as she places the receiver down and comes to my side. She grasps Honey's hand tightly. 'The emergency services are on their way. Come on Honey, stay with us.'

Honey coughs again, and I think she tries to speak, her lips forming a single word as her eyes flicker open, and for a moment I meet her gaze. I don't know if she can see me, if she's still really there, but I hold my gaze steady, reassuring her that I won't leave her, and I'll do everything in my power to save her. After all, that's why I'm here, isn't it?

–

'So, Miss Jones, can you go over things one more time for me?' The detective sits back in his chair, looking far more relaxed than I feel. He crosses one ankle over his knee, pushing back his black fedora, smoke from his cigarette coiling around his head. The whole thing gives me a *Maltese Falcon* vibe, with Detective Schwartz as Bogey's Sam Spade, which would make me a less femme fatale version of Brigid O'Shaughnessy. 'I know it's difficult, but we need to get a clear picture of what happened to Miss Black today.'

Today. It's barely six o'clock and I feel as though I have been awake for days. How can it be less than twelve hours ago that I was downstairs with Tilda, planning the best way to keep Honey safe? Less than six hours ago I was speaking to Honey herself. A shudder runs through me, and I have to blink hard to fight back a fresh wave of tears. We are sitting in a side room at the hospital, while surgeons operate on Honey. The stab wound missed her heart by a matter of inches, but it did nick her spleen, so the doctors had to operate to remove it as a matter of urgency. I feel sick with the knowledge that a few inches higher, and she would have been dead immediately. A few minutes later, and she would have been gone, bled to death in the Paul Williams Suite, just like the book on Hollywood scandal said. *Only she didn't*, a voice whispers in my head. *I might not have been able to stop it from happening, but I* did *manage to save Honey's life.*

'I told you; Honey was staying in her room today. She didn't feel well. Someone gave her a brownie with nuts in yesterday, knowing she was allergic. She had a severe reaction to it, and she didn't feel up to going out.'

'Ahh yes, the brownie.' Detective Schwartz raises an eyebrow. 'If you thought someone gave her the brownie deliberately, why didn't you call us? Knowing that someone had potentially made an attempt on her life? I understand she was in a car accident a few days ago, too?'

'Because Honey asked us not to call the police. I already told you this,' I say wearily. I have already told Detective Schwartz everything I know – within reason – including the fact that a man threatened me in the hotel corridor. 'Honey was worried Leonard would fire her if he thought she was causing trouble or attracting unwanted attention. There had been some… issues, I guess, with some scandalous headlines.' There'll be more now. As Honey was carried out to the waiting ambulance on a stretcher, the paps had swarmed, camera flashes and cigarette smoke filling the air, the thrill of a front-page scoop on their lips.

Detective Schwartz taps his pen impatiently on the table in front of him, a noise that scrapes my nerve endings. 'Miss Jones, someone attempted to murder Miss Black today, and I want to know who is responsible.' He pulls out a sheet of paper covered in scrawled handwriting. I recognise it as a page torn from the notebook Tilda had the night of the car accident. 'Care to explain this list to me?'

'These are the people that we – that *I* – think could be responsible for trying to kill Honey.' Maybe he's actually listening to me after all. 'If you speak to all of these people, I'm sure that one of them is responsible. One of them sent a man to threaten me. One of them was in the hotel at the time of the attempted murder. They all had one reason or another to get Honey out of the picture.'

'Well, that's the thing.' Detective Schwartz sits back again, grinding his cigarette out in the hospital ashtray as I cough, waving a hand in front of my face. 'We've spoken to all of the people on your list. Every damn one of them.'

'And?'

'You did a pretty thorough job. But things still don't quite tie up.'

'What do you mean, they don't tie up? Did you look at Magnus? Where was he when Honey was attacked?'

'He was having lunch at Googie's with a Ms Jessica Parks. She corroborates his story.'

I feel winded, as though I have been punched in the stomach. I was so sure this morning that it was Magnus. I wasted precious time sending Tilda up to his room to check on him, when all the time he wasn't even in the hotel. While I was fretting about Magnus, someone else was in Honey's room, stabbing her through the chest.

'What about Leonard?' He could have done it. He could easily hush it up and get away with it too, just like the rumours said.

'The rest of the people on your list also have alibis – Jean Lawrence was at the public library this afternoon; Leonard Langford had a meeting with a screenwriter – a Mr Robert Pirosh – and then met with Miss Lawrence and they worked in his trailer. Billy Walters was in his hotel room – he called room service a short while before Miss Black was discovered; he and the waiter talked about the baseball game between the Brooklyn Dodgers and the Pittsburgh Pirates that was played this afternoon. Mr Walters is a Dodgers fan, apparently. Cynthia Lake was in Burbank for an audition.'

I wonder if Cynthia is back yet from her imaginary audition. 'So, everyone on the list has an alibi?' I blink, feeling something inside give a little, as desolation steals the remaining air from the stuffy, overheated room. I was looking in the wrong place all the time, it seems.

'The only person who doesn't have an alibi for the time Miss Black was brutally attacked,' Detective Schwartz says slowly, and I realise that a tiny, twisted part of him is almost enjoying this, '...is a Mr Joseph Faulks, of Little Creek, Kentucky.'

'Joseph... Joe?' The ground seems to fall away beneath my feet, and tiny black dots dance in front of my vision. 'You don't mean? Oh God, not Joe.'

'Miss Jones, we have arrested Mr Faulks on suspicion of attempted murder. You're free to go for now, but please don't leave town.'

'Don't worry, detective, there's very little chance of that.'

Detective Schwartz gets to his feet and gestures for me to do the same. I stand on legs that feel numb, as if I've plunged into ice cold water, barely registering as I pass by the detective and out into the hall.

Louis is in the parking lot, Tilda beside him, as I emerge into the dying light of the day. The sun has dropped behind the buildings, but it's not the twilight that brings a chill to the air. It's the idea that Joe – *Joe!* – is the one who tried to kill Honey.

'Lily.' Tilda rushes towards me, but it is Louis who wraps an arm around me and pulls me close. 'I'm so sorry. Is there any more news?'

I pull away and shake my head, reaching into my purse for a tissue. I blow my nose, and then say, 'No, Honey is still in the operating room. But I got it all so wrong.'

'What do you mean?' Tilda asks.

'They've arrested Joe,' I say quietly, picturing the station house, where Joe is presumably locked in a cell for the night. 'They say Joe did it. He's the only one without an alibi.'

'*Joe?*' Louis looks incredulous. 'But he was so thrilled to connect with Honey again. They were going to get *married*. I can't… I can't believe it… we were so sure it was one of the others.'

'He was the only one left alone in the hotel room with her though,' Tilda says, her mouth twisting as if the words taste bitter on her tongue. 'Realistically he could have done it. He could have stabbed her, and then come out to see what was going on in the lobby. He could have been the one who leaked the story of his and Honey's engagement. That's what people will believe.'

303

I shake my head, not wanting to believe it. Not wanting to believe that sweet, mild Joe was really here to kill Honey, not admit his undying love and swoop her away for her dream wedding. That he had it in him at all. That he fooled us all so badly.

'She said something,' I say, 'as I was pressing on her chest, Honey tried to say something.'

'She did,' Tilda says, her eyebrows raising. 'I wasn't sure if I imagined it, but she did try to say something. Did you hear her, Lily? What was it?'

'Chess.' Something falls away inside me, and I raise my eyes to look at Louis and Tilda. 'She said *chess*. Honey told me she and Joe were going to play chess, and I thought she was joking, but the board was set up when we… we found her.' I press my fingers to my mouth, almost wanting to hold back the words. 'Honey knew Joe would come back to the room. She couldn't say his name because he would be there. She was telling us who did this to her.' My voice catches, the words too big to be spoken.

A wave of exhaustion claws at my bones and for the first time in two weeks I wish I was back in my own time. Safe at home (well, my crappy apartment anyway), my only problem figuring out a way to bump into Guillermo del Toro or Jordan Peele. And then I look at Louis, at his familiar green eyes, his mop of dark hair that just begs for my fingers to be run through it, the kindness that practically radiates from him, and I take it back. Even after everything that has happened today – even after *Evelyn* – I would never forfeit meeting Louis.

'Come on,' he says, guiding me towards the car. 'Let's get you home.' As if sensing my reluctance, Tilda puts out a hand.

'Not the hotel,' she says, with a swift glance in Louis's direction as she takes my other arm. 'Let's take her *home*.'

Chapter Thirty-One

The house is quiet, despite it being early evening, and in the kitchen a note from Louis's mother tells us that she and his father have taken the younger children out for ice cream and won't be home until late.

'Good old Mom,' Tilda says as she moves to the stove to put water on to boil. 'Always knows when to make herself scarce.' She busies herself with mugs and loose-leaf tea. 'Are you happy to stay here tonight, Lil?'

'Yes, thank you,' I say. I can't believe I'm still here. Part of me thought that when I burst into the Paul Williams Suite to see Honey lying on the chaise that I would just… *disappear.* That I'd wake up to find myself lying on the bathroom floor in 2019. I'd thought the same when Honey took a breath, and again when Detective Schwartz told me they'd arrested Joe, but here I am. Still in 1949. Just the thought of stepping into the hotel lobby where only hours before I had tried to calm the baying mob of reporters makes me shiver, an icy finger running across my shoulder blades.

'Tea.' Tilda places a steaming mug in front of me and throws herself down in the chair across the table. 'Drink up,' she instructs, and I take a sip, the tea hot and sweet.

'So, Detective Schwartz told you all the others have alibis?' Louis asks, reaching for his own mug.

'Yes. When he said it, I thought maybe he was going to blame me, say I did it – after all, Jean did say in front of Leonard that all this stuff only started once I came on the scene – but I was in contact with Tilda for most of the day. I just can't believe that Joe…' I trail off, unable to vocalise the thought of Joe hurting Honey. 'This is all my fault.'

'What?' Tilda is razor sharp. 'How can it be your fault? You did all you could to try and stop this from happening.'

'Is there any way it couldn't have been him?' Louis taps his fingers on the table, before crossing the room and fetching Tilda's legal pad and scrawling down the names again. Next to each name he writes their alibi, crossing lines between names who said they were together. 'Some of the others were alone at different points in the day… do we know how long Jean stayed at the library?'

'She did look cagey this morning,' Tilda pipes up. 'You said so yourself.'

'Honey said *chess*. I don't see how it couldn't be Joe. I just feel so… stupid,' I say eventually. 'I was so sure I had things, if not certainly figured out, then at least halfway. I was more concerned about Leonard and Magnus because they were the ones who had shown that they were capable of being physical and losing their tempers with Honey. I even said when we first started *this*—' I jab a finger towards the legal pad, 'that I didn't think Joe was worth noting as a suspect.' Tears threaten again and I take a hurried swig of my tea. 'Who was I kidding? I thought just because I had a little bit of prior knowledge that I could come swooping in here, like Jessica Fletcher or bloody… bloody Inspector Morse and solve the whole fucking case, when really, I knew nothing. Just two shitty paragraphs in a battered paperback, and a crappy half story that Eric found on Wikipedia.'

'Inspector Morse?' Tilda mouths at Louis, who shakes his head.

'Lily, I don't know who this inspector guy is, but you couldn't have really known what was going to happen.'

'Could you?' Tilda raises her eyebrows.

'Lily?' Louis turns to face me, and my heart stutters in my chest. 'You did say you'd tell me, Lil. Once you knew…'

I don't think I'd actually agreed to that, and now my stomach churns as I grope desperately for something to say. I can't tell them the truth, it's simply too unbelievable, and the last thing I want is for them both to think I'm spinning them a yarn. So I do the only thing I can do – the thing I'm desperate for them to *not* think I'm doing. I lie to them.

'You were right, sort of,' I say, after a pause that lasts a beat too long. 'When you asked me if I was psychic.'

'You mean, you are? *Wow.*' Tilda breathes, leaning forward and resting her chin on her hands. 'I knew it. Didn't I tell you, Lou?'

'So you can like, see the future?' Louis frowns, a trace of scepticism in his voice. 'But if that's the case, how come you couldn't see who was responsible for killing Honey?'

Oh boy. It's a good question, and I fumble for a moment, before I think of *The Hollywood Book of Scandals*. 'Imagine a page in a book,' I say slowly. 'The only information you have is what is written right there in front of you – even though there might be more pages to the chapter. That's kind of what it's like.' *Technically, am I still lying?*

308

'OK,' Louis gets to his feet, starting to pace as he tries to make sense of what I'm saying. 'So, you can just read what's on that page?'

'Uh… yeah.'

'And for Honey, all you could read was what happened and when, but you couldn't see who was responsible?'

Feeling on more stable ground, I nod. After all, that was the case. 'Right. I wish I could have, but I… couldn't. It's patchy, fragmented. Like the ink is faded. I can't see what I want, only what I'm shown.' What I wouldn't give to be able to go back and look up everything ever written about Honey Black.

'This is incredible,' Tilda says, awe etched all over her face. 'So you can really tell the future?'

Unease prickles at the back of my neck, and I rub my hand under my collar. 'I guess. Kind of. It still didn't do me any favours though, did it? I still didn't manage to stop it from happening.' A wave of exhaustion breaks over my head, and my nose starts to tingle. Everything feels too big, too heavy, and after two weeks here, I am still petrified of saying the wrong thing.

'Hey. Hey, don't cry.' Louis pulls me towards him, wrapping me in a hug, and the dam breaks. 'You did do something – you managed to save Honey. What if you hadn't gone to her room when you did? Things would have been very different.'

'Sorry,' I sniff, as Tilda hands me a handkerchief.

'Oh shush,' she says, but as her eyes meet mine there is something new there, a fascination that makes the tears flow ever harder.

Louis guides me to Tilda's room, and I slip into the bed I slept in before, as Tilda and Louis head back downstairs, presumably to talk over the bomb I've just dropped. Sleep is elusive despite my exhaustion, and I toss and turn, the blankets tangling around my calves as I think everything over. Louis has a point – I did manage to save Honey, even though she was wounded. So if that was my reason for being here, how come I didn't magically disappear after she was found? Why didn't I wake up in the bathroom of the Paul Williams Suite in 2019?

Everything written about the murder of Honey Black said Leonard was the main suspect, although nothing was ever proved, but there wasn't even any mention of Joe. *Joe.* Heart pounding, I sit bolt upright. There was no mention of Joe, because no one was there to introduce Joe back into Honey's life. *I was the one who did that.* I'm grasping at straws, but the way Joe behaved before Louis and I confronted him, I think he would have skulked back to Kentucky without saying a word to Honey if we hadn't taken him to her room. So, would Honey still have been stabbed even if Joe hadn't been brought back into the mix? If so, it can mean only one thing – Joe can't be the one responsible. *Can he?*

With shaking hands I flip the pillow over to the cool side, and lie back down. *If Joe didn't attack Honey, then who did? And is Honey still in danger?* Maybe, just maybe, that's why I'm still here. Not just to save Honey, but to bring her would-be killer to justice.

Chapter Thirty-Two

I wake at dawn but keep my eyes tightly closed, listening to the birds begin to chirp outside the window. *Am I home?* I can hear the steady rush of my pulse in my ears as I delay the moment for just a little longer, not sure exactly where I want to wake up. *Do I want to be back in 2019? Or still in 1949?* And then there is the rustle of bedclothes, and I open my eyes to see Tilda stretching in the bed next to mine. Tilda had come to bed around midnight, but I had feigned sleep as I mulled over the possibility that I am still here because Joe is innocent, trying to wrap my own head around it all.

'How you doin' today?' Louis asks half an hour later, as I get into the car. He smells of toothpaste, and his hair is slicked back and damp from the shower. He looks at me curiously and I wonder what he sees now. Still the same old Lily, I hope.

'I'm OK, a little tired.' I press my hand to my mouth as a yawn pulls at my throat. 'Are *you* OK?'

Louis turns the key in the ignition but doesn't pull away. Instead, he just watches me for a moment, a faint smile on his lips. 'Yeah. I mean, I'm still trying to understand what you told us last night, about your... what is it? Power? Gift?'

'Ermmm... I don't know if I'd call it a gift as such.' I shift in my seat, the leather already warm and sticky. Roll on air conditioning. 'I don't know for certain, but I really don't think Joe is responsible for this.'

'You don't?' Louis fixes his gaze on me, and I know he's trying to figure out if it's part of my 'gift'. 'Is it a feeling, or...?'

'I'm not sure, but something just doesn't sit right with me about it.' I reach out and squeeze his hand. 'Thank you. For believing me. You won't... you won't tell anyone else, will you? Evelyn or...'

Louis is already shaking his head. 'I won't tell, I promise. Listen Lil, about Evelyn, there was something—'

The car door flies open, and Tilda throws herself into the back seat. 'What's the plan for today?'

Louis breaks off. 'Well, I have a shift – I'm going to try and pick up a double so I can be around all day. I'm going to watch the bar area and see if any of the others make an appearance.' He glances at me. 'If Joe really is innocent, then one of them might let something slip.'

I feel highly doubtful about that, but then Louis doesn't have the true crime podcasts and Ann Rule books that I have had access to. With my twenty-first-century knowledge I feel almost as qualified as Detective Schwartz.

'I have to go and get my hair set.' Tilda scowls in the back seat. 'I'm seeing Reggie for dinner – with his parents. I think tonight might be the night,' she says gloomily.

'The night?' I twist in my seat to get a good look at her.

'Come on Til.' Louis glances in the rear-view mirror, an amused smile on his face. 'Not so long ago this was all you wanted.'

Tilda scowls harder and I get the feeling they've had this conversation before. 'That was before,' she snaps.

'Tonight's the night for what?' I ask again.

'Tilda thinks tonight's the night that Reggie is going to propose to her officially.'

Oh. 'And you're... not happy about it?' Frowning, I look from Tilda to Louis. 'I thought you wanted to get married? And what makes you think tonight is the night anyway?'

Tilda sighs. 'It's obvious – Reggie told me to go and get my hair set, and he's coming over to speak with Dad before we go for dinner. With his parents. It's going to happen, Lil, I know it is. And I'll have to say yes.'

Louis pulls into the parking lot, the familiar pink of the hotel a deep rosy blush in the early morning light. I wait until we are out of the car before I turn back to Tilda, putting one hand on her arm to stop her.

'Til...'

She stops rummaging in her purse and looks at me.

'You don't have to say yes, you know. Not if you don't want to.'

'I feel guilty,' she says. 'We've been dating for two years, and I do really like him – I suppose I do love him, really – and I did want us to get married, but since I met you... everything's changed.'

'Oh Til...' My heart breaks for her – for all the women that came before, who wanted something and were told they couldn't have it. 'What do you want? What do you really want to do with your life?'

She smiles then, her whole face lighting up. 'I want to be a reporter, Lily. I do want to marry Reg, and maybe have a kid, but not yet. I want to write other people's stories – not just Honey's story, but other stories too, about real people – get the truth out there.'

'Lily? Are you coming?' Louis calls from the side entrance to the hotel.

'One second!' I turn back to Tilda. 'Who decides what we can or can't do? Men? Why should they get to say how we live our lives?'

Tilda stares at me for a moment, her hand hovering over her mouth.

'Just because this is the way things are now, it doesn't mean they have to stay that way. But if we want change, we have to *make* the change. You can go to college, and write stories, and even marry Reg later if that's what you want. You can do *anything*, if you really want to, you just have to brave enough to stand up for what you believe in.' I hug her, and then pat her on the back before she can reply. 'But for now, get out of here – I'll meet you back here this afternoon for an update.'

–

Cynthia Lake's is the first face I see as I walk into the hotel. Louis has ducked away through the staff entrance, and I am walking through the hushed quiet of the lobby when I hear her call my name. Or at least, some semblance of it.

'Lila! Lila, come here!' She waves me over, covering her mouth dramatically with her hand as I approach, her eyes wide and shining. 'Oh Lila, isn't it awful?'

'It's Lily.' I force a smile, trying not to grit my teeth.

'Lily, Lila.' She flaps a hand, her tears miraculously drying up. 'Isn't it just the most awful news about Honey? I mean, here at the hotel as well. I'm not sure I feel safe, even with Billy staying in the same suite.'

'I'm pretty sure you're good.' I try to move off, but she grips my forearm, her bony fingers digging into my skin.

'No, Lily, I don't think you understand. If this could happen to Honey, it could happen to... well, not any of us, but some of us! I am a *household name*, what if he was really coming after me?'

'Like I said, I think you're good.' I can't resist a parting shot. 'I hear you had a big audition yesterday; how did it go?'

Cynthia narrows her eyes at me and before she can open her mouth to retaliate, I hurry away, heading towards the Polo Lounge. It's breakfast time, and the room is busy – busier than it was yesterday – and I wonder how much of it is people gathering to speculate about Honey, to gossip and compare notes on how they were *right here* the weekend someone tried to murder Honey Black.

Billy sits alone at a table, a cup of coffee in front of him. He looks tired and haggard, his face a washed-out shade of grey. Even if his alibi isn't quite cast-iron – hotel staff can be bought, after all – the cast on his foot would have made it almost impossible for him to hurt Honey and get away in time, seeing as Joe only left the room for a few minutes. The buzz of chatter in the restaurant dims as people realise who I am, and I feel oddly nervous as I ask for a cup of coffee and a pastry that I don't really want. Eyes prickle on the back of my neck, and abandoning the coffee, I fold the pastry into a napkin and tuck it in my purse, striding out of the restaurant more confidently than I feel.

I stand in the elevator, watching the numbers above my head tick up as I make my way up to the second floor. A visit to Honey at the hospital is on the cards too, but first, there is someone I need to see. The elevator doors open on my floor, and when I step out, instead of turning right to head towards my room, I turn left and head towards Jean's.

'Yes?' Jean's face peers out from the crack in the door, and I force myself to smile. She looks exhausted, her hair an unusually wild tangle instead of her smooth, sleek bob.

'It's just me, Lily.' I press one hand lightly against the door. 'Can I come in?'

Jean looks wary. 'Not really, I'm afraid. It's not terribly convenient.'

'Please. I just wanted to talk to someone… about Honey.'

Her face softens slightly, but she keeps a firm grip on the door. 'It's so shocking, what happened yesterday. She's a lovely girl, really, if a little feistier than I'm used to working with. But I can't help you, Lily. I've already spoken to the police.' She looks away, her face flushing. I get the impression that before yesterday, Jean has never had to deal with the police in her life.

'And did you tell them *everything*?' I hold my breath, hoping my bluff comes to something.

'What the heck is that supposed to mean?' Jean snaps, as she steps out into the corridor and pulls the door closed behind her. 'What exactly are you insinuating? I was away from the hotel all day, and I told the police the same thing.' Her voice catches and she shakes her hair away from her face. 'I had nothing to do with Honey's… with what happened to her. I can't believe you'd accuse me…'

'I'm not accusing you Jean, relax. I just wanted to talk about her, about what happened. Try and make sense of it all – the police seem to think that Joe was the one to attack her.'

'He did seem the type… very strong and possibly with a temper.' Jean sniffs, calmer now. I say nothing, still not convinced of Joe's guilt. *If Joe is guilty, why am I still here?*

'Don't go disturbing Leonard,' Jean says quickly as I say goodbye and turn on my heel.

'Leonard? Why not?'

'He's very busy today. He's got to try and figure out what will happen with the movie.'

'He's still going ahead with it?'

'He has to. People have invested in it,' Jean says, a little sheepishly, the expression on her face telling me that she doesn't necessarily agree with it. 'We've only shot a few scenes, so things can't be held up for too long, and he'll want Honey back on set as soon as she's able. And of course, he'll be dealing with his wife.' She looks as though the word slices into her tongue as she speaks. 'So, please don't go knocking on his hotel room door, give him some peace.'

'Right,' I say thoughtfully, wondering why she is so keen to keep me away from him. I watch as she goes back inside, hearing the chain slide across the door before I step back towards the elevator, to head downstairs to see Jessica.

Louis is already in the elevator, a room service cart in front of him.

'You got promoted?' I tease, butterflies tap dancing in my chest as he winks at me.

'I'm a jack of all trades,' he laughs, before he grows serious. 'I just delivered another bottle of bourbon and a grilled cheese sandwich to Magnus.'

'You did?' Questions dance on the tip of my tongue. 'What did he say? Did he mention Honey? Was he—'

'He was passed out.' Louis wrinkles his nose. 'This is the bottle he rang down for in the early hours of the morning, apparently.' He lifts the cloth on the cart to show an empty bourbon bottle and a half-eaten plate of fried chicken.

'What's your vibe on him?' I ask, as Louis frowns. 'Your view, I mean.'

'To be honest? It's hard to have any views at all on a guy who's passed out in his underwear, with the stink of two-day-old bourbon reeking from every pore. I'm sure the attack on Honey will have hit him hard, but it doesn't mean he didn't do it.'

The elevator pings, and the doors open on Honey's floor.

'This is me.' I step out. 'I'm going to see if Jessica is here, and see if Magnus said anything to her yesterday before I head to the hospital.' I glance along the hall, towards Honey's suite. The doors slide closed, and I am alone in the corridor. It feels much as it did the previous afternoon when I had come to check on Honey. I feel that same prickling sensation on the back of my neck, as if someone is watching me, and for a moment, I imagine twenty-first-century Lily standing behind me and egging me on.

With Honey in mind, I walk past Jessica's room and head straight for the Paul Williams Suite. Police tape flutters across the door, and I had thought that maybe there would be a police officer standing guard, but the hallway is empty. Rummaging in my purse, I pull out the skeleton key left there by Tilda this morning as we waited for Louis. With a quick glance over my shoulder, and an overwhelming sense of déjà vu, I slide it into the lock and open the door, apprehensive as I duck under the tape.

It feels so empty. The room is still filled with Honey's things; her bath oils still line the bathroom shelf, and her script still sits on the coffee table as it did the previous day, but there is something missing. *She is missing.* Her scent is still on the air, mingled with the faint coppery smell of blood, and if I close my eyes, I could almost imagine she is still here, in the next room, and any minute now she'll call for me to help her with something. But she's not. She's still at Cedars of Lebanon Hospital – known in 2019 as Cedars-Sinai – recovering from her emergency surgery.

Please, Honey, I pray silently, *if you want me to figure out who tried to kill you, give me a hint. Anything. Anything at all.*

Nothing. I peer between my lashes, but nothing has changed. There is no arrow pointing to a clue, no huge sign clearly showing the events of the previous afternoon, everything is as it was. Champagne glasses on the table, chess game half finished.

'Lily?'

I open my eyes with a start and turn to see Jessica in the doorway. I hadn't fully closed the door and she lingers there now, uncertainty on her face. 'What are you doing here?'

'I was…' I flap a hand uselessly. 'I just wanted to see if I could find anything that might help.' I puff out a short breath, trying to erase the image of Honey, blood-soaked and pale on the chaise.

'I saw the door was open, I was just passing. I wondered who was in here. I thought perhaps it was the police, back again looking for something.' Jessica ducks under the tape now, trailing her fingers over the piano, picking up and inspecting the gifts that still lie on the top. 'So, they arrested the guy. Joe.'

'Yeah.'

'What a piece of shit.'

'I thought it would be Magnus,' I say, watching Jessica as her eyes comb the room as if looking for proof that Honey was ever really here.

'Magnus?' She turns to me with a short bark of laughter. 'Don't be silly. Magnus might be a selfish, arrogant bastard but he doesn't have the balls to do this. I always had my suspicions about Joe — after all he fed her the brownie, didn't he?'

'I don't think Joe forced her to eat it.'

'Honey knew she was allergic to nuts — why would she pick up the brownie herself? It must have been Joe who sent it to her, and then he made sure she ate it.'

I frown, still not convinced, even though Joe told me himself he thought feeding Honey the brownie would be romantic.

Jessica smiles and shakes her head, her teeth a brilliant shade of white. *Did they have teeth whitening in 1949?* 'It's the only thing that makes sense, isn't it? Anyway, I've told everything I know to the police. I'm sure you have as well.'

'Oh yes, of course. Although I'm not sure that anything I had to say was of much use,' I say miserably, before I think of Honey, her lips desperately trying to form a single word. 'She tried to speak, as I was pressing on her chest.'

'What?' Jessica's smile drops, her blue eyes widening. 'What did she say? Oh my God, Lily, I had no idea!' As if unable to hold herself up, Jessica slips into the armchair beside the chaise.

'Chess,' I say, my eyes going to the board. 'She said *chess.*'

'Chess?'

'They were playing chess that afternoon.' I blink, my eyes stinging. *Maybe I do have it all wrong. Maybe it* was *Joe, and I'm still here because it was all my fault for bringing him back into her life.* 'I was so sure it couldn't be Joe, but maybe...'

'Did you tell the police?' Jessica asks, her fingers knotting together in her lap.

'No.' I shake my head. 'I was so upset and confused; it completely slipped my mind until I left the hospital.'

Jessica presses her hands to her cheeks and gets to her feet, pulling me into a hug. I can feel the knobs of her spine as she squeezes me tightly. 'You poor dear. It's terrifying for all of us, the idea that he was just *there*. A potential murderer walking among us, hiding in plain sight. The very thought that he was here in the hotel, all the time. It's not your fault, Lily, people like that... they're very clever. They can fool us all.'

Chilly fingers walk down my spine, and I shudder at the thought.

'I'm just so upset that I wasn't here,' Jessica is saying as I tune back in, pulling out of her tight embrace. 'Maybe I could have stopped him.'

'You were at Googie's, weren't you? Yesterday afternoon when...'

'Yes.' Jessica pulls out a cream handkerchief and dabs at her eyes. 'With Magnus,' she sniffs. 'I met him for lunch. I wanted to keep an eye on him, just as you asked, although there really was no need. The man is a mess at the moment.' She dabs at her eyes one last time and straightens her shoulders. 'I'm sorry Lily, it's all just so terribly, terribly shocking. I don't think I can bear to be in here.' A sob erupts and she presses the hanky to her mouth, shattering any illusions of pulling herself together.

'No, of course not.' I put an arm around her shoulder, casting one more look around the suite. 'I'm leaving now anyway. Come on, I'll walk you back to your room.'

Chapter Thirty-Three

Honey's eyes are closed, her face pale and still, eerily reminiscent of the previous afternoon when I found her on the chaise, as I tiptoe silently across the hospital room and perch on the edge of the bed, taking her hand in mine.

'Honey, I'm so sorry.' Stroking her hand softly, I listen to the rhythmic sound of her breathing, the faded bustle of the corridor outside. 'I tried so hard to stop this from happening – I know I managed to save you, but I still didn't do a very good job, did I? I wanted to prevent anything from happening to you at all.' A tear slides down the side of my nose and plops onto the pristine white cotton of the bedsheet. 'Even though I knew this was going to happen I still couldn't stop it. Maybe time should be left alone. I just hope I haven't made things worse for you in the long run.' What if whoever was responsible for this – if indeed it wasn't really Joe – tries again? Only I'm not here to save her this time?

'Lily?' My name is a breathy whisper and I look up to see Honey's eyes are open. She winces at the bright light above her head, and I slide off the bed.

'Honey. You're awake.' I swipe at my cheeks, hoping she hasn't overheard what I said.

'Yeah.' Honey blinks slowly, her hand pressing to her side. 'Hurts.'

'Keep still. You've had an operation. You're still in the hospital.'

Honey frowns, her eyes opening again and finding mine. Despite the pain meds pumping into her via the IV beside the bed, her gaze is clear. 'Someone did this?'

'Yeah.'

She licks her lips, silent for a moment. 'What happened?'

'You were attacked, in your suite. Someone stabbed you in the chest.' I watch her face as she absorbs my words, pain flitting across her features. 'Honey, do you remember anything about that afternoon? Anything at all that could help?'

Honey gestures for me to raise the bed, and I angle her so she can look directly at me without the overhead lights in her eyes. 'Joe was there…' she says slowly, as my pulse starts to gallop. 'We were just talking and kissing a little… spending time together.'

'Did you argue?'

Honey shakes her head, the tiniest movement. 'No. We had a drink… I rang down for a bottle of champagne and we started a game of chess. Joe says I'm terrible at it…' She looks over my shoulder to the doorway. 'Lil, where is Joe?'

Oh man. 'Joe is… Honey, they arrested him.'

The words strike like barbs and Honey's eyes fill with tears. 'Joe?'

'He's at the station, I guess. No one has seen him. Honey, this is really important, and the police are going to be back here to ask you the same questions as soon as they know you're awake. What's the last thing you remember about that afternoon?'

Honey frowns, her fingers worrying at the soft cotton of the sheet across her lap. 'The chess game… the press? Did the press come to the hotel?'

'Yes!' A jolt of excitement runs through my veins, sharp and fizzy. 'They did! Do you remember anything about that?'

'I wanted Joe to go and see what was happening…' She bites hard on her lower lip, the strain of remembering etched into the deep V between her brows. 'That's it. That's all I remember.' Tears swim as she looks up at me, and my excitement fizzles out. 'Do they… did Joe do this? Is that what they're saying? Is that why he was arrested?'

'Yes,' I say reluctantly, as her face crumples. 'But… I'm not sure he did, Honey. I can't explain it, but I think someone else is behind it all and I'm going to do my best to figure it out.'

'Joe wouldn't do this,' Honey gulps, 'he never… he wouldn't. Lily, you have to help him.'

'I'm going to do my best, Honey, I swear. If Joe is innocent, then I'll find out who did this to you. Don't cry.' Awkwardly I lean in to hug her, as the door behind me opens.

'Ahh, Miss Black. You're awake.' Detective Schwartz steps into the room, looking every inch the Marlowe-esque film noir detective. I pull away, feeling my skin prickle as he glances me over, just the sight of his pencil-thin moustache putting me on edge. 'Miss Jones. What a surprise. If you'll excuse us, I need to speak with Miss Black.'

'Of course.' Kissing Honey on the cheek, I whisper into her ear, 'If you remember anything else, anything at all, you call me.'

'So, did you find anything?' Tilda is waiting for me at the bar when I arrive back at the hotel for a well-earned drink.

'The whole day was a bust,' I sigh, throwing a wearied smile at Louis as he slides a gin and tonic across the bar to me. 'I went to the hospital – Honey is awake, but she doesn't remember anything after asking Joe to go and see the press.'

'So that could be a good sign,' Louis says. 'If she remembers asking Joe to leave, then maybe he really did leave and he is innocent.'

'Or maybe she asked him to leave, and he refused,' Tilda counters. 'They argued and he attacked her. I'm not saying that's what happened, but it's a possibility.'

'I tried Magnus,' Louis says, leaning on the bar on his elbows and lowering his voice. 'I went back up to collect his room service cart and he was in the shower, so he's still alive, at least. I think he'd had a visitor while I was gone. There was a pair of ladies' gloves left on the nightstand, but they could have been Honey's.'

'What did they look like?' I ask.

'Cream. Cotton or linen or something like that. Light, summer gloves anyway.'

'Jessica's.' I visualise her pulling them on, as she left her hotel room to meet Magnus the day Honey was attacked. 'She wore them that day. I suppose she could have visited him earlier. I think you're right, Tilda. I think I need to find out who tried to kill her, but after today I'm not sure it's going to be that easy. Everyone seems to have accepted so quickly that Joe is the guilty party.'

'I tried to see him today,' Tilda announces suddenly, and I realise her hair is the same as it was this morning. She hasn't been to the hairdresser at all.

'Wait a minute, what are you even doing here?' I ask. 'Aren't you supposed to be sitting down to supper with Reggie's parents in less than half an hour?'

'Supposed to be,' Louis smirks. 'I'd love to hear what reason you gave for not showing, Til.'

'I'm changing my own destiny,' Tilda says, throwing a grin in my direction. 'I went to the station instead to see if I could talk to Joe.'

'Any luck?'

'No, unfortunately.' Tilda shakes her head. 'They didn't believe I was from the lawyer's office, for some reason. But...' She leans in close. 'Reggie's cousin is a police officer, and he works out of the same station where Joe is being held. I begged a cup of coffee with him and tried to get some information.'

'What did he say?' I lean in too, barely registering as Louis steps back to take a drinks order.

'That Reggie would be making a huge mistake if he married me, and I should probably learn to keep my nose out of other people's business.' She raises an eyebrow, and I can't help but laugh. 'But then I told him, just because I was a woman didn't mean I didn't know my own mind, and that this was my business, because Honey Black was a friend. That soon shut him up.'

'Good for you. What about Joe? Did he say anything about Joe?'

Tilda sighs. 'It's not looking good, Lil. They all think it's him. He knew she had a nut allergy, and he's a farmer, he would know how to tamper with a vehicle...'

'So, it's *really* not looking good?' Despite everything, I can't shake the nagging feeling that things are all wrong.

'It's not,' Tilda says, 'but Frank – Reggie's cousin – he agreed with me that it all seems a little too pat to be true. Like, everything has slotted into place too easily. His feeling is that Joe didn't do it, but all the evidence is against him. Apparently, all Joe has done is cry and protest his innocence, but that's what they all say in the slammer. Sorry, Lil.'

'It just doesn't feel right,' I say, something burrowing under my skin every time Tilda says Joe could have done it. I've already changed things so that Honey wasn't killed, and I'm still here, so Joe *must* be innocent. That's the only explanation for my still being here.

'You really don't think he did it.' Tilda eyes me closely. 'I don't know if this is just a hunch, or this crazy psychic thing of yours, but if Joe is innocent that means whoever did it could try again. There is a potential murderer here, in this hotel.' Her words are a mirror to Jessica's earlier, and the idea that whoever is responsible is here, right now, hiding in plain sight causes a kernel of fear to lodge itself deep in my chest.

I slump back in my chair, suddenly feeling defeated. I have no idea how on earth I am going to prove Joe's innocence – or if he even is innocent. *Come on, 2019 Lil*, I mutter under my breath, *give me a hand here. Give me some sort of clue at least, I can't do this without your help.*

And then Jean Lawrence walks in.

'Lily, I'm so glad I caught you. I went to your room but…' Jean stops, as if only just noticing Louis and Tilda. 'Can I talk to you, alone? It's about Honey.' She swallows, and on closer inspection I can see her eyes are rimmed with pink, as if she's been crying.

'It's OK, Jean.' I guide her gently into a booth at the back of the lounge, noticing that her blouse is crumpled, and her hands shake slightly as she tucks her purse onto the seat beside her. 'Here, sit. Can I get you a drink?'

'Martini.' Jean looks up at Louis. 'Can I get a dirty martini? A large one, please.' Louis nods, and we wait in silence until he returns, gently passing Jean a huge drink. She takes a gulp, wincing as the alcohol hits.

'Jean, it's OK,' I say again. 'Whatever you have to say you can say in front of Tilda and Louis. They're helping me figure out what happened to Honey.'

'So, you don't believe Joe did it?' Jean looks from one to the other, before nodding as if in agreement. 'All right.' She takes a deep breath, dabbing at her eyes again. 'Lily, I did something awful.'

Tilda hisses in a sharp breath and I give her a pointed look. 'Go on Jean, I promise you can speak freely here.'

Jean nods, her eyes fixed on the drink ahead of her. There is a momentary pause and then she says, 'I lied to the police, Lily.' The words tumble out in a hasty river, as if she has to spit them out before they drown her.

'You lied? About Honey?' I lick lips that are suddenly dry, glancing up at Louis, who shakes his head.

'About where I was.' Jean lets out a sob, pressing her napkin to her mouth. 'I did go to the library, but not for as long as I said I did, and I did work with Leonard in his trailer... well, sort of. But in between...'

'In between?' I prompt.

'In between, Leonard and I met for lunch. At Googie's.' Jean raises her tear-stained face to look at me. 'It wasn't a work meeting, Lily. Leonard and I... we've been seeing each other.' She stares at me, as if challenging me. 'That's why I didn't want you to knock on his door earlier. He... he wasn't there. He was with me, in my room.'

'I kind of had an idea,' I say eventually, ignoring Tilda's shocked expression. 'I saw you two together in Googie's last week, and it didn't look strictly professional.'

'Really?' Jean looks devastated. 'We've tried so hard to keep it a secret, and Googie's was the only place we felt safe. Leonard is... I'm not proud of myself, Lily. I lost my beau in the war, and I promised myself after that I would never marry, never be with anyone again but...' Jean pauses. 'Life is so short. You know Leonard is married, but he's so unhappy with her. We want to be together, but Leonard wanted to finish the movie before he left Eliza so that we could be together.' Her voice lowers to a whisper, and I fight to be able to hear her. 'That's why he was so furious with Honey, when the newspaper ran those pictures of her and Billy falling out of the nightclub.'

'Because he was worried that she would attract unwanted attention to the movie, and the two of you would be discovered?' Tilda asks.

'Yes,' Jean says, 'and then Honey challenged him, that day when they argued in the trailer. You left your clipboard in there when you ditched out of the window by the way.' Jean looks at me and I flush, remembering the panic I'd felt as Leonard had railed at Honey. 'Honey had come to Leonard and told him she knew about us.'

'So, Leonard was angry?' Louis says. 'Jean, doesn't that give Leonard a motive to try to kill Honey?'

'Oh no.' Jean looks horrified. 'Leonard *loves* Honey – she's like a daughter to him. She came and told him that she knew about our affair, but she didn't threaten to tell Eliza. She was furious with Leonard *on my behalf.*' Jean's eyes well up again. 'I had thought she was a silly little girl, but she really cares about me. She told Leonard I was worth more, and that if he loved me, he should move heaven and earth to be with me.' Jean looks down at her bare ring finger. 'He took me to Rodeo Drive the next day, and we visited a jeweller.'

'So,' I frown, trying to get things straight in my head. 'Honey knew about the two of you, and she challenged Leonard. He wasn't angry, but he was glad that she knew, as it forced him to make a decision.'

'Yes,' Jean nods.

'But the two of you agreed to keep things hush hush until after the movie wrapped, to avoid any unwanted scandal, and that's why you lied to the police about where you were on the day Honey was murdered? You didn't want them to know you're together?'

'That's right,' Jean sniffs again, 'but now things have changed, and I can't lie any longer. I have to tell you the truth, because I'm not the only one who has lied.'

Yikes. The whole situation seems to be getting more complicated the further I try to dig.

'Who else lied?' Tilda asks the question for me.

'Earlier this evening I saw Jessica leaving Magnus's room,' Jean says, 'and of course I stopped to see if she was all right. I was expecting her to be devastated, being Honey's best friend. We talked a little, about how terrible it was, and she asked me where I had been that day.' Jean colours slightly. 'Obviously I told her that Leonard and I had been working in the trailer on set, just as I had said to the police, even though it wasn't strictly true, and then I asked her where she had been, and she told me that she and Magnus had been having lunch at Googie's but...'

'But?'

'She wasn't!' Jean cries. 'Leonard and I always sit in the same booth at Googie's at the back, so we can see anyone who comes in, just in case we need to look as if we're in a meeting. Jessica wasn't at Googie's on Saturday afternoon. Magnus was there, alone, for maybe an hour before he got up and left, but Jessica didn't come at all.'

'Oh my God,' I breathe, and when I look at Tilda and Louis, they both carry the same shocked expression that I imagine I do. 'Jessica lied?'

'Yes,' Jean nods emphatically. 'Jessica Parks wasn't at Googie's on Saturday, even though she said she was.'

Chapter Thirty-Four

'What do you think this means?' Tilda hisses, as Louis guides Jean towards the elevator.

I shake my head, stunned by Jean's revelation. There can only be one reason for Jessica to lie, and the thought of it brings a sour taste to my mouth. As if summoned by magic, voices filter in as the heavy doors to the Polo Lounge open, and Cynthia Lake enters, followed by Jessica herself. Cynthia speaks to the hostess, as Jessica surveys the room and I find myself pulling back into the booth, out of sight. Jessica wears a black dress, modest at first appearance as it falls to mid-calf, but as she follows Cynthia and the hostess to the table the fabric clings to every curve. She wears a black pillbox hat, her hair beneath falling in carefully curled waves to her shoulders. She looks pale, her face serious. Exactly what you would expect from a woman whose best friend was just brutally attacked and left for dead in her hotel suite. Doubt clouds my vision and I turn my attention back to Tilda, who also watches the two actresses cross the room.

'She plays the part well,' Tilda says. 'I'm going to call Frank.' Tilda slides out of the booth, and I turn to Louis, who has returned from escorting a shaky Jean back to her room. He follows Tilda's gaze to where Jessica is sliding into a seat, giving the hostess a gracious smile.

'I need to get into her room,' I say. 'I still have the skeleton key... if Jessica really was behind the attack on Honey, there must be something there, some kind of proof that can help Joe. Bloody hell, Louis.' I let out a shaky breath, adrenaline pumping in fierce spurts through my veins. *Hiding in plain sight.* 'Why else would she lie?'

'I'm going to go over and take a drinks order, offer her a menu. I'll try and gauge how long we've got until she's finished here,' Louis says. 'Don't do anything stupid until I get there too, OK?'

'OK.' Tilda is walking towards me, and I give Louis a shaky smile before we both head to the corridor.

'I called Frank and told him Jessica lied to the police,' Tilda says. 'He's coming to the hotel, but he needs to track down Detective Schwartz first. You go to Jessica's room; I'm going to knock on Magnus's door and make sure he's not going to cause us any trouble.' We part ways at the mouth of the corridor and I pause for a moment before I press on towards Jessica's room, my mouth dry and my pulse pounding.

This has to be the reason I'm still here. I might not have been able to save Honey from getting badly hurt, but I *could* save Joe from a life in prison. *And find my way back to 2019.* I don't know how I feel about that part. Stepping into the corridor, I take a deep breath, my heart knocking painfully against my ribcage. Raising a hand and forgetting Louis's instructions to hold off until he arrives, I tap on Jessica's door, then pull out the skeleton key and let myself inside her hotel suite.

The same thought strikes me as my previous visit – it's immaculate, and much smaller and less grand than Honey's, as if Leonard has made a clear statement as to who will be the star of his movie. The bed is neatly made, a thin, battered paperback lying on the nightstand, along with another pair of gloves and a small pot of night cream. Bouquets of flowers line the shelf in the main area of the suite, but when I check there are no gift cards and no way of seeing who sent them. On the coffee table lies a copy of the *Goodtime Gal* script, the same underlined version I saw when I visited Jessica previously. As I pick it up, I notice something unsettling.

'I thought I said to wait for me.' The suite door swings open and Louis peers over my shoulder at the script. 'Jessica and Cynthia are ordering appetisers. We have some time, but not a lot. What's that?'

'The script for *Goodtime Gal*,' I say, shoving it towards him. 'Here, look. These lines are marked up… but these are for Honey's part, not Jessica's – this is the script that went missing from Honey's suite.'

'You mean…' Louis frowns as he scans the page.

'She was learning Honey's lines,' I say, 'but I saw her with this script before Honey was attacked. Almost as if…'

'…as if she knew Honey wouldn't be able to play the part of Sophia. Jeez Louise, Lily, this could be proof.'

'Keep hold of it.' It's good, but it's not enough. I turn my attention back to the suite, my eyes searching for something – anything – that will prove beyond all doubt that Joe didn't try to kill Honey.

'Lily, over here.' Louis's voice is loud in the silence of the room, and I look up to find him holding a familiar pink box, a match to the one I handed over to the police.

'The brownies.' I take the box, peering inside. There is no card, and the box is empty apart from a few stray crumbs. 'I guess on the surface it doesn't mean anything, but it shows that Jessica knew about the brownies. She could have ordered them to Honey's suite, along with the handwritten note. She also knew Honey had an allergy — Honey said she hadn't told anyone, but that night when Honey was sick, Jessica mentioned that Honey knew she had to watch what she ate. I assumed she was referring to that ridiculous low-calorie diet Honey was on, but what if it was the allergy?'

'It all points to Jessica,' Louis says. 'I guess she thought her alibi meant she wouldn't be questioned too hard, especially when Joe was with Honey all day and didn't really have one. I don't understand why though. I thought she and Honey were best friends?'

'They were,' I say slowly. Now I know Jessica lied, the whole thing has taken on a very *All About Eve* vibe, and I feel foolish for not seeing it before. 'I think Jessica did want to help Honey in the beginning, but she didn't realise how ambitious Honey was, or indeed how talented. She had to stop Honey before she stole her thunder completely.'

There is something else niggling at me, something that at the time I thought felt wrong and I hold up a hand to hush Louis. 'Wait,' I say, 'there's something else, I just can't quite...' I close my eyes, thinking over all the times I have interacted with Jessica over the last two weeks. *Her face, the shock as I told her Billy would be in the car chase scene, the way she had excused herself as if unable to watch. Jessica, hurrying along the corridor to meet Magnus, only she didn't meet him. The room service trolley outside her room...*

'Room service!' I shout. 'I knew there was something not right.'

'Room service?'

'The day Honey was attacked, I was watching the hall and Jessica ordered room service. I can't believe I didn't realise... why on earth would she order steak and fries, if she was going to meet Magnus for lunch? She barely eats,

335

there's no way she'd eat twice. And the tray... there was something off about the tray when I lifted the dome, but I couldn't figure out what it was.'

'What was it?' Louis asks, and I feel a bubble of excitement burst in my belly.

'The steak knife,' I say triumphantly, feeling like Nancy Drew, Columbo and John Luther rolled into one. 'The steak knife was missing from the tray. The police never said if they found the knife Honey was stabbed with. It could still be here.'

'I guess she would have had time to slip back here, wait until the coast was clear and then slide out the back entrance before coming back in as if she'd been to meet Magnus,' Louis says, his eyes sparking. 'If she had called the newspapers herself, she would have known there would be enough of a diversion for her to get to Honey and away without anyone noticing her.'

'We need to search the room,' I say. 'Quickly. You take the bedroom, I'll take the bathroom and living area.'

We split up, and I head straight for the bathroom, shoving make-up and various lotions out of the way to get to the cupboard behind. I search the toilet cistern (empty) and the bathroom cabinet (also empty) and am on my knees, about to pull off the bath panel, when a shout comes from the living room.

'Lily, I found something!'

My knees protesting, I hurry into the sitting room, to see Louis standing just inside the entrance to the bedroom, as Jessica lets herself into the suite, eyes wide with shock as she spots me from the hotel room doorway.

I freeze, my blood running cold, as Louis pulls back out of Jessica's line of sight, one hand behind his back.

'Lily!' Jessica steps forward, a smile on her face now. 'What are you doing here?'

Her smile looks genuine but the ice in her voice is like liquid nitrogen. 'Jessica, I—' *I what? Was hoping to find something that proves you're an attempted murderer?* 'I was looking for you.'

'Well, here I am.' She moves to the bar at the end of the suite, dropping her purse on to the couch as she goes. 'What is it you wanted?'

I watch as she pops the cork on a bottle of champagne, something chiming in the back of my mind as the bubbles fizz over the top, splattering the surface of the bar. 'Honey's awake.'

Jessica stills, pale bubbles only halfway up her glass. 'Really? Well, isn't that wonderful news. I'm not sure it's worth breaking into my suite for though.'

'Yes, it is,' I say, watching as she resumes pouring the champagne. 'Now she'll be able to tell Detective Schwartz exactly what happened in her suite.' *Three glasses.* My pulse gallops and I can feel the adrenaline spiking in my veins. *There were three champagne glasses on the table in Honey's suite. She said she and Joe had a drink – she must have poured another drink for the person who tried to kill her. She would have automatically poured a drink for Jessica.*

'Did I invite you to my room, Lily? Only, I don't think I did. I should probably call security.'

'You do that.' I lift my chin, pressing my shaking hands against my thighs. 'I know what you did, Jessica, I know it was you.'

'What did I do?' she smirks, raising her glass to her lips. The façade of concerned best friend slips, her face changing. Her eyes are only on me, and I realise she hasn't seen Louis. She doesn't know he's here.

'You're the one who tried to kill Honey.' I risk a glance towards Louis, who still stands just out of Jessica's sight in the bedroom doorway. He raises his arm from behind his back, and in his fist, I see the steak knife. 'Why did you do it?'

'Oh Lily,' Jessica sighs. 'You had to meddle, didn't you? I thought we had this all figured out. It was supposed to be all sewn up with Joe. Do you really want to know?'

She doesn't even attempt to deny it. 'Yes, I want to know. Honey is kind and sweet, and you were supposed to be her best friend.'

'Best friend, pah!' Jessica rolls her eyes. 'I'll admit I loved her once. She was a sweet, adoring little girl who hung on my every word – what wasn't there to love about that? I would see her, waiting on the edge of the set, rushing over to speak to me once I'd finished shooting for the day. It was like having a little sister who thought the sun shone out of every part of me.' Jessica smiles, mistily. 'But I soon saw her for what she really was, even if she never quite realised it. Honey wanted to be famous – she was utterly desperate for it – and once Leonard saw her, he decided he had to have her in the movie, so he offered her a bit part.' She spits the words out, full of spite and venom. 'After he saw her performance, he was so enamoured with her, he offered her the part of Sophia. Naturally I was furious – that was supposed to be *my* part – but what could I do? One thing Leonard hates is a hysterical woman. I told everyone I had given up the part for her, but then I discovered Honey had gone directly to Leonard herself, begging him to be Sophia.' Jessica pulls out a cigarette, offering the pack to me.

'No. Thank you.'

I wait as she lights it, breathing in and holding it before exhaling a long stream of smoke. She even looks glamorous confessing to attempted murder.

'And then Magnus got involved.' Jessica's mouth turns down. 'He was supposed to string her along – get her hooked, then tell her he'd changed his mind, and he'd made a dreadful mistake, and leave her heartbroken. She'd skulk off back to Hicksville, Kentucky, and that would be the last of her. Leonard would appreciate my talent even more, Magnus and I would be married, I'd have it all. But Magnus fucked it all up.'

'Magnus bullied Honey,' I say, picturing the way he stood over her, the way she had flinched from him. The skin on my wrist feels hot, as though his grip has branded me.

'He fell in love with the silly little bitch,' Jessica spits, ash falling to the carpet. 'Everyone knows Magnus has a jealous streak, but it went too far. She told me he left her, but I knew it was the other way around, and I could see everything falling apart around me – she had Magnus still lusting after her and she had my part in the movie. You can't honestly have believed me when I told you I was happy playing second fiddle to a little country mouse like Honey Black?'

My mind is working nineteen to the dozen as I try and recall everything I've ever read about Jessica Parks. *She marries Magnus in 1953. Wins an Oscar in 1955. All because she got rid of the one woman who was a match for her. Not if I can help it.*

'No, of course you wouldn't be,' I say, moving towards the doors that lead to the patio, forcing Jessica to turn her back on the rest of the suite as her eyes follow me.

Louis starts to move sideways silently behind Jessica's back, towards the suite door. 'Does Magnus know it was you?'

'Magnus,' she snorts. 'Magnus was the one who was supposed to do it. He cut the brakes and he couldn't even do that properly. And then he bottled it, refusing to order the brownies. Said she wouldn't eat anything delivered by him.'

'But why? Why would Magnus want to kill Honey? He still loves her.'

Jessica tuts. 'For Pete's sake Lily, do I have to spell everything out for you? There's a fine line between love and hate. After she left him Magnus came to me, drunk and raving about how he wanted to kill her. Well, that would work out perfectly for me. Only he backed out once he'd sobered up. I threatened to expose him for the violent bully he really is, and I told him I'd leak the truth about their separation, giving Honey the chance to tell her side of the story. He'd be ruined – his career, his reputation, everything – but still I had to do the job myself. It's pathetic, the way he is about her.'

I remember Magnus in the hospital, waiting for news of Honey. He'd been agitated, and it had looked as if he and Jessica were arguing. I'd heard him say something about trying again and I had assumed he was telling Jessica that he wanted to try again with Honey and Jessica was angry, because Honey had moved on at last and Jessica didn't want to see her hurt. Now, it makes more sense – Magnus was telling Jessica he didn't want to try and hurt Honey again, and she was furious with him for refusing.

The door eases open, and Louis holds up one finger as he slides out of the suite. Jessica pours herself another drink, and I exhale as he disappears into the corridor.

'So, you sent her the brownies?'

'Of course I did. Magnus is useless.'

'And the threatening notes?'

'Those too.' Jessica shrugs. 'I thought she'd be scared off, but she was a tough cookie. She did ask Jean about them, and of course good old Jean told her everyone got them. She mentioned them to me too, and I told her the same thing – I couldn't have her going to Leonard and complaining. But the notes didn't work, and neither did the car accident – I didn't mean for Billy to be involved, by the way – so I had to escalate things. Hence my pal paying you a little visit in the corridor. I was quite annoyed when that didn't work. He charged me a lot of money to threaten you.'

The memory of that sour, fleshy palm pressed against my mouth makes me shudder. 'You could have just spoken to Leonard about it, told him you wanted a bigger part in the next movie.'

Jessica laughs, high and shrill. 'That's not how it works, Lily! The news had just broken that *Kentucky Queen* was a smash hit in Europe and it wasn't me everyone was talking about! It was Honey – and once *Goodtime Gal* came out everyone would fall in love with her even more. She had to go, Lily, I was finished. I told Magnus to meet me at Googie's – the least he could do was provide me with the perfect alibi – and then I slipped out and called the reporters to leak the news of Honey and Joe's engagement. Once they all turned up, I could sneak back in. I knocked on Honey's door and of course she let me in – she thought I was coming to tell her what was going on.'

'And instead, you stabbed her in the chest.' I look Jessica dead in the eye. 'Honey never said *chess* at all, did she?'

Jessica gives me an indulgent smile. 'Oh Lily, you were so sweet. So thrilled that you thought you had it all figured out. Of course, I was a little worried at first when you told me Honey had spoken. I was convinced she had told you it was me.'

'She did though, didn't she? She did tell me it was you. She said *Jess*, not chess, and I misheard her.'

'It doesn't matter now anyway,' Jessica shrugs, and there is nothing left of the woman I believed to be Honey's best friend, nothing left of the woman I poured my heart out to in my hotel room the evening I found out about Evelyn. Say what you want about Jessica Parks, but she is a fine actress. 'Who's going to believe *you*? I'm a movie star. You're nobody. And nor is Honey Black. In fifty years, no one will remember her name, but everyone will know mine.' She steps out from behind the small bar, raising her clenched fist as she steps towards me. 'So, what are you going to do, Lily?'

Horrified, I look down to see a letter opener in her hand, the razor-sharp blade pointed in my direction. My armpits prickle and my palms grow slick with sweat as I move back towards the sofa on trembling legs. 'Jessica, please... just wait a second.'

'Are you gonna call the cops, and tell them they got it all wrong?' She steps closer, her face curiously blank. 'Go ahead.'

Her breath hits my cheek, the tip of the letter opener brushing the underside of my chin as I step back, my calves hitting the sofa behind me. 'Jessica—'

'I'll tell them it was you all along.' Jessica smiles, pressing the blade harder against my skin, making it hard to swallow. 'After all, all of this only started when you showed up. Just ask Jean. You broke into my room while

342

I was at lunch with Cynthia. You waited, hiding in my bedroom, and then you attacked me. I had to defend myself somehow.'

She presses me back, and I fall onto the sofa, my breath screaming in my lungs as I try to fight her off. *Was this how Honey felt?* I feel the blade press against my ribs, as Jessica laughs, her knee hard against my stomach. I struggle beneath her, but she's too strong, her weight pushing down on me until I can't breathe, and black dots dance at the edges of my vision. And then abruptly her weight is gone, the pressure of the letter opener against my side disappearing.

I open my eyes to see Louis holding her tight around the waist, Jessica snarling and kicking, while Detective Schwartz steps in and deftly swipes the letter opener from her hand.

'Lily, are you all right?' Schwartz runs his eyes over me.

'Yeah.' I breathe, my gaze coming to rest on Jessica's face. 'It was Jessica who attacked Honey. She entered the Paul Williams Suite, and stabbed Honey Black in the chest to get rid of her once and for all, and she leaked the news of the engagement to make it look like Magnus killed her out of jealousy. It was just pure luck that Joe was in the suite with Honey all day,' I say, my breath painful and ragged. Pressing my fingers to my side, there is the tiniest smear of crimson.

Detective Schwartz holds out a hand and helps me to my feet, as an officer I assume to be Frank snaps a pair of handcuffs around Jessica's wrists. 'Jessica Parks, you're under arrest for the attempted murder of Honey Black.'

I watch as the two officers lead her from the room, her words coming back to me, as she struggles and protests.

Playing nice goes a long way in Hollywood. And I don't think for a second that Jessica Parks ever believed that.

Chapter Thirty-Five

I am still here. Joe is out of jail, Jessica has been arrested, and Honey is alive, but I am still here. Everything has taken on that strange dream-like quality again, the way it did when I first found myself here, as I walk the hospital corridor towards Honey's room. *Am I being given the chance to say goodbye to Honey? Why haven't. I jumped forward to my own time?* A thick lump sits in my throat as I force myself to swallow and paste on a smile as I tap on the door to Honey's hospital room.

Honey sits up in bed, more colour in her cheeks now, even as tears stream down her face. Joe stands beside her, his face scratchy with stubble, and he can barely tear his eyes away from her.

'I just can't believe it,' Honey sobs. 'I thought she was my friend.'

Leonard shakes his head, as Jean slides her hand into his. 'She fooled all of us,' he says, an unreadable expression on his face.

'In a funny way, I don't think it was personal, Honey,' I say, as Joe frowns at me. 'It could have been anyone – anyone who stole Jessica's thunder could have been in this position. She was a very convincing actress, that's for sure, and she was determined to do whatever it took to get what she wanted.' *A bit like Honey herself, really.*

'And things could have been a lot worse if it wasn't for you, Lily,' Jean pipes up. Now that she and Leonard are openly together, she has lost the sour look on her face, and she seems five years younger. She's someone I could picture myself being friends with. If I was staying. 'How *did* you know that someone was going to try and hurt Honey?'

Yikes. 'It's kind of a long story,' I say, feeling my cheeks flame. 'Maybe we can talk about that another time? Honey's been through a dreadful experience. Perhaps we should let her rest.'

'Absolutely. You've a long road ahead of you, young lady,' Leonard says to Honey, with a paternal smile. 'That is, if you still want to be a movie star after all of this?'

'I think you know the answer to that,' Honey says. We move towards the door, and I linger for a moment, watching as they take turns to kiss Honey goodbye, as Joe stands guard over her. *I did it*, I think, *I saved Honey Black, and now I have to try and get back to my own time.* So why do I feel so miserable?

–

A few hours later, back in my hotel room, I splash water on my face, but despite my fatigue, the gloom that had descended on me in Honey's hospital room has eased, and I feel light and strangely untethered now that Jessica has been arrested and Honey knows the truth. Jessica had fought as Frank cuffed her, telling Detective Schwartz that I was a liar and a fantasist, obsessed with Honey Black. Detective Schwartz had held up the steak knife, bagged as evidence, and called in further officers to search her suite more thoroughly.

'You guys want to call room service?' Tilda shouts from the bedroom. 'I'm kinda hungry, all this crime fighting takes it out of you.'

It does. There were no words to describe the emotion I felt as Jessica was led away, and then Frank and another officer had emerged from the bathroom, a sheaf of hacked-up newspapers in their hands. It turns out I'd been on the verge of discovering them behind the bath panel myself when Louis had called to me. Further proof that Jessica had been behind the threatening notes to Honey.

I dry my face and step into the bedroom where Louis and Tilda sit on the bed. Tension crackles in the air and I get the feeling that they have been talking about me while the water was running.

'You did it, Lily. I guess you really do have a gift.' Louis grins at me. 'Tilda wants to celebrate with burgers.'

I laugh, but it's forced. Now I've done what I came here to do, I have to go back to my own time. Despite the fact that I love it in 1949 – I have friends, a job, I've felt far happier here than in 2019 – I don't belong here, and God only knows the damage I could cause if I stay. 'You know what guys? I'm kind of beat. I think I'm just going to get an early night.' *I'm going to head to the Paul Williams Suite to try and time travel to seventy years in the future.*

'No problem. You had a rough day.' Tilda's fingers brush the spot where the bandage lies across my stomach. Jessica had nicked the skin with the letter opener but not enough to do any real damage. 'See you tomorrow?'

'Yeah.' I can barely force the word out, as Tilda kisses my cheek. 'Wait, Til…' I grab her arm and pull her in for a tight hug. 'You're amazing, you know? I couldn't have done any of this without you.' I pause, that pesky lump back in my throat. 'You're going to make a brilliant reporter.'

'Yeah?' She pulls away, a slight grin on her face. 'You sure Jessica didn't bump your head too?' She swats my arm, and heads for the corridor, leaving Louis and me alone.

'See you tomorrow, Lil.' Louis steps forward, gazing at me with those familiar green eyes, and my heart rate speeds up as he links his fingers through mine.

'Louis, I…' I swallow, afraid to carry on. 'I just wanted to tell you that… you mean more to me than you will ever know.'

Louis looks puzzled, a blush creeping up his cheeks. 'Oh gosh, Lil,' he says. 'I don't know what to say. You waltzed into my bar, demanded to know the date, and then choked down a drink that you didn't really like and that was it.' He grins and smooths away the tear that snakes down my cheek with his thumb. 'It's been an adventure, these last couple of weeks.'

'It has,' I say, my voice thick. 'I'm sorry for pretending to like your cocktails, and I'm sorry I dragged you into all of this.'

'Like I said, it's an adventure.' He grows serious. 'Lil, meeting you… I've been trying to tell you that… well, Evelyn and I – we're not a thing anymore, we haven't been for a while.' He blows out a long breath.

'I know,' I say. 'Tilda told me.' *Fuck it.* How much can one kiss affect the future? I lean in and press my lips to his, letting him kiss me, long and hard, until I forget how to breathe.

'The moment you walked into the bar, I knew you and I would have something special.'

'I think I knew that too, Louis…' My hand flies to my mouth. 'Oh my God, I don't even know your last name!'

A laugh erupts from Louis's chest. 'It's Jardine. My name is Louis Edward Jardine.'

My mouth falls open and I have to remind myself to breathe. *Jardine.* No wonder Louis's eyes are so familiar – they are Eric's eyes. Eric Jardine, my best and only friend in LA.

'What?'

'Nothing.' I shake my head, unable to tell Louis that his great grandson was there the day I ended up here. 'I've never met anyone quite like you before, Louis Jardine. I'll miss you.' I reach up and kiss him again. Eric's words come back to me, from the day we talked about the Beverly Hills Hotel. *There's been someone in my family working at the Beverly Hills Hotel for decades, right back to my great grandfather. He had a thing with a British girl once.* 'Remember me, won't you?'

'Lil? What are you talking about? I'll see you tomorrow, won't I? You're exhausted, and you're not making any sense. Get some sleep, and then we can talk tomorrow. Properly.'

Blinking back tears, I say, 'Yeah. Of course. See you tomorrow.' And then I close the door behind him and sob my heart out.

–

Once darkness falls, I change into my old housekeeping uniform and sneak along the corridor towards the Paul Williams Suite, the skeleton key – which will surely be missed any day now – held tightly in my hand. I let myself in, and again I am struck by how empty the room is without Honey's bright presence. Leonard has arranged for Honey to move into a bungalow in the hotel gardens, and someone – housekeeping presumably – has cleaned the room, and all traces of Honey's effects have gone. It looks eerily similar to the way it looked in 2019, when I first entered the room with Eric. Maybe this is how it is supposed to be for me to be able to get back, control conditions, if you like.

I step towards the bathroom, suddenly terribly nervous. How will I explain my absence to Eric? Will he have been worried about me? Probably not; he probably thought I just took off. Or will it be like an alien abduction, when people think they've been gone for days when in reality it's been only a few minutes? I don't know which I'd prefer. The thought of waking up in Honey's tub, and then carrying on cleaning her room as if nothing has happened, makes me feel a little queasy.

I just need to go for it. 'Like Harry Potter running through the wall at Platform 9¾,' I say, my words strangely echoey in the empty bathroom. 'Yeah, maybe that's for the best.' I rest my hands lightly on the cold marble surrounding the tub. 'I just have to…' *Smack my head on the tub.* I lean over, poised and ready. 'Wait. Give me a minute.' Standing up, I suck in a deep breath and lean over again, the bass line of my heart loud in my ears. 'Lily, just do it. Bang your head on the damn tub.' Gripping the edge of the bath tightly I try to, I really do but… I can't do it. I can't wilfully knock myself out.

'Think, Lily.' I press my fingers to my forehead, where the lump has long since faded. 'It can't be the head-banging that brought me here. I'll end up with concussion.' Opening my eyes, I scan the bathroom. It's this place that is magic. This suite. It has to be. There has to be a reason why it's been left untouched for so long in my own time. And specifically, this bathroom. This *bathtub.*

Maybe I don't need to bang my head. Maybe the bathtub works as a portal by itself. Climbing into the tub, I lie down and close my eyes, trying to remember exactly what I was thinking the moment I fell. *Honey. I was thinking about Honey.* So maybe I should think about home, and I'll transport myself back there? I think of Hyde Park on a summer's day, of nights out at the Viper Room in LA, loud music, and cold drinks. And... I crack one eye open. Nothing happens. Everything is exactly the same. Sitting up, I rest my head on my knees, blinking back hot tears. I must be doing something wrong. There must be a way back.

Water. The word comes to me, bright and clear. Magic always requires some sort of element, doesn't it? Maybe time travel is the same. I eye the gleaming bath taps. When I fell the first time, I was cleaning the bath, and the water was running. Maybe water is the key. Feeling a lurch of excitement, I stand up and strip off my housekeeping uniform, folding it neatly and placing it on the corner of the bath. Then, I fill the tub to the brim.

I wonder what they'll say tomorrow when I don't show up. The thought of Louis thinking I won't meet him tomorrow because I don't like him, or don't want to be with him, breaks my heart. *Maybe this won't work.* Maybe I'll sit up in the tub in a few minutes, soaking wet and miserable, still here in 1949. Maybe I'll go and meet Louis tomorrow and I'll let him take me for dinner, and then I'll let him kiss me again, only this time I won't pull away. I step into the water in just my underwear, goosebumps sprouting all over my skin. It feels different this time.

You don't belong here, Lily. It's time to leave. The voice I hear is my mother's, and I slide down into the water, knowing she's right. As the water closes over my head, I think, *People. It's the people who are important.* I think of my mother, and the way she looked in her hospital bed in the last days of her life, of Eric, and the way he makes me laugh until my stomach hurts, of London and LA in the twenty-first century and all the hustle and heartache that goes with it, and the last thought I have before my head hits the enamel is that I really, really don't want to go.

–

I am lying in the empty bathtub, the enamel cold against my wet skin. The water has drained away, but everything else looks the same. *Did it work?* Shakily, I push myself up to a sitting position. I feel weirdly refreshed, as if I've just woken up after a really good night's sleep. I sit for a moment, preparing myself to get to my feet, as a wash of images run through my brain. *Honey, turning to smile at me as I enter the suite that first time, Leonard and Jean sitting together in the diner as James Dean pushed past me, Ingrid Bergman and Clark Gable dancing together at Honey's birthday party, watching as Honey's car smashed into the tree, Louis leaning in to kiss me, seeing Honey lying on the chaise, her chest crimson.* Is this the moment I realise it was all a dream? Or am I still in 1949? Closing my eyes, I try to see Louis's face, but I can't make out his features. Can't quite catch the soft drawl of Honey's voice, or the tone of Tilda's laughter.

My housekeeping uniform still sits on the corner of the bath, so I reach for a towel and dry myself off, before pulling the dress over my head.

'Lil?' A voice floats through the open bathroom door, familiar and welcome.

'In here.' I step out into the suite, empty of any trace of Honey. No dresses draped across the foot of the bed, no lipstick-stained tissues in the trash.

Eric peers around the door frame, and I offer up a weak smile. *A dream, that's all it was. A horribly realistic, lucid dream.* 'Sorry, I lost track of time. How long have I been in here?'

'Maybe forty-five minutes?' Eric glances around the spotless suite, edging my trolley out of the way and coming towards me, his eyes running over my damp hair. 'I thought I should come and check on you. Are you OK?' He steps closer, frowning. 'You look like you've seen a ghost.'

My breath stops for a moment, and I think I might cry. 'Ha ha, very funny.'

'Huh?'

'*You look like you've seen a ghost,*' I mimic, pushing past him, and wheeling my cleaning trolley out into the corridor. 'All that stuff you were saying about Honey Black, and how the suite was haunted.'

Eric follows me out into hallway. 'Lily, I have no idea what you're talking about.'

'You said Honey Black haunted the Paul Williams Suite, that's why I went in to clean instead of you...' I turn back to the now closed door of the suite, my heart simultaneously sinking and lifting, if that's even possible. 'But...'

'Lily, you've lost me. Whatever happened to Honey Black anyway? I thought she was still alive...' Eric frowns, as I close my mouth with a snap, my knees trembling with a familiar wobble. 'Did you bump your head or something?' He lifts my chin, inspecting my forehead. 'Are you sure you're all right?'

'I'm... perfect.' I let my gaze linger on the closed door, holding on to what happened behind it for just a few more moments. 'Right as rain. In fact, everything is just as it should be.' And with a small smile that does nothing to drown out the sharp pain in my heart, I turn and walk down the corridor, away from the Paul Williams Suite.

A Letter From Lisa

This book is a pandemic baby, written while I was supposed to be on a break from writing anything at all. The idea came into being as I sat beside my husband, watching a TV show about the world's greatest hotels, while we dreamed of being able to travel again. The show featured the Beverly Hills Hotel, and referenced the Paul Williams Suite, with the host saying that the suite has remained more or less untouched since Williams – a prominent African-American architect – first designed it in 1948.

'Imagine,' I said to my husband, 'waking up in that suite. You wouldn't know if you were in 2020 or 1948.' And so, the seed of Lily's story was planted.

In January 2022, once the world started opening up again, I travelled with my husband and one of my best friends to Hollywood, to visit the Beverly Hills Hotel – and more specifically, the Paul Williams Suite – in person. The only problem was, someone booked the suite the night before we arrived, and they wouldn't let me in! We did, however, get to tour around the rest of the hotel (including the Crystal Ballroom) and the gardens and grounds, and it was everything I imagined and more.

I've tried to recreate the Beverly Hills Hotel – and the surrounding areas in Hollywood – as accurately as I can, but I have taken a few liberties to make the story work. You would never get a scrum of paparazzi outside the hotel, let alone inside! The hotel is one of the most elegant, discreet places I've ever visited and it's easy to see why the A-listers love it so much. I didn't see a single celebrity on my visit, although according to the bartender at the Polo Lounge, I was sitting on the stool that Al Pacino sat on just the week before (allegedly). And of course, we ordered the McCarthy salad for lunch.

Googie's, the diner, existed until 1988/1989 when it was demolished, and the Palomino Club closed in 1995, but you can still get a table at Musso and Frank, and then play a couple of games of bowling at the Highland Park Bowl.

Hollywood has always been crammed full of scandal, and they do a pretty good job of covering it up. The scandals that are briefly referenced in this book are allegedly true, some of them only coming to light recently – here's hoping that will change with the #MeToo movement. Lily references a book on Hollywood scandals, where she first read the scant information that was available on Honey Black. While Lily's book doesn't really exist, there are plenty of others that do, and I lost hours immersing myself in the so-called 'Golden Age' of Hollywood. If you want to read further, a few books that I highly recommend are *This Was Hollywood* by Carla Valderrama, *A Woman's View* by Jeanine Basinger and *Scandals of Classic Hollywood* by Anne Helen Petersen.

I've loved every minute of working on this book, so thank you, dear reader, for adding it to your TBR. I hope you love Lily and Honey just as much as I do.

Acknowledgments

I have a raft of people to thank for bringing this book to life. My agent, Lisa Moylett, and her assistant, Zoe Apostolides. Thank you for accepting the dirtiest first draft I've ever written (and there have been some filthy ones – not in a good way) for a book that I hadn't been contracted to write, in a genre I'd never tried before. Your insight, patience and hard work have made this book a completely different beast to its original incarnation, and I am so lucky to have you.

Keshini Naidoo, Jennie Ayres and Iain Millar. Thank you so much for your passion and excitement for Honey. I knew from that very first Zoom call that you guys were going to be the dream team to work with, and I wasn't wrong (it's been a long time coming, Kesh!).

My writing buddies, Darren O'Sullivan and Annabel Kantaria. You two are the absolute best – thank you for reading the horrible drafts, spurring me on when I thought it was all a big bin fire, and for letting me vent. I live for your voice notes.

Diane Jeffrey, a magnificent writer, friend, and grammar queen. Thank you for tidying Honey up, when I could no longer see the wood for the trees.

My mum, for reading the hideous first draft and telling me it was brilliant. And the same for the next draft. And the next.

Charlotte Seddon, for the *hawt* new author pics. We just won't talk about the ones that got deleted.

Karen Crawford. Thank you for being the best of the best – for always making me laugh till I cry, for being an LA adventurer, and for splitting the McCarthy salad.

The folks I met on my big night out in Hollywood, especially Tommy Fradenburgh (I have not drunk Jack Daniels since). I also have to thank the kids of *Vanderpump Rules*. Not only have you shown me what it's like to be young in Hollywood, but you've also provided light relief after a long day of writing, and excellent gossip fodder.

Nick, Geo, Missy and Mo, and of course, Hats and Sam. Thanks for the cups of tea, the sausage sandwiches, the biscuits, and pretending you know who I'm talking about when I try and unravel plot and character over the dinner table. You are my raison d'être.

Finally, thank you to the readers and bloggers who have shown me such incredible support since that very first book. I can only keep doing this because of you.

If you do enjoy reading I would love it if you would consider leaving a review – it helps to spread the word and us authors are eternally grateful!

If you'd like to keep up to date with news, you can follow Lisa here:
Twitter: @lisahallauthor
Instagram: @lisahallauthor
Facebook: https://www.facebook.com/lisahallauthor

Honey Black's Soundtrack Playlist

I've never felt the need to create a playlist for a book I've written before but something about the world of Honey and Lily made me feel that this story needed one. I've tried to choose every track carefully. Some songs I chose because I felt they fit the story perfectly (I'd like to think that if Honey turned twenty-one in 2023 she would have claimed Taylor Swift's *Bejeweled* for her own at her birthday party!) and some I chose for more personal reasons. For example, one of the characters in this book is named after my grandfather, and I've included a song that he used to sing to me as a child. I hope you enjoy this playlist, and it helps bring Honey and Lily to life…

- BEVERLY HILLS – Weezer

- BEJEWELED – Taylor Swift

- FAST CAR – Luke Combs

- JAMBALAYA (ON THE BAYOU) – Hank Williams

- SWINGING ON A STAR – Bing Crosby

- JAMES DEAN – Tash Sultana

- HOLLYWOOD'S BLEEDING – Post Malone

- THE LUCKY ONE (TAYLOR'S VERSION) – Taylor Swift

- VOGUE – Madonna

- ADORE YOU – Harry Styles

- FILMSTAR – Suede

- A SKY FULL OF STARS – Coldplay

- HOLLYWOOD – Marina

- TWENTY ONE – The Cranberries

- MOVIES – Alien Ant Farm

- ISN'T SHE LOVELY – Stevie Wonder

- KILL THE DIRECTOR – The Wombats

- KENTUCKY – Jake Bugg

- DRINKING IN L.A. – Bran Van 3000

- ANTI-HERO (COUNTRY VERSION) – Josiah and the Bonnevilles

- BARTENDER – Lady A

- RIDERS IN THE SKY – Vaughn Monroe

- NATURE BOY – Nat King Cole